THE HUNTER
OF HERTHA

OTHER BOOKS BY TESS COLLINS

FICTION

The Midnight Valley Quartet::
Notown

The Appalachian Trilogy:
The Law of Revenge
The Law of the Dead
The Law of Betrayal

Helen of Troy

NON-FICTION

How Theater Managers Manage

Casebound: 978-1-937356-40-8
Trade: 978-1-937356-41-5
ebook: 978-1-937356-42-2

Library of Congress Control Number: 2015901212

Publisher's Cataloging-in-Publication Data

Collins, Theresa.
  The hunter of Hertha / Tess Collins.
  p. cm.
  ISBN: 978-1-937356-40-8
    1. Murder–Fiction. 2. Kentucky–Fiction. 3. Appalachian Region–Fiction. 4. Environmental toxicology–Fiction. 5. Radioactive pollution–Fiction. 6. Magic realism (Literature). 7. Visions–Fiction. 8. Coal mines and mining–Fiction. I. Title.
  PS3553.O476324 H86 2015
  813.6–dc22

                        2015901212

Published by BearCat Press: BearCatPress.com
BearCat Press logo by Golden Sage Creative
Front Cover Photograph by Paula Melton
Book design by Frogtown Bookmaker

THE HUNTER OF HERTHA

Tess Collins

BearCat
PRESS

San Francisco

For my brothers and sister

Jesse Collins,
the smart one of the family with whom I share my green eyes.
You probably don't remember this, but it was me who fought off
those two neighbor kids who were trying to kidnap you when you
were two. Well, until Mom came to the rescue.

Mark Collins,
the one that drives me crazy but I'd still want you on my side
in a bar fight, and the one I claim as a brother even when I
unfriended you that one time on Facebook.

Cindy Collins Code,
the other smart one who is much saner than the rest of us
because she missed our childhoods, but that's okay because I'm
counting on you to take care of me in my old age.

PROLOGUE ONE

May 1938

What a seven-year-old sees as magical, mysterious, or even frightening, an adult knows as hard reality: an eclipse is the paltry darkness of nature. Preachers point to sin, blaming the hardworking for their own diseases, leaving the bitter taste of hopeless despair. In those years of poverty and hunger when leaders promised a New Deal, people in Appalachia distrusted political recovery. Very little of it had come their way, and what good was in their lives came from scratching a living from absentee employers made wealthy through their toil–employers with names like Rockefeller, Delano, Morgan, Mellon, and Ford.

The Cumberland Mountains held its people in a bottomless cauldron; they were a barricade blocking the greater view. In an earlier age, these mighty bulwarks were thought to be gods, a sweet mother giving food from her crust to fill a belly, a passionate father raining down self-righteous anger in a moment of jealous folly. But neither ancient nor modern deities can match the true power of Nature when an infant ceases breathing for no reason, and only a child finds death curious.

Temperance Herne paced around the kitchen table looking at the body of her dead baby brother. The little girl's eyes, just above the level of the table, resisted blinking just in case something else awful might happen. She squeezed her hands until her knuckles cracked. Where was Mother? Empty rooms. Back door open wide. Night. She hated being left alone, and outside a monster was eating the full moon.

Maybe it was the end of the world like the traveling preacher had said. The image of the black-suited man on the street corner, preaching that Armageddon was at hand, festered in her imagination. Mother had pulled her along, and now she wished they'd stopped and listened.

Her brother's skin looked as gray as the lizards along the creek bank. She knew he was dead. She'd seen a dead man before. Ulysses Stark, who'd gotten shot in the head on the steps of the Crimson County courthouse. She and her father had watched men load the body on a bench and carry it away. Ulysses had been gray, too, just like her brother. She poked the baby's arm and jerked back from the cold, doughy feel.

Out the rear door, the moon was a sliver smaller and a blood-red color gripped the outer edges. She hadn't imagined it. The moon was disappearing. She wished they'd never come to Kentucky. Their house in Pennsylvania was bigger, and they had a yard with a tire swing. But Poppy had lost everything in the big flood and said they needed a new start in this patch called the Rhine, on the backside of a swamp named Quinntown. She hated this place, with its nightly gunfire and drunken people on the roads at all times of day. Pop had said if it didn't work out, he'd move them over to East Tennessee where the TVA was busy building dams and making 'lectricity. Temperance was tired of moving, so like her mother she held on and looked past the sins of her black-hearted neighbors.

2

A sob in the darkness caught her attention. Temperance hid in the shadows of the kitchen, every muscle tight, expecting the Grim Reaper to cut her down. If only her father were here. She studied the other houses. A few lanterns blew golden glows from their windows. No one else seemed worried about the fading moon. A violin played in the distance, a haunting, deep melody that wrapped a sense of safety around her.

Emboldened, Temperance stepped into the night. Following the crying voice, she paused at the canal bank. What was left of the moon created a white sheen on the stinky water where all the trash and sewage of the Rhine ended up.

Below, Mother was on her knees, sobbing. Temperance had never seen her mom cry before, not even when Poppy left for the old country to save Grandma from a mean man named Adolph Hitler. Before leaving, Poppy had sat her on his knee and told her about Hitler violating the Versailles Treaty. His words confused her as he recounted fighting a war in the old country when he was a young boy. He said another one was coming, so he had to rescue Grandmother. It would take a long time, but she'd promised to be strong and help with the baby. But now, Brother was dead.

The hilt of a shovel stuck in the dirt reflected a little piece of moon, and Temperance could see a deep hole in the ground. Now, she understood. This was where they'd bury Connor. This was where people from the Rhine tossed out things they didn't need anymore. And now baby Connor was one of them. Her mother stood straight and wiped her brow. Temperance wanted to run to her, but Mother's temper might snap to find she was out of bed.

Temperance hid underneath the porch as Mother started up the canal bank. The porch slats creaked and rained wood slivers on Temperance as Mother got Connor's body and took it back to the hole. Night filled with a creeping blackness, and Temperance shivered, afraid the whole world would be dark. Would the moon ever come back? Would the sun? Would the monster grab her? Would she vanish into the ghostly mist?

A whine interrupted her terror. Mother noticed it too. She watched as Mother peered into the darkness, looking for the sound. Temperance expected the world to explode any minute. She trotted toward Mother, who moved toward the shadows, looking for that whiny pitch. Then, Mother was gone, the moon as well. A hollow night surrounded the little girl. Her ears popped, and breathing in was like inhaling water.

"Momma?" She turned in a circle, having lost all sense of direction. Straggling curls fell onto her forehead, obscuring her sight. The dark swallowed her whole. "Momma, please." She pressed her knuckles, causing them to crack, and each snap released more fear. Tears streaked her cheeks and she collapsed. A hand clamped her shoulder. She screamed.

"Hush!" Mother scolded. "You'll wake the baby."

Temperance clasped her mother's legs. "I'm scared."

Mother pulled her along, back to the house, fussing that she was outside. Something in her arms whimpered. Inside the kitchen, Mother laid a baby on the table. She tossed out the brown-spotted, filthy cloth covering it and inspected its limbs, counted its toes, brushed dirt out of its blond hair. Temperance stood in the corner, every part of her shaking. Mother crossed her arms over her chest, one hand on her lips as if she was thinking deeply or maybe saying a prayer.

The little girl couldn't have known that this Daughter of the American Revolution was not of the starving Irish or indentured English who'd settled these fertile hollows in the last century. Wallis Herne's Pennsylvania Dutch ancestors had never known a debtor's prison, and she embraced her native ambition, despite these fallen circumstances. She found no pleasure in children or meaning in death rituals, she only knew the function of living. Her offspring would be raised Christian, work the good Lord's earth, and return to His glory in their time, not because she believed, but because in this world it was the expedient way to live. Her son was dead. Her husband would grieve, but then he would want another. If Wallis doubted the wisdom of her Maker for taking her baby, she hid those thoughts as she observed the foundling that had fallen into her care. Its mother, lying dead on the creek bank, wouldn't be the first person to die on that stinking shore, but her child would be the luckiest soul to escape its fallow darkness.

"Get in bed, Tempy," Mother said. "You've kept your brother awake long enough."

"That's not Connor," Tempy said, pointing at the pretender.

Mother slapped her. Temperance ran to bed, pulling blankets over her head. The sting on her cheek faded as she fought back tears. When her sniffles disappeared, Temperance got up and tiptoed into the kitchen. The new baby was in her brother's bassinet. He gazed up at her with blue moon eyes, and she looked away, a seed of distrust sprouting within her. Brother was dead and another had taken his place. Mother had struck her and told a lie. She squeezed her hands to keep them from trembling. Cracking her small knuckles was the only sensation that eased her worry.

Temperance pulled a chair to the window and climbed up. Down the embankment, Mother dug a larger hole. Temperance watched her drag a bundle toward the hole. A body! A woman whose long blond hair trailed in the dirt. Momma rolled the woman into the pit and dropped baby Brother on top of her, then covered them with dirt.

Temperance got down from the chair, wondering if what she'd seen was something she could believe, or if Mother would say it

5

hadn't happened. She peeked over the edge of the bassinet. The new baby's pink skin contrasted with dark pupils peering at her. She stepped back, expecting its eyes might shoot out poison. What was this thing Mother had brought into their house? This creature born of a dead woman and the dark moon would surely bring them misfortune.

THE BLACK DAHLIA

August 1948

Connor Herne ran the uneven ground of Beans Fork Hollow. Out of breath, he pushed himself up the hill, protecting a sack under his arm, and hopped rocks across a snaky creek. At the peak of the next ridge, he looked west toward the setting sun to judge how much light he had, then, speeding up his pace, he jumped onto a dirt road and trotted toward a giant beech tree beside a stone bridge. Choir practice hummed from a Holiness Church on the far side. Connor ran around the beech tree and looked up at a red-lettered sign reading *Renegades Hide Out. No Girls Allowed.*

"Rusty, you up there?"

A freckled face peered down at him from a tree house twenty feet above. "Hurry up." Rusty Haskew motioned with a hand.

Connor anchored his feet onto square boards nailed into the tree and held the brown bag with his teeth as he climbed.

"Got it?" Rusty asked as Connor fell onto the floor.

Connor spit out the bag at Rusty's feet. "Got yours?"

The auburn-haired boy fell on the sack and pulled out buttered biscuits that he stuffed in his mouth. Rusty nodded toward a tattered magazine.

Connor took the coverless journal to the door and held it toward the setting sun. He flipped through the pages until he found it. "Ugh," he said, looking up at Rusty. "They cut her in two."

"Told you," he said with a jaw full of pork. "Look how they sliced her mouth."

"Whooooa." Connor traced the black-haired woman's mouth, cut up each side like a clown. He glanced over at Rusty. "You get enough?"

Rusty nodded as he bit into the second biscuit and a piece of pork. "Sure your Mom ain't noticed?"

"Naw, she just reckons I eat a lot." He turned the page and looked at a half-page photo of a smiling dark-haired woman, a small cross on a cord around her neck, white flowers behind each ear. "The Black Dahlia," he read. He turned back to the picture of the woman's body, staring at the gap of open flesh that split her into two pieces, and he swallowed hard. "Who in the world would think to do such a thing?"

"A monster," Rusty said.

"Can you get this back without the other boys noticing?"

Rusty waved his hands. "Detective magazine's ours. I ain't afraid of them."

Connor's eyes widened at his friend. He had to be the bravest or the craziest boy in the world. Living in an orphan house with boys twice his size, he regularly stole from them: their dirty magazines, their hidden candy, sometimes even their clothes. He'd shown up at the tree house with a black eye more than once, but his stories told of how he'd given more than he got. Connor brought him food because he was always hungry, and sometimes when they swam in Big Creek his ribs showed under his skin.

"Herman seen this?" Connor asked.

"He's on watch." Rusty nodded and slowly punched his fist into his other hand. "Tonight, Little Preacher Boy gets his."

"Without mercy," Connor laughed, rubbing his belly at the thought of what they had planned for their nemesis: a ten-year-old, self-righteous shortie that went door-to-door spreading his version of the word of God that had nothing to do with anything Connor had ever read in the Bible. More like whatever Preacher Boy wanted, people better do or he'd denounce them from the pulpit. One time he'd embarrassed Connor's parents into going to Wednesday night, Sunday morning, and Sunday evening services. Connor had thought he was going to fall over and die if he had to listen to one more hell-fire sermon from the white-shoed tyke. People came from all over the county to hear the Little Preacher Boy, who didn't have his own ministry but hired himself out as a non-denominational evangelist, and was currently leading a revival at the church across the bridge. Connor thought that little as he was, Bryson Pomeroy was still a punk worth whipping.

The trill of a whippoorwill caused both boys to head down the ladder. Next to the tree trunk stood the third renegade, Herman Cahill. He took off his glasses and pointed toward the bridge. "He's yonder down the road."

The boys hid on sloping support braces of the stone bridge and waited. Dusk washed out the outlines of trees, but glow from the church gave enough light for the boys to watch their plan play out. And here he strutted, ten-year-old Master Pomeroy, dressed in his checkered suit with striped tie and his signature white shoes. Flattened against the rails, the boys raised their heads as he passed.

11

Bryson slipped and waved his arms to keep from falling. An afternoon thunderstorm had made the bridge all the more slippery. He slid again and let out a shrill "Shit!"

The boys stifled their laughter. "More'n he knows," Herman whispered.

A third step took Bryson to one knee. "Holy damnation!" he yelled, sliding in dog poop that the boys had collected for the last two days. He let out a string of cuss words. The boys giggled, unable to control themselves any longer. Bryson scraped his white shoes on the bridge rail, but they were hopelessly mired. "I see you heathens," he yelled at them. "You're going to burn in hell with Satan and his minions, and I'll be there on the Day of Judgment to testify against you!"

The boys hopped the creek, holding up middle fingers toward Little Preacher Boy, who continued to cuss them. Downstream, they climbed onto a castle-shaped rock protruding in the middle of the water. Herman flicked on his USA Lite Mickey Mouse flashlight as they fell to their backs, holding their sides from hard laughter. "Reckon he went to pray for our salvation," Connor joked.

"He didn't get a good 'nuf look at our faces." Herman smacked his own cheeks. "God won't know who he's talking about."

"Anyways, the Lord don't listen to people who cuss worse than a drunk soldier," Rusty chortled.

"But we have to figure a way," Connor sat up and emphasized each word, "to get rid of him for good." He cocked an ear upstream. "What's that?"

The boys listened. Sounds of the early night faded into a gentle roar. They looked at each other, alarm overtaking their features. "Water from the mines!" Herman yelled.

The boys jumped rock to rock to get on high ground. Herman held the flashlight while Connor grabbed onto wild honeysuckle vines and pulled himself up the creek bank. Behind them Rusty slipped into ankle-deep water. "Come on!" Connor yelled, and Rusty, again, started up the slope. The roar upstream grew louder as Connor and Herman stretched out their hands toward their friend, who had frozen in place.

"Yonder it is!" Herman yelled, pointing at a wall of water barreling toward them.

The wave hit Rusty, sweeping him from their sight. Connor and Herman stared at their empty hands. "We'll catch him at Big Creek," Connor said and began running.

The two friends sprinted through the dark. Herman lit a path through backyards, gardens of cornstalks, and both boys jumped a beehive as they raced through the woods lining the creek bank. Out of breath, they'd beat the flood to Big Creek, a large tributary where Little Creek emptied. Huffing for air, Connor looked upstream where the bank of water would emerge. He turned in a circle, looking for something to hold on to. "There!" he yelled, and jumped on a low-hanging branch of a young birch tree. "Hold it down, Herman. After I catch Rusty, let loose."

Herman anchored the flashlight between two rocks and pointed it upstream, then put his weight on the tree limb as Connor crawled out over the water. The rush of wind over the water grew stronger. "It'll get you, too," Herman yelled.

"Yonder he is!" Connor pointed upstream at a bobbing head and flailing arms. He circled his legs into the branches. "Get me down low!"

Herman leaned on the branch with all his strength. The crest of the water hit Connor, and he struggled to hold on while reaching out into the flood. He snagged Rusty by the hair and one shoulder, holding him tight. Herman released the branch, and it sprang upward, taking the boys out of the waves.

Rusty coughed and wheezed as Connor held him. Slowly they made their way along the branch to dry ground. The boys collapsed on the shoreline, Rusty spitting water, and Herman patting his back. "Damn coal mines," Rusty said, his shoulders trembling from exertion. "Their dams break every hard rain, and everything floods."

"I thought you two were goners," Herman said.

"Take more'en mine water to get shed of me." Rusty shot out his middle finger at the flooded stream. "I swear, one day I'm gonna break a window in a mine owner's house."

"I'll help," Connor agreed.

"Me, too." Herman shook a fist.

"Think we lost our big rock?" Herman wondered.

The boys sat quietly, watching smaller stones tumble into Big Creek. In a few seconds, their castle-rock hiding place crashed into the larger stream.

While Connor and Rusty dipped themselves naked in an upstream pool to clean off coal slurry, far away two men inspected the break in the coal mine's holding pond. They were unconcerned that their flood had claimed a dog, three chickens, half a dozen gardens, swamped the backyards of every creek-side home, and washed away a boy. It didn't matter that the poison in the coal ash would stunt the growth of every tree whose buried roots now withered, or that the toxic sludge would contaminate the well water of all the homes in the hollow. There was no concern that the fish were dead. It'd been an accident, after all, an act of God. The men couldn't be held responsible . . . that is, if anyone found out, if anyone could prove it was their fault. People didn't know what to do when these things happened, people didn't know whom to call or even if there was anyone to call, and the men . . . they liked it that way. Acts of God always worked in their favor.

Rusty's clothes were mud-caked, and Herman snuck into the backyard of a nearby house and stole a pair of overalls off the clothesline. They hung loose on Rusty, but they were good enough. Connor's clothes were more splashed than covered and he figured he could blame it on playing in the creek beside his house. "Gotta get home before the folks notice I'm not in my room," he said.

Herman shined his flashlight as far as Beans Fork where he turned off. They made their secret handshake and promised to meet at the tree house the following day. House lights lit a path down Notown Road. When they came upon the orphan house, Rusty motioned for Connor to give him a lift. Connor fell to all fours underneath an open window, and Rusty stood on his back to get inside.

A screen door slammed. The wooden porch creaked with heavy footsteps. The boys held in place. Rusty's fingertips dug into the window ledge, toes balanced on Connor's back. "What in tarnation!" a high-pitched voiced yelled.

Both boys crumbled to the ground. Whirling around the side of the house, Judge Rounder swung a razor strop through the air. He caught Rusty by the arm and thrashed him. Rusty trotted a circle around the guardian of the orphan house, but was unable to get free of the grip. Connor sprinted away. At the main road, he turned and watched as Judge Rounder beat Rusty to the ground, then jerked him inside. When the door slammed, all went silent.

Connor stared, teeth clenched, perched on the balls of his feet as if ready to pounce. In his mind he could see himself beating the tar out of Judge Rounder. But Mr. Rounder was a respected jurist who took in orphan boys for the good of the community. Connor hated him for the bruises he saw on his friend. Beatings and an empty belly were hardly worth the bed Rusty got, and Connor wished Rusty could move in with him, but Mom had already said no. Sadly, he left, knowing there was nothing he could do, but as he walked, he calculated . . . first, Preacher Boy; second, the mines; and then Judge Rounder. One day, he'd get them good.

Connor continued up Notown Road and cut through his neighbor's backyard to jump the fence over to his house. He didn't need a lift to the open window. Earlier, he'd left a ladder against the wall. As he dropped into his room, he saw his father sitting on the bed, arms folded.

"Thought I saw a bear," Connor said. "Went to check it out."

Pop pointed at the dirt on his shoes. "No fibbin', young man." He handed Connor a set of pajamas. "Mom finds you sneaking out, and we will never hear the end of it. Now, where were you?"

"With Rusty and Herman," he said, and looked at the floor.

His father sighed and glanced at the ceiling. "You've got the rest of summer to play, but promise me you'll stay inside after dark."

"Promise, Pop," he said, and crossed his fingers behind his back.

"Okay, get in your pjs," Pop said. "I told Mom I'd make sure you said your prayers."

Later on, lying in bed, looking out the window at the moon, Connor mused on the difference between his and Rusty's lives. He was lucky to have a father who never hit him and a mother who only occasionally hollered. Could have done without the bossy sister, he thought, and closed his eyes. But he didn't sleep easily. His rage at Judge Rounder overtook any annoyance he felt toward Bryson Pomeroy or some nameless mine owner, and merged with images of the murdered Black Dahlia. Ghosts of the monster who tore her up hid in the shadows of his dreams. He jerked awake more than once as the dead woman clawed to be part of his landscape, to live behind his closed eyes.

2

Connor thought he was going to die from boredom as he waited for his parents in front of a Quinntown grocery store they were thinking of buying. Sitting in the suffocating midday heat drenched his armpits with sweat. It didn't help that his hair had been shaved to the scalp because of a lice infestation. The sun crackled his noggin like it was melting through a layer of wax, and he slipped on a gray work cap his mother had let him buy after losing his blond locks. He wished he were out in the cool woods with Rusty and Herman. It'd been a week since they'd pooped ole Pomeroy, and they needed to stage another attack if they were going to get rid of him for good.

Flies circled a browning apple core that a policeman had tossed in the gutter. Along the three blocks of Quinntown, men, women, and children strolled up and down the street, pausing for Saturday gossip when they saw someone they knew or joining a discussion already in progress.

Connor knocked his head against the back of the bench. Beside him, his sister Tempy had no trouble sitting still reading a library book. She'd graduated high school last May, and Connor couldn't help being envious because he had to return to school in a couple days. If he'd already graduated, he'd never read another book. The novel, *Bedelia*, had his sister entranced, and he made faces to see if he could get her to look up. She didn't, and he groaned, "How much longer?"

"Keep hitting your head like that," Tempy said without a smile, "you'll crack your skull and your brains will leak out."

"Will not." Connor hawked in his throat and spit on the sidewalk.

"Vulgar." Tempy shuddered and went back to her book.

Connor tapped his toes on the sidewalk around his spit, and the dance seemed to amuse his grandmother, parked in a wheelchair beside the bench. "Quinntown smells like rotten eggs," he said, bouncing on the balls of his feet.

"It's surrounded by sulfur springs," his sister murmured.

"Don't want to live where it stinks."

"Notown was always for the short term."

"Why didn't we stay in Sevierville? Tennessee had good fishing."

"We don't talk about that," Tempy snapped and looked over at their grandmother. Grammy's head was weaving in a figure eight and her tongue lolled around her lips. "Give Grammy a drink."

Connor picked up the soda they'd bought earlier and held the paper straw to his grandmother's lips, hoping she wouldn't squish it. As she sucked in cola, he squinted and held a hand over his eyes, looking down the sidewalk. "Holy damnation."

"Mom hears you cuss, and you'll not see the light of day–"

"Little Preacher Boy!"

"Horsefeathers!" Tempy gasped, and slammed shut her book. "Quick, inside, maybe he'll walk past."

18

Brother and sister ran into the store and flattened themselves against the far wall. An outside thermometer embedded in a metal tin reflected the street and Little Preacher Boy strutting down the sidewalk, Bible in both hands and nose in the air like he was looking for Heaven to anoint him. He'd cleaned his white shoes and wore casual short pants and a buttoned-up white shirt with sweat stains around the armpits.

"We forgot Grammy," Connor whispered to Tempy.

"No time to get her," Tempy said.

As Bryson Pomeroy approached, Connor held his breath. Preacher Boy said hello to everyone he passed, inviting them to church or chastising anyone who didn't attend his revival meetings.

"Praise Lord," Grammy hollered out.

Connor and Tempy cringed.

"Praise Lord to you as well, Sister." Bryson took her hand. "What has you out on the Lord's sizzling day?"

"Devil's tickling my toes."

Bryson cocked his head to one side. "World's full of temptation," he said. "I'll pray for ye."

From behind them, Connor heard his mother's footsteps and poked Tempy on the arm. "Gotta do something," he said. "We leave her out there, Mom'll holler at us for sure." Tempy's face scrunched up, unsure what to do.

Connor bolted out the front door. "Bryson Pomeroy, what are you doing haranguing my grandmother?"

"I was just a-praying for her. She's got the Devil on her."

"She's an old lady and don't need your caterwauling. Get on down the road."

Bryson gave a girly gasp of insult. "You're going to Hell," he charged.

Connor stamped his foot, causing the runt to jump back.

"Connor Herne!" His mother jerked him by the arm. Her cheeks colored beet-red, and Connor knew this was going to be a talkin'-to. Mom turned toward Preacher Boy and smiled her best penance. "Master Pomeroy, enjoyed your June revival so much. Come back to our church again soon."

Connor swallowed his ire and wanted to spit. "He was bothering Grammy," he tried to explain.

"Preaching at Calvary Baptist for the next month," Bryson started in on Connor's mother. "Not that far out of your way."

Connor shot a look at Tempy in the doorway, and she rolled her eyes as they listened to their mother promise to make both services on Sunday. Only Grammy seemed to absorb the gist of the pledge. "Demons dancing in your aisles. I saw 'em lick your privates." She cackled a laugh that made Connor join in, and Tempy covered her mouth with both hands.

"What's wrong with that woman?" Bryson clutched his Bible to his chest.

Grammy let out a string of German words Connor didn't know the meaning of, but Preacher Boy's expression looked like he had swallowed throw-up.

"We'll come Wednesday, too," Connor said. "I'll push Grammy to the front row."

"She's possessed by the Devil." Bryson stepped back and pointed at Grammy, who mocked the gesture and hissed. He held up his Bible. "Don't you bring the Devil to my church! The Lord'll strike you down."

"Nnnn . . . no." Connor's mother scrambled to explain. "She's ill."

Preacher Boy backed away, holding his Bible like a shield, praying as he went. Connor bent over in laughter, but when he looked up, his mother's glare closed him down. He might have to listen to her fuss, but down the block, approaching, as Preacher Boy walked on, was the most beautiful gal he'd ever seen. For an instant, he wondered if she was an angel, with a pale blue dress that drifted in the breeze, even though there was no wind. Her walk seemed to make her and the dress float. Strawberry red hair, loosely twisted atop her head, with ringlets drifting down her neck, and skin so whitely pale that Connor wondered if she ever got in the sun.

"*Excusez-moi*," she said, then bit her lip, blinking eyes so blue they were almost lavender. "I . . . mean to say . . . excuse me."

The four of them turned toward her, and even Grammy seemed mesmerized by her beauty. Connor's mother's exasperated expression ripened as she looked the girl up and down.

"I . . . look for zee *Lune Sur le Rhine?*" She read from a folded clip of paper.

"She's speaking French, Mom," Tempy said.

"Rhine girls belong on Marcescent Street," Mom whispered in an aside.

"*Oui, s'il vous plaît*, zee Rhine." She smiled, nodding her head and pointing at her paper. "Moonuver . . . zee Rhine."

"Good Lord," Mom huffed in frustration. "Every speakeasy in the county is on that street." She pointed toward the west and said, "That way, that way."

Connor offered the beautiful girl his hand and helped her around Grammy. He escorted her to the corner until his mother hollered for him. The vision turned to him and said, "Thank you." Then, slipping her hand under his chin: "*Beau garçon, vous êtes mon sauveur.*"

Connor repeated the strange words in a whisper as he returned. Her soft fingers on his skin left a memory, and he closed his eyes and imagined them still there. His daydream abruptly ended as his mother collapsed on the bench and buried her face in her hands. "I can't believe this," she said. "We get run out of Sevierville 'cause my mother trots down the road butt naked, end up in Notown, and now, even Quinntown'll know we're harboring an insane person. How can I live here, where even the floosies walk up and down the main street?"

"Grammy's not crazy," Tempy said. "She's sick."

"What's a floozy?" Connor asked.

"Hush," his mom growled, "all of you be still so I can think."

They sat quietly, only his grandmother's occasional nonsensical words breaking the tension. Connor rubbed Grammy's shoulders. He felt sorry for her. The last few years, she'd begun to do crazy things, put on her clothes backwards, eat food with her fingers, talk about the old country and, sometimes, believe she was still there. Mom took her to doctors who could only come up with a lame diagnosis that occasionally old people lose their minds. Connor thought she just had a unique way of looking at life. He'd been the one to find her when she disappeared in Sevierville. He led her home . . . naked, while people turned their heads away. Some boys laughed, pointing their fingers and calling out names that upset Grammy, but Connor calmed her down, covering her as best he could with a blanket one of the merchants had handed him. He'd made a mental note of every person who'd laughed, and if his family hadn't moved so soon afterwards, he would have egged a few houses but good.

Pop came from the store holding a black metal tube and handed it to Connor. "Found a telescope in back, needs cleaning."

"Wow, Pop," Connor said, peering through the eyepiece.

Mom stood up and clapped her hands. "Not this place, Pop," she said. "It's all wrong. Better we move to Contrary, bigger store, better living space."

"But honey, that store won't be up for sale 'til next year."

"This one's too close to the Rhine. I hate the Rhine."

"Now, Wallis, ain't much to the Rhine anymore, not since the fire of '42 and the flood of '46."

"I hate the Rhine," she said again and wheezed out a breath. "Asa," she mouthed sternly, pointing toward the store. "Inside." She clamped onto Pop's arm and pulled him along.

Connor wiped the telescope lens with the hem of his shirt. "I'll be able to see the moon," he said, and aimed the scope toward the sky.

"Man in the moon," Grammy whined, "has relations with the stars."

"What's a speakeasy?" he asked Tempy.

"Don't ask questions right now, Connor." Tempy watched after her parents, anxiously cracking her knuckles.

"Why doesn't Mom like the Rhine?"

"We used to live there."

"I don't remember that."

"You were born there. Most of it burned down. Now it's full of ... places where men go." She glanced at him but was distracted by their parents' exchange.

"Rats in the bread," Grammy whispered.

"Why does Mom hate it?"

Tempy shot him a nervous glance. With one hand she checked her hair tied in a topknot. She bit her bottom lip, looking like she was about to tell him a secret. " 'Cause there's floosies there," she said.

"What's a floozy?"

"Connor, be quiet for two minutes, okay?" Tempy studied Connor and cracked her knuckles.

Connor rolled his eyes and smiled when Grammy rolled hers, too. Before Grammy went crazy, she'd told him stories about the

23

great German hero Siegfried, who killed a dragon and drank its blood, and then afterwards, he could talk to birds. Connor wished he could find some dragon blood. It'd be fun to speak to a woodpecker.

"You always wind up with a present," Tempy smirked, pointing at the telescope.

"I'll let you look at the moon," he said.

His sister stared at him oddly. "I know what the moon looks like."

"But up close you'll be able to see mountains and lakes. Maybe we'll even see some moon floosies."

"That's not funny."

Connor aimed the telescope down the street. Maybe he'd see the pretty red-haired girl. He suspected floosies were bad. It was okay that Tempy wouldn't tell him about them, he'd just ask Rusty. Rusty knew all kinds of things. He focused the telescope and settled on a blond-haired man running from store to store.

The man wore brown alligator boots, and Connor looked up as the shoes ran past him. The man's short-sleeved khaki shirt overhung moleskin work pants that looked well-lived in. "Hey," he called out and jogged back toward them. "You seen a girl, 'bout that tall?" He held out his hand. "Red-headed."

"She went to Marcescent Street," Connor said dutifully.

"Marcescent Street," that man repeated, wiping his brow. "Who in God's name would send a child there?"

"My mom," Connor volunteered, pointing inside the store.

The man looked inside the store, studying Connor's mother. "Why?" he said, almost a whisper.

"'Cause she's a floozy," Connor said helpfully.

The man cocked his head and stared at Mom, then sprinted down the street, no longer stopping at the stores. Grammy looked after him, raised a finger to her throat and sliced across it, making a zip sound.

Soon his parents came out of the store. Pop looked exhausted from arguing with Mom. He pushed Grammy's wheelchair, and as they strolled to the car his father put a positive spin on staying in Notown for another year. Connor was just as happy in Notown. He had made friends, and Herman had said the Notown School wasn't too hard. "Pop," he asked. "Did we have a big house when we lived in the Rhine?"

His father explained that they'd only lived there a couple years, but it was his mother's reaction that he noticed. Her shoulders hunched up into her neck as she shot a swift glare at Tempy. His sister clutched her hands and rubbed her knuckles with a thumb. He'd have to ask Rusty about the Rhine.

As Connor climbed into the backseat of the Chrysler, across the street he noticed a glistening restaurant sign, *Moon Over The Rhine*. He wondered if that was what the red-haired girl was looking for. The sign's moon was full and tinged a bluish color. Would the real moon be blue through a telescope?

On the corner, Little Preacher Boy stood on a vegetable crate, Bible raised and shouting about the Devil. Most people walked past him, but the ones who stopped and listened nodded their heads, held their palms to the sky, and occasionally shouted "Praise the Lord" and "Amen, brother." Connor looked back at the blue moon. It was sheer, inviting, and otherworldly, almost like the beautiful red-haired girl. The blue moon had a face and one of the eyes winked. Connor smiled. He knew how to scare Bryson Pomeroy out of the mountains forever. Preacher Boy was about to meet the Devil head-on. Connor knew Rusty and Herman would help him, but they'd need one other person. They needed a Blue Fred.

Another dead woman. This one in their very own town. Connor stared wide-eyed at Rusty's mouth as he spoke. He could read the words *dead woman* on his friend's lips, without having to hear them.

"A dead woman," Rusty repeated. "Called Bette Moss."

"Done like the Black Dahlia?" Connor asked.

"Worse." Rusty walked ahead on the path, hopping onto some tree roots that humped up out of the ground. Holding one hand onto the thin papaw tree, he swung around in front of Herman and Connor. "Cut off her head. Body propped on a rock under one of the canal bridges in Quinntown, hands folded on her lap, dress drenched red with blood that gushed from the stump of her neck." Rusty jumped back on the path. "You sure the Blue Freds live this way?"

"Yep," Connor said, hardly hearing his own words. "Pop traded with 'em at the farmers' market, a case of Hershey's Kisses and fourteen boxes of Cheerios for a side of butchered hog meat."

"Tell me about the head again?" Herman asked.

"The law can't find the woman's head," Rusty said. "Cut clean off from her body. Sheriff brought his hunting dogs, you could hear 'em bark for miles around, but much as they tracked, no head."

"How'd you find out?" Connor asked, his curiosity mixing with a dark stirring deep in his belly.

"Tom Dixon, used to live in my house. He's joined the police department. Darius Stark is sponsoring him. Said they might do the same with me when I'm older."

"Who'd take her head?" Herman asked.

"A monster," Connor whispered, unable to get the image of the blood-gushing neck out of his mind, just as the photos of the Black Dahlia had occupied his dreams. "Reckon she'll be in a magazine like the Black Dahlia?"

"Same book as your blue people," Rusty smirked.

"They really blue?" Herman asked.

"For the hundredth time, yes." Connor's voice squealed with the same exasperation as when he'd first explained the plan. Neither friend believed him. "Pop didn't have enough chocolate at the farmers' market to pay off the hog meat, and they trusted him to bring it up their holler. I talked to 'em. I played with 'em. One of the boys gave me an Indian ring." He pointed at a faded scar on his index finger.

They walked on for a while in silence. "We're far enough back in the hollow now, if'n there's blue people back here they probably ain't human," Rusty said.

"They're blue cause their blood is closer to their skins than ours," Connor explained. "Not a thing to hold against a body. The blue ones rarely come to town. Folks make fun of them."

The land sloped into a flat basin with dirt footpaths leading to a circle of houses. Other cabins hung on the hillside all the way up to the far ridge. Blufred Hollow, people called it, land of the Blue

Freds. The Manfred family had settled the area back in the early 1800s. The Dyers, the Goes, and the Claxtons joined them in time. Connor figured they must have all gotten along because most of them had stayed up here, rarely leaving their territory. Only difference between them and other people was that some of them had a bruised skin tone that ranged from lilac to the blue underbelly of a fish.

Connor peered among a clutch of fourteen or so children playing ball in a dirt patch behind the cabins. He saw who he was looking for . . . Blue Toomey. Connor stepped out from behind a tree and waved at the tall, barefooted blue boy wearing dungarees rolled up around his shins. Toomey fell out of the game, as did two of his cousins. They sprinted up the hill, grabbing sticks along the way.

"Good Lord," Rusty said, "that boy is blue as a smashed thumb."

"Sure they're human?" Herman asked, staying behind the tree.

"He's even got blue fingernails," Rusty said, shielding his eyes with a hand for a better look at the sloe-eyed youngster headed his direction.

"Don't make him mad," Connor warned, "or he'll turn purple."

As the young men got closer, Toomey waved off his cousins. "It's okay," he said. "I reckon one of 'em." The cousins stayed by his side, sticks in hand.

"Brought you some candy, Toomey." Connor held out a bag of leftover Hershey's Kisses. It'd been fuller when they started, but Rusty had eaten half of it on the way up.

"Fer from home," Toomey said, sitting down with his cousins and emptying the bag. Popping chocolate into his mouth, he said, "Ain't killin' another hog 'til next spring."

"Got a proposition for you." Connor sat cross-legged in front of him.

Toomey sucked the candy, closing his eyes as sugar focused his senses. "What's in it fer me?"

"There's a blight on the land." Connor steadied his voice to sound serious. "Name's Pomeroy. Working his way toward your people, and if'n he gets here, you'll be at church morning, noon, and night. I already been this morning, and I'd had to go back again tonight except I convinced Pop to take us boys up to Pinnacle mountain to see the stars. It was a big fight between Mom and Pop . . . church, stars, stars, church."

Toomey and the cousins opened their eyes wide, stuck on every word coming from Connor's mouth. "Our women folk is like that, too." Toomey looked over his shoulder toward a few blue women tending clothes in a large boiling pot over an open fire. He nudged his cousins. "Women folk finds out there's a traveling preacher nearby, they go all loony. Remember last time."

Both cousins nodded. One explained, "Thought things would never get back to normal. Got whipped when we hollered, whipped when we fought, even whipped when we danced. Everything we did was against God's law."

"We don't need no more church," the other cousin agreed.

"What's to be done about it?" Toomey asked.

Connor smiled. "Remember the farmers' market?"

Toomey looked at each of his cousins, then back at Connor. "Hell's bells, man! I almost got shot that day. This crazy sheriff thought I was an escaped South American monkey." He wiped his forehead as if to say he'd dodged the bullet with his name on it. "Daddy ain't let me go to town since."

"Pomeroy don't carry weapons, he fancies hisself a man of God." Connor leaned in. "Real scared of the Devil."

"Meet us at the creek rock bridge on Beltline Road, Monday night at dusk," Herman said. "There's potluck after the revival service. He's always the last to leave 'cause his daddy packs up all the extra food and takes it home."

29

"Always promises to bring it to the orphan house," Rusty sneered, "but only half of it makes it, if that."

Toomey looked aside, then demanded, "Another bag of candy and a pig-skinned football. One we got's losin' air."

Connor huddled with Rusty and Herman and figured out that they could steal a ball from the Contrary High School while Connor got more chocolate from his father.

"Ain't enough," a cousin argued. "We're taking all the risk."

"And my dignity is worth a little extra." Blue Toomey grinned. "But I'll throw in a set of red peppers taped to my head as horns."

Connor, Rusty, and Herman looked at each other, trying to figure what else they could give.

"I got something for you," Rusty volunteered. "I'll show you where a woman got her head cut off."

"Naw," the cousins groaned simultaneously.

"Yep," Rusty said. "Blood all over the place. On Marcescent Street, under a bridge in Quinntown. Heard said there's even a bloody sheet on the creek bank."

"How much blood?" Toomey asked.

"Marcescent Street," Connor repeated. "You never said it was on Marcescent Street."

"There's a hoochie house there, too," Rusty said to the Manfreds. "Could be Bette Moss worked there. Could be one of her men who sliced her neck."

Connor felt dizzy and swallowed hard. The Manfred cousins put out their hands, and he, Herman, and Rusty put theirs out as well as they shook on the plan to make Bryson Pomeroy think the Devil was after him. But the Devil wasn't on Connor's mind. Bette Moss was. As they journeyed back to the main road, Connor again said, "You never said it happened on Marcescent Street."

"What's it matter where it happened?" Rusty asked.

"What did Bette Moss look like?"

Rusty laughed heartily. "Without a head, who knows."

"Don't say that!" Connor pushed him. "Why don't you pay more attention to things!" he hollered. "All you ever know is killing and candy and bloody death!"

"You gone crazy?" Rusty fussed back at him.

"We don't have to see the bloody sheets," Herman said, swallowing hard.

A wave of nausea surged through Connor's stomach. "I know somebody who went to Marcescent Street."

"Couldn't be a person you know," Rusty smirked. "Heard some of her hair was caught on a bush. Red hair. Red as scarlet. Red as blood. That's why I think she was a hoochie girl. Your girl a hoochie girl?"

"She is not!" Connor shoved past Rusty and ran down the mountain toward home. In his mind the words repeated . . . *Vous êtes mon sauveur. Vous êtes mon sauveur.*

The boy ran with the wind, his feet grabbing the terrain like a fox that knew its territory. Once inside his home, he shut the door to his room and closed his eyes to the stark territory of his mind. Gray with amethyst sky. A small boulder off to the left. The Black Dahlia sat there, her raven hair cascading down her back. She stared at the ground between her knees. She stirred, looking over her shoulder, expecting someone.

A sharp knock jarred Connor from his reverie.

"Suppertime, son," Pop called out. "We'll head out to look at the stars just before dark."

Connor pulled the telescope off the shelf, holding it tightly to keep his fingers from trembling. He inhaled shivery breaths, wondering at this world he'd created behind his closed eyes. Was the Black Dahlia really alive there? Was she safe? Was Bette Moss the lost French gal? Could she hide from her killer in this daydream he could almost touch? Had he and his mom pointed that beautiful girl to her death?

The jostling of Pop's car on the Notown Road caused Connor's leg to touch the thigh of Iona Stark, Tempy's new best friend. He stiffened and scooted closer to the door. She was a string bean girl, and he couldn't figure out why she wouldn't shift more to the center. Tempy, on the other side of her, was sprawled sideways, knee up on the seat, and taking up most of the room.

Connor leaned forward and shot her a look. She didn't take the hint, probably because her lips flapped nonstop about a movie called *Black Narcissus* that she hoped to see at the Rosa Drive-In next week if one of the two girls could borrow a car. Connor was certain Pop wasn't going to loan her the family Chrysler. He wished he'd sat up front with Herman, but they were leaving that seat free for Rusty 'cause he usually smelled too bad to sit with the girls.

They turned down a lane that had no name. The indigo-colored orphan home sat three houses down. Connor jumped from the car, but stopped short of the fence. What if Judge Rounder remembered him as helping Rusty sneak back in the house a couple weeks ago?

"Pop," Connor asked, "reckon you could ask Judge Rounder if Rusty can come?"

"You lacking in a wee bit of self-confidence, son?"

Connor nodded and glanced toward the ground.

Pop chuckled and opened the car door. "How 'bout I stand behind you?"

Connor climbed the stairs of the wraparound porch while Pop waited at the bottom of the steps. Holding his breath, Connor knocked just above the lock. A skinny brown-headed boy cracked the door. "Looking for Rusty Haskew," Connor said. "He's needed for a scientific expedition."

"Rusty!" the boy yelled.

"Don't holler in the house!" spit a tinny voice as a fleshy hand slipped behind the boy's head and smacked him. The child moved aside, rubbing the back of his noggin. The door opened wider.

Judge Rounder looked down at Connor, his bulbous blue eyes showing the whites all around and brown hair parted in the middle slicked back behind his ears. "What needs ye?" he asked, a sideways cock of his head acknowledging Pop.

Connor cleared his throat, his back warming with sweat. "My pop is taking us to look at stars on top Pinnacle Mountain with a telescope. Wanna see if Rusty Haskew can come."

Judge Rounder's lips pressed into a thin line. Close up, he was a younger man than Connor expected, and behind him, a circle of boys gathered to see what was going on. "Orphans aren't allowed out after dark," the judge replied, his curious gaze whipping from Connor to Pop. "Lessen it's church, and I go with them."

"It'll help us in school, Judge Rounder," Connor said, just as the idea popped into his head. "Want your boys to make good grades, don't ya?"

"Boys?" he asked. "Are all the boys invited?"

Connor looked down, biting his bottom lip. "Only got room for one."

"I hear that from so many families." He mouthed a snaky smile. "That why most of them are here."

"Sir?"

"If all can't attend, then none of them can go," he said in a soft voice that flowed like water.

Rusty bounded down a back staircase, having heard that the goings-on were about him. He broke through the circle of kids and anchored himself beside his guardian. "Please, Judge Rounder," he pleaded. "I'll do extra duties."

"No argument from you!" he spit at Rusty, and held him back with an arm across the door.

"Sir," Pop interrupted and came up a few steps. "I'll be responsible for the boy. Maybe another day we can round up a bunch of cars and take everyone up there. I'm sure Connor will lend his telescope."

"I'll thank you, sir, to cease stirring trouble in my house. I let one boy have privileges, the rest are out of control."

"Surely, just this once–"

"Do I come to your place of business and tell you how to operate?" The Judge stepped out the door, his lips set in a trembling line.

Pop rested a hand on Connor's shoulder. "Come on, son," he said.

"But, Pop?" Connor tugged on his father's arm.

"They'll be no convincing here," Pop said.

"Wait," Connor called out and ran to the car. He grabbed the sack of baloney sandwiches and brought it back. "I can give him his birthday present, can't I?"

"He has no birthday." Judge Rounder's face wrinkled in a ball that reminded Connor of a large cabbage.

35

"Mr. Rounder–" Pop started.

"Judge Rounder," the judge interrupted.

"What's the harm in it?" Pop continued. "My boy wants to give one of yours a gift. It's a kindness."

Judge Rounder stepped aside and motioned toward Rusty.

Connor leaned in and handed his friend the bag of food. Rusty snatched it and bounced toward the staircase, a gush of boys chasing after him. Connor knew Rusty would be lucky to scarf down two of the sandwiches before the others took them from him, but at least he'd have that much in his belly.

Judge Rounder's lips frowned on Connor. "That beating's on you."

Connor jumped off the porch and stood behind Pop. His father put an arm around him and called out to Rounder. "I hope you remember, Judge, that one day those boys will be men."

The Judge slammed the door, scoffing as it closed, "Bringing trouble to my house."

As Connor and his father walked back to the car, Pop's arm tightened around his shoulder, and it made him feel safer. "Pop," he asked, "why do people forget about orphans?"

"Guess seeing them reminds them of how they've failed," Pop told him. "Doesn't take that much to choose kindness. You did that, son."

Tempy rolled down the window and fussed at him. "You gave away all our baloney sandwiches, Connor."

"Hush, Tempy," Pop said. "Connor made the decision of a wise man."

Tempy glared at him as he climbed into the backseat. He spread his legs like a boy, causing Iona to shift toward his sister. He wasn't going to give any more ground to cranky people, not even if he was related to them.

36

The stars . . . as Connor had never seen them. Constellations that he'd looked at from his home appeared like they might reach down and touch him on the top of Pinnacle Mountain. Before the sun went down, Pop showed the youngsters the slope of the Cumberland Gap, telling them stories of how frontier men had carved out the Wilderness Road through that natural formation and led early settlers into the dark and bloody ground of Kentucky.

The waning crescent moon rested like a tear in the sky. Stars poured out of the cup of the Big Dipper. Pop pointed out the town lights of Middlesboro, Kentucky and Cumberland Gap, Tennessee, but Connor couldn't take his gaze away from the diamonds blanketing the sky. Letting Herman take his turn at the telescope, Connor listened to Pop tell the story of Sagittarius the centaur, a half-horse, half-man creature that shot arrows across the sky.

"Bet he can shoot lots of rabbits from up there in the sky," Connor said. Tempy and Iona had followed a path up to the top of the hill, where sandstone rock formations made for good sitting places. Connor turned in a circle, becoming dizzy from the perspective of all that was above him. Mixing with the majesty was the wafting aroma of pine trees. Fireflies dotted the mountains like fairies playing hide-and-seek. Croaking frogs and slithering nocturnal creatures he could only imagine caught him up in a vortex of scent, sound, and image. He stepped away from the others as if being pulled by starlight. "Pop, going to the top of the hill."

"Take a flashlight, son," Pop called out, "and watch for snakes."

Snakes were not on Connor's mind, but rather sitting on the highest peak under the cover of the brilliant galaxy and pawing the ground like a wolf ready to howl at the moon. Could the night be any better, he wondered. He illuminated the path until he found a worn staircase of rocks embedded in the earth. Closing his eyes and turning off his light, he stood quietly, letting his feet get the feel of the ground. When he looked ahead, he followed shadows. The arch of his foot hugged the ground. Even though Connor had never been to this mountain before, he felt a sensation of comfort. Beneath his boot he could tell the difference between a pebble and a twig, a tree root and a vine. He revolved in a circle, breathing in the night that fed his imagination with a moist cloak of familiarity. A shuffle off to the side caught his attention.

Pulling his flashlight from his pocket, he aimed it and pressed the button, revealing two entwined figures. A giggle burst from his lips, and Tempy and Iona broke apart. "I see you k-i-s-s-i-n-g," he sang, pointing at them.

Tempy flashed her own light in his direction. "Turn that off!" she hollered.

"You first," he teased back.

"Tempy," Iona said, voice stressed and high pitched. "Do something."

Tempy stomped through the brush between them, took hold of his arm and jerked it toward her. "Little brat!"

"Hey," he yelled, "that hurts."

"You'll more than smart if you say a word."

"You don't get to tell me what to do!" He tugged away from her, but she held him tight.

"Little woods colt, been nothing but trouble since the day we found you."

"Ain't a woods colt," he said, insulted by being called a foundling child. "What's wrong with you?"

"You tell, and I'll let Pop know the truth. Mom found you on a creek bank. You're not even part of this family. Pop finds out, he'll send you to the orphan house. You'll live just like that stinky little friend of yours, Rusty Haskew."

"You're crazy, Tempy." He knocked the flashlight out of her hand, and she let him go. He flipped his flashlight off and stepped off the path into the darkness. The shadows of the woods hid him. He wrapped his arm around an elm tree, holding to the furrowed bark as if to make himself part of it.

"Tempy," Iona called out. "Can't see a thing."

Connor watched the outlines of the two girls reaching for one another. Their hands clasped and his sister pulled Iona to the main path. They spoke in whispers that he couldn't hear. When they passed him, he leaned down, searching the ground, and found their flashlight. He rolled it into the path and Iona kicked it. Both girls fell to their knees, hands sweeping the path until one of them found the light.

The girls made their way toward Pop, and Connor was glad to be alone. There was peace to it, and he wasn't afraid of the woods. Tempy's mean words blistered his feelings. Suddenly all the odd looks she'd given him through the years blossomed with a different meaning. Everybody in his family was dark-headed except for him. Tempy and Mom had blue eyes, but Pop's eyes were brown like his, he rationalized. His sister was crazy, he decided, and squeezed the thoughts from his mind, but those words left a scar on him, and in his imagination, the scar became a creek, a slow meandering stream off to the right of this land behind his eyes. A girl sat on the bank, her red hair twisted loosely into a bun on her head, long tendrils streaming down her neck. She let her fingers dip into the cool water. The Black Dahlia still sat on the rock opposite her, face turned up toward the lavender sky. The red-haired girl looked toward him. It was her . . . the beautiful red-haired girl he'd seen in Quinntown. She dipped her eyes, then smiled, her lips parted and formed the words *"Beau garçon."*

39

"Connor!" Pop yelled out, breaking his imagining. "Come on down, we got to get home."

"Coming, Pop," he hollered back, and flipped on his flashlight. He took a breath, thinking on what he'd seen his sister and Iona doing. They were silly. Acting like boyfriend and girlfriend. Practicing for the real thing.

Connor cut his own path down the hill and emerged from the woods several feet in front of them. Pop laughed and called him a jackrabbit. Herman commented that Connor could find a path even in a briar patch. Tempy and Iona, following behind, stared at him with worried expressions. Connor flipped his flashlight on and off in their eyes and stuck out his tongue.

On the way home, Pop turned on their newly installed car radio, and Dinah Shore sang "Buttons and Bows," followed by Art Mooney crooning "I'm Looking Over A Four-Leaf Clover." Connor couldn't sing along with the songs like the others. Tempy's words played in his head, and after they dropped Iona and Herman off, he climbed into the front seat with Pop. He decided not to say anything to Pop about what he'd seen the girls doing. What he'd done to Tempy was meant to tease her. He hadn't realized she would take it so seriously. He'd keep their secret, just to have something on his sister.

"Think we might take Rusty next time?" he asked his father. "You don't mind that he's an orphan, do you?"

Pop answered, but Connor couldn't concentrate on his words and instead stared out at the outlines of houses they passed. The world behind his closed eyes was like that . . . outlines in moonlight. He wondered if the Black Dahlia and the red-haired girl were happy in that other place. Maybe if he thought hard enough, he could put some flowers there, maybe a farmhouse where they could live.

Thinking about ways to protect the women kept Connor's mind off Tempy calling him a foundling. His sister had to be lying, he told himself. But what if she wasn't? Maybe that was why he hadn't said anything to Pop about his sister kissing a girl. If she told Pop that he wasn't his son, Rusty's situation could be his. Connor knew he could survive many things, but not the place where Rusty lived.

He didn't speak to Tempy the rest of the night, and decided he might not talk to her for a month. What he hated most was the doubt she'd put in his head. If Mom had found him on a creek bank, would Pop really send him to the orphan house? And if they weren't his parents, who was? He might as well live in the gray world of his mind, and with each visit, he'd bring the women more color.

5

Connor could hardly believe that the first day of school was a Labor Day parade, and it wasn't even the official holiday. Schools from the surrounding area joined in for a picnic, games and races, even a tug of war. Families were invited and local politicians showed up to solicit votes for the November election. Connor watched as two men supporting Thomas Dewey for President started shoving another man carrying a Harry Truman poster. Policemen broke up the fight and the Dewey supporters were hauled off to jail.

For the games, Connor had signed up to run in the fifty-yard dash and a rope-climbing contest. But before that, he and his buddies planned to sneak away at Marcescent Street and look for the bloody sheets left on the canal bank. Connor had been unable to find out any more about the identity of the murdered woman. Even the boys at Rusty's house were clueless. Connor wondered if the whole story had been made up. Then, at least, his red-haired girl was alive . . . somewhere.

Later that night, he and his friends were meeting Blue Toomey and his cousins to scare the dickens out of ole Pomeroy. If all went well, by tomorrow Connor's life would be in order. Church only once a week, and who knew, maybe he'd see the red-haired girl again. Maybe seeing her in that place in his mind was just his imagination. Least he could do would be learn the meaning of the words she'd said to him. *"Beau garçon,"* he whispered to himself, hoping those words meant that she liked him.

Today was more than the first day of school. Today would change his life. He watched a marching band pass, followed by a convertible carrying Quinntown's grim-faced mayor. Connor twisted his cap on sideways, his head itchy now that his hair had begun to grow back.

After the parade, Connor, Rusty, and Herman let the younger children line up in front of them to march to Copperhead Fields. Miss Singer held a hand high so everyone could see her. With so many young ones in front to keep the teacher's attention, the older boys lagged back. As they crossed Marcescent Street, Rusty pointed. "Yonder it sits, the snot-colored one." He pointed at a green building called the Regal Hotel, the hoochie place as he usually called it.

Beside them a blond-haired girl asked, "Where ya going?"

Rusty whipped around and snarled, "Hey! Who said your mouse-face could come back here and listen?"

"She only asked a question." A tiny black-headed girl stepped in front of her friend and wrinkled her nose at Rusty. Connor's cheeks flushed as he recognized Randi Jo Gaylor, one of the girls who'd been at Pop's store the day his head was shaved. She'd come out to the creek afterwards and told him where to find the gray caps, and even offered him a nickel to buy one so he could hide his bald head. He'd thrown a rock at her.

Now, a rush of embarrassment heated Connor's cheeks, but she didn't look his way or back down from Rusty's orneriness.

"Get your hind ends back with the little kids or you might end up like Bette Moss," Rusty snorted.

The blond looked like she was about to cry, and Herman went over to her and rubbed her shoulder. "Go on," he said to her. "Girls don't need to be around Marcescent Street."

"Follow me." Rusty motioned and leaped up on the sidewalk. Connor ran after him with Herman not far behind. He turned to look at the lines of children continuing down the street. The black-haired girl watched him, her lower lip pouted.

The boys hopped a cinderblock wall behind the Regal Hotel and landed in a backyard. A clothesline stretched between two poles was heavy with female undergarments. Red bra, black garter belts, a girdle, several pairs of white panties. Rusty pointed and sniggered while Connor and Herman looked at each other in embarrassed titillation.

The boys ran under the clothing and emerged into an alley where they trotted up the back steps of a brick building. Inside, they snuck down the hallway and came out the front of the building onto Lester Street, then made their way to the end and a concrete traffic bridge over a canal. Built by President Roosevelt's New Deal workers, it had a pipe sticking out at one end that brought up a waterspout from an artesian well. The boys got a drink and then spit. The reek of sulfur wafted around them, but after a while their noses got accustomed to the smell.

"Maybe we oughta go back," Herman said.

"Chicken?" Rusty blurted.

"Nobody's afraid," Connor defended his friend as he surveyed the marshy land and stream so still that the muckish water hardly seemed to flow.

Rusty peered over the bridge and pointed. "Last one down's a stinky toe." He hopped the railing, landing on a steep bank, and slid down on wool-grass and sumac shrubs.

"Can't leave him there," Connor said, looking at Herman and thinking he likely had the same chills in his stomach.

"Nobody knows where we are," Herman said. "What if something bad happens?"

"It's three of us," Connor said. "We're renegades. Nobody hurts us." The two boys hopped the rail and slid down to the rocky shore.

Connor held his breath as he looked under the bridge. A cool breeze blew from the shadowy corners and the air he inhaled was smooth as water. He stepped underneath the bridge and his ears popped. Above, a car passed over with a howling sound. Tumbled stones sloped to the water's edge, and the boys spread out looking for evidence of murder.

The far side of the bridge sloped up in a dark curve as if something were sitting there watching them. Connor studied the shaft where it met the ground. Spider webs nested in the cracks and the cool, watery breeze gave him the feeling of being in a cave.

Whatever had happened under this bridge, he realized, now haunted it. Perhaps the cauldron of events was still considering itself, trying to decide what it would be, and the boys were intruders upon whatever it was becoming. The boys would never know the true horror of what had gone on here. It was between that girl and the darkness, and only she and the killer could surmise the rich tapestry of their dance.

Connor moved out into sunlight. Overhanging the banks were bushes of red berries. His foot scuffed a paper that was half buried in sand. He pulled it loose. Old English lettering said *Dragon Blood*. He glanced toward Herman and Rusty, who'd crossed the canal on protruding stones to inspect rocks on the other side. Conner looked again at the words, *Dragon Blood*, thinking about the stories Grammy used to tell him about Siegfried drinking dragon's blood, and then the hero could understand the language of birds. The trees overhanging the canal had plenty of good places for birds. A raven could have seen what happened. A starling might have heard. They'd know if the woman killed here was his redheaded lady. They'd know who'd killed her. The birds could tell him.

He tore off a small cluster of berries and bounced it in his hand. That was just one of Grammy's stories, he thought. Surely not true. People couldn't understand the language of animals. That was silly . . . but if there was a way . . . Could it be possible that dragon blood would allow him to speak to birds? As much as he doubted it, he wanted it to be true. He bit his bottom lip, weighing myth with his own common sense tugging against his desire for the world to send him a message.

Rusty hollered for him and he answered, "Be there in a minute."

"Gotta see this!" Herman enthusiastically squealed.

Connor popped a handful of berries in his mouth. The sour taste made him gag but he forced himself to swallow, telling himself that dragon blood berries would give him the answers he needed. He put another handful in his shirt pocket for later. He didn't know how much he'd need, but for sure, he'd know what happened on this creek bank if Grammy's stories had even a trace of truth.

"Look." Herman pointed as Connor came up behind him.

"Blood." Rusty voice expelled in a flat breath. "I smell it."

The boys bent down, studying stains, unsure of what they were seeing. Connor stepped into the sunlight. His friends followed him, then all three halted.

"There," Connor said, pointing at the creek bank where green foliage was dotted brown, not scarlet red like he expected, but a nasty mud color that gave off a metallic smell. Flies circled the area like rodeo riders and their buzz heightened in an irritating drone.

"That ain't so much," Rusty said, disappointed.

"Cops must have already taken the bloody sheets," Herman surmised.

"This is where she ran," Connor said, pointing out what was the easiest way back to the street.

"She tried to get away," Herman mused, his eyes following the path. "But he caught her and . . ." The boys grew quiet, trying to imagine the atrocity that had taken place, each lost in a silent vision.

"This ain't enough to pay the Blue Freds." Rusty broke the silence. "Gonna bring some red paint down after school and make it look better."

Connor's stomach cramped and he coughed, hoping the nausea would pass. A woman had died here in the most horrible way and all they could think was making the place where it'd happened more gruesome. He leaned on a bridge piling, one hand on his stomach. He took off his cap and hung it on a spike. Wiping sweat from his brow, he realized that the weather was not all that hot.

"Better get to the picnic," Herman said, "before we're missed."

They jogged around the canal bank until they got to the woods on the far side of Copperhead Fields. Once they crossed through, they could join the festivities and no one would notice that they'd been absent. Connor reached up to wipe his forehead again and realized that he'd forgotten his cap. "Gotta go back," he called out. "Meet you at the games."

He trotted down the canal bank, under the bridge to the shaggy, bloodstained greenery, and found his cap hanging on the bridge spike as he'd left it. He stepped under the bridge again. Cars passing above made it groan, and in the sound, he thought he heard a baby cry. The familiar feel of a presence nosed up to him. His throat burned and his stomach lurched. At first he thought he might throw up. He looked over at the trees growing along the top of the canal bank. Must be birds in there, he thought as he stepped out on the other side of the bridge into sunlight.

"Do you know what happened here?" he asked. The branches shivered and burst into a kaleidoscope of sparks. Were the trees on fire? A spear of lightning struck the ground beside him. A rush swished through his head. In the canal water, an inky ribbon of blood curled past. He stepped on higher ground, watching it spread when a woman's hand shot up out of the dirt beside him. He yelled and ran into a stinging wind that chafed his cheeks.

Hopping across the water on some moss-covered stones, he missed his footing and landed in mud. He made it to the woods and grabbed onto a dogwood tree. Not far to go, he thought. The birds were not going to speak to him, but every manner of Devil was. As he looked back, the banks of the canal simmered with boiling blood. Women were caught in its flow as it fried them like acid.

Connor fell to his knees, hands on the sides of his head, praying harder than he'd ever prayed. This had to be a dream, a nightmare, and he had only to wake up. Acid blood began to drip from the trees. He curled into a ball, knowing he was about to die, when a wet nose touched his forehead. He looked up into a large brown eye. White fur surrounded it and above that a long white ear. A white rabbit rubbed its nose on his cheek, then hopped off down a path. Connor followed it, not sure what else to do.

Soon as he stepped onto the rabbit's path, a roar of fire consumed the world behind him. The rabbit seemed to know how to outfox the fire, even as walls of flame tunneled over him. Connor jumped for the ground on which the rabbit sat. Then, the rabbit was gone. Before him all was ash. Smoking tree stumps. Ground burnt and the sky gray with haze. The white rabbit lay on a rock, but it wasn't the full-bodied rabbit he'd chased. This one was starved, its ribs poking out of its belly, dying just as the earth around him was dead.

He pulled himself from tree to tree until he saw the back of a female with dark hair. The Black Dahlia? Maybe he was in that landscape where she kept herself. He came up behind her . . . she turned. No. Not the Dahlia. That little black-haired girl. The one with the boy's name. Randi Jo. She stared at him with big green eyes and, for a moment, Connor worried that she might not be real. He tried to speak but wasn't sure words came out.

"Your sis's hunting you," she said, shaking his shoulder. "I'll lead you back."

Connor realized he was at the pond next to the picnic site. His family would be on the far side. He bolted, leaving the girl standing there. All he could think of was getting to his Mom and Pop.

When he found them, he settled next to Grammy under a willow tree. Mom was making sandwiches, and Pop was off to the side talking to some men. Connor could hear the yells of children in the games. He must have missed the races he'd signed up for. He shifted closer to Grammy, wanting the comfort of her touch.

She leaned toward him, passed a hand over his scalp and sniffed. "You're not of me," she said, staring at him, passive eyes round as quarters.

Connor wondered if he was still in the horrid dreamscape. "I drank dragon blood, Grammy," he said, burping up the nauseous taste. "Birds didn't talk to me, but a white rabbit saved my life."

She put a hand under his chin. "Did she mark you? Did she rub her nose and whiskers on you?" Connor nodded, and Grammy cackled.

"What's it mean?" he asked.

"You've been marked–by the hare of Hertha."

"Why am I so sick?" Connor's stomach twisted in knots. The din of voices drowned out his own as he tried to tell her about what had happened to him. But his grandmother's voice penetrated all of it.

"Once you've been marked by Hertha, she keeps her eye cocked your way for the rest of your life."

"I'm sick, Grammy," he said. "Get Mom."

Grammy petted his head and seemed not to listen. "The hare saved your life. Someday, she'll demand the same of you."

Connor realized that his grandmother was crazy. Nothing could be done for her and she'd die crazy. Maybe he was dying, too. He pushed himself up. Getting to his feet took all his strength.

"Mom," he called out. She was twisting the cap off a pickle jar. "Pop," he said. Vaguely aware that they turned simultaneously at the sound of his voice, Connor's sight blurred and the world became a series of waves as he tumbled to the ground.

The Milky Way . . . a spiral that glistened with diamonds, and Connor was working his way to its center. Whispers in the distance. Were the stars talking? Connor listened to the voices that were near and then far. He drew closer to the voices and realized he could feel his fingers, but they were in a different place than him. He digested a swallow, also in a different place. While wondering at how he could be in two places at the same time, a single voice cracked through the mural of the galaxy.

"Please, God," it said.

Was he about to be in the presence of the Almighty? Connor wondered if he was dead. He opened his eyes. He was in his own bed. Tempy knelt on the floor beside him, hands folded in prayer, eyes squeezed shut.

"Please, God," she said. "I know I've done wrong. I swear to reform my ways. Just please, dear Lord, let my sins stay hidden in this lifetime, and take my brother to Your mighty halls."

Connor coughed, realizing that his sister wasn't praying for him, but to keep herself out of trouble for kissing Iona Stark. He didn't give a hoot who she kissed. She could smooch a walrus for all he cared. He moaned, half sorry for losing the starry world of the cosmos.

Tempy stood, staring down at him. Some of her hair had come loose from the topknot and she looked like she'd run a mile. "Thought you were rid of me, did ya?" he smirked.

"You foolish boy. Eating those berries. It's a wonder you're not dead." She held her hands in front of her, then cracked a knuckle. Her red-rimmed eyes watered up and she grabbed his hand and patted it. "I'm sorry, Connor. I didn't mean anything I said. I was looking everywhere for you to tell you. I lied about finding you on a creek bank. I was mad at you, and I'll never say a mean word again, just please don't say anything about me and Iona."

"Why would I care about that?" He pushed himself up, a nauseous wave flowing through his body. "What time is it?" he asked, remembering that he had to meet the Blue Freds at dusk.

"Lay down. The doctor said those berries could give you nightmares, maybe even hallucinations."

Connor swung his legs over the side of the bed. "The berries?" Suddenly the nightmarish landscape rolled upon him, infusing memories of boiling blood and dead arms shooting up out of the earth.

"Don't you got sense enough to spit out something that taste bad?"

"Like your cooking," he smarted off to her.

She bit her bottom lip, refusing to challenge him. "I'll get Mom and Pop. They're with the doctor."

Connor swallowed hard. He let his feet touch the floor. The reality of something concrete steadied him. For several seconds he let his toes tap the boards. Yes, this was the real world. Yet his other worlds were real as well. It was as if in his mind, every thought had a different universe: The world where Pop might not be his father; the nightmarish landscape of boiling blood and white hares; the growing haven of Bette Moss and the Black Dahlia; even the darkness under the bridge. The worlds were equally real, and yet, only in this one could he touch the floor.

Out the window, the sun was low in the sky. He had a couple hours before having to meet his friends and the Blue Freds. He could see his parents beside a black sedan, talking to Dr. Mead. Tempy came up to them and began to explain, and they all hurried toward the house. Before they got inside, Connor knew there was one thing he needed to do. He trotted around his bed and across the hall to his sister's room. It smelled like Ivory soap, and a stuffed black bear from a Smoky Mountains souvenir shop lay on mismatched pillowcases. On a shelf, he grabbed a French dictionary and hurried back to his room, stashing the book under his pillow just as Mom came rushing in, arms wide to hug him.

"Mom, air," he mouthed into her chest.

"You scared the chickens out of me," she exhaled, letting him go and placing him against the bed. "If I was a whipping woman, you'd sure get one now."

Pop stood behind her with an expression of relief as he reached out and touched Connor's shoulder. "You worried us, son," he said.

Dr. Mead put a stethoscope against Connor's back and asked him to breathe deep. Tempy stood in the doorway, lacing her fingers together in front of her, probably to keep from cracking her knuckles.

"I'm fine," he grumbled. "Thought they were cherries."

"Good thing we found the berries in your pocket, young'un," the doctor said. "We might've treated you for the wrong thing."

"Well, it's done," Mom said, unable to look away from him. "You'll know better next time." She had a pressed-lip expression like she wanted to grab Connor up and hug him again, so he figured to use the situation to his advantage. He coughed and rubbed his throat.

"You don't have a fever, do you?" Mom asked.

"Just a mite hungry. Got cravings for Hershey's chocolate. Funny thing." He looked up at Pop. "Reckon I might have a bag of Kisses?" Surely, he thought, being sick and all, he'd not be denied a whole bag.

"Anything you want." Mom looked over at Pop and nodded for his agreement. Tempy turned away and went into her room.

Minutes seemed like eternities as the doctor pronounced him well enough to go to school the next day. He made Connor take two tablespoons of a queer-tasting medicine and left the bottle on his nightstand. Mom promised to bring him supper in bed and said he could have two helpings of apple pie if his stomach was up to it. Pop watched him, saying nothing, and Connor couldn't help wondering what his father was thinking. Maybe that no son of his would have been foolish enough to swallow sour berries. Tempy had said she'd made the whole story up to bother him, but ragged fears scratched his insides like hungry rats.

Mom left to walk the doctor to the car, and Pop sat down beside him. "A whole bag of candy?" Pop put an arm around his shoulder and guilt made Connor look away. "Want to tell me?"

"Just hungry, that's all."

"You don't have to let me in on your secret, if you think that's the right thing to do."

Connor studied his father's eyes that hadn't left him since he'd entered the room. He looked aside, feeling uncomfortable doubt, wondering if his father would always love him. His dad had a way

54

of knowing when he was hiding something. Surely that said something . . . meant they were connected. "I promised it to the Blue Freds," he admitted. The scheme he and his pals concocted tumbled out of his mouth. Connor glanced up at Pop, trying to gauge his reaction. "Mad at me, Pop?"

His father twisted forward on the bed, hands clasped between his knees, staring at the floor. "Think it will work?" Pop asked.

Connor hesitated, half wondering if he'd heard correctly. "Worth a try," he said timidly.

"Hmmm." Pop stood and put his hands in his pockets. "Let me think on it. Now to bed, young man."

"But Pop, I've got to meet Rusty and Herman."

"Those boys are clever enough to get by without you tonight," Pop insisted, pointing to the bed.

Connor got under the covers, thinking that after Mom brought dinner, he'd pretend to be asleep and sneak out the window. "Whatever you say, Pop."

He got back into bed and pulled out the French dictionary. Sounding out the words, he looked them up one by one. *Beau garçon, vous êtes mon sauveur.* Beautiful boy, you are my savior. *Beautiful boy, you are my savior.*

Connor closed the dictionary and dropped it to the floor. He said the words over and over in his mind, both the French and the English. He wished he knew if Bette Moss and the red-haired girl were one and the same. He didn't feel like a savior. He could have escorted the redheaded girl to her death.

The doctor's medicine wound through his muscles, leaving him in a drowsy slump. He wished he could keep his eyes open. Part of him was afraid of returning to the nightmare world those berries had opened up. He drifted as if floating on water. For several seconds he saw the amethyst sky and jerked awake. Darkness filled the room. He held to the blankets, tapping his toes against the bed frame to keep himself centered and in the real world.

Outside the window, three stars arced like a bow. He realized he must have slept several hours. He wondered about these worlds of his. The nightmare landscape of acid blood where only a white hare could lead him to safety; the refuge he'd made for Bette and the Dahlia; the concrete place where his toes tapped the floor but where women were in fact torn apart by monsters. One place was as real to him as the other. Other people must not see these things, for surely someone would have spoken about it. Better to keep them to himself, else people would think he was crazy.

Cautiously, he closed his eyes, and there it was . . . the trickle of water, a fragrance of gardenia, gray outlines forming. The pale purple sky had darkened. It must be night there too, he thought. The quiet stillness of it fixed like a portrait. Then a movement . . . slight, as if a dance: the Dahlia repositioned herself to look up at a waning crescent moon. Bette moved as well, falling on her back in a patch of clover and letting her fingers dip into the stream. He thought about calling out to them, but was afraid he might scare them. He was satisfied with watching as his breath became deep and rhythmic. He realized that the gray landscape of his mind, stark as it was, gave him the same feeling of belonging that surrounded him in the woods. He also realized that was the reason why the Black Dahlia and Bette Moss stayed here. They were safe—the Dahlia and Bette. He'd given them sanctuary in this place where no one would ever hurt them again. Here, they would never encounter monsters.

Connor exhaled a breath of rest. Some part of him knew he'd missed meeting up with his friends. They'd have to tell him what happened with Preacher Boy and the Blue Freds. Had his plan worked? Would Little Preacher Boy be defeated this night? Drifting in and out of dreams, he saw the little girl with the black hair shaking his shoulder. She had an expression like she knew him, like she was his best friend. Her voice sang, "Your sis's hunting you." But maybe he didn't have a sister. Not if what Tempy had said was true. Why else would she pray for God to take him to His mighty halls, his own sister praying for his death. A real sister would never pray for such a thing. That could mean Pop wasn't his father; his mother just a woman who'd picked him up off the creek bank. Who was he? Who was Connor Herne? "I'll lead you back," the little black-headed girl said, her voice echoing all around him . . . "I'll lead you . . . I'll lead . . . I'll . . ."

He woke up. Daylight streamed through the window. On the pillow beside him lay two bags of Hershey's Kisses.

PROLOGUE TWO

September 1956

English folklore says that the mirror is an instrument incapable of reflecting a demon. This story came over on ships to the New World and worked its way deep into the mountains until now it's an old Appalachian saying. This tool in the hands of a narcissist can fabricate fantasies even for a homely girl, letting her slip on the sin of vanity to balance the flaws with strengths. But it hides the wicked streak the same way a vampire is unable to see its likeness.

With the prospect of facing a lover she'd not seen in six years, Tempy Herne was ready to lie to herself. She was pleased that her milky skin showed no blemishes, but she'd given up on her hair. Spiral locks stuck out from her scalp, making her head look like one misshapen triangle. She'd used half a bottle of Tame Cream Rinse and her tresses were still one frizzy mess. Nothing worked. She'd ironed it and only had burns on her fingers to show for it. Large rollers made of Campbell's soup cans helped, but sleeping in them gave her the worst headache and the style lasted all of fifteen minutes before her springing curls did whatever they wanted. After working in a dab of Brylcreem, she held up a mirror so she could style the back. Mother Mary couldn't have prepared her for what she saw . . . a nickel-size bald spot on the crown of her head.

She threw the mirror, shattering it into three pieces, and covered her face with both hands. She had to meet Iona Stark in twenty-five minutes and felt like she was going to throw up.

A million questions swirled through her mind. *Have I changed? Has she? Will she resent me for not writing? What if I embarrass her? Does she have a boyfriend? I have a bald spot. Oh, my God, I have a bald spot? Hide the flaw. Have to leave in ten minutes. Iona. Haven't seen her. Six years. Iona. What to do? Iona.* Tempy's fingertips balanced on the sink as she stared into her own panicked blue eyes. It never occurred to her that the object of her affection might be equally nervous, only that she might not measure up. In Tempy's mind, the mirror showed the plain-faced girl all she could have become–a teacher, a hairstylist, a bank teller, instead of a part-time store clerk who spent her nights living through characters in library books. She had haunted the Salinas Valley as Cathy Ames in *East of Eden*; gone on a quest for stardom with *Marjorie Morningstar*; and breathed in the Alexandrian sand with *Justine*. I can't do this, Tempy told herself.

"You break something?" her mother's voice pierced through the bathroom door.

"Mirror slipped," she lied. "I'll clean it up."

"That's seven year bad luck."

Tempy pressed her hands over her ears, wishing all the voices in her brain, and her mother's as well, would shut up. Twenty-three years of living in her parents' house and they still treated her like a child. Tempy had thought of leaving home only one time in her life and that was to follow Iona to college. Much as she didn't want to admit it, going away with Iona might have meant she would lose her love to the world. Better to stay in Contrary and live in the memory of their perfect days as young church ladies of the town.

Tempy grabbed the brush, smoothing her hair into a ponytail at the top of her head. She wound the mane into a topknot, covering the bald spot and looking the same as she had most of her adult life. This style was all her hair knew to do.

"Be back around eleven," she told Mom as she passed through the kitchen.

Mom's arms were elbow deep in soapy water. "That's a little late," she said without looking at her. "There's a church social for the young people, stop by there and say hi."

"Young people, Mom, means teenagers. I'm not a teenager anymore."

"There are still plenty nice boys there, and don't backtalk me, daughter."

Tempy had been brilliant at scaring off any suitor that came her way with her prim and proper *I don't do that and never will* attitude. "Leave those dishes for me, Mom," Tempy said with overly friendly enthusiasm, hoping to redirect her mother's thoughts away from boys. She searched her purse, making sure she had Chap Stick, extra bobby pins, and a rubber band in case the one tying up her hair broke.

Mom pulled her arms out of the dishwater and dried them on her apron. "Wonder if Conner will come in this weekend?" She tenderly lowered herself into a kitchen chair as if her knees hurt and blew out a sigh. "Have to remember to tell him he can invite his roommate some weekend if he wants."

Tempy fought a roll of the eyes. "He only left last week, Mom."

"Duke University is so far away. Don't know why he couldn't stay closer to home."

"Like me," she snapped. "I make you so happy."

"Being flip is not going to win you any friends in this world, Temperance Herne." Mom sighed again, looking aside. "People go away to college, they change."

Tempy bit her lip, knowing Mom wasn't talking about Connor. "Pop wanted him to go to Duke, and he did win that scholarship."

"People who leave, most times, don't want the same things they might have wanted when they were young and silly. Things that probably embarrass them now."

Tempy ignored the hints Mom knew how to stick in her gut so well. Sometimes she wondered if her mother even loved her. Connor was all Mom talked about, and since he'd left, her parents seemed stunned by his absence. Tempy hadn't missed him at all. Her brother's departure gave her more time in the bathroom. She paused at the top of the steps, thinking . . . *except, he's not my brother.* The words no longer frightened her. She'd thought them many times through the years but had never said them aloud. Nor had she and Mom ever discussed what happened all those years ago. Those events were like an ancient, frozen dinosaur, something she could observe through a blurred scrim of frost, but she lacked the skills to thaw its icy grave.

"Be home by ten," her mother called out after her.

Tempy clipped the door closed and pretended not to have heard. She waved to Pop as she passed the store underneath their apartment. He'd started work at five a.m., getting up to drag in frozen beef and chicken left in ice-filled crates on the sidewalk at four in the morning. Except for Tempy and Mom relieving him for lunch and dinner, he'd not had a break and she felt a little guilty going out. "Want me to push in the vegetable carts, Pop?" she called out to him.

"'Nother hour 'fore closing." He waved her off.

She nodded and stared at the vegetable stands in front of the store and the handmade signs her father had put up advertising a sale on potatoes and squash to compete with the new Kroger supermarket that had opened out near the highway. She was wasting time, she realized. Holding off walking the two blocks to the Contrary library. Iona Stark was there by now. Waiting on her. "Be home by eleven, Pop," she said, letting her fingers roam over a head of lettuce and a slick red pepper.

Every step rattled her insides and her heart pattered until she wiped sweat from her upper lip. She checked her profile in the reflection of the Dollar Store window. If only she had tried one more time with her hair. She found herself cracking her knuckles and shook her hands to ward off the nerves. Stop it, she told herself. A good friend returning home. Nothing to be nervous about. But what if school had changed Iona? What if Mom was right? Good Lord, she thought, I'm in my twenties and acting like a teenager in love.

Up the library steps, pulling open a solid oak door with a lion carved in the center. The comforting smell of old books puffing in her face like department store perfume. Nodding to the librarian, she coasted off toward the fiction section and pretended to look at a selection of Patricia Highsmith's novels. Iona's four years at a university and another two at a teacher's college would have given her a new perspective on life outside of Contrary. She had taken a job teaching French at the Crimson County High School. Suddenly Tempy regretted that she'd never sought higher education. Iona might not consider her an equal any longer. In an instant, she resented that Mom and Pop had sent Connor to college. She'd been so glad to get her brother out of the house that she hadn't really considered what it gave him over her. The apartment was finally quiet of his Dizzy Gillespie and Charlie Parker music. In many ways, it was the home that should have been, she thought. Me,

Mom, and Pop. Connor made daily life seem like it was on fire, and she resented the noise.

"Stupid," she said aloud.

"Shhhh," came from a librarian sitting at a nearby desk.

Tempy went to the farthest stack to be alone. All these thoughts of Connor had her so upset she could hardly think. Iona wasn't here. Maybe she'd changed her mind and this was her way of telling Tempy goodbye. Tempy sucked in breath through her teeth, causing a whistling wheeze, and turned the corner of the stack, knocking heads with a girl coming the other direction. Iona.

Stunned from the blow, the two looked at each other for several seconds. All Tempy could think was those dark black eyes melted into the core of her being, and she knew in that instant that if Iona pushed her away, she might as well jump off the nearest tall bridge.

"That hurt," Iona said, rubbing the spot on her head where they'd connected.

"Deserved it. You're late." The girls had a secret place in the far stack that was intersected by another, giving them a corner where they couldn't be seen. "In back?"

"Don't think I will." Iona stared at her, biting her bottom lip, and slowly wet the upper with a stroke of her tongue.

"Fine with me." Tempy's mouth tasted pasty and her breath quickened. Her insides tangled as she tried to read the puzzle of Iona's expression. Gently, Tempy let her fingers drift forward, caressing Iona's.

"I can't stay," she whispered. "Have to meet some French friends of Aunt Renita's. I'm the only other person in the family who knows that language."

"Of course." Tempy turned away, fighting the urge to crack her knuckles.

"We have to figure something out." Iona clasped Tempy's arm and pulled her behind the stack, watching over the books in case the librarian turned around.

"Speak plain," Tempy said, inhaling Iona's spearmint breath.

"Missed you." The words tumbling through her lips like small stones skipping across a still lake. Iona glanced again at the librarian, then inserted a hand behind Tempy's head and brought her face closer. Their lips touched. The soft feel of her flesh darkened Tempy's every other sense, and she lived in the honeyed taste she remembered so well. "Wasn't sure how you'd be."

"I'm still me."

"Good. I'm still me."

"We can't tell."

"I'll never tell. Just let us be this."

As if love was a dream, Tempy watched Iona move off, check out books, and push through the lion-headed doors, leaving them bouncing in the frame. Tempy sat at a maple table, turning pages of a newspaper she didn't read. When the library closed, she walked three blocks to the Westminster Cinema and watched *The Searchers* for the third time. Home by ten after ten, she found Mom sitting at the table, drinking a cup of milk and reading last Christmas's issue of *McCall's Magazine*.

"You're late," Mom said, turning a page.

"How come you never tell Connor to be home by ten?"

"How's Iona?" Mom asked, without looking up at her.

Tempy didn't answer.

"I forbid you to be alone with her," Mom continued, the dry clip of her voice like the snip of scissors. "Church, a social gathering, I can live with, but not alone."

When Connor goes over to that Notown church, he's eyeing that trashy Randi Jo Gaylor, and it'd serve you right if he dropped out of college and gave you a load of snotty-nosed grandchildren that'll be no more Herne than he is. Tempy hesitated and swallowed hard. For a second, she thought she had actually blurted those words. "Night, Mom," she said, and moved around her mother. Like a robot, she changed into her nightgown, washed her face, and took down the topknot, checking the crown of her head with a broken piece of mirror to see if the bald spot was any bigger.

Later on, she lay in bed staring into the dark and lost in the memory of Iona. With one touch of their lips, her spirit soared above all the frippery that was her life. But it wasn't enough. One touch. One kiss. The taste of the sole person who stole her breath. It wasn't enough.

As she tossed and turned, a plan formed. She sat up in bed and stared into her own dim reflection in the dresser mirror. Even then, she could not see the hissing vipers all around her. The mirror reflected back her pain. It lied, saying she would always be the victim, concluding that this situation was not her fault. She swallowed a congested sob. All her concentration was on her plan, her needs, *her world*. She could do it, if her resolve was strong, if she wanted Iona bad enough. She could turn Mom's attention toward Randi Jo Gaylor. Dropping hints around Mom, but discouraging Connor–that'd be all either of them would respond to, innuendo and a dare.

She didn't believe her brother would bother marrying somebody like Randi Jo. The girl lived in Notown and was from a family of eleven kids crowded into a five-room shack that barely clung onto the mountainside. Connor was, if anything, ambitious, full of big ideas that wouldn't include a nobody from Notown. Now that he was in college, he'd likely have his eye on some Southern debutante . . . but Mom didn't know that. Tempy would spur his interest in Randi Jo by telling him to stay away from Notown. Connor always wanted to do what he was told not to do. Yes, finally her pretender baby brother could be useful to her. A word here, an insinuation there, and she could keep the two of them spinning in directions they never thought they'd go. Mom would forget all about her and Iona.

Tempy licked her lips, the taste of girl still in her mouth. When would the next hidden minutes come? Her mind thrashed like a worker ant, concocting reasons to see Iona, places they could go that wouldn't draw suspicion. She twisted the blanket around her legs, closing her eyes to an internal world of sensation. Life could be so much easier if she didn't have these feelings, and yet, *this* want was all her heart knew to do.

MRS. WORDEN

Snow blanketed the woods like ironed linen. Pawpaw trees, ash, hickory, redbud, oak, maple, and poplar stood like ancient sentries. Before the primordial forest witnessed Daniel Boone cutting his way to the dark and bloody ground of Kentucky, its existence flourished with only wind, rain, or lightning daring to alter its shape. The sole foot upon its skin was of the nature of rabbit, cougar, bear, or deer. Even the Cherokee and Choctaw followed the Warrior's path, a natural trail cut by the great bison winding around the forks of mountains to the salt licks north. It might be that on this particular piece of land, eighteen-year-old Connor Herne was the first man to stand at the tip of the sharp ridge. He looked down at a coal mining operation hugging the fold of the parallel slope. A rickety tipple fed the coal down the mountainside and into train cars, its hurried drone marring the fresh whoosh of the outdoors.

Stepping off his perch, he wound his way through the trees until the harsh whine of the mine disappeared. This side of the mountain, unmarred by industry, filled him with a wild fervor. He stopped. Listened. A dull scratch of scampering. Connor swung his rifle around and aimed into a beech's skeletal limbs. He squeezed the trigger, the bullet cracked the still air, and a gray body silently fell.

Connor kicked through a snow bank, powdery as baking soda. A splash of red colored the vines where the squirrel landed. He picked the animal up by a bushy tail. Clean shot through the head, just the way he liked it; that way no bullet fragments ended up in the meat. Hunting ran deep in his blood, and before each shot, he made a silent pact with whatever beast he was tracking that this was the way of their world.

A shrill whistle cut the air from the ridge alongside him. Connor squinted into the white brightness. Rusty waved an arm over his head. "I got seven."

Connor glanced into his hunting sack at his nine squirrels. "Six," he called back.

A loud "ha!" exclaimed Rusty's glee. "Whoever gets skunked pays for the beer."

"Pfff. Willie's paying for the beer," he called back, referring to their wealthier friend who thought hunting was banal. Rusty signaled okay.

Herman trudged through the snow toward him, pointing his rifle skyward. "Counted nine shots from your hollow."

"Missed a few." Connor shrugged.

"You ain't miss a shot since junior high."

Connor pulled out three squirrels from his hunting sack and stuffed them in Herman's. "Let Rusty think he won."

Herman shook his head, "You don't got to apologize for yourself."

70

"Don't want to listen to his complaining about coming in second." Connor pointed to the tracked path for Herman to go ahead of him.

Over the hill Rusty waited with Pickles, a beagle he'd borrowed from Darius Stark, the man on whose property they were hunting. Herman set his bag on the trunk of his 1949 Buick and opened it up. "Five for me,"

Rusty punched the air. "Leave it to the army man to get the most kills." He pounded the hood in childlike glee. "How 'bout that, beat me a college boy and a businessman."

"I pump gas," Herman said.

"I'm all out of practice, not been hunting since I left for Duke last fall." Connor spread his hands to explain.

"Ante up." Rusty pulled a feed sack from his jacket and the boys deposited a portion of their bounty to the landowner for letting them hunt. Rusty pointed toward a two-story cabin. "Darius usually has beer."

"Can't," Herman said, opening his trunk and laying in his rifle and hunting bag. "Gotta get this car back. You don't know this, Connor, happened after you left for school, some sonnavagun stole Daddy's brand new Nash Ambassador. Right out of the church parking lot. This old Buick's only one we got between the two of us."

"Notown Holiness?" Connor asked, mouth ajar. "Reckon Pop was right not letting me take my car over there."

"Meet up tonight with you and the girls at Pinkie's," Herman called out and waved as he gunned his car through snow sludge.

Connor followed Rusty an acre back from the main road to a cabin surrounded by an unpainted plank barn and scattered store-houses. He noticed the hundred-and-eighty-degree view. Darius could see anyone coming toward the house from three directions and the three-hundred-foot vertical cliff behind the property blocked rear access.

"In the army we string somebody upside down and leave 'em to drink their pee for stealing a car," Rusty said, more a brag than a statement of fact. "Bet you don't get to roughneck at your fancy-smancy university."

"Know what I get in college that you don't have in the army?"

"What?"

"Pretty girls."

They scuffled in jovial play, then raced toward the front porch, sliding on ice along the way. Rusty stopped short of the steps and turned toward Connor. "Army uniform walks into a bar and I guarantee you every dame in the place swoons, so don't you think you're competing with the likes of me."

Connor saluted. The boys hopped onto the porch and kicked snow off their boots. Rusty pushed open the door, scraping it along the floor. A honking snore rattling from the couch came from a bulky man asleep on his side. Seemed odd since it was three in the afternoon, but the Starks ran a lot of businesses that were open late into the night, bars, restaurants, hotels, so maybe sleeping during the day wasn't so strange for them. Connor followed Rusty, eyes shifting around a room of empty beer bottles, scattered papers, and a stench that suggested unwashed clothing. "Maybe we oughta gut 'em at my house."

"Darius'll bug out if he wakes up and we ain't left him nothing."

Connor glanced around the living room while the property owner snored loud as a horn player. A strand of garlic hung on the back of the door, and at the top of three windows upturned horseshoes were nailed. "Your friend a little bit superstitious?"

Rusty looked in from the kitchen. "Oh, that. Get this. Darius is afraid of ghosts. Don't ask me why. I don't get it."

Connor puffed out a chuckle. Beside the couch, an overturned bottle spilled the contents of pills around the barrel of a snub nose, pearl-handled pistol. Rusty ripped the hide off a squirrel, releasing the metallic smell of blood and innards. Connor gingerly picked up the pistol and slid it underneath the couch. Best to avoid any misunderstanding should Rip Van Winkle wake up, he thought, then turned the pill bottle upward and read the name Seconal. Unsure what it was, he figured the drug had knocked Darius out and was probably the reason for his ghosts.

"Knife won't cut worth a damn," Rusty called out, leaning into it to snap off a squirrel paw. "Slate's out in the barn, shelf next to the horse harnesses." He nodded for Connor to go get it.

Connor followed a snow-packed path with Pickles following him. The barn door swung against icy slush. Inside, bales of hay formed a wall dividing the barn. Two horses stalled next to each other shifted to look at him. A worktable, as messy as the house, steadied the wall of hay. Connor searched through scattered tools and found a block of slate beneath a greasy cloth. He turned to go when he noticed a gleam between the bales of hay.

Walking around the hay, Conner saw a trio of cars covered with tan tarps. The shiny wheel hubs drew him like magnet. He fought a heavy feeling of stones in his stomach as he pulled the tarp on the car closest to him, revealing a dark blue Nash Ambassador sedan, silver chrome grill and bumper shiny like new. On either side was parked a white Cadillac and a tan Chrysler. In the sedan's back seat lay a church bulletin for Notown Holiness. A cold wind whipped through the barn slats, leaving Connor stiff and holding his breath.

"Find the slate?" Rusty asked.

Connor jerked at the sound of the voice. Rusty stood at the end of the hay wall, the butcher knife in his hand. His friend's eyes coasted from Connor to the blue sedan then back again.

"I found Herman's car," Connor said, unable to vary the flatness of his voice.

"Naw," Rusty said. "That ain't Herman's, couldn't be."

"You know about this?"

"Nothing to know about." Rusty stared at the ground. "These are Darius's cars."

"Got a church bulletin in the back, Notown Holiness."

"Darius goes to that church. I've seen him. You been gone to college, how would you know?"

"You've been in basic training. How would you know?"

"I'm way past basic training. I'm a private first class." Rusty's voice shot up a pitch, and he nervously passed the knife from one hand to the other. "Darius wouldn't steal a car," he said, staring at the rafters. "He comes from a rich family. He doesn't need to steal. He lets me stay here on my weekends home. Don't you think I'd know if he pinched cars?" Rusty pressed his lips together, eyes on the rear fender. "You making an accusation?"

Connor focused on the same spot on the blue sedan. He wasn't certain this was Herman's car. Could belong to Darius. Rusty was a loyal person to his friends, wouldn't take up for a car thief, especially one who stole from their klatch. Connor handed Rusty the slate, spread the tarp back on the car, and patted the roof. "Guess I'll get cleaned up," he said, swallowing the uncomfortable notion that he was accepting a lie. "Meet you and the girls in a few hours."

Connor shuffled out of the barn, feeling Rusty's eyes follow him. Once, he started to turn back and tell Rusty he needed to get away from the likes of Darius Stark, but he didn't. He wanted to pretend like it hadn't happened. He wanted to maintain his friendships just the way they were when he was a boy, wanted Rusty to feel equal and quit resenting that Connor was in college. He wanted life in Contrary to always stay the same. If that meant believing a lie, maybe that was a small price, but still, misgivings seeped into his gut, and Connor couldn't help noticing how tightly his friend gripped the handle of that butcher knife.

8

Connor coasted Trooper, as he called his '55 Dodge, into a vertical parking space in front of Herne's Food Market. The store's green canopy shaded vegetable and fruit carts, and hand-printed signs spelled out today's bargains. This *better* store that Wallis Herne had had her eye on years ago had indeed been prosperous for the family. Situated in the middle of Contrary's most fashionable block, with a men's clothing store on one side and a women's on the other, it made for convenient shopping with ample parking along the avenue. Last year a Kroger had opened out near the highway, but as of yet they'd not lost business to the big brand store. Their customers' loyalty was rewarded with friendly service and a free lollipop for every child. Above, an eight-room apartment looked out on Laynchark Avenue.

Waving to Pop inside the store, Connor held up his sack of squirrels. Pop pointed the thumbs-up. The exchange with Rusty weighed on Connor's mind as he unlocked the door to the apartment. Darius Stark had given Rusty a place to live after he left the orphan house. Connor was never clear on why a man from such a prominent family had an interest in his friend, but at the time, it'd seemed an answer for the aimless Rusty Haskew. Connor wished he'd gotten the license numbers of the cars. Then again, if he was wrong and the cars belonged to Darius, he'd look like a darn fool and mess up Rusty's living arrangements. Harsh words shot over him as his mother and sister passed down the hall, making him pause on the steps.

"Don't see why I can't have the car," Tempy said, her steps thumping the linoleum. "It's a poetry reading. Twenty other people'll be there."

"Twenty people who'll spread lies about you all over this town," Mom countered sharply.

Tempy glared at Connor, finally noticing him as he stood with a hunting sack in one hand and a rifle slung over a shoulder. "You could do more than hold up the wall."

"Honeybun," Mom called out, coming toward Connor and taking the hunting bag as she pulled him into the kitchen. She peered inside at the squirrels. "I'll fry one up for supper. Pop's been talking about going hunting since you left but hasn't had the time." She dumped the game onto the side of the sink.

"I'm eating at the drive-in tonight with the gang."

Mom glanced at Tempy, who'd slumped in a kitchen chair, arms crossed over her chest. "Now, put on a face, your brother's home."

His sister's foot tapped impatiently and she leaned forward to say, "Saw Randi Jo Gaylor in front of JC Penney earlier today. Window shopping wedding gowns with Holly Waller."

"Wish you'd stay home, Connor," Mom interrupted. "You've only the weekend, and those high school girls, well . . ." She didn't finish the sentence as she flopped one of the squirrels onto a cutting board. Pulling a knife from drawer, she snapped off the paws and ripped the skin off the squirrel with bare hands.

In the corner, Grammy rested in her wheelchair. Her snowy hair was long on her shoulders and her expression a soft mixture of confusion and amusement. Connor knelt down and took her hand. "How's my favorite girl?"

"Who are you?" she asked.

"Siegfried," he grinned and cocked an eyebrow at her.

"Smelly Siegfried." A low chuckled as if to say that in this world where she lived, where everyone she loved was a stranger, she was pleased that they were, at the least, entertaining.

Tempy leaned in behind him. "Can I borrow your car, Connor?"

"Hare!" Grammy yelled.

Connor fell back, caught off guard by her outburst as much as by the word Grammy hollered. For an instant, he was flung into the memory of sitting beside her at Copperhead Fields, but he couldn't recall the circumstances. He stuttered, "N-n-no, squirrels."

"Hare!" she yelled again.

Tempy pulled Grammy's hair from behind the pillow. "Her hair gets caught," she said. "You have to adjust the pillow."

"Take Grammy to her room, Tempy," Mom said. "The overhead light in here agitates her."

Tempy dutifully turned the wheelchair and pushed it toward a suite of rooms on the far side of the kitchen. "Get the door for me, Connor?" she called out, and motioned with her eyes.

Connor glanced at his mother as she ran a blade up the belly of the squirrel with the skill of a butcher, and he couldn't help thinking how good she was at getting to the meat. As cantankerous as Tempy could be, she still couldn't stand up to Mom.

Inside Grammy's room, Tempy grabbed his hand. "Can you drive me to Quinntown?"

"Kinda out of my way, but I guess." A cautious relief fell over his sister, and he wondered why she was meeting someone in Quinntown.

He helped transfer Grammy to bed, and afterwards, Tempy instructed him like a military man. "Pick me up at ten fifteen, not a minute late, or I'll never hear the end of it."

He nodded, aware that he hadn't agreed to pick her up, only take her; however, starting an argument about it now seemed pointless. When he returned to the kitchen, all the squirrels had been gutted. Mom rested her bloody hands on the edge of the sink. "Think Randi Jo Gaylor and Holly Waller will be there," she asked, "or is it just the boys?"

"Maybe. Holly is going out with Willie."

"Willie's a nice boy, but somebody like him, with his family connections, he can do better than Holly Waller."

Connor exhaled a deep breath. "I don't tell my friends who to date, Mom."

"Bring your girlfriend home some weekend. I'll move Tempy in with Grammy and she can have a room to herself."

"Don't have a girlfriend, Mother," he said, working to keeping irritation out of his tone.

"Tempy wants to go to some poetry reading tonight," Mom said, intuiting that it was time to change the subject, "and I bet she meets up with that Iona Stark. You know Mayor Stark wants to change our entire main street to parallel parking. Pop is so upset. It'll kill business."

Conner started to say something, started to point out how Tempy was an adult and maybe she should have a car of her own, maybe parents shouldn't be telling her who she could spend her time with, and it wasn't the town's business, but he held his tongue on a touchy subject. He went into the bathroom to shower, turning on the water hot as he could stand. Since he'd left home, he'd learned to value his independence, and yet, he couldn't see a way out for his sister. Least he could do was give her a ride.

❦

Connor could smell where the snaky road from Contrary crossed over into the sulfuric swampland of Quinntown. Tempy sat beside him, holding her purse in the center of her lap. White gloved and in her new red Christmas coat, she seemed more tense than usual. Her hair, pulled atop her head, had been sprayed with White Rain hairspray to keep the strays in place and the overpowering smell made Connor sneeze.

"Who's reading poetry tonight?" he asked.

"Few schoolteachers, nothing formal." She popped a Lifesaver in her mouth and didn't offer one to him.

He made a U-turn in front of the Quinntown library, a redbrick square building that used to be a union hall. "Sis, sorry Mom gave you so much trouble. You know, she won't let me drive the car over to Notown to go to church."

"Let me out at the corner."

"Quinntown doesn't strike me as the poetry capital of the–"

"I said at the corner." She pointed at the place for him to turn. His sister scooted out the door, preaching as she moved. "Silly of you to drive to a Notown church. Get your gas siphoned if not the car stolen. Our church in Contrary is the best. Only thing in Notown is, well, nothing good."

"I–" The car door slammed as she bolted up the library steps. "Meant to say I felt sorry for you," Connor said to himself. "And by God, if I want to go to church in Notown, I blessed-be will, no matter how many buses I have to take!" His last words echoed in the car, and he realized he'd reacted as he had only because she'd taunted him. Funny, she usually knew that's how he'd react. He passed it off as a brother-sister clash, pressed the gas to get going, then slowed just as quickly as he caught a red light.

Quinntown hadn't changed much since they'd moved out of Notown years before. The storefronts were updated and the streets wider, but here it was January, and they hadn't taken the Christmas bells down off the streetlights yet. As he turned onto Laynchark, a red flash caught his eye in the rearview mirror.

Tempy trotted down the library steps. "What in the world?" he pondered. His sister darted across the street and hopped into a mint green Hudson Rambler. Connor pulled into a gas station, hiding his car behind the pumps, and waited until the Rambler pulled even with the stoplight. Iona Stark drove and her mouth flapped with the rhythm of her hands as she explained something. In the seat next to her, Tempy listened as if focused on President Dwight D. Eisenhower himself.

Connor chuckled, his sister's deception an amusing stain on her proper facade. He couldn't blame her for sneaking around. Might be the only enjoyment she has, he thought.

"Don't get too wild and drunk, girls," he called out, and saluted as the Rambler sped passed without either woman seeing him. Connor wheeled Trooper around and headed toward Pinkie's Drive-In. Time for fun!

9

Pinkie's Drive-In had opened in the early 1950s and become an instant hangout for Crimson County rebels, hooking its hat on the bobbysocks and beatnik trends. Teens flocked to the phosphorescent building as if it were a shrine to outlander heroes, icons the mountain kids could watch only in movies or on TV, characters who lived lives of angst and trouble—Marlon Brando, James Dean, Dobie Gillis, and Maynard Krebs.

As Connor turned Trooper into the parking lot, a fistfight landed on the hood. Two boys slid to the ground, but Connor caught a glimpse of Rusty's auburn hair and ripped the gear into park. In the headlights, Wayne Bacon was about to punch Rusty in the nose. Catcalls erupted from a pack of kids speeding over to see who was top dog. Connor jumped out and delivered a kick to

Wayne's kidney. He fell sideways, giving Rusty a chance to roll him over. By that time the flock surrounded them. His friends, Herman Cahill and Willie Carmack, cheered Rusty on while three others yelled for Wayne.

A horn tooted, and Connor looked that direction. The girls were nice and warm in Willie's '57 Chevy, and Randi Jo waved at him through a foggy window. He glanced toward the fight that was heading toward a bank of dirty snow, then jumped into Trooper and parked beside the Chevy.

Sissy Renner rolled down the front window and said, "Those fools are going to freeze to death. Get in with us, we've got french fries."

Connor hopped out of his car and the back door of Willie's opened. He slid in beside Randi Jo Gaylor. "How long've they been going at it?"

"Ten minutes," Randi Jo said, twisting a strand of black hair behind her ear and offering him french fries.

"Who p-o'ed who?"

Holly Waller twisted around from the driver's seat, her flaxen mane flouncing over the seat. "Hate to say it but Willie started it."

"Your boyfriend?" Connor sassed, glancing at the fight. "Who doesn't seem to be doing any of the fighting."

"You know Rusty." Lynn Moore fidgeted, looking after the boy she'd had a crush on since grade school as he tumbled into a row of garbage cans. "He's gung ho daddy-o since boot camp."

"Think I'd save the fighting for what counts."

"That's why you made it to college." Randi Jo scooted closer to him. "More brains than the average bear. Fries?"

Connor gobbled a handful and watched the gang of kids. Police lights flashed down the road. "Now they've done it." Connor jumped from the car and shot into Trooper. Before he knew it, Randi Jo had climbed in beside him and Lynn jumped into the backseat. Holly whipped out of her parking place and gunned the Chevy toward the fight. Connor followed, skidding to a stop.

Lynn rolled down the window and yelled, "Tear ass, Rusty!"

Teenagers ran all directions. Willie and Herman sped toward Holly, and Rusty, wetter than a catfish nesting in sludge, dove through the back window of Connor's car. Both autos sped out the rear exit as the police cruiser turned into the front. Connor followed Holly fifty miles per hour around the curvy beltline road toward Quinntown. He watched and the girls screamed as Holly and Willie switched positions in the front seat of their car, accelerating to sixty. Finally, they reached Copperhead Fields and pulled into the picnic area.

"Can't believe they're still alive," Randi Jo said, pointing at Holly and Willie as they clung to each other in a groping kiss in the beam of their headlights.

"I'm sopping wet," Rusty complained. "Gotta warm up 'fore I die of pneumonia."

"My hunting overalls are in the trunk." Connor tossed Rusty the keys and nodded that he'd start a fire.

After the blaze got going, the boys examined Rusty's bruises. He'd held his own, but would return to Fort Knox with a few more bruises than he'd left with. "Gonna hurt," Herman said and packed a snowball for him to hold against his lip.

"Why in the world would you start a fight with Wayne Bacon?" Connor asked. "You know he's done time."

"Adlai Stevenson," Willie smirked. "Bacon's an Eisenhower man."

Rusty didn't answer, his expression sheepish and equally embarrassed that he'd been losing the exchange.

"Wayne's from Coalfire," Holly said, bringing Willie a beer. "They're nastier than poked snakes. No shame in a draw for that fight."

"Well, I'm a Notowner," Rusty quipped. "Ain't nobody meaner than me. I'm the meanest sonnavagun in Midnight Valley. Ouch!" Part of the snowball stuck to his lip and he sucked in some of the ice so his skin wouldn't pull off. "Just this week I blew up a platoon of enemy combatants plotting the downfall of America."

Willie chuckled. "Army games don't qualify, but Daddy's got some tree stumps in his backyard that need dynamiting."

"Got to get warm or I'll freeze to death." Rusty's voice shivered.

"Best we all get home," Willie said, "Cops'll be looking for somebody to take in for fighting."

Connor and Herman exchanged a glance while Willie whispered to Rusty. Connor had come upon the fight in mid-exchange, but suspected Willie had probably goaded Rusty into fighting what should have been his own fight. Son of a wealthy coal mine operator, Willie was a year younger than the other boys, still in high school, but he had a smooth way of talking people into doing his dirty work, and that he was easy with the buck kept him more friends that he might normally have had.

Randi Jo, Lynn, and Sissy came over with the last of the beer. "We just burned the box," she said. "Fire'll be out soon."

"Rusty's spending the night at my house," Willie said. "Got some talking to do." He kicked snow on the fire while Holly hung on to his arm. "You drop off the others, Connor?"

"You won't drive your own girlfriend home?" Connor asked.

"Think you might wrestle that chip off your shoulder, college boy?" Willie's tone killed the jovial din of the evening, and the other kids traded glances with each other but avoided the two boys.

Connor flicked at his shoulder and grinned. "There, it's gone." He shot a challenging stare at Willie.

Willie circled his arm around Rusty's shoulder. "First you disparage Rusty's judgment on the fight and then start with me–"

"Don't aim Rusty at me the way you did Wayne Bacon." Connor stepped in front of Willie. "Somebody like you . . . you'll never come between us."

Willie's cheeks colored cherry red, and Rusty stared at the ground. "Come on, guys," Rusty said. "You know I like fighting."

"Be glad to take everybody home," Connor said, daring Willie to look him in the eye. "But only if Holly gives me a goodnight smooch."

"My kisses are only for my man," Holly interceded, and planted a kiss on her boyfriend's cheek.

Willie wrapped an arm around her, ignoring Connor. "Sorry, baby," he said to Holly. "I gotta go to the mines with Daddy early, otherwise I'd drive you home." He led her to his car, kissing her several more times before jumping into the Chevy with Rusty and gunning the gas.

Connor stamped out the last of the fire and shoved his hands into his pockets from the instant cold. "Pile on in," he said to the five people he was chauffeuring. The gang situated themselves, Randi Jo next to him. No one talked as they drove, and the wind, whistling through a crack in the passenger's side window, sent icy air against the car's heater. Connor wondered how Willie had even gotten into their circle of friends. It wasn't as if he knew how to hunt or fish, and his only contribution was beer.

⁊

Randi Jo and Holly were last to be let out. Randi Jo held her hands to the heater while Holly stretched out in the backseat like a cat. Connor hadn't been all that mad about having to drive everybody home as much as irritated at Willie and his entitled ways. He glanced in the rearview mirror at Holly's overly endowed bosom and adjusted it to see that she was watching him. As women go, she scared Connor; her in-your-face attitude matched her kittenish sexuality in ways that only a seasoned man could handle. Randi Jo, on the other hand, exuded a sweet shyness that only wanted to be liked. Connor fanned her hair, and she giggled.

"When spring comes, I'm gonna sing a song to the sun," Randi Jo said, voice shivering.

Connor pulled a neck scarf from behind him and with one hand draped it over her knees. "I'll try and get up the hill to your house if you want."

"Lord no, you'd never make it. Ice puddles in every dip in the road." She pointed at the gravel parking area in front of Wink's Market.

"Turn on your porch light so I know you made it all right."

She paused before getting out. "See you in church tomorrow?"

"Back row, save me a seat."

Her eyes beamed, but she seemed to suppress a smile to avoid appearing too eager. As she trotted up a dirt road and crossed the railroad tracks, she lost a shoe a couple times and had to stop to reposition a piece of cardboard in the sole. Her house was the furthest up the hill, a tin-roofed structure hanging onto the mountainside like an owl with talons dug into the ground. Soon she disappeared into the darkness.

"Somebody's got a crush," Holly sang and draped a leg on the front seat.

"She's sweet," he said, deflecting Holly's sassy remark. "Never seems to resent that she has so little. I mean, really, cardboard in her shoes."

"Got cardboard in my shoes." Holly heaved herself over the seat and landed beside him. "She's hooked and head over heels for you. Now I got to ask myself . . . big college boy like you . . . can you take a Notown girl seriously or are you gonna leave her all starry-eyed and broken-hearted?"

"Can the son of a rich coal mine operator fall in love with a Notown girl?"

"How do the French say it, '*too-shay*'." Holly's voice hardened, and she stared ahead, her frosty breath panting as if she wanted to say more but held back.

"I shouldn't have said that," Connor said. "Willie loves you."

"And I love Willie, and if that's all it took then I guess Notown won't be in the way."

"No reason for it to be. Of all the reasons two people should be kept apart, that'd be the last."

She sat up, one hand on the dashboard. "Notown's a mean bitch. Every time you think you got her sweet-talked, she'll flip you the bird and knock you on your ass."

Randi Jo's front porch light flipped on and off, and he started the car. Holly's house was only a few hundred feet down the road, just short of the hairpin curve that turned into Notown Road. He punched the gas and let the car drift off the shoulder just short of her turn-in. "See you in church?"

She swung her long legs out the door and turned halfway around. "Hell no," she said. "Last time I spoke to the Lord, lightning knocked out the TV. Missed *Gunsmoke* a solid month." Then, she kissed her fingers and touched them to Connor's lips. Without looking back, she skated on the icy ground toward a tar-papered cabin at the edge of the creek bank.

Connor watched until her porch light flipped on and off. He scratched his head and wrapped the muffler back round his neck, shaking off a stirring below the waist.

Instead of making a U-turn on Laynchark, Connor drove down Notown Road, slowing down to take in the same houses, trailers, and abandoned cars that he used to walk past as a child. He parked on the bridge next to his childhood home. The store where his father had cut hair had washed away in a flood caused by the coal mine's settling ponds. Connor remembered the day Rusty had been swept away by such a wall of water. Willie had once argued that settling ponds holding the mine's processed water were emptied in a controlled release and only after the particulates had settled to the bottom, so that the clear water didn't harm the creek. The flood destroying Pop's old store had been caused by several of these dams bursting when rain softened the ground. The ground where the sediment and water settled wasted the earth. Connor wasn't sure what to believe. He only knew that where once was an apple and a cherry tree, now stood withered shrubs whose puny fruit tasted sour.

Connor's parents still owned the Notown house, renting it to a family named Trent. He sat on the concrete bridge rail, looking at a single light illuminating his old room. He wondered if the children who lived here ever climbed the walnut tree the way he used to do. Did they find the gooseberry bush on the backside of the barn, and did they swing in the tire hanging on the dying apple tree? Inhaling a deep breath, a chill took him. He wasn't sure why he missed Notown. He'd only lived here a few years, but the backyard, the woods behind his house, the tree house up Beans Fork . . . most fun he'd ever had. Being outside every day, playing in the creek, all this was so different from living above the store in Contrary. Tomorrow afternoon, he'd be headed back to North Carolina and he'd carry with him the quiet stillness of this place. In his mind, Notown wasn't the bitch Holly believed. Notown was a place of memories that filled up every part of him and held him like a kind mother saying, *Don't forget me, son. I'll always be a part of you.*

10

There are many locations on earth where holiness is self-evident–
a mountaintop at sunrise, a grove of secluded trees, the sky on a
moonless night. Only the individual can consecrate other places as
hallowed. Connor did that with Duke University. He seldom visited
the mountains in North Carolina that weren't all that far of a drive
from the campus. Instead, he held his breath each time he entered
the library, marveling at the volumes of learning that might as well
be the Athenaeum of Alexandria for him. Every classroom spilled a
world of alchemy with every teacher a wizard. Connor knew how
lucky he was to be here. No more of the antiquated rote learning
dribbled out by the teachers from Crimson County High. At Duke,
his imagination soared with possibilities of what he could learn
about the world and what he could one day contribute to it.

Connor's favorite instructor, Professor Herzog, teetered on a
stepladder in front of the blackboard at morning physics class.

Connor yawned and shook himself awake as he slowly waited for the teacher to finish spelling out the Heisenberg Uncertainty Principle. He'd driven most of the night and had to sleep in the backseat of the car because the dorm wouldn't let him back in after midnight. The professor swayed, whirled around on one foot, and hopped off the ladder as he pretended to do a swan drive. A few girls giggled. He pulled the unit to the other chalkboard and began writing on it, too.

Everybody wanted to be in Professor Herzog's class. He had known Albert Einstein, and standing in the same room with the professor made it seem a little like Mr. Einstein was here as well. A poke in Connor's ribs caused him to sit upright and glance to the row behind him.

A pretty black-haired girl smiled. "You the boy from Contrary?" she whispered and smiled again.

"How'd you know?" he asked, sizing her up. She was dressed in a peach-colored sweater and blue pencil skirt. Her shapely calves nudged up to the edge of his chair and he noticed a scar on one leg.

"Your roommate told me."

A sandy-haired boy beside her snapped his pencil on the desk, leaned in and quipped, "Of course he's the weirdo from Contrary, can't you tell from his *far* not *fire*, his *har* not *hair*, and constant use of, ugh, *ain't*."

"Shut up, Fitch." She smacked his knee. "My mother's aunt lives there."

"Yeah, shut up, Fitch," Connor mimicked and shot the girl a grin. "I got a parrot that talks like he's from Savannah." He twanged the last word and shot Fitch a sassy head tilt, then he leaned back, taking in her single-pearl necklace and pale pink lipstick that look good enough to lick. "Connor Herne." He extended his hand, shaking hers and holding on several seconds longer than was necessary. "You?"

"Rory Parker," she whispered. "I'd love to catch a ride with you some weekend. Haven't seen Aunt Edna since I was thirteen."

"My car's got plenty room."

The professor turned around and clapped his hands as Fitch muttered the word "philistine" under his breath. Connor sat upright and angled his pen to paper.

"Who wants to explain the Uncertainty Principle to me?"

Connor and Fitch raised their hands. The professor pointed at Fitch.

Fitch stood, gangly with a head too big for his body. His slippery Savannah accent gave him an air of entitlement that made Connor want to puke. "Uh," Fitch said, clearing his throat to give himself time to think. "Measuring a thing means that the thing being measured really can't be."

"Uh-huh." The professor blinked and scratched his head. "What's your take on that, Mr. Herne?"

"It's a little more complicated than that," Connor said, rising. "Let's say, we're trying to get a statistical measurement of whether the lovely Miss Parker here will have lunch with me or Mr. Fitch."

"I'm intrigued," Professor Herzog said. "Continue."

"Just a minute," Fitch objected.

"We could point out that Mr. Fitch says *hair* not *har*, *can't* not *cain't*, *hour* not *our*, and never misses an opportunity to let us know he's descended from some lord muckety-muck who witnessed the signing of the Magna Carta that, uh, I believe was never actually signed." The girls who'd previously giggled were sniggering again, and some of the boys who often dozed in class were upright and focused. "So we might say Mr. Fitch measures up as a higher choice for Miss Parker than does my humble self."

Professor Herzog twirled his hand for Connor to go on.

"What we've failed to consider is all the other worlds that exist."

"Ah, other worlds," Professor Herzog repeated. "Now, you've got me out on a limb."

" 'Cause he's a confused country hayseed," Fitch interrupted, and continued, "Measurements can only be relative in the world they're taken in. In this world where, let's face it, I have a higher grade point average than you, I'll take Miss Parker to Dexter's Emporium for lunch, and you might manage the student union. For her birthday, I'll throw a fur stole around her neck. Will you bring her a coonskin cap?"

Connor stepped around his desk, closer to Rory. Her cheeks pinked up and she stared at the floor. "I'm not enjoying this," she said.

"But there are other worlds, other considerations." Connor rested his hands on Rory's shoulders. "Right here, in Miss Parker's mind, is an entirely different reality than the one we're standing in. And neither you nor I can measure that, for while we as a class tried to measure this choice, the essence of the Heisenberg Uncertainty Principle tells us we can never know anything for certain. Perhaps Miss Parker is thinking, 'My, what a good-looking fella that Connor Herne is,' or maybe she's thinking, 'What a conceited ass Mr. Fitch is making of himself.'"

Fitch stepped toward Connor, challenging him. Professor Herzog burst out laughing. "I haven't had such a lively discussion since the King of Sweden gossiped that Niels Bohr belched during his Nobel address," he said. "Sit down, gentlemen, and let's talk about the totality of systems."

Connor and Fitch made slow curves away from each other and took their seats. Rory's hand brushed against Connor's as he passed, and he winked at her.

Once class was over, Rory moved to the empty desk beside him. "I've never been a component in a physics equation before."

"Didn't mean to embarrass you."

"Fitch got the worst of it." She glanced at the door where Fitch impatiently waited for her, until, with a huffy twirl, he finally stomped down the hall.

They both chuckled. Connor leaned closer. "Be going to Contrary in a couple weeks, why don't you ride up with me? Farmer's Almanac says we got an early spring coming, so maybe we'll get some green."

She opened her mouth to respond, but his roommate, Brody Hatfield, hollered his name from the hallway. He was flushed from running and waved an envelope. "This came for you." He handed Connor the paper. "The Dean brought it himself, said to get it to you right away."

Connor cleared his throat, irritated that Brody had interrupted his time with Rory, but intrigued that he'd received what looked like a telegram. "These are usually good news," he joked as he tore it open. "Wonder if I won something?"

Connor had read passages in books where characters felt their blood drain from their face. He'd always thought the description maudlin and melodramatic, but now he could feel the life source drain from him. "My grandmother died," he said.

"Connor, I'm sorry." Rory covered his hand with hers while Brody put a hand on his shoulder.

He coughed and stood, bringing up his books with him. It wasn't as if her death hadn't been expected, and in some ways was a blessing for the last decade she'd spent in a confused oblivion. "'Nother world," Connor whispered.

"What?" Rory asked.

Connor had taken several steps, not realizing he'd left Rory and Brody behind. "Nothing," he said. "I have to go home."

11

Of what do the dead dream? Lying peacefully on satin they might never have owned while walking this earth, did they object to the lines of people filing by to see what they looked like on their last day before being closed up in a coffin in their Sunday best and stuck in the ground? Connor knew that Matilda Schumacher, in her lucid years, would certainly have objected.

Grammy looked serene, but Connor couldn't help wanting to stand guard, protect her from these gawkers. Very few had even known her. All came to see the crazy lady. Alzheimer's, the doctors had finally named the disease that stripped her every bodily function a slice at a time. Connor wondered if the same beast might be lurking in his own blood. Would this be an unwanted inheritance passed to him by Grammy, or did her nonsensical ravings of long ago, telling him that he was not of her, spare him that fate? What in the world had she meant? Or had her words been the irrationality of a mind lost in its own muddle?

He turned away from her casket, walked the length of the First Baptist Church, and scooted into a pew on the far side next to Randi Jo, Sissy, and Lynn. Willie and Holly sat behind them, with Herman standing in the aisle. "Nice of you to come," Connor told them as each nodded politely. What does one say to the living about the dead? Sorry for your loss; she was a wonderful person; that she's finally at rest is a blessing. Connor had heard all of these today and was grateful for his friends' silence.

Pop stood with Grammy's open casket behind him and told about having to drag her to the ship that would take them back to America in 1938. Seems Grammy was part of an underground movement against Hitler and was working to overthrow his government. "When World War II began," he said, "she blamed me, saying if I'd let her stay, she would have taken down the Third Reich single-handed." People near him murmured a light laughter.

Connor swallowed hard. He'd never known this story, and as he looked at Grammy's pale face, cheeks painted with pink rouge that she'd never worn in life, he wished he'd talked to her more, tried to glean some coherence from her confused thoughts so that he might have understood the kind of person from whom he was descended.

To break the cycle of his thoughts, Connor indicated he was going outside. In the vestibule, Tempy and Iona stood closer than they should, whispering and touching hands. They stepped apart and stared at him. Connor managed a flat smile that neither woman returned. A slight fear in Tempy's expression sent him quickly out the door and into the cold January air.

He walked half a block to the Courtesy Cafe and stopped to listen to the TV set playing President Eisenhower's second inaugural address: *"We cherish our friendship with all nations that are or would be free. We respect, no less, their independence. And when, in time of want or peril, they ask our help, they may honorably receive it; for we no more seek to buy their sovereignty than we would sell our own. Sovereignty is never bartered among free men."*

A polite round of applause for the President, and Connor wondered if freedom was a state of mind and less tangible than Eisenhower was suggesting. A tap on the window drew his attention. Willie, Holly, and Randi Jo stood outside, and Willie motioned him to come out.

"Taking you for a stiff one," Willie said. "Time like this . . . calls for it."

"Naw, rather watch the speech," he began, but both girls grabbed an arm and ushered him into Willie's car, and the brief impression of freedom to choose left his mind. They drove through Indian Hills, through two-and three-story houses where lived the townsfolk who never worried about whether their sovereignty would be sold because if it was, they'd be the people to make a profit. Pulling into a gated driveway past a marble fountain and bronze statuary of deer and gnomes, the Carmack house . . . mansion . . . sprang into view. Before Willie's parents divorced, the kitchen had been featured in *Ladies' Home Journal* with his mother displaying a pan of biscuits.

Inside, the cavernous living room smelled of cigars. Willie poured a caramel-colored liquid into a glass and handed it to Connor. "Bourbon," he said, "best in the state."

Connor took a sip and found it bitter.

"Randi Jo and I'll make some baloney sandwiches," Holly said.

"Clean up afterwards." Willie pointed toward an arched doorway. "Don't want Daddy fussing when he gets home."

The girls disappeared into a brightly lit room with mint green tiles, and Willie plopped down on a pink, frieze-covered couch with gold tassels hanging off the bottom. He motioned Connor to join him. "I swear, Holly eats every time she's here. Have to wonder if they ever feed her at home." After a few seconds, he continued, "Randi Jo's skinny as a beanpole, too."

"People like you and me, we never had to worry about food," Connor said. "Don't you get that?"

Silence. The two boys stared at the tri-colored hooked rug under a tortoiseshell coffee table. The furnace kicked on, sending a wave of warm air through the room. A grandfather clock counted the seconds, then its deep, brassy tone called the hour.

"I've missed three days of school," Connor finally said, "probably won't make it up next weekend to hunt. You'll tell Rusty?"

"Sure," Willie said. "Daddy's wanting him to do some security work on his weekends off, so just as well."

"Nice of you, Willie . . . to help him like that. Nice of you." He pointed toward the kitchen. "Guess I said some stupid stuff last time I was in town." Connor tried to mean the words he spoke. After all, Willie had brought him into his home, given him bourbon, yet through the years of knowing him, every kind act always had a price, and Connor wondered what Rusty would have to do for that part-time work, or what he might have to swallow for the privilege of being invited inside. Looking down into the swirls of russet-colored liquid, he placed the tumbler of liquor on the coffee table.

Willie waved his hand as if none of it mattered. "Tell you something, Connor. Something I haven't told Holly. Mining's had a bad decade. Real bad. Money . . . that's the reason my Ma left. Imagine that. Leavin' a good man because you can't buy New York designer clothes any more. Daddy's hoping to strike a deal with the Tennessee Valley Authority to supply coal for their dams. He don't get a sell . . . we're out of business. That's why friends count. They're the only ones to stand by you when times get tough."

Connor swallowed hard, never expecting to hear of money troubles from a boy who'd grown up with everything. "I'm sorry," he said, saying words he thought were expected of him. "Anything I can do." Willie nodded, and again, they sank into a vat of silence, letting the stillness unexpectedly bond them in this hard-fought world of men.

Randi Jo came in with a plate of sandwiches and placed it in front of the boys. "Holly's gonna make some chocolate pudding but can't find the mix," she said. Willie shot up and trotted toward the kitchen as Randi Jo picked up a baloney sandwich and handed it to Connor. "This one has mustard."

"You go ahead," he said. "My stomach's jack-rabbiting."

"Got something for that." She held out a yellow package of Beechnut gum.

As he pulled a stick of gum, their fingers touched. Hers were icy and he took her hands, rubbing them between his to warm her up. Her tiny hands disappeared into his and the connection to her flesh held him like a magnet. Maxwell's equations on magnetism and electricity popped into his mind as he interlaced his fingers with hers. Einstein had used those laws as inspiration for his theory of special relativity. This elfin girl before him was indeed special, and he didn't know why he'd never realized that before. Centuries ago, the ancient Chinese had invented the lodestone compass. The lodestone attracts the needle, finding true north. He looked into her eyes. "You're a nice girl, Randi Jo."

"Known you since we were kids in Notown, Connor. Even when you moved to Contrary, I sorta kept track of you."

He chuckled for the first time today. "When I go back to Duke, I'll be looking over my shoulder."

"I'll write you a letter and let you know I'm still in this old town. Let you know the things that are going on here. Which Stark gets elected mayor, who got in a fight at school, how much honey the bees make."

"Ah, don't waste the three cents on a stamp. I'll be back in a week or so."

"Kinda want stay close to home after something like this, hmmm?"

Connor nodded, not having realized that was exactly how he felt, and she knew it. She'd read him like a page of newspaper. He needed these people. More than physics or Dr. Herzog or Duke University, he needed to hold on to the friendships that defined him more than any life he might try to make outside of the mountains. It impressed him that Randi Jo could intuit his feelings in a way that he hadn't completely understood.

"I want to talk to Pop more," he said. "Find out about where he came from, what kind of people his parents were. You know, he's a lot older than Mom, and I didn't know those grandparents. Wish I had now. Wish God had given me more years with Grammy. If I'd known to do it, the things I could have asked her when I was a little boy. I didn't think of it. I didn't know." He stopped, his voice catching in his throat. "I wish that disease hadn't happened to her. Why'd it have to happen to her? And where'd she go? Where do any of us go after the energy leaves our bodies? Are we nothing? Do we get trapped in some ether world where we watch the living and some poor bastard watches the dead?" Connor stared at the wall, realizing he saw the gray land of Bette Moss and the Black Dahlia full-blown in his mind. He held his breath, watching as they moved in a staccato motion, vibrating themselves to awake. He held out a hand, hoping to close that world off, glanced at Randi Jo, who only looked at him. She didn't see it. Connor scoured the landscape, hoping and even praying that he did not see his grandmother in this dour place. He looked aside and wiped his eyes on the back of his sleeve. He hadn't thought of this world since he was a boy, but it had popped out full-blown as if it had never left him. "I see my mistakes now, and I wish I could undo them."

Randi Jo moved to the couch beside him. She rubbed his arm and that imaginary world faded as the women cried his name, fading to an echo: *Connor, Connor, Connor.*

Randi Jo leaned her cheek onto his arm and said, "Things I've seen in my seventeen years, sometimes makes me wonder what the Lord is thinking to have let them happen." She paused, bit her bottom lip, and looked up into his eyes. "But if there is a Heaven, somebody like your grandmother, somebody who endured, I got to think that's the place she would be."

Connor focused on her irises, the greenest he'd ever seen, the color of grass in the shade of a tree. "I want to believe it, but I'm not sure I do," he said. "Thank you, Randi Jo, for trying."

"No appreciation needed. It's a thought anybody could have had."

From the kitchen, a radio played a tune by the Platters, "The Great Pretender." Randi Jo stood and pulled him up. Slowly they moved, not quite dance, not solely an embrace. The warmth of her body melted into his, and for those few moments Connor forgot about what happens to the dead and the haunted women in his mind.

When Connor returned to Duke, Rory had left him a sympathy card, but it was Randi Jo who was on his mind.

12

By the beginning of March, Connor found himself lost in Maxwell's equations and Planck's hypothesis. After class, discussions put him into endless arguments with his fellow students about matrix mechanics and Schrödinger's Cat. He wanted to understand everything . . . from Galileo's thought experiment that led to the law of inertia to Newton's laws of motion and how all of it laid the groundwork for Einstein's theory of relativity. The complexity of the universe left him swimming in possibilities that confounded him as much as they left him in awe.

Professor Herzog offered him an internship the following semester, a job that would be mostly erasing blackboards and answering correspondence, but would give him access to some of the most brilliant minds in the world. Dr. Herzog often spoke of twenty-page arguments he would send off to Max Born or Hideki Yukawa, both Nobel Prize winners. Connor couldn't wait to type them up. The elderly physicist inspired him so much that Connor declared a double major of physics and mathematics.

Connor and his roommate, Brody Hatfield, spent their free time playing pranks on their fellow dorm mates or tossing a football in the grassy areas around the gothic Duke Chapel while Brody compared certain students to Falstaff and Richard III and Connor pointed out the students riding on Einstein's light beam who were going places in life and the slower ones on asteroids who didn't know their arse from a persimmon pit. Sometimes they'd sit quietly and watch the world pass by, and other times the world offered opportunities they could not resist.

Brody nudged Connor as they lounged on the grounds near the statue of The Sower, a bronze figure of a man sowing seeds that was often referred to as Johnny Appleseed. "The moon rises on yonder break," Brody said.

Connor glanced up at Rory Parker prancing down the steps of the East Duke Building, her black hair bouncing with each stride. He sat up, hoping she'd walk their direction. "Think she'll see us?"

"The speck of dirt in thine eye offends."

"Can you talk in something other than Shakespeare?"

"Fitch is skulking," Brody blurted.

Connor spied the gangly Fitch milling behind a magnolia tree, doing his best to look inconspicuous. "One of the primary rules of physics is an object in motion will continue forever unless something interferes with it."

"And Fitch is plotting his course."

"Like an asteroid being pulled by the sun," Connor said. "But I move at the speed of light." He hopped up and aimed himself into Rory's path. "Hey, girl," he called out.

She turned, not seeing Fitch, who had strategically meandered to where she would have all but tripped over him. Rory pushed her hair back from her forehead and smiled as she touched Connor's arm. "Got the article you left for me on tobacco," she said. "Not sure I agree, but I'd love to discuss it with you."

"Student union. We'll hash it out over a soda."

"I'll be late for class," she said, checking her watch. Her lips pressed together as she thought, then she said, "What's a few minutes?"

They linked arms and headed that direction. Connor offered to carry her books, but she declined. He realized she liked being self-reliant, and he gave her every consideration.

"Rory!" Fitch yelled. "Why're you going that way?" He trotted up behind them. "Biology class is in twenty minutes."

Connor halted and in a half turn quipped, "She can find her way to class without a guide dog."

"Hate to break it to you, Peckerwood," Fitch said, "but Rory Parker is going to be one of the few women physicians in the state of North Carolina, and she doesn't have time to waste on twaddle."

Rory hesitated and looked toward the ground. "Be along in a few minutes, Fitch."

Connor couldn't help the smirk he shot toward Fitch and linked arms with Rory as they walked forward.

"Cracker!" Fitch called out behind them.

Connor swung his body backwards, hardly seeing the motion of his fist as it connected with Fitch's jaw. The taller man hurled sideways, one hand on his cheek, but he bounced back and grabbed Connor by his jacket. Rory hollered at both of them, but her voice disappeared with the blur of the two men tumbling to the ground, fists flying. Connor was unaware of how long it took, but soon Brody and a few other boys had pulled them apart. "This *cracker* just whipped your ass," Connor spit at his opponent.

"You embarrass yourself," Fitch shot back.

Connor went for him again, but Brody held him firm, whispering in his ear that he could be kicked out of school. "And you showed your tail," Connor shouted back.

Fitch extended his hand toward Rory. "Do you now recognize how uncouth this hillbilly is, completely out of place with civilized people?"

Rory froze, embarrassed by the stares of the gathering crowd, eyes darting from one boy to the other. Connor jerked free of Brody and stomped away. He entered the East Campus Union, darted into the men's toilet and inspected the bruise over his eye. He felt like a dang fool, being pulled into Fitch's trap. The Savannah blueblood had baited him, and he'd fallen for it like a prize sucker.

Holding a wet handkerchief to his eye, he moved to a lobby and plopped on a couch away from the other students. A nearby TV played an afternoon soap opera and though he had no interest, he watched two people declare their everlasting love. In the reflection of the TV set, he saw Rory standing behind him. He wanted to turn around, but pride kept him from acknowledging her.

"Never fight about facts, Connor. You are a hillbilly," she said. "You should have shown him that is something to be proud of." She rounded the bank of chairs and sat across from him. "Most of us are here because a destitute European peasant got tired of being filthy, hungry, and used as fodder in a tyrannical king's war."

"Fitch was right. I embarrassed myself." He stared at the floor between his feet, turning the wet compress to the cold side.

"My father punched out our mailman once," she said.

"Glad to be in good company."

"Mailman made the mistake of calling our Jack Russell a waste of dog. Father was quite fond of the mutt."

Connor looked up at her. Those blue eyes studied him, and he couldn't help but think he'd never seen such a brilliant color. He and

Rory continued chatting like they'd known each other all their lives. He might have continued with her all afternoon, but his train of thought was interrupted by a familiar twang. He paused mid-sentence while explaining The Meissner effect to her. Not only the voice, the accent. Connor peered around Rory at the television set. He could hardly believe what he saw and burst out laughing. Rory followed his line of sight. "Little Preacher Boy," he said between wheezes.

On the TV, a commercial featured Bryson Pomeroy inviting people to his tent revival at the fairgrounds near the edge of town. He had matured, but hadn't grown much taller. His familiar pompadour had a little more pomp and quivered like a rat lived in it each time he moved his head. Connor explained to Rory about the white shoes, the bridge, the blue kid dressing up like the devil, and she didn't stop laughing until tears filled both eyes. "Worst part is I was sick and missed the whole thing."

"But you were the instigator, I bet." They both watched the TV for another commercial. "We could go out there next weekend and see if he's still wearing white shoes," she giggled.

"Would love to, but it's my weekend home."

"I'm coming with you," she said. "About time I visited Aunt Edna, and you have to promise to show me the bridge."

"Maybe introduce you to the blue people if there's time."

"Time," she exclaimed, suddenly looking at her watch. "Good Lord, I'm late," She scooped up her books and ran out, turning briefly at the door to look back.

Connor waved and leaned back in the chair, his eye throbbing, but his humor back intact. Who'd have thought he'd ever see Preacher Boy again. He paused and looked up at a poster of the football team, Duke University's fighting Blue Devils. He scared a preacher with a blue devil, surely he could maneuver a Savannah blueblood to show his yellow without resorting to violence.

As the afternoon passed, he found himself thinking about his childhood days in Notown. His thoughts landed him, oddly, on a memory of Randi Jo leaning over the bridge and offering him a nickel to go buy a cap after Pop had shaved his head from a lice infestation. He often thought about what she'd said to him at Grammy's funeral and wished he'd kissed her that day. He had known Randi Jo for so long and couldn't help but compare her with Rory. They were both exceptional in their own way. Rory was book smart and polished, but Randi Jo had a way of understanding him that was extraordinary. Something about Rory was new, fresh, smelled like roses, but Randi Jo was a comfort where he could rest and be himself, and in many ways he couldn't live without that simplicity.

The two girls gelled like statues in his mind, but then they weren't themselves, only gray outlines that split apart in a burst of atoms firing across a sparkling universe. Connor knew immediately where he was, but he didn't know why he was there. It was that place . . . the land of dead women. The women were shadows, stiff and unnatural like they moved through water. Connor stood, trying to shake off the vision, but the ladies were stirring, and as much as he tried holding on to daylight, this other world was waking up. More than that, the girls were looking out at the world through his eyes, their hands rubbing together in anticipation.

He knew what that meant. *They were waiting on someone.* More than Fitch, or his throbbing eye, or being expelled . . . that worried Connor.

13

The drive to Contrary revealed that Rory Parker liked dill pickles on grilled cheese and had won first prize in the Halifax County Dressage Competition. She'd grown up in Virginia, daughter of a teacher and a tobacco farmer. After losing her father when she was sixteen, she and her mom moved to North Carolina to be near family. She'd once kicked a fence that her horse, Feathers, wouldn't jump and that was how she got the scar on her leg.

Connor reminded himself to keep his eyes on the road each time he glanced over at her. They'd started out at three a.m., skipping their Friday classes and hoping to make it to Contrary in time for breakfast. His mother had insisted Connor bring Rory and Aunt Edna for a late lunch, and even Pop had said he'd take an hour off from the store and meet them. A strand of black hair dangled like a fish line from the side of Rory's headband, and he reached over and pushed it back behind her ear. Her cheeks flushed and she fiddled with the radio tuner as static interrupted banjo playing on the Knoxville station.

"Closer we get to the Cumberland Mountains, you won't find any shake, rattle, and roll."

"Was hoping for some Elvis." She bypassed a gospel station only to land on another. "Let's just talk," she said, switching off the radio.

Connor slowed as they pulled off the U.S. highway and turned toward Contrary. As the sun rose behind them, he pointed out the ridgeline where he'd often hunted, showing her a place where a cave dropped into the earth nearly a hundred feet down. "Remember me to show you the court house where the Stark family had big shoot-outs in the 1930s and '40s."

"Interesting history," she remarked, head swiveling this way and that as he recited each story as he had been told. "Do the Starks still live around here?"

"Mayor of Contrary, Quinntown, and a hotbed called Coalfire 'bout forty miles up the road. Get a parking ticket, fifty percent of it goes into their pockets, but if you need anything, they'll arrange it, long as you know you owe them." Passing a rabble of clapboard shacks with children playing in the yards, Rory shot him a tentative smile. Men with rifles slung over an arm walked on the shoulder of the road and women rocking on porch swings stared suspiciously at the unfamiliar car. Rory studied each scene of poverty or menace. Her fingers, clasped around her knee, turned white at the sight of men target-shooting in a side yard while toddlers played around their feet. Poor Rory, he thought, she's in a world she never dreamed existed.

"Why do people keep electing them?"

"Who?"

"The Starks. They sound like hoodlums."

Connor slowed as they swerved on a curve, her words drawing a defensive streak out of him. "'Round here we call 'em colorful," he said. "Guess we get used to it after a while." They passed out of the hollows section of Contrary and into a series of avenues with English names: Cornwall, Cumberland, Kent, and Essex.

"I've finally let out my breath," Rory commented but didn't look at him.

Connor didn't respond, a surge of embarrassment heating his cheeks as he realized he should have chosen another route around the hollows. He turned into Indian Hills neighborhood, and three roads down pulled in front of a two-story white house with a wraparound porch. Aunt Edna's house rivaled any well-to-do North Carolina abode, and Rory's expression registered relief. "See you 'round one o'clock," he said. "Tell Aunt Edna to dress comfortable."

Rory smiled and touched his arm as she got out of the car, pulling her green hatbox and suitcase from the backseat. Connor drove away, contemplating Contrary's hollows and the downtown neighborhoods. People in the hollows were not unlike the populace in Notown on the far side of Quinntown. He'd found them at times defensive, with a spit-in-your-eye attitude, but given time and conversation, most hollow folks weren't all that different from the downtowners. As he rounded the corner of Essex in the Marleybone neighborhood, Willie's Chevy passed him and its horn tooted. Both cars stopped and reversed toward each other. Willie rolled down the driver's side window and Herman called out. "Follow us to the pool hall."

Connor checked his watch. He had a few hours before lunch, and while remembering he had promised Pop he'd start on the painting job in the stockroom, he made a U-turn and followed Willie to a two-story building with cedar siding. An overhead sign hitched into the roof spelled out *Critter's Pool Hall*. Hopping out of Trooper, he came up beside the boys. "Can we get in?"

"Willie's got connections," Herman said and walked ahead as if they were expected.

110

"I got connections," Willie repeated with more swank. "And if I'm gonna skip school, gotta make it count."

Rusty emerged from the side door marked *Private Entrance*. Still wearing his army fatigues, he waved them inside. "Told you I could get us into an upstairs room," he bragged, pointing to a black curtain. Beyond was a smoky room overcrowded with out-of-work coal miners, a few high school boys skipping school, and a handful of blue suited businessmen who hadn't yet made it to the office. The boys cut a path along the rear wall, following Rusty. "Room for us is upstairs," he said over his shoulder. He paused in front of a man dressed in black sitting on a stool in front of a red door. "Raccoon," he whispered to him, naming the critter of the day for passage. The man unlocked the red door.

Up a spiral staircase and down a coral-carpeted hall, Connor's shoes sank into the plush rug. Paisley wallpaper centered in a square of muted gray made him feel like he was walking to meet a queen. They entered a billiard room. Velvet purple drapes and silver candelabra wall sconces centered between large mirrors dressed the sides. Sunlight from three wall-size windows lit the room. Willie racked up the balls as a butler entered and took drink orders.

Connor was amused that Rusty was the contact that got an upstairs room. He wondered how he'd managed it, as these rooms were usually reserved for the town's politicians and businessmen, rarely for boys their age. Rusty looked surprised to see him, and he wondered if his friend had been deliberately coming home on weekends when he knew they'd not run into each other. They'd never spoken about the cars in Darius's barn, but Connor had not forgotten it.

After a few games, the butler brought in a plate of fried chicken, and the boys, all except Connor, devoured it between stories of how their time had gone since their last party. He sipped a foamy draught beer that tasted like it had been watered down.

"Can't get out of this damn army fast enough," Rusty complained after Herman had described the May wedding he and Sissy were planning.

"You just don't like people telling you what to do," Herman observed. "Never did. Don't know why you even joined."

"Might be sending me to Korea. Now why would I want to go there?"

"Knock-knock." Herman tapped the side of Rusty's head. "Ain't you who gets to choose."

"Least I get to blow stuff up."

Connor rested his elbows on the bar, looking out at a copse of pine trees. Willie seemed nervous, tapping greasy fingers on the bar and swallowing Scotch in gulps. "Everything turn out with the TVA?" Connor asked, turning away from the other boys.

"Daddy thinks so. Right now, he's keeping his eye on a man named Hoffa. Jimmy Hoffa. Got arrested by the FBI. Daddy's hoping John L. Lewis is right behind 'cause his damn representatives are saying Carmack mines ain't safe."

"You did have three miners die last year."

"Slate fall," Willie spit. "Act of God. Ain't 'cause we're non-union."

Connor didn't know that much about unions. He listened as Willie pontificated all his knowledge of how the mine owners were more than fair in wages, and mine accidents . . . well, that was the nature of the job.

"Gangsters, all of them," Willie spit, shaking his head. "Hoffa'll unionize even the little grocery stores. Your daddy oughta be aware, could affect him too."

"Nobody works for us but us. We could unionize ourselves." Connor chuckled, but Willie did not.

"Daddy says his thugs come in and rough people up."

"I'd put Tempy up against any gangster."

"Laugh now," Willie said in a low voice, "but beware the unions."

Connor looked at his watch. "Gotta get home," he said, sliding from the stool. "Friend of mine from college is coming to lunch."

"Friend?" Willie smirked.

"Randi Jo's gonna be crying crocodiles," Rusty said, scrunching his fists into his eyes.

"We're just friends," Connor insisted. "Rory Parker, you'll meet her tonight at the cookout."

"So," Willie smirked, "who'd be top dog in a knock-down-drag-out?"

"Money on Randi Jo," Herman joked. "Notown girls are tough."

"Rory's too classy for that," Connor said, not amused by their conjecture. "So is Randi Jo," he added, even as a shot of worry settled in his gut.

Beer-inspired snickers filled the room, and Connor wondered if it was a mistake to invite Rory to meet the gang. He saluted Rusty and bowed to Willie and Herman, who threw a chalk cube against the door as he closed it.

As he walked down the long, paisley hall, sharp voices drew his attention. He peered inside a banquet room at Darius Stark waving a fork in the face of a red-haired man who couldn't have been much older than Connor himself. Darius looked like a different person from the man Connor had seen passed out on the couch. An open-collared shirt showed a thick-necked man with a pug nose and sharp eyebrows that had a tendency to peak in the center when he spoke. He gobbled the steak lunch and swigged from a quart bottle of bourbon.

Darius, Connor thought, *that's how Rusty got us in here.* Glad he was leaving, he wished he hadn't drank the beer. Dolled up like a movie star, a woman next to Darius wore a low-cut purple dress and a glittery barrette holding back one side of her platinum-colored hair. The man opposite Darius had no food, and his sour expression made him look like he wanted to puke.

"Kiss my ass in a pan of fried lard," Darius snorted sharply, shooting up a middle finger in the redhead's face. He continued eating, cutting the meat with hard grunts that spoke his contempt.

"Jonas says sit tight," the redhead replied, avoiding Darius's disdainful glare.

"I don't give a blast what Jonas thinks. He parks his fat ass up in Coalfire, thinking he can rule the roost while I'm farting all the risk."

The redhead sighed and dipped his head.

"Got three jalopies to go out by next week," Darius spit, "not a minute longer."

The blond woman noticed Connor in the hall and rose in a sensuous curve. She seductively walked toward him, their eyes connecting in a mesmerizing gaze. She smiled with cherry-colored lips as she slowly closed the door.

14

During lunch, Connor couldn't keep his mind off the Cadillac, Chrysler, and Nash Ambassador in Darius's barn. How could Rusty be friends with Herman after what they'd both seen? He had to be mistaken, he thought, trying to convince himself, even as what he'd heard at the pool hall gnawed at him.

Rory touched his arm and pointed to the dinner rolls. He let his fingers slip over hers in the transfer. She'd enchanted Mom, and even Tempy couldn't take her eyes off the charming girl with the deep blue eyes. She told them stories of her North Carolina ancestors fighting Indians and how some of the Parkers traveled the Wilderness Road with Daniel Boone. Aunt Edna chuckled and confirmed that every word was the gospel truth. Pop patted Connor on the shoulder as if to say he'd made a good choice. As uncomfortable as Connor was with their assumptions, he didn't say anything to correct them.

Lunch flowed like a scene from *The Adventures of Ozzie and Harriet*, taking a surreal quality of glossy togetherness as if they talked and joked with each other like this every meal. As Connor ate the last of his red velvet cake, something Mom only made for Christmas, he realized his food tasted like Fitch. That was it, he thought. None of this concocted setup was him. Fancy dinnerware reserved for holidays. New cobalt goblets with ice water and smaller ones for pink lemonade. This lunch was a scene one might find at Fitch's Savannah estate. His family put on for Rory, hoping to win him this prize. Connor played along politely, but doubt mixed in with his food and every swallow coated his insides with brine.

As he walked Rory and Aunt Edna to their car, he wondered if he'd made a mistake letting her come to Contrary. "Got directions to Copperhead Fields?" he asked.

"We drove it on the way over here to make sure I wouldn't get lost," Rory said. "Can't wait to meet your friends."

"See you later this evening." Connor watched as they drove away. He wasn't the only one watching. The Black Dahlia and Bette Moss scratched to reality behind his eyes, watching, waiting, wanting to come out and play. "Stop it," Connor said to himself. In his mind, he heard a girlish giggle.

༄

When Connor returned upstairs, Pop had retired to take a nap, and Tempy had gone to cashier in the store. Lunch dishes were still on the table, which wasn't like Mom, and he poked his head into the front rooms but didn't see her. Out the widows he observed Laynchark Avenue, its Old English architecture looking worn from last winter's harsh weather. He watched pensively as two men shook hands outside the National Bank, a gaggle of teenage girls window-shopped Josephine's Dress Shop, and a small boy eyed hunting knives in a John's Store display. He'd grown up watching this slice of street, and even the simplest of scenes took hold in his mind like treasured Christmas tree ornaments. A scrape from Grammy's room drew his attention, and he found his mother sitting among the keepsakes of Grammy's life. "Too soon to box all this up, Mom."

Mom let out a tearful breath and squeezed a housecoat between her hands. "I never got along with my mother when I was a young girl."

Connor chuckled. "Kinda like you and Tempy."

"Tempy's stubborn," she said. "I was the practical type, and Grammy, she was out to change the world. Had no use for a husband or a family. That I was even born was a miracle."

"Well, thank good Louisa for that, 'cause otherwise I wouldn't be here."

She looked up at him, biting her bottom lip as if she held her breath. Looking at the child on whom the sun rose and set, Wallis Herne let words slip from her lips, words that had never been spoken aloud. "My father wanted a boy."

Connor had never seen a vulnerable moment in his mother's life. The woman who'd always been so exactingly perfect rarely spoke of the past, and he saw his chance to know more about his ancestry. "Don't think Grammy had much use for boys," he said. "She told me I wasn't of her."

"That was the disease talking," Mom exclaimed, a hint of shock in her voice.

" 'Course, Tempy told me the same thing."

"Connor," she said firmly. "You sister has lied so much in her life, she has trouble knowing the truth."

"We were kids. I didn't think much of it." He picked up a floral printed housedress and folded it into a square, placing it in a box with the other clothing.

117

Mom opened up a sock drawer and pulled out a green rabbit's foot with a tiny chain laced through the paw. "I wondered what happened to this." She handed the key chain to Connor. "She won that at the Crimson County Fair last year, picking plastic yellow ducks out of a fountain. You might as well take it."

Connor swallowed hard and his eyes stung. "I'll put my car keys on it," he said. The soft, dyed fur caressed the back of his hand and a tingling sensation spread up his back. "Maybe you could tell me more about the old days?"

His mother's lips pressed together, head nodding slightly. "I'm going to make this into a sewing room." She stood up without acknowledging Connor's question and pushed the clothing box under the bed with a foot. "Best to move forward."

"Great idea," he said, standing with her. "Painting the stockroom's gonna take me three or four weekends, we'll have lots of time to talk." He turned but paused at the door. "By the way, I need my birth certificate."

"What in the world for?" she asked, a tremor in her voice.

"Dr. Herzog offered me an internship. I have to fill out employment papers, and the school needs my birth certificate."

"They didn't ask for any of that for your scholarship. Just tell them, you're here, so obviously you were born."

Connor chuckled. "No worries, Mom. I'll call Dr. Carr who delivered me," he said. "He'd have one on file, don't'cha think?"

"No," she said sharply. "Don't worry about it." She moved toward Connor, smiling, and patted him on the arm. "I'll find it."

Connor thanked her and headed back through the kitchen, stopping in the hallway leading toward the stockroom, where he picked out a gallon of white paint. As he crossed over the threshold of a utility room that separated the apartment from the stockroom, he glanced down the hallway. Mom was on the floor, cross-legged beside the file cabinet, riffling through handfuls of paper. She ripped several into pieces and threw them into the garbage pail. Connor watched as her previous unguarded openness washed off her like soap. She snapped shut the file cabinet drawer, holding the handle for several seconds as if to glue it in place. A tight grimace about her mouth told Connor she was ready to move on, she would let the past be as dead as her own mother.

15

Much to Connor's relief, Randi Jo said the first kind words to Rory, complementing her on how she pulled her hair back with a headband. They ate hotdogs, and he toasted a marshmallow for Rory. She was polite but uneasy around his gang and hid her apprehension behind an infectious laugh. Connor was impressed with her natural friendliness among people who were looking her over as if she were a prize calf. Earlier Rusty had started an argument with him about civil rights legislation as Connor defended the colored students who were set to register next fall for high school in Little Rock, Arkansas. When Rory arrived, Connor tried to avoid politics as best he could, until Rusty swaggered back, half drunk, and leaned into Rory.

"Bet this little lady agrees with me," he said, his breath foul from beer and hotdogs. "Bet where you're from, people know segregation of the races is the natural way of the world."

"Nobody tells this girl how to think," Connor spit. His cheeks flushed, unable to understand how Rusty could take such an ignorant view of the world.

"I don't hear her speaking for herself," Rusty said and lurched away, leaving Rory and him sitting atop a picnic table, a single beer between them.

"Seems my presence has stirred the pot," Rory said cautiously. "He wouldn't be acting that way if I weren't here."

Connor waved his hand through the air. "Contrary has its name for a reason." He looked over her shoulder at the group gathered around the fire. A record player had been wired to a battery and played The Five Satins singing "In The Still of the Night." Sissy held weenies on a stick for herself and Herman over the flame, and he wrapped his arms around her as the two swayed with the music. Willie and Holly snuggled together on a log, her hands deep in his coat pockets while they stared into each other's eyes. Lynn sat off to the side, trying not to notice the couple's intimacy. Randi Jo danced by herself on the far side of the campfire. Sparks shot up into the air, making her seem as if she moved behind an otherworldly curtain of fire. She swayed hungrily, not so much to the music but to the sensuous wave of flame. "You get used to them," he said, bringing his gaze back to Rory, but glancing off again as Rusty came up behind Randi Jo and placed his hands on her hips. "Before you got here," he said to Rory, "Randi Jo pointed out something I never thought of, even though I support civil rights. You realize integrating the schools will put the colored teachers out of work?"

"Your friend is quite unique in her thought process," Rory said, and looked off into the dark woods. "Something no one talks about, and yet, I guess it's true."

"Yeah," Connor said, as he watched Randi Jo and Rusty, then realized he didn't know what Rory had said. "What?"

121

"I said Randi Jo had it right about . . ." Rory scanned the ground, then threw a quick glance over her shoulder. "Little tired after all that driving today," she said. "Maybe I ought to go."

"No," Connor said, his eyes darting to Randi Jo as she upturned a bottle of whiskey and gulped several drinks. As she brought the bottle down, she wiped her mouth with the back of her arm, flame reflected in her eyes like fire snakes. "Uh, I, I'll get you another hot dog," he said to Rory.

"I don't want another hot dog," Rory replied. She stood and dusted her pants.

Then, the dancing stopped as Randi Jo bumped the record player. The needle swerved over the album in a drone, drawing everyone's attention. Randi Jo put a hand over her mouth as she stumbled backwards and bolted into the woods. Everyone stood and looked after her. Lynn uprighted the turntable but didn't put the music back on. Sissy and Holly shot brief glances at Rory.

Connor stepped toward the woods with Rory following him. He stared into the darkness. The vague outlines of poplar trees, recently planted full-grown as a windbreak, spread before him like bars on a jail cell.

A flash of burning mountains held him where he stood. A recollection of a white rabbit, leading him out of hell, gelled in his memory. His grandmother's voice, teasing him, "You've been marked—marked by the hare of Hertha . . . She saved your life. Someday, she'll demand the same of you."

Connor had not returned to these woods since the day of that hallucination. He'd avoided learning about Hertha, dismissed his memories of the scorched earth, but he knew Randi Jo had run toward that same place, the mound of dirt where he'd collapsed, ready to accept his own death.

"Somebody ought to go after her," Holly said with a flip of her eyes up toward Connor.

"I'll go," Rusty said, emptying the whiskey bottle onto the ground.

"Stay, Rusty," Connor interjected. "You're the one who fed her that poison."

"I look like a bartender?" he said defensively, letting his hands rise in a not-my-fault gesture. "Grown-ups make their own decisions."

"Hope she's all right," Rory said, coming up beside him.

"Canal's that way," Connor explained. "Not deep, but if she were to pass out . . ." His own words echoed in his mind as he spoke to Rory. He already knew part of himself was in another place, but he wasn't sure where it would land him–in the hell of ashes where only the Hare of Hertha could lead him to safety or in that gray land of his own psyche where he could feel murdered girls clawing to look out his eyeballs as if they were windows. The Black Dahlia and Bette Moss asserted their presence from a slumbering sleep. They danced and sang themselves into his consciousness, excited and expectant. Their song was an echo to him now. So faint he couldn't make out the words. Connor knew *someone was going to die.*

Holly patted Rory's shoulder. "I'll walk you to your car, hon, but make sure you stay on the path behind me 'cause there's lots of cottonmouths around here."

Rory's eyes widened. "Snakes?"

"She's joking," Connor said and took her hands. Rory hesitated and looked up into his eyes. Connor knew she wanted him to walk her to the car, but the thought of Randi Jo out in those woods with only the dying embers of their fire to lead her back scared him more than facing the hallucinatory world that had frightened him as a child. "I'll pick you up Sunday," he said to Rory, "right after church."

Rory nodded, a hint of disappointment in her eyes. Holly wrapped an arm around her shoulders, and Willie followed them, shooting him a thumbs-up as they headed toward to parking lot.

"Need a flashlight, Connor?" Herman asked. "I can run to the car and get one."

"Take a piece of torchwood." Lynn pointed at the fire. "It'll give some light."

"I can find her," Connor said, and stepped off into the darkness.

Their voices faded. Only the whoosh of wind between the trees mixed with the coo of an owl. He stood, silent, eyes closed, and imagined the landscape around him. He'd never been afraid of the dark, not like most children. He found a comfort in the unseen, almost like it gathered around him, forming its own creation. It was the known that Connor feared. He listened and moved to his left, his feet sure on a path that he created in his imagination and found, oddly enough, that it existed in the world. He discovered Randi Jo holding to a tulip tree, more embarrassed than sick. She looked up at him, the tilt of her face the only angles in the glow of faraway parking lights.

Connor helped her to his car and rolled down the windows. She leaned her head on the door, letting the breeze dry the sweat on her forehead. As they drove, he struggled with the war inside his brain. Never had the dead women struggled so hard to come forward into his reality. He thought briefly of his argument in Dr. Herzog's class that different realities exist in people's minds.

"Let's stop at the church parking lot and get some air," Randi Jo said. "Like to clear my head before facing the folks."

He pulled into a gravel lot at Notown Holiness Church, and they got out of the car. Connor grabbed an RC Cola from a six-pack he'd put in the backseat for his and Rory's trip and opened it on the door handle. Handing it to Randi Jo, he shook off his other world even as a persistent knocking pestered his mind. "Pop'll settle your tummy," he said.

He peered into the graveyard behind the church, and the imaginary women scurried back and forth, upset. They didn't like the dead. Graves gave him the creeps, too, dead people in the earth and the living dead in his mind. He wondered why them—why the Black Dahlia, a woman whose name he'd never known. She was a noir photograph in a pulp detective magazine he'd seen as a boy. Why Bette Moss, a girl he'd met once? Why not his grandmother? His sixth grade teacher? Why did some women have a consciousness of their own in his imagination and not others?

Randi Jo spoke to him and looked as if she were feeling better. During the course of the conversation, his sense of reality expanded and contracted, and only gazing into her eyes kept him from losing all sense of himself. He scuffed a foot in the gravel. In this land, he walked with a name; he once again saw the majesty of the mountains and the fruitfulness of its legend. Now he remembered this was his home and no one would scare him away. He didn't belong to specters that wanted more death, and the women backed away from him, afraid. "I never realized what I had around here," he said, then reached out and touched Randi Jo's cheek. "What a good place this is to grow up. Not perfect, but good."

A sliver of the moon reflected in the clear green color of her irises. Her words fractured into his consciousness and he heard her say, "I hoped it would be perfect for you."

School . . . they were talking about his college.

He saw the sweetness in Randi Jo, sincerity as strong as the belief a child has in Santa Claus. Their fingertips touched and hers were cold. He slid his hands around hers, bringing her closer. As he leaned in and kissed her, all thoughts of the dead slipped back into their dusty abyss and her touch kept him grounded. Her lips tasted of her mint gum, the smell of her hair sweet almond, her neck soft as down. He lifted her onto the car and she pulled him on top of her. Her hand slipped between his legs and, for an instant, breath held in his throat. "Are you sure?" he whispered.

Her body answered as she wrapped her legs around his. Once he looked to the sky: stars poured through the black film of night, spread like dots of ice melting under moonlight. Only the fervor of sensation coursed through his veins and in her touch was all life. No dead women could get to him here.

16

First sex. First sexual relations. Connor pondered the awkward words as he slathered a second coat of paint onto the storeroom wall. Sexual relations was what his high school health teacher had called it. He recalled Coach Eastwood standing in front of the blackboard, a somber look on his face as he explained that someday the boys would marry and have sexual relations with their wives. His friends called it other things. Willie had once said *screwing*. Rusty usually called it *getting some*. He knew that they'd both done it but suspected it was Randi Jo's first time. He wasn't sure what he'd say to her when they saw each other at church tomorrow. He hadn't expected this to happen, but also wasn't sorry. He wondered what this meant for him . . . for Randi Jo . . . Rory . . .

Tempy came halfway down the steps from the apartment above, holding her nose to avoid breathing the paint fumes. "Rusty called to say the guys are hunting critters tonight but to use the word skunk."

"And?"

"And I'm thrilled it makes sense to you!" she said with an annoyed expression, like taking the message was a bother in the first place.

"Do they want the privilege of my company?"

"I guess you could read entitlement in it."

"Ever think of running away, Sis, maybe joining the French Foreign Legion?" Tempy shot him a middle finger, and he flicked the paintbrush her direction, sending white drops spattering the floor in front of her.

She jumped back. "You can't join the Legion. However would Notown's maidens get their swoons?"

As she turned to leave, he called out to her, "Hey, where's Mom keep our birth certificates?"

"I don't have one. I was born at home. You had the privilege of being one of the first babies born at the newly opened Marleybone Clinic." She cut the last word short, her face scrunching up. "Least that's where I think you were born.

"Where does she keep my birth certificate?"

Tempy let her lips slip into a half smirk that caused her cheek to puff out. "Where she keeps everything, file cabinet in the dining room." She paused at the grated gate that separated the stockroom from the apartment. "There was an eclipse the night you came into the family," she said, resting an arm against the door.

"Neat."

"I thought a monster was eating the moon."

"Moon," he repeated, as she locked the barrier gate from her side. She'd done that on purpose, he realized. Now he'd have to go out the back way in his paint-spattered clothes and reenter through the front. He sealed up the paint buckets and walked into the alley back of the store. From there, he stared into the bluish dusk as it settled onto a deserted factory field that he used to play in as a boy.

The cool air felt good against his sweaty face. An orange feral cat darted into a vent of a deserted redbrick building. The windows made targets for boys with rocks or older ones with guns. Children told stories about how it was haunted. Looking at the darkened structure, he could sense ghostly residents reaching out. That was the nature of specters, he realized. They needed to be acknowledged. He felt sorry for the lonely presence trapped behind those murky panes that seemed to sweat tears of desperation. He wondered why Darius Stark was so afraid of ghosts. They weren't evil souls wanting to do people in. They were sad memories of the past that people gave voice to. They were imaginings whipped up to a fury by those who wanted to give meaning to their losses. The old factory had gone bankrupt a generation before he was born, and still the sadness of all that loss lived behind those walls. That's what a ghost is, he thought.

On the back porch above him, Mom had hung out his clothes that she'd washed that morning. He hopped on top a trash bin, climbed onto the porch and put on jeans and a white shirt hanging on the line, then jumped back onto the trash bin and circled the block to find Trooper. Let Tempy marvel at the mystery, he snickered to himself.

He drove a beltline road out of Contrary toward Quinntown and parked on the Lester Street Bridge. Down Marcescent Street, music competed from the Regal Hotel and a restaurant across the street. The blackout windows couldn't blot out the sound of slot machines. When there was a break in the music, an ethereal melody played from somewhere above him, on an instrument he couldn't identify. Just as quickly, the jukeboxes overtook the wistful sound.

Connor glanced at the single spout of sulfur water coming up from a pipe on the far side. He slurped a drink, looking down into the coffee-colored canal. A street lamp reflected eerie, wavy lines on the motionless water. Relieved that the burnt world of Hertha's warning had not appeared when he went into the woods to rescue Randi Jo, he turned his thoughts to the dead women who would not leave him alone. "You died here," he said to Bette Moss. "Why don't you stay here instead of being in my head?"

Bette smiled like he was a silly child, prancing around a set of daffodils in her world, flowers that wouldn't bloom in this one for several more months. He got back into his car and drove toward the pool hall, putting Bette aside. Tonight, he'd not think of her or any woman. Not Rory, not Randi Jo. Tonight was for men.

By the time he arrived, the lot was full and he parked on the side of the road. The door of Critter's swung open and a cloud of cigarette and cigar smoke hung in the air like a fogbank. He pushed through men stacked three deep at a weathered oak bar and nodded to the bartender that he needed to be let upstairs. "Skunk," he said. The bartender unlocked the red door, and Connor sprinted up the steps.

At the end of the hall, laughter erupted like someone had told a joke. He followed and found Willie, Rusty, and Herman playing pool and drinking beer. They were not alone. Darius Stark was sighting a ball and the blond-haired woman he'd been with last night sat on a stool at a side bar, watching the shot like it was the most boring action on the face of the earth. She adjusted an ankle-length silver sequin gown, then fanned herself with a silver lamé purse.

"There's my man," Willie called out, walking toward Connor and handing him a bottle of Pabst Blue Ribbon.

"Button it," Darius growled, concentrating on his shot.

Willie put a finger to his lips and whispered, "We're waiting on Minnesota Stinks to make his fortune."

Connor sipped the beer and made his way to the other side of the room, where Rusty and Herman were waiting their turn. Both nodded but kept their focus on the table. The cars in Darius's barn floated like an unwanted dream into Connor's thoughts and he had trouble looking at the cocksure man without a knot of suspicion tying up his insides. He was taller than Connor remembered, barrel-chested, with greasy auburn hair and black eyes that reminded Connor of a dead animal. The beefy man studied each angle as if he were drawing it out in his head before making the shot.

Rusty leaned Connor's way. "Randi Jo okay?"

"Probably had a headache this morning." He nodded.

"Sorry about last night," Rusty said, exhaling a deep breath. "All this army bullcrap."

"Blue ball, right corner pocket." Connor motioned with his eyes.

"Hate getting up early," Rusty complained. "Hate being told what to do, when to eat. They'd tell you when to take a dump if they could. Wish I'd never joined the blamed army."

Darius snapped the green ball too hard and it ricocheted the wrong direction. "Damn it!" He threw the chalk cube at the wall and barely missed hitting the blond wrapped around a bar stool on the opposite side of the room.

"Hey!" she said, looking up from a compact and red lipstick she'd been reapplying.

"Shut the hell up," he barked at her.

Herman moved to take aim, shooting Connor a nervous glance. Willie stepped into the hallway and snapped his fingers. A tuxedoed waiter appeared. "Bottle of Johnny Walker," he said and moved over to Darius, patting him on the shoulder. "My Daddy's favorite. A taste of Johnny W. sliding down your throat and you'll forget one bad shot."

"Would've dropped it if you hadn't snapped that powder case closed," Darius mocked the blond. He pulled a silver lighter from his pocket and lit a cigar.

"I did not," she said.

"Did," he spit back, snapping the lighter closed and tossing it onto the bar.

She sat quietly, not challenging him again, putting the powder compact and lipstick into the silver lamé purse. She clipped it shut then sipped from a glass of white wine.

Herman missed his shot, and Rusty gingerly slid off his stool for his turn.

"Orange in the side," Connor whispered.

"I see it," Rusty said under his breath and dropped the ball easily, which brought a clip of the whiskey glass onto the bar from Darius as he sucked his cigar and sent smoke rings out into the air. Rusty moved to set up the green ball at the end of the table. As he stroked the cue back and forth, his fingers trembled. Darius coughed, and Rusty glanced at him without changing his position. Connor watched. Something about Rusty's stance, his hunched shoulders, hand flimsy on the table, said he was going to miss and Connor wasn't sure why.

"Heard Pete McCarthy is retiring from the police force next year," Willie said, opening the Johnny Walker and pouring. "Wish we could get Rusty back home so he'd apply for that job. Don't'cha think that'd be a good idea?"

Darius grunted, swallowed the contents of his glass and poured more whiskey.

Connor sensed that the forced strangeness in his friends' behavior had to do with Rusty. The boys wanted that job from Darius. The

Starks had a cop in every pocket. Outside, a neon sign cast a green glow across the red velvet room. Breeze from an overhead fan spread the sharp smell of liquor. Connor wondered why he'd even come. Watching them kiss this barrel-chested man's butt wasn't fun. It was painful. Willie's wide, fake smile set a tone of phony congeniality. Herman followed along, barely saying a word, and Rusty smothered his usual self-assurance to let Darius look like the top dog. Only the blond seemed uninterested or unaware of the game.

Rusty missed the shot he should have made and opened his hands toward Darius. "Got your second chance, old man." He waved Darius to the table. "I learn something every time I watch you play." He slapped Darius on the back as he leaned down to study the billiard balls.

"Didn't leave me an angle worth piss," Darius grumbled, eyeing the balls at table level.

Connor sat at the bar and picked up Darius's silver lighter. His initials were engraved on the side in a script DS. He looked over the pool table and calculated a triangulation of the billiard balls. "Bet you could get three with one."

"Pfff," Darius spit, and swallowed the remainder of the whiskey in his glass. "Can't be done."

"Simple geometry." Connor pointed to the green ball and traced his finger up toward the red one. "Bank off the side and knock the red into the back pocket."

"Screw geometry. What it takes is skill." Darius got the bridge stick and slid the cue into a groove. Steadying the stick, he popped the red ball. It went spiraling nowhere. "See, told you."

"My fault," Connor said. "You should have hit the green first."

"You're nuts, that shot can't be made." He replaced the balls as they were before and offered Connor his cue.

133

Connor glanced at Herman, Rusty, and Willie. The three of them appeared to be holding their breath. Connor eyed the angles and made a silent calculation of the length between the pockets and the balls. Gently he rapped the green ball, sending the red and purple spinning into pockets and ricocheting the blue ball sideways. It banked off the side and time seemed to stretch as the lone blue ball rolled across the table in slow motion and curved sideways before tipping into the far corner pocket.

"Set up them balls again," Darius ordered. As he waited, he studied the table, chalking the tip of his stick. He modeled Connor's stance and bent over the table, hitting the green ball. All the balls missed their mark. "Again," he demanded, biting his lip and marching to the bar to finish off his drink. Once more he hit the green ball too hard, bouncing balls in every direction. "Bloody damn!"

"It's hard to get the exact trajectory," Connor said, figuring he'd made a mistake trying to teach this shot to an impatient man. "You were right. I got lucky. It was a once-in-a-lifetime shot."

"And I'm, by God, going to make it before I leave this room!" Darius tossed the pool cue aside and got another off the wall, balancing it in his hand as if that would make the difference. "I got damn bad luck devils following me, and if I make this shot, they'll be gone." He missed the shot three more times. Connor, Herman, Willie, and Rusty shifted tensely. Only the blond yawned like a bored and distracted house cat. After he missed again, he dropped his cue and anchored both hands on his hips. "Damn, how did you do that?"

"Guess some people have the touch and some don't," the blond said, her voice a singsong whine as she snapped open her compact and combed her fingers through her hair.

"No!" Connor yelled, as his mind projected Darius's next action. Swinging the pool cue, Darius struck the woman across the back. She collapsed to the floor and he hit her again.

The boys froze at the sight of the blond scrambling to escape. Then, their wits returning, all but Willie moved to pull Darius back. He shoved the boys off and slapped the woman, who flipped backwards from the blow. Connor got hold of one of Darius's arms as Rusty held him around the waist. Herman put a chokehold on his neck. The man's strength was that of a bear and he shook the younger men off as if they were children. Coming round the bar, he backhanded the woman, and she crashed through the glass window.

Connor registered the horror on her face as she realized she was falling, hands clawing the air, dress ballooning, legs kicking as if she were swimming. Willie shut the door. The sound of the lock clicked in Connor's ears. No one knew what had happened in this room. She'd fallen to the side of the building and with all the noise downstairs, it was doubtful anyone gave any thought to the commotion. Seconds of silence ticked. No one moved. The woman's compact and red lipstick stood on the bar like she was ready to pick them up.

"What have I done?" Darius said, looking down at his hands. "What have I . . . I didn't do that. You know I didn't do that. It was the ghost. One of them devils got into me." He turned in a circle, pulling a pill bottle from his pocket and swallowing a handful without water. "You gotta help me, boys," he said in a panicked laugh. "Gotta get rid of the body. Somebody help. Don't nobody call Jonas."

Connor bolted for the door and knocked Willie aside, followed by Herman. They raced down the back staircase. Outside, a long stretch of tarp from an overhead canopy alongside the building had broken the woman's fall. She lay splayed on the ground, pushing herself up on one arm and holding the other to her chest. Whimpering, she looked around, trying to decipher what was glass and what was ground. "Can you walk?" Connor asked.

She looked at him with the eyes of an injured pet.

"She's in shock," Herman said.

"Pick her up," Connor said. "I'm parked on the road." Connor wasn't sure why the woman didn't scream. Most people would have. She had cuts covering her face, arms, and legs. The left arm looked broken. Only the canopy catching her had kept her from being killed. He took some of that ripped material with him, wrapping her upper body to steady the arm against her chest.

"Can't take her to the hospital," Herman said. "He'll find her. He ain't gonna let somebody like her go to the state police about him."

"I'm taking her to Knoxville." Connor jumped in the driver's seat. "You okay?" he asked Herman.

"Go!" Herman said. "I'll cover for you here."

Connor punched Trooper's gas pedal. In the rearview mirror, the woman's eyes stared at him. "You're going to be okay," he said, fearing all the same that he might be lying to her. A deep gash on her forehead streamed blood. He pulled a handkerchief out of his pocket and handed it to her. She didn't take it. At a red light, he put the car in park and turned to hold it against the head wound. The material was soaked before the light turned green. He was going to need some help. Racing into Contrary, he sped toward Indian Hills.

The woman hiccupped and began crying. "He's killed me," she said.

"I'll get help." Connor parked in front of Aunt Edna's house, turning toward the woman and cupping her cheek. "I'll get you out of here."

Still in shock, she could barely acknowledge him. "I loved him."

"You're safe," was all Connor could think to say. He jumped from Trooper and raced to Aunt Edna's door, tapping as gently as he could, but knowing adrenaline rushing through his blood had made the knock an urgent bop.

Through the window, he saw Rory jump from a chair and drop a book she'd been reading. No sight of Aunt Edna. She came to the door.

"What in the world–"

"I need your help. We have to go now. Get some towels."

"Connor, what's going on?"

"Towels," he said, the word hyperventilating from his throat. "Please, we have to go now."

Rory glanced over his shoulder. "Who's in the car?" She placed a hand on his shoulder, then stepped back as she saw the blood on his shirt. "Are you hurt?"

"No," he said, her touch calming him.

"Just a minute." Rory stepped off to a side cadenza and opened a bottom drawer, pulling out a handful of towels and napkins. "Is this what you need?"

He grabbed her wrist, pulling her with him out to the car. "I need your help."

Rory peered through the window and saw the battered woman. "Connor." She hesitated and stepped back. "Who's that woman?"

"I don't know. I have to get her to Knoxville."

"We're taking her to the hospital."

"In Knoxville."

"No, here. Contrary has a hospital, doesn't it?"

Connor pushed his hands through his hair. How could he explain to her? What could he say to make her understand? Biting his lip, he realized there were no words to describe what would happen to this woman if she stayed in Contrary. To understand the dynamic of people like the Starks, a person had to know them all their lives; had to know they were capable of the cruelest deeds without a thought for consequences; had to know that no matter what the crime, a Stark would never pay Lady Justice her due; had to know this was just the way it was in the mountains. Connor stared at Rory, wishing she knew what he knew. "Come with me now, or take the bus back to school tomorrow, but I've got to go." He opened the car door, and Rory hesitantly got inside, then fast as he could, he sped toward the Tennessee border.

17

The drive was silent except for the woman. Her whimpers at times melted into outright bawling as she detailed a scene where Darius had once held a gun to her head, then just as quickly she pleaded with the two kids to take her back to Contrary because she loved Darius Stark no matter what he'd done. If the complex emotions of a broken woman confused Connor and Rory, they set their bewilderment aside to deal with the situation at hand. It never occurred to Connor to seek the aid of an adult; perhaps his inner knowing that he should never have been there with Darius in the first place enriched a sense of embarrassment. If Rory thought about it, she, too, wanted to hide her involvement with such unsavory people. She held towels to the worst of the woman's cuts and did what she could to calm her down. Toward Tazewell, Tennessee, the woman, who'd said her name was Brenda Crider, seemed to come to herself and looked around as they drove through town.

"Turn here," she said. "There's a hospital. My mother works there."

Connor followed the directions and soon they pulled up to a redbrick building. Inside, Rory stayed with Brenda, who wouldn't let go of her hand until the mother arrived. While he waited, Connor paced in front of a pay phone. He jingled coins in his pocket and felt something cold and metallic. He pulled out Darius Stark's lighter. In the disruption, somehow it'd ended up in his pocket. Connor traced the DS engraved on the side, his eyes flipping to the pay phone as he thought. There were many reasons, so many, to forget this had ever happened. He could almost see himself and all his friends the next time he came in—none of them speaking of this night, acting as if a woman hadn't been beaten and shoved through a window. But sometimes it's an impulse that changes the world, not the well-thought-out consequence. Connor grabbed the receiver and dropped money into the slot. "Operator," he said, "get me the Kentucky State Police." He nervously tapped his foot against the wall as she connected him, then without saying his own name, he told an officer where to find a barn full of stolen cars and who was responsible. The state trooper laughed when Connor said Darius's name, and for a few seconds, Connor wondered if they'd do anything.

"Son," the trooper said, "we been trying to catch that crook for a decade. Hope what you're saying pans out."

After he hung up, Connor went outside and sat on the hood of his car. The fresh air cleared his head, and he fought reliving the vision of the woman being thrown through the window. Her terrorized expression haunted him, especially how it'd changed in seconds when she realized she was falling. An instant. But he had seen it. An acceptance of the inevitable. Her features had relaxed and her focus turned from the room to death below. The thud of her hitting the ground thumped in his ears. He shook it off. She was alive. She hadn't died. She was inside the hospital getting treatment. But there was someone asking *"why?"* Voices inside his head echoed like a church choir. *Why? Why? Why?* The dead women were curious . . . *why had he saved her?* Why didn't he let life live itself? Why did he always try to challenge fate?

Rory came out of the hospital. The tense furrow of her brow grew deeper as she approached him. "She told the doctor she'd been hit by a car." Rory paused. "I don't think her mother believes her, especially with the way that woman's dressed."

Connor slid off the hood, hands deep in his pockets. He felt the cold lighter against his fingers. "Good," was all he could think to say.

Rory swung and hit him on the arm. She punched his shoulder with a balled fist and pushed him with all her strength. "What's wrong with you! Why'd you get me mixed up in a mess of beaten-up, cheap women and talk of guns? What's wrong with you to think I'd want any part of this!"

"I'm sorry," he said, staring at the ground.

She struck him again, this time on the cheek. "What's wrong with you? How am I going to explain to Aunt Edna, who has no doubt called my mother at this point? My clothes are back in Contrary! What am I going to say to my mother? Why did you do this?"

"Because I don't want any more dead women living in my head!"

She backed away from him and put a hand to her forehead, holding back hair that'd tugged free of her headband. "It was crazy for me to drive up here with a stranger," she said more to herself. "This world isn't mine."

"I'm sorry," he said again. She held to the hood of the car, thinking. Connor wasn't sure she'd get back inside with him, but he couldn't leave her out here so far from school. "Let's not talk about it anymore," he said.

She circled Trooper and got into the driver's seat. "I'll drive." She looked at him, defiant, and held out her hand.

He realized that was the only way she'd feel safe and tossed her the keys before getting into the passenger seat. They didn't speak again until they came upon the Duke campus. She put the car in park and got out. "Rory," he called to her.

"Don't talk to me," she said and walked away.

He watched as she rounded the dorm, jimmied open a side window, and crawled inside. She was lost to him, and he knew it.

~

A few days later, Connor got a letter from Herman. By the time he got back inside everyone had run except the intoxicated Darius. With all the pills he'd taken along with the booze, he had no idea what had happened. When he sobered up, Herman told him the woman was dead and buried. The lie seemed to work, Darius thinking that he'd picked out the burial site in a place where she'd never be found. *At least this way,* Herman wrote, *he'll never go looking for her. The funniest part is the big dunce thinks he owes me, so we'll probably get that policeman job for Rusty after all.*

Connor chuckled, knowing his friend had done the best he could with people who thought every breath was a lie. Whatever fear Darius Stark inspired, at least Connor believed none of what happened would come back on him.

In physics class, Rory moved to the other side of the room with Fitch. Connor passed her from time to time on the campus, but she never spoke to him. The rejection opened an isolation inside of himself that he unwillingly let be filled with melodic, haunting ballads sung to him in his dreams by Bette Moss and the Black Dahlia. He tried not to listen as they chastised him for allowing a friend to get away. They'd made a nice place for the girl with the blond hair. They would have healed her wounds, bathed her scars in primrose oil, and given her a safe home where her story would create their landscape. He shook himself out of their illusion each time they tried to open a dialogue with him. He'd had enough of other worlds. Connor only wanted to live in this one.

18

Every plant and shrub sprang alive with buds. Connor watched a red-tail hawk soar skyward as he anchored each foot on wooden wedges loosely held by rusty nails. Up above, the Renegades' tree house was still sturdy. He heaved himself onto the floor and looked around. A few green-hulled walnuts were scattered on the floor, a layer of accumulated dirt, and in the corner, a wet stack of girly magazines left behind by whatever herd of boys had found this perch after his gang had abandoned it.

Connor wasn't sure why he came out to the Notown woods. He'd always felt safe here, away from downtown and alone with memories of when his friends were steadfast in their loyalty, and thoughts of girls were nonexistent.

He'd been home from school for two days without seeing anyone other than family. Most of that time had been spent finishing up the painting of the stockroom. But both evenings before dark he came up to the tree house and watched until the sun set. Today, he'd brought the *Crimson County Sun* to read about Darius Stark's arrest for hiding stolen automobiles in his barn. Darius's brother Jonas was quoted as saying the state police had a vendetta against the Stark family and he'd go to the governor about judicial malfeasance.

Far as Connor could tell, no one associated him with the arrest. What had happened on that night in Critter's was never mentioned among his friends. Rusty had only been home from Fort Knox twice and if he'd seen Darius, he didn't let on. Willie said his father had taken a dislike to Critter's, which meant rumors of what'd happened circulated among the town's wealthy. Not even Herman brought up the incident, but he kept his distance from Rusty, and each time the boys looked at one another, both glanced away quickly. Connor was fine to leave the situation alone and hoped the ill will would fade in time.

Connor wadded up the newspaper and tossed it behind him. Climbing back to ground before the last of the light, he breathed in the pine-scented air and climbed to the road where Trooper was parked. As he drove toward Contrary he thought maybe he'd bring Randi Jo here, violate the Renegade creed of *No Girls*. He wondered what it'd be like making love in a tree house, up above the whole world. She might like seeing where he'd spent his time in Notown since she'd grown up here too. Every visit home he and she went parking in a nearby national park, but lately teenagers had found their favorite necking place behind a fenced-off Civil War canon. He would return to Duke on Sunday to escort one of the May princesses to the Spring Cotillion. Rory was a candidate, but he doubted she would allow him to walk her down the aisle.

Afterwards, he showered, shaved, duded up in his weekend clothes, and splashed his jaws with Old Spice. He could hear someone banging around in the kitchen and hoped it wasn't Tempy as he wasn't in the mood for an argument. She'd been as curmudgeony as a badger every time he was home, yelling about his music, making smart-alecky remarks about his going to church in Notown, rolling her eyes every time he talked about Duke.

He peered around the doorframe and saw Mom rearranging a shelf of pots and pans.

"We got rats?" he joked.

She giggled and set a flour canister with the pans. "Thought I'd make a raisin cake for you to take back to school. Maybe you and Rory can have a get-together with your friends."

"Don't see much of her these days."

"Spoke to her Aunt Edna and she thought the two of you had eloped last time she was here."

"Not likely," Connor said uncomfortably. "You know, Mom, I've been seeing Randi Jo Gaylor."

Mom looked at the cake pans, then stacked them back on the shelf without speaking. "Have to be careful, Connor. Small-town girls are looking to get married."

"Got no plans to get hitched, but Randi Jo is a nice girl. She's a lot like me."

Another round of silence as Connor slipped on his socks and loafers.

"She's nothing like you, Connor. A Gaylor'll get you in trouble. That older brother of hers has already been in the county jail and the younger ones are walking that same road. Now, somebody like Rory, that's the kind of girl who'll support a husband . . . that is, after college . . . when it's time to get married."

"Randi Jo is as good as any college girl, maybe better, and her younger brothers are nothing like that oldest one."

"You're meant for different things, Connor. You'll do great work in this world. A Notown girl'll drag down any man she's with."

"Mom, that's an awful thing to say."

"Truth needs to be spoken . . . before you make a ruinous mistake."

"How do you know I was meant to do great things?"

"What do you mean?" Mom sat in a kitchen chair opposite him.

"How do you know I wasn't meant to be a postman? What if my talent was digging ditches or banging on a banjo? Maybe I'm meant to run a store like Pop."

Mom winced and leaned toward him. "I know because I raised you, and I've seen it in you." She bent over the table and pulled an envelope from between the napkin holder and saltshaker. "I got Doc Carr to issue a new birth certificate for the one I lost," she said, handing it to him. "Here, you take that internship with Professor Herzog, and you show up Einstein and Newton and whoever else he knows."

Connor laughed aloud. "Professor might be a mite resentful of you thinking he is as old as Newton."

The telephone rang and Mom picked it up. He started down the steps when she called him back.

"I told you not to go over there," Mom said into the phone. "That's why you don't get the car, you're irresponsible." She put the receiver on her shoulder and huffed a frustrated breath. "Can you go get Tempy at the Quinntown Library? She missed the bus."

"Sure," he said with a grit of his teeth, knowing it would make him late.

"Your brother will pick you up," Mom barked at Tempy. "Be waiting outside 'cause he's got things to do." She clipped the phone down and shook her head. "I swear that Iona Stark will get her into trouble. I can see it coming."

Connor couldn't suppress a smile, but his mother's scowl quickly wiped it off his face. He scampered down the steps before she thought of something else for him to do. He stuffed the envelope with his new birth certificate into the glove compartment and sped Trooper to Quinntown.

Tempy wasn't waiting in front of the library when he arrived. Great, he thought, looking around for her. This branch was due to close in half an hour, so he reluctantly parked. While waiting, he opened the envelope to look at his birth certificate. "Connor Erstle Herne," he read, "born April 1, 1938, 9:30 a.m." That's odd, he thought, remembering Tempy telling him there had been an eclipse the night he was born. She wouldn't have been able to see the moon that early. The certificate was typed out and certified by the county clerk, not like birth certificates issued by the local hospitals. Maybe Mom forgot, he thought, laying the envelope on the passenger seat, maybe she simply pulled 9:30 a.m. out of the air or maybe Tempy was just wrong.

Growing impatient, he finally got out and went into the library. He checked through the few stacks, and clearly his sister wasn't there. He parked himself at one of the tables and looked out the window. Across the street the abandoned Moon over the Rhine restaurant looked like a shivering pup. A crack through the winking moon made the glass appear like it might shatter. Connor picked up the nearest book. The title *Folklore of Germany* didn't interest him, but he thumbed through it to keep from looking out at the spooky, winking moon. Landing on a paragraph about the ancient Germanic goddess Hertha, he paused. The name stunned him. In all these years, he'd not gone out of his way to find out about Hertha; instead, every cell in his body tried to forget he'd ever heard the name. He scanned a paragraph about the earth mother who bathed in a black lake where only her consecrated servant might observe her. He looked at the index and found no other mention of the deity. What had Grammy said . . . "*marked by the hare of Hertha.*" Connor closed the book. *"She saved your life. Someday, she'll demand the same of you."* He pushed the book across the table as if it had burned him and squeezed his eyes closed to block the memories. Rising, he stared outside at the slow moving traffic, determined to stay connected to this world.

Down the street, Tempy came trotting around the corner. She hadn't been at the library at all. She raced to Trooper's passenger side, out of breath and pink-cheeked. Connor hustled out of the library and chastised her as he approached the car. "I been here nearly twenty minutes."

She had opened the envelope with his birth certificate and was reading it. "Sorry to have held you up," she said without looking away. "Mom got you a new one, certified by the county clerk and all." She stuffed the paper back in the envelope as he hopped in.

"And you're a liar," he blurted, starting the car and ripping out onto the main road back to Contrary. "Says there I was born at 9:30 a.m.; you can't see a moon eclipse that time of morning."

Tempy shot him a closed-mouth grin, her eyes darting around his face. "I'm a liar," she repeated, her inflection amused. "I'm not a liar," she said, facing forward. "Found Connor Herne's real birth certificate ripped to shreds in the trash pail beside the file cabinet."

"Why would Mom do that?" he asked cynically.

Tempy shrugged, "Guess she wanted you to have a nice new one."

"You're not making any sense."

"Guess not." Tempy laid the envelope on the dashboard.

Connor didn't say anything else to her. She already had heck-to-pay waiting for her when she got home. He'd leave her to that.

"You know," she said, "I'm an embarrassment to my family." She hesitated and looked at her clasped hands on her lap. "Because of Iona."

"No secret Mom's got no use for the Starks."

"That's not why."

"Stop it, Tempy. What's wrong with you?"

"Maybe I'm just crazy, saying things nobody wants to hear."

"Then let me say a few things," his temper rising. "Iona's a girl."

"Got that," she railed.

"You two can be friends. Friends!" he said louder than he intended. "Is it more?" He coasted Trooper to the corner between their store and the next block. " 'Cause if it is . . ."

"What?" she said. "What?"

"I don't know what."

Tempy laughed, a half-hysterical giggle. "Yeah, I found your birth certificate. So cute, those tiny baby hand and footprints of yours on the back. Wonder why Mom would have torn that up." She nervously laughed but wouldn't look at him. "But hey," she said, opening the car door as they pulled in front of the store. "You've got a nice new one all your own, you don't embarrass your family, and monsters do eat the moon!"

Connor steamed, biting his lip so he wouldn't say what he was really thinking–that Tempy wasted the life she'd been given; that she seemed to enjoy making everyone miserable; and that if she had the least bit of gumption, she'd get herself out of this corrupt, mobbed-up little town and live whatever life she wanted rather than wallowing in her wretchedness.

⌇

All this silliness and doublespeak upset Connor more than he realized, and he wished he hadn't come home this weekend. Only the thought of hooking up with Randi Jo tonight kept his spirits up. Talk of birth certificates and monsters filled his head, agitating him, and he nearly ran a stop sign. Slamming on his breaks to keep from hitting a blue truck, he squeezed the steering wheel tightly, working to get control of the boil inside of himself. He could hardly wait to see Randi Jo and now wished he'd called her earlier. She always knew what to say to him when he was bothered. That's what he needed, someone who understood him. Randi Jo. Randi Jo would know how to get him out of this mood. In that cute way of hers, she would have him chuckling at how the grass grows or deep in thought about how Venus cradled above a crescent moon looks like a pendulum. She'd know just what to do. Yes, Randi Jo, he thought, that's the girl he needed to see.

He steered into Copperhead Fields and saw Willie, Herman, Sissy, Holly, and Lynn at their usual picnic table. He didn't see Randi Jo until he was almost upon them. She sat on a rock out near the water, away from the group. Connor waved at them as he approached and Willie tossed him a beer.

"Just in time to get your bet down on the Kentucky Derby," Willie said. "My uncle's taking money up to bet on Iron Liege."

"Rusty make it home this weekend?" Connor asked.

"Naw." Herman looked aside as if glad he didn't have to face him. "But Lynn's got a big plan to get him out of the army." Herman held his hand out from his belly and gave Connor a wink.

Connor rolled his eyes. "Yeah, that's just what Rusty needs."

Willie shrugged his shoulders. "Just as well. My father wants to put him on as a security guard. Some dirty sons-of-guns been stealing equipment from our mines."

Connor looked toward Randi Jo. Sissy had joined her and both girls glanced his direction. Connor had a feeling they were talking about him. He smiled, and Randi Jo's expression tensed like she was afraid of something. Watching Sissy return to the party, he pondered that maybe Randi Jo was about to break up with him. Maybe she

151

had another boyfriend. After all, he was gone for weeks at a time. Maybe she was tired of waiting on him. His gut clenched, but he hid his distress from the boys. He'd have to do something about that. "See you chaps after the important stuff."

"Woo-hoo," Willie whispered as he walked away.

Connor made a run and slid on a patch of grass, deftly landing beside Randi Jo. "What'da'ya doing over here all by yourself?"

"Thinking," she said. "Tempy said . . . a dance. I figured you'd be with–"

"My sister rarely gets to approve my whereabouts," Connor interrupted, irritated that Tempy had been talking about him. "Since Thursday I've been painting Pop's storage room. Here I am in college, and Tempy still thinks she calls my shots." He scooted closer to Randi Jo, noticing that her eyes were bloodshot. "Besides, Cotillion's not 'til Sunday. I get to escort one of princesses at a presentation dinner, but I'm not sure it'll be Rory. Wish you could come down and see me."

"I thought . . ."

Connor cupped her cheek with a hand and pulled her toward him. He kissed the side of her head, breathing in a sweet fragrance. "Nice perfume."

Randi Jo sat upright, pushing him back with one hand on his chest. "Connor, I missed my period."

Connor was aware that he had stood up, yet at the same time his limbs were losing the texture of the ground underneath. "You're sure . . ." She didn't answer and all his focus went to her large green eyes, wide like those of a child in trouble. For a second, he flashed on the eyes of the blond woman as she clawed for air, trying to hold on to what was not there. "You're sure?" he said again. Even as he walked away, he knew the right thing to do. He knew he should have comforted her, the way he should have comforted Mom when she was upset with Tempy, the way he should have comforted Tempy when she was upset with Mom. "Everything's ruined." He knew Randi Jo heard him, knew his words must have torn her apart, but he couldn't make himself turn back.

He got into Trooper and began driving. Before long he was halfway back to Duke. Heavy fog obscured the road. He drove into the bank of white, unsure of the centerline. An intense bright light blinded him. A horn. He swerved to avoid hitting a car coming the opposite direction. He stopped on the side of the road, his heart pounding. The fog rolled past, opening up onto a panorama of the Smoky Mountains. He couldn't see the details of the landscape, only the giant orb of the full moon rising in the folds of forbidden valleys. Storm clouds gathered from all sides, taking bites out of the moon glow. He had had a future that could have taken him anywhere, and he'd thrown it away by not being careful. He'd given in to frenzied rumbles in the backseat of a car and had lost sight of the grand prize. Now he understood how monsters could eat the moon.

19

As Connor waited in Dr. Herzog's office, he watched the students hurrying to class outside of the arched window. Two squirrels climbed an ancient beech tree, scurrying skyward, each with a hickory nut in its jaws. A group of boys tossed a football, dodging around the giant oak trees. All this was lost to him now. He had to laugh at himself for all his hubris and ignorance. He'd missed Contrary as long as he knew he could go back to it on weekends, but now that he had lost Duke, all he could think was how trapped he would be back in the mountains. One day he'd had a future and the next his prospects had disintegrated into a plethora of particles, only to reform into who knew what. Einstein would have said his view was an illusion. He would have used the example of the light beam and the asteroid, pointing out that while the light beam appeared to be moving faster, the two were, in fact, traveling at the same speed. For the first time, Connor didn't understand. His reality was stuck. How could he have messed up his future so completely?

Down the tree-lined walk, Rory traded girl-talk with three of her friends. He breathed in step with her movements until she turned the corner. She'd won May Queen, and Fitch had had his picture taken with her for the local newspaper. Even this trivial rivalry was gone. None of it mattered any more.

His eyes drifted across Dr. Herzog's books on chemistry, physics, and philosophy. He wished he could lock himself in the office and devour each volume. This level of study would never come near him again. A dissertation on planetology drew his attention and he pulled it off the shelf to thumb through it. One of the appendices had data on eclipses for the last hundred years. He slid his finger down to 1938.

"Hmmm, no eclipse on April 1st." Either his mother or sister was lying, he realized, but now, even that didn't matter. The nearest eclipse to his birthday was in July. He'd lived down every April fool joke known to creation growing up, so if he'd been born in July, he'd own it.

"Here we go." Dr. Herzog entered. "I've signed the necessary papers. You can transfer your credits to Kingsley University with no problem."

"Thank you, sir. I'll really miss your classes."

Dr. Herzog shook his hand and Connor had trouble letting go. "You have a fine mind, Mr. Herne. Don't ever forget that."

Connor looked at the floor. "I've let you down."

Dr. Herzog smiled kindly. "My dear boy, World War I interrupted my work the first time. Don't even ask me what World War II did to my colleagues and me. All you have to worry about is a little baby. I think you're up to it."

A knot in Connor's throat throbbed and he could only nod. Outside, he memorized the hallway and counted the steps out of the building. Stopping at the statue of The Sower, he laid his hand on the cold stone as if communicating his sorrow.

"Connor?" Rory said from behind him.

He didn't turn toward her, and she didn't come around to face him. "I'm leaving, Rory."

"Your roommate told me. I'm sorry."

"Nothing to be sorry about."

"But why? Your grades are so good. If it's money, can't you get another scholarship–"?

"It's not money," he said, cutting her off.

Silence for several seconds, but he knew she hadn't left. Her breath stroked the space between them. "I want to give you this," she said, and moved even with him. She held out a photo of herself dressed up for the Spring Cotillion, May Queen crown on her head. "Don't forget me. I won't forget you."

"After I nearly got your name on the Starks' list of no-goods in need of a comeuppance."

"I don't hold that against you. You were helping someone, and I should have been more understanding."

"I can't take the picture," he said, not even reaching for it.

"Connor, who knows what will happen. We're just starting our lives. Maybe we'll end up at the same graduate school, or you'll be able to figure out a way to come back, or maybe–"

"Randi Jo is pregnant."

He heard the breath she exhaled as she circled to face him. Her expression reminded him of the blond girl falling. Betrayal, disbelief, injury, and her words confirmed it. "How could you?"

Eyes moist but she didn't cry. Goosebumps spread up her arms. For the first time, Connor realized that he'd meant more to her than she'd ever let on, but now he could do nothing about it. Rory tucked the picture in her pocket as if she suddenly felt silly. Her forehead gently leaned against his shoulder, then Rory walked away. Connor didn't turn to watch after her but he could see it in his mind: The slow drift of students moving around her, sun on her face, one hand raising to shield her eyes, and she moved on, while he stood inert, stuck, and motionless in the muck of his own making. All his former classmates were on moonbeams and he sat on an asteroid.

20

The months passed. Connor and Randi Jo lived in Grammy's old rooms, turning the sitting room into a nursery in the final months. Wallis Herne hadn't been happy about losing her new sewing room, but Connor owed it to his father for smoothing over what might have been a miserable existence. He and Randi Jo grew out of their teenage romance and settled into necessary routine. Whatever discomfort came from the origin of their marriage faded with the companionship of the night and the kick of the growing baby. Connor enrolled in classes at Kingsley University and worked part-time at the grocery. His dreams of Duke faded. Even Rory became a distant memory of what-might-have-been. Randi Jo worked hard to make herself fit in with the Hernes, helping with housework, cooking, even sweeping out the stockroom. Connor saw her efforts and appreciated her small kindnesses to his family, who didn't always appreciate her. Many girls wouldn't have tolerated

Tempy's sly remarks or Mom's disgruntled perfectionism. But in all, life found its pace, and they journeyed forward as a couple.

In late December, the family gathered to celebrate Wallis's forty-second birthday. As Mom Herne grinned and started to blow out the candles, Randi Jo let out a similar whoosh, prompting an impolite stare from Tempy until all realized that she was in labor. The frantic rush to get her to the hospital was followed by agonizing hours of waiting.

Connor paced the length of the waiting room, stepping over two of Randi Jo's little brothers. What were their names? Cain and Able? No, Cane and Hector. She had eleven living siblings, five of them below the age of ten. Connor had seldom seen the older teenagers or the oldest brother, who was currently in jail for public drunkenness. Her mother, Malva Gaylor, a resolute woman who'd had given birth to her twelfth child several weeks earlier, blocked the door of the waiting room so her children would not run out, all the while cradling the infant and keeping one foot around her four-year-old, a rambunctious toddler named Butch who was partially blind, deaf, and mentally deficient. Butch wailed a high note, swinging his good arm as if practicing to be a ball player. Connor had no doubt that if he'd put a baseball in the boy's hand, he'd've cracked a window the way he whipped his arm around, hitting his own opposite shoulder.

All these children made Connor a nervous wreck. He finally went down to the soda machine and bought four Dr. Peppers. When he returned, Malva was on the pay phone trying to raise her husband, who was working at the Black Ice Mines. She shifted the infant and corralled Butch with one leg. Connor handed out the soft drinks to the other kids and hoped it would keep them occupied.

"My husband's on the way," Malva said, turning the corner. She looked down at the youngsters chugging pop and frowned. "You shouldn't have given them that, they'll be up all night."

"Sorry," he said.

"Don't say you're sorry, they'll see it as weakness," she whispered.

"Mommy." A shaggy-headed boy tugged on her skirt. "Cane has to pee."

"You're gonna have to hold it," she snapped.

"That's probably my fault," Connor said. "I'm sorry."

"What did I just say about sorry?"

"Don't fuss at Connie, Momma," the tyke exclaimed. "Bad 'nough po' feller had to marry Randi Jo."

"Hush up." Malva pointed for him to sit in a nearby chair.

Connor thought he might faint. He'd been here eight hours and still no birth. The doctor had come out several times, but when he related details of cervixes and centimeters, Connor would cough to hold back a gag.

As if the cavalry had arrived, Randy Joseph Gaylor rushed in, his twin pre-teen daughters in tow. With a nod from their mother, the girls corralled the younger kids like they were miniature stallions. Mr. Gaylor had come directly from work and was covered in black soot. He started to shake Connor's hand but pulled back his soiled palm. "Been too long in there, Malva," he said, nodding toward the delivery room, "this'ne keeping us waiting."

"Mr. Gaylor," Connor interrupted, "I don't mind about your work clothes. Think you might help me sit down? 'Cause I'm frozen where I am." Connor licked his lips, his throat tickled from dryness, and he swiped Hector's soda and drank. The child screamed. Mr. Gaylor smiled wide like he knew the signs of nervous fatherhood and helped Connor to a chair.

"Deep breaths, son. Little'un'll come in its time." He patted Connor on the shoulder and stuck a dusty cigar in his shirt pocket. "I'll get these young'uns home, and it'll be tolerable in here." With the help of the older girls, the pack of kids marched past him, all staring at him like they wanted something. He didn't know what to do and blithely waved. How was he ever going to raise a child? "You get used to it," Mr. Gaylor said, as if he'd read Connor's mind.

Connor recalled nodding at his words but wasn't sure what he was agreeing with. Soon, Mr. Gaylor and the twins–what were their names? Patsy and Rhoda–had gathered the clan for home to wait for news.

Malva sat next to Connor and felt his forehead. "You're just pitiful," she said.

"I know it," he agreed.

Connor's own parents and Tempy came and went, driving Mrs. Gaylor home around midnight. Holly, Willie, Lynn, Sissy, and Herman had also popped in but there was no news to report and soon they left as well, leaving Connor dozing in an orange plastic chair with no arms. He jolted awake and stared out the window as the L&N train rumbled past. A caked snow covered the ground, tinting the landscape in shades of blue. Connor picked up a newspaper that another couple had left earlier in the evening. He recalled their singsong accent as they waited for their grandson, who was getting forehead stitches after a sled collision with a fence post. Not from around here. *The Minneapolis Star*, he read. He glanced down the headlines, eyes stopping on the words *Killing*. Mr. Ed Gein, a fifty-year-old Wisconsin farmer and his house of horrors. Connor examined the photo of the slight, pasty-faced man, wondering how he could have hung fifty-eight year-old Bernice Worden by her heels and carved her up like wild game, laying her internal organs about and putting her heart into a pot on his stove. As Connor continued to read, he could feel the rush of the dead women hurrying to his shoulder, peering onto the page, salivating for information.

He stood and peered down the empty hall. Fluorescent lights hummed, illuminating a dozen closed doors in a green tone. Returning to his seat, Connor tossed the newspaper in a trash pail. How fair was that? he thought. A woman minding her own business, tending her store, and a man eviscerates her like a Thanksgiving turkey. What if she'd not come to work that day? Asked her son to stay home from deer hunting? A tiny instance changed her history and put her in the crosshairs of a monster. Connor reflected that it was the tiny incidents that changed people's lives. What if Rusty's parents had kept him? He'd not have grown up beaten and hungry in a tyrannical orphanage; yeah, there was a dirty trick of fate.

These thoughts pestered him as he stared at the murky landscape, hands tucked deep in his pockets. His fingers touched Grammy's rabbit's foot on which he'd attached his keys. He pulled it out and stroked the soft fur, dyed a vivid green by circus folk to attract attention. Carefully, he took the paw off the key chain and tossed it into a nearby trashcan on top of the newspaper. Carrying a rabbit's foot for luck was superstitious at best, unsanitary at worst, he thought. People make their own destiny . . . *Just like I made mine.* Time to start living in reality, not wishful thinking, he told himself. He wondered if Heisenberg had such problems. There would always be the unknown element that popped up when least expected, but he'd deal with them. Where would he be now if he'd not gone into Darius's barn? If he'd told Herman what he saw that night. If he'd made love to Rory rather than Randi Jo. Would there even be a baby? After witnessing the clamor of the Gaylor clan, he felt like giving up before he'd even started. From the trash, the crumpled photo of Mrs. Worden gazed at him

The clock on the mint green wall rolled round to three a.m. Today was the darkest day of the year. At least tomorrow would be a start toward spring. Connor heard shoes click on the tiles and the crusty static of a radio. Rusty rounded the corner, wearing his policeman's uniform. Having recently been hired as one of Contrary's finest, his rookie status earned him the night shift. He settled into the chair across from Connor and took off his police cap. Rubbing his eyes, he yawned and said, "What'd we get ourselves into?" Lynn had given birth a few months before, and Rusty complained about no sleep and twenty-four-hour squalling like his child had invented it. Rusty scooted down, stretched his legs out, and leaned his head against the wall. "Darius used to say a married man is like a caged animal."

Connor flinched at the mention of Darius Stark. "Got its benefits."

Rusty leaned forward, bracing his arms on his knees, and stared at the floor. Eyes closed, he yawned and continued, "Went to the state pen last weekend." A low buzz of fluorescent lighting backgrounded the pad of a nurse's steps as she passed. "He's mad as fire. Said he'd kill the person who reported him, ever he caught him."

Connor swallowed, looking out the window at the dark, weighing the words. "Why the hell do you defend that man?"

Rusty sat up straight and folded his arms over his chest. "Thinks he can get the governor to pardon him next year or so."

"He stole Herman's car," Connor blurted, sitting up.

"Got nothing to do with Herman."

Connor stood, hands on his hips. "Listen to yourself. Why stand up for such a man?"

"I'm a policeman 'cause of Darius. He gave me everything I am."

"Everything?"

"All that matters."

"I'm your friend, and I'm telling you that man wants something of you and it's not gonna turn out good."

"Not the same." Rusty stood as well, but didn't face Connor. "This is adult stuff, our friendship is made up of a tree house and a handful of pranks. We gotta be real men. Now we got kids. Gotta think of how to feed 'em."

"How can you even face Herman?"

"I'm square with Herman," he said. "He knows how it is."

"Really, or is it that the whole family is afraid? Cahills got their windows shot out the night Darius was convicted."

Rusty gently beat a hand on the wall. "Darius finds out I had you at his house, finds out you were in that barn, he'll always suspect you."

"He doesn't trust you?"

"Haven't proven myself yet. But I will, and I know you didn't have anything to do with sending him to jail." Rusty swallowed, eyes pinned to the floor. "I told Darius I hadn't had anybody in the house and any hunting we did, I kept everybody in sight."

"See, he's already turned you into a liar."

"Better that than a dead man."

A nurse emerged from swinging doors. "Hurry, she said, motioning with a twirling hand. "You have a baby, Mr. Herne."

Connor followed her down the hall through the swinging doors, around the corner, and up to a glass window. He stared in at a row of cribs: a nametag said *Baby Girl, Herne*. The baby's tiny fingers had worked their way out of the blanket and touched its lips . . . her lips. Except for the size they were also his lips. He became aware of how breath needled through his lungs and out his nose, giving him a sensation of pleasure so intense that he knew the life that was in him was also in her, and somehow it had woven a magical spell, creating a little girl. He got it. Got what Rusty meant about living in the world of adults. It was an unreal world where men had agreements. They lived by those creeds or they paid the price. He knew that he'd do anything to protect this child.

Despite Connor's determination, he thought forward to the day he'd have to let her go. What tiny incident would haunt her life? Into what swamps would the world lead her? He didn't know, but for now, in this state of purity, he'd keep quiet about what he knew was true. Darius would get out of jail. He would steal, fight, maybe kill . . . and Connor would look the other way. This was not the world he wanted to believe in, but it was the one he lived in now.

On impulse, he ran back to the waiting room and dug the green rabbit's foot out of the trash. He squeezed it in his hand, brushing the fur and attaching it to his keys. If he was going to father this child, he'd need all the luck he could get. Rusty was gone, and Connor was glad. This was how they'd leave their young manhood behind, a kiss goodbye to steadfast camaraderie as they steadied themselves on unsure ground. It might not be perfect or what they'd expected, but it was life. Mrs. Worden's reflection stared out at him from the face of the clock, her horn-rimmed glasses showing him his own face.

He laughed a cynical cackle as he returned to the nursery, the faint imprint of dead women dancing behind him. He'd not try to control life anymore. It had to live itself the way it did. He was no more in charge of life than he was of death. "Come on in, Mrs. Worden," he said. As the elderly lady surveyed her surroundings, the Black Dahlia and Bette Moss rose to greet her. They took her hands, pulling her along. Stroked her arms, pointed to a cabin and the rocking chair on the porch. And here she was, another lost soul living inside his mind.

He looked through the nursery window. The infant lay motionless. "I'll always keep you safe," he said. His breath frosted the glass and the elderly lady lowered herself into the rocker. "Welcome, Mrs. Worden," he said. "We're both victims of tiny circumstances." He choked back a sob, not of fear, or loss, or frustration, but of amazement. He realized in that dull hospital hallway that he was exactly where he wanted to be. Here was the light on the darkest day of the year. A trick of fate, he thought. All seven pounds of her.

PROLOGUE THREE

April 1968

Some people thought the world went crazy in the1960s. The decade started with friendly, good-looking presidents and ended up with foul-mouthed replacements, one that lifted his beagle up by the ears and another who'd once used his pup as an emotional cover for being a crook. The Beatles knocked the likes of Pat Boone off the record charts and Martin Luther King Jr. back-talked the establishment and got away with it. There were riots in Watts and an assassination of the handsome president as well as the man who'd shot him. Medgar Evers, Malcolm X, Ngo Dinh Diem, and George Lincoln Rockwell would join John F. Kennedy in martyrs' graves, while their ineffectual Camelots limped forward into iconic mythology.

The counterculture came to the mountains in dribbles. Not that the citizenry didn't know about the big picture. They'd watched it on their black-and-white TV sets; listened to their ministers preach about the evils of LSD and marijuana; sat through politicians' speeches as their young men marched off to Vietnam. On occasion, when the outside world clashed into their own, such as a hippy cousin coming for a visit or a local band playing a Jefferson Airplane tune at prom, the good people of Contrary smiled and looked aside, never judging their brethren as long as his or her manners were polite. The din of the outside world simply needed to stay away from the ring of hills that insulated them from the frivolity and horror of the new world order.

The good people of Midnight Valley carried on and lived their lives, as did the not-so-nice and the downright contemptible. Vertical parking on Laynchark was repainted to parallel spaces. The merchants on the main street, including Herne's Market, took a sixty percent reduction in business as people traveled out to the highway where car-friendly shopping centers peppered the landscape. Mayor Floyd Stark was having trouble finding ways to deposit the thirty-thousand-dollar payoff he'd taken for convincing the city council that wider streets would alleviate traffic congestion. Various uncles, cousins, and brothers owned the companies that paved the parking lots, constructed the buildings, and hung the billboards, but in his mind he kept straight the percentage he'd get off those deals. No one cheated a Stark out of a nickel, not even a relative.

None of this mattered to Tempy Herne because for the second time in her life she was in love. Tempy never thought anyone could steal her heart the way Iona Stark had years ago. But it had happened, sure as the moon rises. She didn't even guess how this eleven-year-old bundle of kinetic energy worked her magic on Tempy's duplicitous life. Tallulah Herne shined, and the little girl accepted Tempy heart and soul. Tempy couldn't keep her mind off the child. Blond and hazel-eyed, she had a gift of penetrating thought that bordered on brilliance. Connor may not have been Tempy's brother, and she could barely tolerate the woman he'd married, but Tallulah was for sure her spiritual niece and she would do anything for her. Maybe the girl reminded her of herself, full of potential and unrecognized promise. What had been crushed in her life would be nurtured in Tallulah–that Tempy would make sure of.

"Ready?" Tallulah asked from the next room. "Cover your eyes."

"I'm all set," Tempy said, one hand blocking the line of sight. Tallulah came in and cleared her throat. Tempy removed her hand and smiled as her niece stood at a makeshift podium of a cookie sheet balanced on the backs of two kitchen chairs.

"Four score and seven years ago," she started, "our forefathers brought forth on this continent a new nation, conceived in liberty and dedicated to the proposition that all men are created equal."

Tempy smiled as Tallulah continued reciting the Gettysburg Address. Yet her attention faded from the well-known words, grabbing onto the concept of *all men* being created equal. Certainly not all women, she thought, smiling wider as Tallulah finished. She clapped her hands. "Wonderful!"

"Aunt Tempy," the girl moaned. "You come to critique me not praise me. Pretend we're not related."

The words startled Tempy as she cleared her throat, giving thought to the performance. "If I were giving the speech," she said, templed fingers tapping her chin. "I'd think about what freedom means to one single individual. Liberty guaranteed to one of us translates into the nation."

Her niece stared at her, and Tempy figured the little girl had no idea what she'd been talking about. Tempy was a little unsure herself. "Kinda like when I wanted to join the Boy Scouts and was told I was a girl," Tallulah said. "Like . . . obviously."

An insistent peck on the door interrupted. Tempy leaned back and pulled aside a blue curtain. Iona stood at the door. Tempy could have been struck by lightning, seeing her girlfriend in Notown. "Honey," she said to Tallulah. "Make us some hot chocolate. Miss Stark must have school business with your father."

Tallulah gathered her notes and trotted into the kitchen. Tempy waited, listening as the young girl practiced reciting, then pulled open the door and brought Iona inside. "What are you doing here?"

"Your mother told me where to find you."

"My mother?" she whispered, looking toward the kitchen. "Are you out of your mind?"

"I had to find you."

Tempy paused, studying the tense furrow of Iona's brow. "Who died?"

"Sit down, Tempy."

Tempy sat, never realizing she responded to Iona's orders like a trained dog. Through the years, both women had mastered the art of reading the other. Each knew when to look away, pretend they weren't together, when to interrupt an intimate conversation for a generic one because a passerby hovered, or when to quietly hold their hands prayer-like in front of them as if contemplating their next good deed. "Is someone ill?"

Iona's lips pressed together, and she blinked several times. "I want you to stay calm."

"I am calm," Tempy responded, wiping moist palms on the lap of her dress.

"This is the way it has to be, but nothing is going to change. Do you understand?"

Tempy held her breath, afraid of what would happen next. She would remember it years later as the exact moment her world succumbed to slavery. What peace she had made with the gods of morality was about to be crucified on the cross of social convention. That breath she held came out sour in her mouth, and she nodded.

170

Iona stared out the window through sheer teal curtains. "My family insists that I get married."

Tempy sputtered, waving her hands in front of her face. "They can't make you."

"I asked you to listen, please, this is hard enough."

"Okay, but you don't even have a boyfriend. Fake them out. Date one here, one there, but never let it go anywhere. Your family will get bored after a while. Mine did."

"I'm marrying Wayne Bacon."

Tempy giggled. This had to be some sort of joke. Iona was kidding her. Wayne Bacon pumped gas out on Highway 25E and worked part-time in the Carmack coal mines. He had dirty fingernails and an Adam's apple so large it looked like a cancerous growth bobbing up and down his throat. Spending more than a few weekends in the county jail for fighting, he'd be the kind of brute the Stark men would like, but they could do that without marrying him off to Iona. "He's barely above a Neanderthal ape."

"Shut up, Tempy! Shut up." For the first time, Iona's emotions threatened to spill over. A hand covered her mouth, and she squeezed her eyes closed. "Aunt Renita has made the arrangements," she said with deliberate diction. "Uncle Jonas is giving me away because we can't be sure Daddy will be sober."

"I'm not sure I'll be either."

"Uncle Jonas had a come-to-Jesus meeting with Wayne. He knows what he can't do. He's not allowed hit or cuss me, and when I want money, he has to give it to me. Uncle Jonas will give him a full-time job as an auto mechanic. It'll get him out of the mines, and I get to keep my job at the high school."

"How forward thinking of them."

"That's the only way I'd agree."

"You agreed?"

"And I get to keep you, long as we're discreet. Aunt Renita knows, but Uncle Jonas thinks we're just gossipy girls who are a little too attached."

As the willowy Iona Stark paced the room, pale as a narcissus, her pumpkin-colored blouse making her skin tone even more sallow, Tempy couldn't focus on the spoken word. She watched her love's lips as they moved in explanation, lips she'd kissed; she noticed the crook of her elbows tight to her sides, arms that had held her; the rise of her chest with each intake of air, breath she'd inhaled. This woman belonged to her, and some man dared to take her. "Wayne Bacon" was all Tempy managed to say as her mind realized this was really happening.

Iona let out a shivery breath. "Like I said, nothing has to change between us. I'll have to let some time pass, put up a front and act like I'm happy. Don't fight me on this, Tempy. I know what you're feeling. This is the way it has to be." Iona touched a finger to her forehead. She took small steps to the door, pausing to look at Tempy, who'd held herself as if she was in church since she'd sat down at Iona's order. Lightly touching Tempy's shoulder, Iona gave her a squeeze. "Don't cry," she said, then moved on, closing the door softly and turning to look in at her, letting her palm rest on the glass.

The click of the lock in the cylinder would reverberate in Tempy's mind for the rest of her life. The warmth of Iona's hand on Tempy's shoulder lingered just as the vanilla scent dabbed on Iona's wrist filled her head with an intoxicating heat. Tempy's lips moved, saying words that echoed in her eardrums–couch, chairs, lamps, all things that make a home; all things that make a marriage. She named each item in an attempt to hold herself together in this surreal world of union between men and women.

"In here or the living room?" Tallulah hollered from the kitchen.

No answer. Tempy stared at the wall clock, its insistent ticking like a hammer in her brain.

Tallulah came round the corner balancing a cup of hot chocolate. "I guess in here," she said, and repeated, "Four score and seven years–"

A wail as sorrowful as the song of a death march blew forth from Tempy's core. Then another, and another. Tallulah froze in place, never having seen such a sight in her eleven years. Was her aunt dying? She placed the mug on an end table and tentatively approached her. "Aunt Tempy?" But the child was too young to know that there were no words, no actions, no grace that could make better the shattering of a heart.

Six long, sorrowful wails, then silence. Neither child nor woman spoke. They did not match gazes or touch. Each pulled their thoughts inward and close, aware that life had changed and that this information was not to be shared. The girl, now afraid, had seen fear in a person she believed unbreakable, and though she was too young to articulate the knowledge, some part of her now recognized the world as a place that caused tears.

Tempy had always known that lesson well from when she was far younger than her niece. She unclenched her fists, slowly pushing herself to stand, while the child watched. Tempy walked out into the yard, lifted her arms to the cold sun, but all the world's mercy would soon enough turn to a vitriolic hatred that would scorch every person she knew. If she couldn't be happy, then why should anyone else?

SHARON

21

Even if the world had gone crazy in the 1960s, Crimson County's children still had to be schooled in math. In the worn halls where he'd been educated, Connor Herne now taught high school. The crashing of locker doors mixed with impromptu cheers for the basketball team and the chatter of teens about the big, bad establishment. Connor settled into an academic routine, missing San Francisco's Summer of Love while Russia and the United States blustered about mutual destruction. He read about the first heart transplant, the execution of Che Guevara, and Muhammad Ali being stripped of his title; accommodated the post office giving him a zip code, and his wife going on birth control pills; Cuban exiles invaded the Bay of Pigs, and cigarettes were declared a health hazard. Mathematics, however, never changed. Numbers gave him a stability that was measurable.

Through the years, Connor had kept an eye peeled toward the work of monsters. The Boston Strangler killed as many as thirteen women early in the decade; a disturbed man named Charles Whitman shot over forty people from a Texas university tower; and mass murderer Richard Speck strangled and stabbed eight student nurses in Chicago. Connor also followed the commitment of Ed Gein to an insane asylum. The man who'd butchered Mrs. Worden had finally stood trial just the month before. Charles Whitman was gunned down by law enforcement, the Boston Strangler sentenced to life in prison, while Richard Speck got a date with the electric chair. Connor was grateful no additional victims had come to live in his land of dead women.

When Mr. Herne, as his students knew him, wrote calculus problems on the blackboard, he noted that the women watched–all except Mrs. Worden. She seemed content to sit on the porch of the farmhouse, rocking and knitting, not overly concerned with the trial of her killer. No one ever learned the names of the monsters who ended Bette Moss's and the Black Dahlia's lives. No justice. No day of reckoning. Men such as these made Connor fearful for his own daughter. Some day she would go out into the world, attend college, get a job, walk the same paths as monsters. In his mind, he negotiated with higher powers, hoping somehow to buy her passage through the dark cities. On this day, he would learn that evil was closer to home than he knew.

"Linda Guthrie, come up and conjugate this verb."

The students giggled, and Linda smirked. "I can do it in English, French, Latin, and mathematics, Mr. Herne."

Connor stood by the window overlooking the high school parking lot as one of his brightest students confidently walked to the blackboard and worked the equation. Thank God for this advanced class. He'd gotten these students when they were freshmen and stayed with them through their senior year, taking them through algebra, geometry, trigonometry, probability, and beginning physics. But it was one class; the other five periods were filled with general math dummies whose sassiness and backtalk kept Connor's temper in a slow boil until by the end of the day he was snappish and withdrawn. More often than not, Randi Jo and Tallulah were the recipients of his aggravation. He hated himself when his mood got the best of him, but all the same knew his bad humor sometimes raced beyond his control.

Outside, Connor noticed a Contrary police vehicle, and Rusty jumping from the driver's side. Crimson County High was on the backside of Quinntown, and he thought it odd that Contrary's police would be here. Finding himself hoping that no student was in trouble, he watched his old friend's quick strides toward the door.

Linda Guthrie paused at a particularly tricky part of the equation, then the strokes on the blackboard matched the firm boots on the concrete stairs outside his classroom. Within seconds, the policeman peered into his classroom. Rusty's grim expression woke up the class. Connor crossed the room and closed the door behind him, aware that the students had ceased to focus on the blackboard.

In the hallway, Rusty held his gaze. "Need to take you to the hospital. Pop Herne's been shot."

There were more words, more explanation, but that was all Connor heard. Without getting his coat, he hurried across the hall to Mrs. Bacon's French class and asked her to watch his students, then rushed out with Rusty, who flipped on the police siren and raced to the hospital.

On the drive, Connor heard that two men had held up the grocery store. Pop had shielded Tempy and Mom from the robbers as they wildly waved their guns. Rusty wasn't clear on the sequence of events, but one man had fired, and Pop took the bullet.

179

"Are Mom and Tempy all right?" he asked, his breath panting.

"Fine. They rode in the ambulance."

"Did the police catch them . . . the men?"

Rusty cursed and swerved around a delivery truck parked in the road, his hesitation full like the swell of an overfilled balloon. "One of 'em got away."

"One of them . . ."

"Randi Jo shot the other one. He's dead."

"Randi Jo was shot!" he called out in confusion.

"She's okay," Rusty hollered above the siren as he pulled into the entrance of the Miner's Hospital. "She's back at the store . . . taking care of things . . . cleaning up."

"Cleaning up," he repeated, not clear on what his words even meant and feeling useless with the influx of information that pecked at him with eerie clarity. Before the car completely stopped, Connor jumped from the cruiser and ran into the emergency room entrance, seeing Mom and Tempy huddled together on hallway chairs. Tempy sobbed into her hands as Mom sat, her back straight staring ahead. He fell to one knee in front of them, touching both his sister and mother at the same time.

"Pop's dead," Mom said, dry-eyed and detached. "Pop's dead, and it's all your wife's fault."

❧

After taking Mom and Tempy home, Connor stood in the center aisle of Herne's Market. The steady hum of coolers and fluorescent lights over the cash registers layered an eerie glow though the store. A Black Forest cuckoo clock that Pop had brought back from Germany called the hour. All was in place. The shelves orderly, floor clean, brown paper bags stacked for the next day. Mom had described blood spatter on the brackets of candy bars and packs of cigarettes, the killer crumpled at the door, his blood a red gloss on the linoleum. The store was clean as Sunday morning, with a slight bleach odor. Perhaps the neighbors had cleaned up, maybe even Randi Jo. She'd not shown up at the hospital, and he'd arranged for Rusty to pick up Tallulah and take her home. For an instant, the second gunman, the one who'd escaped, flashed through his mind. He could come back. Were his mother and sister safe upstairs? Maybe he should stay here tonight. He needed his rifle.

A tap on the front window jarred him. Rusty stood there with Connor's car keys, having brought the vehicle from the high school parking lot. Connor let him inside and thanked him for all he'd done this day.

"Just heard. A burned-out Plymouth found out near Coalfire," Rusty said. "Registered to a jailbird named Luther Ballard, the dead one. Other man's long gone. Probably hitchhiked out to I-75."

"Appreciate it if a unit could stay out front tonight anyway," Connor said.

"Not a problem." Rusty said. "I'll do it myself."

"Why did this happen?" Connor asked, his eyes scanning the wall photos of Pop in front of every store he'd ever owned or operated going back to the 1930s. He noticed Rusty glancing at a corner and instinctively knew the place Pop had fallen. Probably where he'd drawn his last breath. "He was protecting Mom and Tempy?"

"That what Randi Jo said." Rusty stepped in the direction and pointed to the floor. "The mean one, barking orders, corralled them over here with the women up against the wall. Pop spread himself wide to protect them. The quiet one started emptying the cash registers." Rusty acted out the crime, leaving out details he deemed too gory. "Guess they didn't count on Randi Jo back in the stockroom sweeping up."

"Pop pays her ten dollars a week to do that."

"Good thing your dad kept that old rifle back there."

"But if she'd just let them rob us?" Connor turned away.

"You're sounding like your mom. She kept saying that at the hospital. Connor, she was huddled on the floor with Tempy, back to the killer."

"Who cares about the money? Pop would be alive."

"Don't blame this on Randi Jo," Rusty said, coming around to the other side of Connor and looking him directly in the eye.

"She could have scared him with the rifle. Fired into the ceiling."

"She came out fighting. Just what I would've done."

"My father would be alive."

"You don't know that." Rusty slammed a hand on the checkout counter. "You could have lost your mother and sister too if Randi Jo hadn't shot that man."

"She killed a man." Connor stared into his own reflection in the mirror over the vegetables. Someone had taken the time to cover them with a white cloth. Randi Jo? Had she been so calm as to take a man's life, then cover over the vegetables as if it were just another thing to do? Did he really know this woman he'd married?

"Get hold of yourself," Rusty admonished. "You wife is one of the bravest people I know. She could have hid in the back until it was all over. She could've been killed herself."

"My father's dead," Connor said as much to himself as Rusty.

"A bad thing has happened. Don't blame it on her."

"Of course not." He shook Rusty's hand, though his mind rebelled against the day's events as if they were a movie he could rewind. How could something as momentous as his father's death happen, and he wasn't here to play his part? He could have stopped it. Another man in the store would have deterred the robbers. Instead, he was teaching a bunch of mouthy kids how to add and subtract. He hadn't even sensed the emergency. This was unfair. Unaccustomed to being a bit player, he agonized: If he'd been here, he could have . . . would have . . . done exactly what Pop had done, exactly what Randi Jo did, he realized. This was not his horror. He was a bystander, useless to have prevented it, and that acknowledgment festered a rage inside of him, so ripe he could barely contain it.

Outside, he looked up at the apartment over the store. The lights were out, though he was sure Mom and Tempy were not sleeping. He nodded to Rusty, stationed across the street, then started his own car and drove toward Notown. Notown. Pop had given him and Randi Jo the Notown house as a wedding gift. That gesture had given them a leg up. Pop, the kindest, best man in the entire world, who never had a bad word to say about anyone except Richard Nixon. Pop carried the wisdom of the ages, and Connor always stood in awe at how his father's advice guided his own life. He could hardly believe this magnificent presence no longer graced the earth.

In Quinntown, Connor turned on Marcescent Street and parked on the bridge about three blocks down. He got out and braced himself on the concrete railing, feeling like he wanted to vomit. Bawdy music from a nearby restaurant mixed with women's laughter from a party at the Regal Hotel. Connor jumped over the railing and scooted down the embankment. Underneath the bridge, a familiar hollow swallowed him. If death was here, let it explain itself. Why take a good man in such a way? "Answer me, damn it!" His voice vibrated the listlessness. Building lights spasmed across the water, but the mute darkness held. Only the ancient goddess Hertha, her essence inert in his psyche, jarred herself awake and pondered this vassal who held her murdered daughters.

An hour later, he walked into the same darkness of his home. Randi Jo was upright, asleep on the couch. Curled beside her, Tallulah's head lay on her mother's lap. How could his wife sleep, he thought, how could she appear so calm after shooting a man? He shook her shoulder, and she jerked awake. Their eyes locked but neither spoke. She shifted from underneath Tallulah and pointed to the kitchen.

"Coffee?" she asked, flipping on the stove light.

"It'll keep us awake."

"Pop?"

"Didn't make it."

She pressed her fingers to her inner eyes and leaned into him. "It was awful."

Slowly, his hands rose around her shoulders, and he smoothed the back of her raven-toned hair. "Where'd you find the rifle?"

"Been sweeping around it for months now. Knocked it over a few weeks ago . . . your mom got so mad at me."

"Doesn't matter anymore."

"I should've pulled the trigger sooner. Maybe then . . ."

"Or later," slurped out of his mouth as he swallowed a sob.

She wrapped her arms around his waist, holding him tightly. "Is there anything I can do?"

"You've done enough." He tilted her chin up to look into her eyes. He studied them, a seasoned green as muted as dried sage. Her gaze held firm, almost braced. He pressed her against him, resting his chin on top of her head. Each of her breaths held a second before release. The heat of her hands warmed his back. His wife was hiding something.

22

The morning of his father's funeral, Connor found himself more agitated than sad. Randi Jo and Tallulah had some sort of mother-daughter disagreement for which he had no time, and the ugly issue of whether Randi Jo was responsible for Pop's death injected an unspoken rift into his family. He taught his morning classes in a daze; his mind kept replaying a murder scene he'd hadn't even been a part of.

At the end of geometry class, Cane Gaylor stopped by his desk. Randi Jo's sixteen-year-old brother was an average student, managing Bs and Cs on most math tests, but Connor always thought he had more potential than he showed. "Momma wanted me to tell you how sorry she is," he said.

Connor nodded as he had to so many well-wishers. "Appreciate it."

"She's sending all the boys but Butch to the funeral, and she says if you need them to do anything, pallbearers, deacons, whatever, you just ask and they'll do it. The girls are at school, but I know they'd be here if they could. I gotta stay in class this afternoon, otherwise I'd be there to pay my respects, and well– Momma said to tell you it was too soon for her to see another good man laid to rest, so she hopes you understand."

"That's very kind," Connor said, eyes moistening. "Tell your mother that I understand." Randi Jo's father had passed away several months previous from miner's consumption, a debilitating and gruesome disease that ate a man's lungs until breath felt like razor blades. The Gaylors had watched their family patriarch waste away like the last of fall's leaves until the vibrant personality that was their loved one could no longer hold onto flesh and bone. "Cane," Connor called out after the boy as he turned to leave. "I do understand."

Cane bit his bottom lip, holding back feelings that must have flooded in from the day of his own father's funeral. "Gotta go," he managed, and hurried from the room.

Connor rested his forehead on folded hands, bracing himself as a new class of students shifted into place. After lunch, he drove to the First Baptist. The funeral wasn't for another hour but he needed quiet. The somber surroundings of the church relaxed him. He looked at his watch. He had time to go pick up Randi Jo. He'd been terrible to her the last few days, cold and irritated with every word she'd spoken. Mom's accusations that his wife had caused Pop's death had eaten at him until he didn't know what to believe. He knew this: he needed to make peace with his wife. He'd have to get past whatever mistakes she'd made and accept that she'd made the best decision she could under the circumstances. Steeling himself, he turned toward the front of the church. The mahogany casket was centered in the chancel. A wave of sorrow rippled through him. That box held Pop.

In the front pew, a bent figure rocked to and fro. He approached an unfamiliar woman, handkerchief pressed to her nose. "Did you know my dad?" he asked.

She looked up at him, red-eyed, and chapped lips pressed together as if she held a breath. Her auburn hair sprouted gray roots, and chipped nail polish indicated someone not usually slovenly. "Paying my respects," said the gravel-voiced woman, rising and tossing the tail of a silk scarf across her shoulder. "Didn't mean to intrude. Recently lost someone as well."

"My condolences," Connor said. "You're welcome to stay . . . if it's not too difficult."

Her lips pursed into a frown and eyes narrowed. "Death is just another fast-talking fella," she said. "Don't'cha think?"

"Can't say I ever thought of it that way."

"Flirted with him a time or two myself." She pulled a cigarette from the pocket of a mink coat and held it between her lips without lighting it.

"People don't smoke in church," Connor said, realizing this woman might be unstable.

"Screw 'im. And he can kiss my ass while he's at it." She looked up at him, perhaps seeing his dismay, smiled as if it were a gesture, and put the cigarette back in her pocket. "Death, that is."

The tap of the vestibule door in its frame caused both to look that direction. Tempy made her way down the aisle, with Iona and Wayne Bacon following, carrying two baskets of white lilies.

"Aunt Renita?" Iona said to the woman.

The woman didn't answer, but her hacking cough caused all of them to look from one to the other. "My sympathies for your loss." Renita Stark paused and put a hand on Iona's arm. "Lovely to see you and Wayne so happy."

"Well, that was strange," Iona said, looking after her aunt, who had left the vestibule door swinging in its frame.

"Said she'd recently lost someone," Connor addressed Iona.

Iona's blank expression seemed to travel to a place she wanted to keep hidden. "Daughter, years ago. Didn't know her well. She grew up in France."

Distrust gnawed in Connor's stomach. Iona's dark eyes always seemed to hide secrets with a bit of disdain. A vacuous French phrase made a slow spiral in his mind, then split apart like repelling electrons. *Beau garçon. Beautiful boy.*

"We brung these," Wayne interrupted, standing like a waiter, holding the baskets of lilies.

Tempy seated herself in the nearest pew, fingers covering her mouth as she stared at the casket.

Tension-filled grief pushed its way among them, mixed with disbelief and salted with umbrage for the living as Connor took the lilies from the uncomfortable Wayne and placed them beside the minister's podium. Tempy leaned forward but seemed unable to rise. "I wish it had been me."

Iona put a hand on her shoulder and dropped into the pew beside her. Wayne reached over and shook Connor's hand, and for the seemingly millionth time offered the same tiresome condolences. When he turned, he looked aside while Iona embraced Tempy. "Time to go, missus," he said in a low voice.

Tempy held on to Iona as she tactfully pushed back. A congested sniff and the two women pulled apart as if they were lining peeled from the same cloth. Wayne took hold of his wife's arm, pulling her up from Tempy's embrace.

Connor touched Tempy's back, and she shot him a glare, then laid the same daggers into Wayne. The two women stared at each other, not wanting to break a delicate connection. Wayne linked his arm to Iona's and nodded to Connor. "Sorry we can't come to the service. Iona only had her fourth period free."

Connor nodded, unsure what to do. As the couple filed up the aisle, Iona looked back only once before exiting. The door tapped again in the frame, then Tempy darted after them. Connor chased her, catching his sister at the door. "You can't," he whispered in her ear, holding her from behind.

"I need her. Today of all days, I need her."

"I know." He held Tempy tight as she struggled to get away and run after the one person in this life she loved. Tears flooded her cheeks and her chest heaved sobs so agonizing Connor felt the pain himself.

"Let me go." Tempy relaxed, palms patting the wetness on her face.

Only then did Connor relax his grip. "It's hard for all of us, Sis. We have to lean on each other."

"You'd be the last person on earth I'd lean on." Hands on her hips, she closed her eyes and panted shallow breathes. "He wasn't even your father," she said, letting the words slip from her lips like wafers she could no longer stomach.

"Enough!" Connor barked. "You've played that malicious, childish game far too long. It's cruel, especially at a time like this. I asked Pop years ago. I'm not adopted, Tempy. He's as much my father as he is yours."

She paced a circle around him. "Lies," she said. "Deceit and fabrication, all for a precious baby boy to carry on the Herne name."

"Pop would have told me."

"Pop didn't know." Tempy straightened her jacket and tucked in a crocheted scarf around the collar. "But you're right about one thing. Times like this call for common sense, so I guess we'll have to let the mighty of the town have their illusions."

189

"This is all about you not getting what you want, not about our parents."

"Just stay away from me."

"You hate me that much? What did I ever do to you?"

"You exist!" Tempy pushed open the foyer door. "Mom," she said, her voice melting to a whimper.

"You two fighting on a day like today." Wallis Herne entered, holding an oversized family Bible. "I can hear your shrill voice all the way to the street, Temperance Herne."

"It's nothing, Mom," Tempy said.

"More than that," Connor interrupted. "Let's get this settled, Tempy. Go on, tell Mom what you've been saying."

Tempy pushed herself in front of him. "Connor's upset that Randi Jo isn't part of the funeral program."

"What!" Connor blurted, exasperated with his sister's diversion.

Wallis shook her head and pushed past her children. "After that woman got him shot, I can hardly stand the sight of Randi Jo Gaylor." She walked half the length of the church, pausing to steady herself on a pew. "Ohhh," she moaned, looking at the casket.

"Go ahead," Tempy whispered to Connor, "destroy her. I'll enjoy the show, but know this, it's on you."

Connor flinched and swallowed his ire; a sister who wouldn't claim him as kin; a mother who still called his wife of eleven years by her maiden name. There were days he wished they weren't his family. But today wasn't about them, or even himself. It was about Pop, and he'd see his father laid to the peaceful rest he deserved. But more than that . . . Asa Herne would always be his father, no matter what anyone said.

Connor remained at the grave long after everyone else had left. A headache throbbed behind his eye and his stomach growled with hunger. Cemetery workers were busy digging higher on the hill and told him to take all the time he needed. He wasn't sure there was enough time to say goodbye to the one man who'd shaped his life more than any other. Cold December. Winter darkness crept along the horizon.

Tempy's words ate at him like worms devouring apples left too long on the tree. Whatever his sister's problem, let it be buried here today, he thought. All their lives would now change. Without Pop, the center was fragile. The family would have to work at getting along. Despite their difficult natures, he'd take care of Mom and Tempy just the way Pop did, just as Pop would have expected him to.

A hearse ambled up the gravel road, followed by a black sedan. He watched as funeral home officials carried a pine coffin up the hill. They nodded to him, though he didn't recognize them. Connor felt sorry for the poor soul who was being laid to rest with no one to mourn him or her. A slamming car door caught his attention, and he watched Iona's Aunt Renita light a cigarette then follow the route of the pine coffin. Catching his gaze, she paused, then walked toward him. Stopping at the edge of the grave, she looked into Pop's resting place, then up at him.

Connor could see the duplicity in this woman's eyes, more complicated than an algebraic equation. "Someone close?" he asked, indicating the procession she'd followed.

"Love of my life," she said and inhaled on the cigarette.

"Iona said–"

"Argh." Her hand flipped a dismissive wave. "What my family knows about me is piss in a thimble."

He paused, thinking of the odd relationship with Iona and Tempy. These Starks were a family of secret keepers. Renita peered again into Pop's grave, her thoughts, even Connor couldn't guess. Biting her lower lip, she seemed to be considering as she stared at Connor's shoes. Connor cleared his throat and said, "I guess every family has a little of that."

"More'n you know." She glanced up, studying his face.

"Is there something you want to say to me?" he asked.

"Just . . ." She stared into his eyes, pupils like darts. "I'm sorry." She swept black sunglasses across her eyes and drew on the cigarette before tossing it away. Connor watched after her as she decided against going to the grave of the *love of her life* and returned to her car.

Curious, Connor climbed the hilltop to the other grave positioned toward the sunset. The pine coffin sat on the ground as the workers prepared to lower it. Funeral home officials stood aside; one opened a pack of gum and the other checked his watch. The pine box was the cheapest available, and Connor wondered why Renita wouldn't spring for better for her loved one.

"Who are you burying?" he asked.

The heavier set of the two men pulled a paper from his pocket. "Ballard," he said. "Luther Ballard."

The name sent lightning through Connor's system. He looked after Renita who was getting into the black automobile. Renita Stark was burying the man who'd murdered Pop. In his mind, he saw the defensiveness in Iona's eyes, remembered the snap of Darius's fist into a woman's face, the smirk of Renita's lips.

"Stop!" he yelled, and ran down the hill. "I said stop! You explain–" Connor fell, hitting the side of his head on a gravestone.

Stunned, he pushed up to see the black sedan pull out of the cemetery. Across his foot, a small root protruding from the ground had tripped him.

He hurried to his own car and shut himself up in the stuffy, confined space. He yelled the rage in his body, beating his palms on the steering wheel. His world spun until he no longer knew where the pieces fit. Lies, deception, and fabrication, even the world in his imagination. Maybe Connor Herne could have made sense of the chaos, but perhaps he wasn't that man. Where was his connection to life, to this construct of a personality that went by a name that might not be him? Truth was a dream he couldn't remember and didn't want to know. Would his cowardice prevent him from asking the questions that he might have in his youth? He feared confronting his mother about his birth; he feared Renita Stark's love for Luther Ballard; he couldn't ask his wife if she was responsible for Pop's death. He hated his own inaction, but this was the life he'd made, and the only comfort he would find in it was the solace of dead women.

23

Over the next week, Connor stopped at the police station daily, each time with the same results. No leads on the second man who'd robbed Pop's store. He worried that the criminal might come back and hurt Mom and Tempy. Rusty had arranged for a cruiser to park outside until midnight, but likely that would end soon. His frustration at not knowing who had scarred his family remained raw and festered.

"Renita Stark buried Luther Ballard," he told Rusty, taking him outside the police station, where any Stark cronies wouldn't have the chance to eavesdrop. "She's gotta know who the other man is."

"Not possible. Luther Ballard was buried by the state," Rusty replied. "He had no kin that we could find."

"I'm telling you, she knew him, intimately."

"How do you know this?" Rusty asked, as he rubbed a hand over five o'clock whiskers.

"She told me," he spat, impatient with Rusty. "Love of her life, she said."

Rusty paced a short distance, hands on his hips, and stared at the ground. "We gotta be careful," he said. "If this is a Stark thing, who knows whose poop we've skidded in." He nodded as if a plan had shaped in his mind. "Let me take it from here," he said, clasping Connor's shoulder "Let me handle it."

Connor waited. He taught his classes each day, checked on his mother and the store, then drove home, where he ate dinner, watched TV, and helped Tallulah with her homework. His insides bubbled in a slow boil. He called Rusty several times, only reaching him once. His lifelong friend advised patience. After a week and a half, he could stand it no longer. Entering the Contrary Police Department, he fought a nervous quiver in his stomach. A chlorine smell overpowered the hallways, and as he waited for Charlie Mandel, the detective handling Pop's case, he held every other breath until he had to release it.

"Sorry, still no leads on that second man," Detective Mandel repeated as he had every other time Connor had come to see him. "Like he disappeared with the mountain mist."

Connor hesitated, then said, "Rusty Haskew tell you our thoughts on this Ballard character?"

The detective frowned. "Haskew writes speeding tickets," he said in a cold and irritated voice. "Sometimes directs traffic when the grade school lets out."

Rusty hadn't passed along the information, Connor realized. He had protected the Starks. As he walked out of the station, Connor considered the disrespect with which the detective had referred to Rusty. Could Rusty have some misguided conception that protecting the Starks would advance his career? Had Rusty betrayed Connor? He didn't want to think that of someone who'd been so supportive after Pop's murder, but it was the only conclusion. He'd have to work around Rusty, even if they were friends.

With some sly misdirection and several lunches at Mrs. Bacon's table, he found out that her Aunt Renita lived with her brother, Jonas Stark, in Coalfire, and that she was home alone most afternoons.

The forty-mile drive to Coalfire went through several small towns, quaint and picturesque with a layer of the season's first snow. Kids built snowmen, and a few leveled snowballs at his car as he passed. Connor found himself wondering how the Starks infiltrated the infrastructures of those boroughs. Were they non-involved politicians who passed by with a wave and a smile, or were they into every shiftless drug den and whorehouse stacked on the backsides of the towns, where most of the residents didn't go? Packages shifted in the trunk, and he tried to pump himself up for Christmas Eve. Perhaps he should have waited until after the holidays, but until the second man was in jail, there was only the insatiable need to bring the guilty to justice.

Coalfire was a splat of a town, hardly a dot on the map, but its proximity to the interstate made it a haven for chop shops and hustlers looking to make a quick getaway. Jonas Stark owned Jumpin' Jonas' Used Cars and Mobile Homes, and as Connor drove by, he glanced inside to see a Christmas party in progress. Tree-lined blocks squared out the east side where the houses seemed to grow in stories as he drove. Odd, he thought, that no children seemed to be out playing in the snow, nor did any of the houses have Christmas decorations. This was a town of adults. Pulling up to a three-story Victorian, Connor was surprised to see a silver tree with red tinsel through the front window.

He knocked, and the door jarred open. "Hello," he called out.

"In the living room," the familiar husky voice answered.

Connor entered into a wave of fire warmth. Turning into the living room, a blaze in the fireplace made the room festive. Renita sat on the couch, elbow propped on the back, cigarette between her fingers. Smoke curled like cursive writing and disappeared toward the ceiling. Flicking ashes into a coke bottle was her only reaction. "You remember me?" he asked.

She sucked on the cigarette and blew upward. "I'm not supposed to smoke in the house. Jonas can't stand the smell."

"I'm not the cigarette police." He noticed that the gray roots were gone and her nails now matched the mahogany shade of her hair. She was a curvy woman with more delicate features than the Stark men. "You owe me some answers."

She chuckled into a hacking cough. "What makes men believe that the scales of life will always be balanced?" She stood and tossed the remains of the cigarette into the fire. "You think maybe somebody should write a book."

"Luther Ballard killed my father."

She looked aside, biting her bottom lip. "Yeah, and I'm sorry about that. He was aiming for your mother."

Connor flinched. "I don't find that funny."

"I wasn't joking." Her expression was a cynical mask. "I look like the type of person to enjoy a good joke when there's so much death?"

Connor's muscles braced as if he might be attacked. "You better explain yourself."

"I don't have to do nothing," she barked, coming around a coffee table and punching a finger into his chest. She picked up a picture from a nearby table and held it to her stomach.

"Why don't we let the police decide that?"

She let out a *pffff*. "Yeah, let's do that. Police in this part of the state are so high minded."

He realized there was no lie this woman wouldn't tell, nothing she wouldn't do to protect her own. He wasn't sure he could believe her, but he had to try and get as much information as he could. "Is my mother in danger?"

She held his gaze for several seconds. "If that's all you want," pausing, eyes narrowed, "then rest your angst. Your ma's a bug in a rug."

"How can you be sure? There was another man. What'd they have against an old lady?"

Renita looked down at the photo, then turned it toward Connor. "This is mine and Luther's baby."

Connor stared at the image of a young woman, and though the photo was black and white, she sprang into full, blazing color in his memory. Strawberry hair, far more delicate features than Renita's, piercing eyes that even in the photo appeared to be light blue. Bette Moss, the red-haired girl that he and Mom had sent to Marcescent Street, the beautiful teenager whose head was never found. "You?" His voice failed him, mouth dried and cakey.

"My baby, Bette."

"A Stark?"

"Her daddy was Luther, but I was married to a man named Moss when she was conceived." She gently placed the picture back on the table, a finger stroking the glass over Bette's cheek. "She's dead."

"I know. I was a boy, but I recall."

"Luther remembered, too. Remembered your momma sending a little girl to Marcescent Street where some monster . . ." Renita's voice broke. She sniffed, one hand wiping her nose.

"My mother didn't kill her. She didn't know. We couldn't understand what your daughter was saying. She spoke French."

"What do you want from me?" Renita's eyes searched his as profoundly as he had made it his mission to wring information from her. "You think 'cause something unfair has happened to you that I can cause it to make sense? Life sucks a big one, in case you haven't figured that out!" She whipped her hands around as if trying to strangle an invisible enemy. "Luther blamed who he could, 'cause we'll never know who murdered her. I tried to talk sense to him, but his mind was gone, buried in darkness he couldn't escape, and that was my fault, too."

"I don't care," Conner called out. "You don't go out and kill somebody."

"Ah, baby, you do when you're that far gone." She leaned against the wall, arms crossed over her belly. "When Bette was killed, Jonas believed Luther had done it. Held him in a cage not fit for a dog, sent him to prison on some trumped-up something-or-other." She stared at the fire, now burning low, and moved toward it, hands toward the heat. "But you don't need to hear all about that. You want to know about the other man, and I can't tell you anything other than Luther was the only one looking for justice. The other, I'm guessing he was in it for the money, so look for somebody who's disappeared."

Connor's knees shook, the tremble rising through his body until he croaked out the words, "You should have warned us."

She didn't answer him, only gave him a sideways, disdainful look that he read correctly. He'd been just as responsible for sending Bette Moss to her death. He'd been the one to point Luther to his mother. If justice was apportioned, his feet were stuck in part of the guilt. It was odd to Connor, standing here with Bette Moss's mother, that the specters in his created world didn't come forth. They hid in the layers of his psyche like slumbering sprites. As he stood there, a level of understanding occurred to him. These murdered women existed in him, for him and no one else, not their previous lives or their loved ones. Visions of the past held no curiosity for them.

He knew in that moment that they were not themselves, but rather constructs that his mind had created, something he could dispose of, if he so chose.

"It's Christmas Eve," Renita said, opening the front door. An icy breeze whipped around them, consuming the warmth. "Happiest Christmas I spent with my daughter was in Nazi-occupied France," she said, staring out at the snow. "We almost didn't make it." Without looking at him, she swept her hand toward the outside. "Be grateful for what you have, Mr. Herne, not what you believe you're entitled to."

Connor drove to the Gaylor house for the family's annual Christmas Eve celebration. Tomorrow, they would be with his family. His thoughts rumbled through the discoveries of the evening, and he realized he'd driven in a trance with no idea how a good twenty of the miles had passed. He had difficulty thinking of Luther as a man looking for justice. Wasn't that what he'd been seeking . . . justice for a murdered loved one? Did Luther love Bette any less than he loved his father? Were he and Luther all that different? What would he have done if someone had caused Tallulah's death? Stopped at a red light, he pondered the unfairness of it all. Pop had taken a bullet for his and his mother's error. Luther Ballard shot the wrong person, and he was dead. Nothing to be done.

He unloaded gifts from the trunk, and Tallulah ran out of her grandmother's house with her cousin Collette to help carry them inside. He smiled at the Gaylors, shook hands with Randi Jo's brothers, gave her mother a quick hug, but he had trouble stomaching the meal of ham, mashed potatoes, peas, and corn bread. When Randi Jo handed him a small box wrapped in gold paper, she whispered in his ear, "Hope you like it." He nodded, his body going through motions that his mind wasn't part of.

After dinner, the Gaylors' large family exchanged presents from names they'd drawn the previous year. Connor noticed a missing family member. Pug Gaylor, Randi Jo's oldest brother was not here. Each time the girls came to one of his gifts, they made an *awww* sound and placed the brightly wrapped packages in a corner. The laughter and joy of Christmas filled the room, yet, all Connor's focus was on Renita's words: "*Look for somebody who's disappeared,*" and those of Detective Mandel: "*Like he disappeared with the mountain mist.*"

As they drove home that evening, Connor asked his wife, "Where's Pug?"

Randi Jo stared ahead at the road. "Think he might have a girlfriend in Tennessee. Doubt we'll see him this holiday."

"Odd he'd ignore his family, especially since your father's death is still so recent."

Randi Jo was quiet as they turned the hairpin curve onto Notown Road, and she looked out at a dilapidated house about to fall into the road. "Tallulah, did you have a good time?" she asked, without looking back at her daughter.

"You and Daddy didn't open your presents," she answered sleepily.

"Here," Randi Jo said, holding out the gift Connor had gotten her. "You open it."

Tallulah ripped the wrapping and held out a Timex watch and *oooo'd.*

"Thank you, Connor," Randi Jo said and caressed his shoulder.

Connor felt the stiffness in his body. His wife's hand touched him, and yet he could only process it as an appendage he didn't want near him. "Here, open mine." He pulled the box from his coat pocket and handed it back to Tallulah. Randi Jo had gotten him a watch as well.

Tallulah laughed hysterically. "Guess you two think alike," his daughter said, putting both watches on her own arm and holding them over the car seat. "Time will tell." She sat back in the seat, transfixed on the matching timepieces as if synchronicity assured her a reliable world.

Connor pulled into the driveway of the Notown house and his daughter jumped from the car, eager to retrieve her gifts. Connor caught Randi Jo's hand. "Still, strange," he said, "Pug gone. I mean, it's Christmas."

Randi Jo exhaled a deep breath. "Guess it's true love," she quipped, opened her car door, and motioned for him to pop the trunk.

"Pug was never one to turn down a load of Christmas presents," Connor said. "Why would he disappear like that?"

"I don't know, Connor," Randi Jo said with an exasperated huff. "Now open the trunk, it's cold out here."

He looked at his wife, her green eyes armored and fearful. Hiding, he realized. Hiding something.

24

January 1969

The clank of the radiator added to the nervousness of the general math student trying to suss out fractions. Connor yawned as he stood in the back of the classroom. The weeks since Pop's funeral moved slow as mud. "Can anyone help him?"

No student raised a hand. No surprise. Four of his six classes were dumber than weeds. How they'd make it after high school would be by the grace of government handouts or becoming military fodder. He'd followed the failures of one graduating class after another, seeing maybe a handful make successful lives for themselves, and those were usually the ones who left the area or had family businesses. "Try keeping the same denominator," he said to the student. "See if that works."

His gaze drifted to the window, out into the parking lot, where a light snow covered the cars. Half an hour and he'd be out of here. Funny, he'd never thought that way when he attended high school. Now he was as eager as his most daft student to finish out the day.

Looking back to the blackboard, he glimpsed a blond mane drift past the door, then return. Holly peered in and nodded to him, then continued on. Connor had come to distrust people showing up unexpectedly. It anchored bad news in his gut as he flashed back to the day Rusty had come to take him to the hospital. Holly hadn't waited or called him out, so he rationalized that there was no emergency, but still . . . had to be bad news.

The bell rang and the students aimed for the door like swarming insects. He waited several minutes but Holly never showed up, so he put on his coat, grabbed his briefcase and headed home. Outside, Holly leaned on the hood of his used Chevrolet, a car he'd never named but Tallulah called "the old clunker."

"Kinda cold," he said.

"Mink is warm." She pulled the fur collar tighter around her throat. "Stopped to see how you were doing."

Connor opened the back door of his auto and laid the briefcase inside. "We could go inside and talk, if you want." Holly Carmack had never cared how another human being was doing in her life as far as he had known, and that she was here inquiring about his well-being told Connor she wanted something.

"Naw," she said, with an involuntary shiver. "Being in that building brought back day terrors."

Connor opened the driver's side door to telegraph Holly that he was tired and wanted to get home. She put a hand across the opening, keeping him from getting inside. "Trouble with you and Willie?" he asked.

"You knew me before you knew him."

"True, but still . . ."

"He's in Palm Beach all week, looking for investors. Got his picture in the paper down there with some New York model, all legs and eyelashes."

"You know how to hold on to a man better than anybody I know, Holly."

"Why is it that women always have to hold on to their man?" she griped. "Why don't men work on holding on to their women?"

"I can't help you with your marriage. Willie is still my friend regardless of how long I've known you."

The tip of her nose reddened, either from the cold or some emotion she would never admit to, as she stepped away from the car. "You hurt Randi Jo, accusing her of being responsible for your Pop's death."

"I never said that."

"You've implied it with every defense of your mother."

"I was upset. She took what I said the wrong way."

"She was a little upset herself. She was the one who had to kill somebody. You ever think about that?"

"Frankly, no," he huffed. "At the time, I was thinking my father had just been murdered. Randi Jo is reading more into it than was meant." He held to the doorframe, his fingers tightening. "This is between me and my wife, Holly. Keep your nose out of it."

She stepped up to him, poking him on the lapel of his coat. "Let me tell you something, mister. People like me and Willie–we'll fight and cuss each other, then we make love and sleep it off, but a woman like Randi Jo . . . she'll hurt inside and never say a word. But learn this, Teach, that's a woman who'll stand by you through anything." Her gaze latched on to his like a hook to a fish. "She's yours to lose."

"I know the two of you are friends, but I highly resent her discussing our marriage with you, and I'm going to speak to her about it."

A Contrary police cruiser sped down Lester Avenue. They wouldn't have seen it except the officer bopped his siren to move the traffic pulling out of the high school parking lot. "Now, there's a friend," Holly smirked. "You'd think the Contrary city council would get a little tired of paying for a policeman who spends all his time in Quinntown."

Connor followed her line of sight. The car was too far away to see the driver. He glanced at Holly, her lips pressed, eyes flipped toward him. She stepped back, letting him in the car, but didn't walk away. Connor ground the ignition, then turned it off, rolling down the window. "You seen Pug Gaylor around?"

"Why would I socialize with the likes of him?"

"No reason. Randi Jo doesn't talk about him much. Was wondering if there's a problem I don't know about."

Holly stared him a chilly expression, tapped the top of his car, and blew out a frosty breath. "Be seeing ya." She turned, heavy-footed, marching toward her red Porsche.

Holly's visit continued to aggravate him as he approached Notown Road. Twice this week he'd been irritated by people he'd considered friends. Rusty had sought him out, jovial and confident, to explain all Luther Ballard was to Renita Stark was an ex-employee fallen on hard times. A piano player from way back, worked in one of their honkytonks, tickling keys for tips. She'd felt sorry for him and paid for flowers for the burial. That was all. As he watched Rusty's lips that day, lying or deceived, he wondered if the Starks' patronage gave his friend the self-confidence he'd always lacked, or if he feared the powerful family like most people. He wondered if it had been Darius who'd given Rusty the explanation.

He wondered if Rusty believed it. He wondered if it was worth it to be in a Stark pocket, always indebted to believe lies. He never told Rusty about his visit to Renita or indicated to him that the Starks were using him. Connor worried that the gulf these Starks had created between his best friend and him would widen further with any discussion of them. He and Rusty hadn't spoken since.

He turned the hairpin curve onto Notown Road and looked out at shacks with yards full of beer and pop cans, rusted-out cars, and outdated washing machines turned on their sides. Least these people could do is pick up their trash, he thought. But they wouldn't, and he knew it. He wondered why he stayed in Notown. His attachment to the place centered on Pop. Pop's memory was here, and he couldn't abandon it.

Home, Randi Jo rattled around in the kitchen. He bypassed her without speaking and went into the bedroom. Peeling off his suit, he sat on the bed, dropping chin to chest, exhausted. Music from Tallulah's room played too loud. He sniffed. An odor. Smoke? Cigarettes? After dressing he opened Tallulah's door. "Turn down the radio."

She lay across the bed, a *Tiger Beat* magazine open to a picture of Bobby Sherman. With a sarcastic huff she pushed herself up and reduced the volume. "Rock and roll's meant to be loud."

"Less attitude."

She smiled wide and insincere. "Okie-dokie."

He stepped inside the room that had once been his. "You been smoking?"

"No," she said. A perplexed expression.

"Don't fib to me."

An expression of hurt crossed her face. "I don't lie to you, Daddy."

He glanced out the window he'd crawled out of as a young boy, and lied about to his own father. "I catch you with cigarettes, you can forget debate camp next summer." Without waiting for a response, he turned and shut the door. The music went up a notch but he didn't return to the room.

In the kitchen, Randi Jo sped through dinner preparations as if she'd gotten home late. "Feeling sick?" she asked. "You're pale."

"You think Tallulah would lie to me?'

Without hesitating, Randi Jo offered her opinion. "It's all that time she spends with Tempy."

"Don't be silly."

Randi Jo dropped the biscuit pan onto the stovetop, harder than she needed to. "Open your eyes, Connor! Your sister has grown into a hysterical old maid, and it's rubbing off on our daughter."

"You're imagining things."

"I don't have an imagination." Her arms opened wide and flapped to her sides. "I leave that to you, walking around talking to yourself all the time like there's a pack of unseen people living in this house with us."

Connor froze, fearing his imaginary world had been spied upon even though he knew that to be impossible. The phone rang and both stared at the other as if the ring built a wall between them.

"Anybody going to answer that?" Tallulah came in and picked it up. "Hey, Aunt Tempy," she said into the receiver.

Randi Jo glared at Connor and began mashing potatoes. He huffed a breath when Tallulah handed him the phone. "Tempy?" he said. She and Mom wanted to see him immediately. Connor made the excuse of being too tired as he watched Randi Jo set the table. Finally, his wife broke a cup and frowned as she dumped it into the trashcan. After he promised to stop by the store before school the next morning, Tempy once again asked to speak to Tallulah. "Not now," Connor said as Tallulah hovered. "It's our family dinner time."

208

Clearly disappointed, Tallulah took her seat next to him, with Randi Jo on the other side. Silence as each scooped out peas, corn, and each took a slice of ham.

"What do they want to talk about?" Randi Jo asked, her eyes fixed on her plate.

"Don't know. Probably the store. Gonna need some help now that Pop–"

"They didn't ask me," she interrupted, a trace of hurt in her voice. "I sweep that stockroom every week. I know where every can of vegetables is."

"You helped out because you're family."

"Let's see somebody else do that for ten dollars a week."

"Randi Jo," Connor said sharply, "can we eat in peace?"

"Watch them. They'll put on somebody else just for spite."

"If I had to listen to this all day, not sure I'd want to hire you either," Connor snapped and threw his spoon down, clanking on the plate. Randi Jo sprang up and left the room. Tallulah sat quietly beside him, pushing her fork through a helping of corn. She swallowed without chewing and held a cup of milk to her lips without drinking. She didn't look at him, holding herself still as if the harsh words might break apart and spin into warring universes.

"Mother's too emotional," he said.

"I guess so, Daddy," she agreed with him too easily.

Connor realized he'd scared her. Guilt laced through him without telling him how to fix this uncomfortable situation. "Go do your homework," he said, taking his coffee to the living room and flipping on the TV set. "Let me know if you need any help." A news story played about the Soviet space program launching Venera 6 toward Venus and Soyuz 4, followed by Soyuz 5, that would dock with it and transfer crew. He shook his head. The Soviet Union was outpacing the United States. Venus, for godsakes, he thought. Why can't our leaders see what is right in front of them. We're lost without innovation. Stuck in the same old routines. He couldn't concentrate on the evening news talking now about the upcoming inauguration of Richard Nixon as president. Pop hadn't liked Nixon, thought he was a crook despite holding up his children's cocker spaniel in defense of his character. It was a misdirection, he realized, something Pop had been able to see, a diversion of a sweet puppy to veer the mind from the real issues. But people had forgotten about the man he was and elected the man they wanted him to be. The masses couldn't see through him the way Pop had. With Nixon in charge, the Soviets might just overtake the U.S. Nixon had no vision, only myopic, self-glorifying self-centeredness. Connor rubbed his temples, his mind exhausted, his thoughts too many places at once. Holly's shrill voice scratched like chalk on the blackboard, but he could not make out her words. Pug Gaylor's absence picked at him like summer gnats. Cigarette smells inflamed his nostrils, giving him a headache. Cigarettes . . . who was smoking in this house? What was going on here that he wasn't seeing?

25

The next morning as Connor drove to Contrary, he thought perhaps it might be a good decision for Mom and Tempy to sell the store. That was probably what they wanted to talk to him about. Pop had left a life insurance policy that would take care of Mom. If they sold the business, that cash would be an added bonus. He wondered what Tempy would do. Her only skills were working the cash register and being difficult.

He parked behind the market, unable to find a spot in front. The parallel parking instituted by Mayor Stark had made downtown shopping virtually impossible. Connor paused at the corner, looking at *For Rent* signs in two abandoned stores. Their own building would be hard to sell. Might have to take a loss on its value, a loss of all his father had worked for. Connor fought the sadness of his father's death welling up inside of him. Sometimes it seemed that the town was in a slow downward spiral as well, but now he had to think of what was best for his family. They were his responsibility.

Mom and Tempy had already pulled out the vegetable carts, and Baylor Grubb, a deacon at his mother's church, came out the front door with hand-printed sale signs he put over a stand of potatoes.

"Baylor," he said. "What are you doing here?"

"Your Mom hired me on to help out," he said, a flush spreading through his cheeks. "Okay with you?"

"Not a problem," Connor answered, steadying his voice to avoid sounding surprised. Connor bit his bottom lip and looked at the sidewalk just as Mom came out with a basket of yellow onions.

"Good, you're here. Baylor, watch the register," she ordered. "Tempy and I will be in the stockroom talking to Connor."

He followed Mom inside. Tempy had moved the lollipop tree to a higher shelf. He'd hoped they would continue Pop's tradition of giving a sucker to every child who came into the store, but it seemed his sister had other plans. Back in the stockroom, Tempy paced and cracked her knuckles. Mom popped on the overhead lights, giving the room a greenish glow. The white paint he'd given the room years ago was starting to flake off the hewed wood.

"Surprised to see you've hired somebody so soon," Connor said. "Thought maybe you might . . ." He paused, their blank expressions confusing him. Tempy twisted her hands in front of her as if resisting the urge to crack a knuckle. A strand of hair from her topknot poked out like a horn. "Randi Jo's available for work. I know she'd appreciate it."

"Tell him," Mom said, motioning to Tempy with a pointed finger.

His sister stood mute, her gaze bouncing from Connor to the floor then back to Mom. She looked as if she wanted to flee, but was held by some irresistible addiction that she couldn't kick.

Mom folded her arms, eyes penetrating like an eagle focused on prey. "We have to protect our good name."

212

Connor thought perhaps Tempy's friendship with Iona Bacon had again come center stage. Since Iona had married, gossip about the two had piped down even though he knew the women saw each other at every contrived opportunity. "Whatever it is," Connor said calmly, "we'll fix it."

"Before I say this," Mom started out, "there's only one path you can follow, and it's got to be set firm."

"It's Randi Jo," Tempy blurted. "She's cheating on you."

Connor laughed, a nervous chuckle emerging from his throat at hearing the unexpected. "Nonsense."

"With Rusty Haskew," his sister said.

Connor realized he was biting the side of his tongue. "Where are you getting this trash?"

"My own eyes," Tempy said in a resentful tone. "Rusty's car at your house when you weren't there."

"He's my best friend. A million reasons he'd be at my house."

"Only one matters," Mom said, matter-of-factly.

"Car was behind the house, hidden so no one would see." Tempy stood behind Mom, her lower lip quivering. "I saw it myself!"

"This is you!" he accused his sister. "You've been jealous of my wife her entire life, and now you're competing with her for Tallulah's affections."

"You need to know," Mom interrupted, staying between the two. "Seen anything suspicious around the house?"

Connor turned his back to them, pressing his hands on both sides of his head. "Nothing goes on in my house I don't know about," he said, even as the cigarette odor popped into his thoughts like a poisonous cloud. "This is you," he said, pointing at Tempy. "You repeat this around town, and I swear to God you'll regret it the rest of your life."

"How dare you," she shot back. "I am not lying. If there's one thing I've never done in my life, it is lie, and that's a hell of a lot more than other people in this family!"

"Tempy!" Mom's voice silenced the room. "Go help Baylor."

His sister's glare fixed pure hatred on him, and he suspected his visage was no different. Throughout their entire lives they'd butted heads, but this was more than a sibling disagreement, this was an attack on his wife. Tempy stomped from the stockroom, turning at the door to stare angrily at him again.

Mom pulled him by the arm. "This is not a thing to let pass." She stared directly into his eyes, her voice soft and cajoling. "What comes of this is a direct reflection on the man you are, the man I raised you to be." She turned to leave, then paused at the door, leaned sideways, and pulled out a rifle. She held it in front of her, eyes surveying the length. "Needs to be cleaned," she said, holding it out. "It's the one that dropped that man, the one who killed Pop." She put the firearm into Connor's hands. "The one your wife killed. Bet you never believed your wife capable of killing. Now you know. If she can do that, what else can she do?" Mom fixed her eyes onto his, not in a pleading manner, nor a stern warning, just matter-of-fact. "Needs to be cleaned," she said again.

Driving to Crimson County High, Connor kept checking his watch. He had twenty minutes before homeroom, but instead of turning back toward Quinntown, he drove another two blocks and stopped at the corner of the police station. A line of three police cars was parked outside, and two were puffing smoke from their tailpipes, likely warming up. He watched as Rusty came trotting down the steps, smoking a cigarette. He took one last draw on it, then flicked it away before getting into a cruiser and driving past without recognizing who was watching him.

Connor's heart raced and his forehead sprouted sweat. Had he changed that much? He was no longer the smart kid with a good future, not the firebrand who could explain concepts most of his contemporaries struggled to understand, not the boy who was going places. He was ordinary, a man who faded into the fabric of small-town life; another cog who would live, learn, wear out, and die, leaving nothing of value behind; a man whose friend thought he could take advantage. A man whose best friend drove past without even recognizing him.

Holly's words, "*Now, there goes a friend,*" tossed about in his mind, but he heard them differently now. She wasn't talking about a friend. She was talking about a snake. He thought back to the times he'd seen Rusty and Randi Jo together. Was there a sign, some spark that had changed the direction of their relationship? He, of all people, should have noticed if there was a rise in temperature, a non-contact magnetism between his wife and his best friend. When did he lose touch with the minutiae of his marriage? When did Rusty start to smoke? Connor's mind juggled these questions with a stomach full of rocks. What else didn't he know?

∽

The school day stretched like homemade taffy. Connor's thoughts pinged from one half-formed reflection to another, finally resting on the concept of ether wind, a theory from the late 1800s that suggested light waves moved via an invisible ether wind. Einstein had proven it false: light waves existed in and of themselves with no physical matter needed. Just because a fast car generates a breeze doesn't mean there's a storm, Connor thought. What he'd heard about his wife and Rusty was as believable as ether wind. He couldn't accept the half-baked theories of his negative sister and mother who wanted the worst to be true.

When the final bell rang, he walked to the car in a trance. A gray sky threatened rain, and a low rumble of thunder echoed around him. He held to the car door handle, his rage hot, but not knowing in which direction to vent it. What was he going to do? Driving two blocks over, he pulled into Herman's gas station and beeped his horn. Herman held open the office door, and Connor braced himself against a brisk wind.

"Gonna storm," Herman said, handing him a mug of coffee.

Connor held the cup to his lips but didn't drink. He breathed in the hot steam, then set the cup down and looked directly at Herman. "I was the one who called the state police about your father's stolen car all those years ago. Found it in Darius Stark's barn that day we were hunting. Rusty said Darius didn't steal it. I believed him." He paused, waiting as Herman took in what he'd said. "I don't think Rusty knew Darius was running stolen cars, but he's in so deep with the Starks now, he can't see that he needs to get out." He waited, watching to see what Herman would do. A King James Bible on the shelf above his head crowned pictures of Sissy. Herman looked at the photos as if asking what he should do. Connor inhaled a deep breath and spoke his fear. "Somebody's told me . . . told me Rusty's having an affair with Randi Jo."

Herman sank into his desk chair as if the information pained him. He didn't know anything, Connor realized. Herman leaned forward, clasping his hands. "Rusty's a dog. No doubt about that. But Randi Jo? Would he? Would he really do that to you?"

"Never thought he'd look the other way about your stolen car." Connor had trouble looking at Herman. Maybe he should have told him about his part in finding the cars years ago. "Rusty's always wanted what I have. He's never felt equal to me."

Herman nodded. "Only one thing to do," he said and picked up the phone. Several seconds passed and Herman asked for Rusty.

Once on the line, he asked Rusty to meet him at Copperhead Fields. "We'll take my truck," Herman said to Connor.

As they drove, Connor wondered if he was making a mistake. Randi Jo had been a good wife and mother. What difficulties they'd had through the years were mundane, silly disagreements of people who'd grown used to each other, except for Mom's accusation that his wife had been responsible for Pop's death. He thought about that. Mom hadn't kept her feelings secret, though she'd never confronted Randi Jo directly. Whispers and dirty looks had done their job. Even his subtle accusations that her brother Pug was involved were unfounded. Had he defended his wife enough? Had he wanted to keep the peace in his family so badly that he'd driven his wife into the arms of another man? But Rusty? An affair with his best friend? She'd never give in to Rusty with his crude ways. He stared ahead as mist wet the windshield.

Herman parked, but left on the heat and windshield wipers. "Thinks I'm here to give him a tip on stolen auto parts," Herman said. "Gave him one a few months ago, and blamed if the fella never got arrested, but his garage got broken into." Herman blew out a heavy breath. "The stolen got stolen."

They watched as a police cruiser pulled up with one driver. Rusty stepped out and lit a cigarette. Connor's heart sank. Any hope that he might be wrong flared out with the flick of a match whirling to the wet ground. The two men got out of the truck.

"Didn't know you were gonna be here," Rusty said to Connor and shot an uncertain glance at Herman. "Something going on at the high school I should know about?"

Words collided in Connor's mind as Rusty pulled up his coat collar and trotted underneath a covered picnic area. A light rain pelted their shoulders as they walked. Connor pointed at the cigarette, "When'd you pick up the habit?"

"Lately," he said. "Nerves, you know."

"Got a lot to be stressed about?"

"Gets me through the day."

An edgy silence hung between the two men, the only sound rain pelting the wooden roof above them.

"Smelling cigarettes in my bedroom," Connor said, his voice a low whisper.

Rusty's stance widened as he bent his knees. Quick as thunder, he went for his service revolver. Herman kicked Rusty's hand just as he dislodged the gun from the holster, and it spun backward several feet away. Connor shoved Rusty with both hands.

"I'm an officer of the law," Rusty called out as if the badge would protect him.

"Face him like a man," Herman said, angling himself so that Rusty was unable to get the firearm on the ground. "Don't use your job as an excuse. You're not a policeman with us. You owe Connor the truth."

"Look fellas," Rusty said, emitting a nervous laugh. "What'da'ya doing here?"

"Tempy says your police car's been at my house when I'm not there."

Rusty took a step back. "Your lesbo sister?"

Connor backhanded him across the mouth. A spray of blood spattered the ground, but Rusty stayed on his feet. He held his fingers to his bleeding nose, eyes wide, calculating. Connor willed himself to keep control of his fury. "What did you think would happen, Rusty? I'd look the other way?"

"What do you know? What do you or you know!" He pointed at both of them. "Gotta have two men to beat me down."

"Herman ain't gonna do nothing to you," Connor said, his lips curling into a smile. "You know why?'Cause he pities you." Connor tracked a half circle around Rusty, who continued to step backwards each time Connor advanced. "I used to feel sorry for you when we were boys, but you're as much of a shameful rascal now as you were then."

"You're weak. That's why your wife turns to another man."

"You ain't took a swing yet," Connor said, holding out his jaw. "And you won't."

"Don't think you know what I'm capable of."

"I know . . . because you can't beat me." Connor halted in front of the man he'd once believed to be a brother and addressed him: "You couldn't beat me when you were a boy, you couldn't kill more game than me as a young man, and the only way you can top me is by bedding my wife? In that sick mind of yours that makes you better? You were always somebody's bitch. Judge Rounder, Willie Carmack, Darius Stark. You just got a different boss-man yanking your choke-chain."

"You think you know!" Rusty hollered at him and punched the air. "You know nothing!"

"You and Randi Jo gonna run away?"

"No."

"Why not?"

"She ain't worth it."

Connor swung on Rusty, connecting with his jaw and knocking him into the mud. He stayed down, looking up at Connor, one hand holding his cheek. In those seconds, Connor forgot that he was a teacher, a father, a husband. An ancient rage flowed through him and but for Herman's hand on his arm, he might have fallen on Rusty and beat the life out of him. "We have to go," Herman said. "Enough. Now you know."

Connor let himself be pulled along, all the time keeping his eyes on Rusty, who pushed up to his knees. Once in the car, Connor stomped his feet onto the floor, every muscle tight as rope. "Let's get out of here."

Herman's worried expression never changed as he pulled into the gas station beside Connor's car. They sat in the truck with the ignition on, heat pumping out of the heater. The rain let loose, coating the truck. "Too much was said."

"Would you have done different?" Connor asked.

"Probably not, but I know what I saw. Look in his eye."

"He deserved every bit of it."

"Never know where it could lead."

"Wasn't a choice."

"Still," Herman said. "Best sleep with your gun at your bedside tonight. Maybe for a while."

Connor nodded, knowing the precarious situation he'd put himself in. He jarred open the door, icy air flooding his lungs. "Sure as hell I am not going to live my life afraid of Rusty Haskew. He wants to take me on, I'm here."

"Rusty's the kind of man that'll shoot you in the back." Herman put a hand on Connor's arm, holding him inside. "Tallulah," he said, holding on to him. "That's who you live for now. Don't let her grow up without a father. You let Rusty Haskew be the past."

Connor closed the door, looking at his friend as if reality had infused itself into his muscles. Squeezing his eyes shut, he knew Herman was right. *Tallulah.* His child was all that mattered now. "Would have thought Rusty would've considered the kids. I mean, him an orphan. If Lynn divorces him, you know the pain it'll cause his children."

"He's not the boy we grew up with. He belongs to the Starks now."

"Maybe so. But Randi Jo still belongs to me, and I got some things to say to my wife."

26

Betrayal stitched together with humiliation is a watery grave. While Connor grasped for the explanation, he tried to convince himself that this whole situation with Randi Jo and Rusty might be a misunderstanding, and he'd overreacted. Maybe he'd get home to find all his friends and family were playing a joke on him. Deeper he sank, until all light of understanding vanished in the murky reality of his fist connecting with Rusty's jaw. He rubbed his palm over the knuckles of his right hand, sitting in his parked car as rain speckled the windshield. He opened the car door, chilly air rushing in, then walked toward a home that would soon become as bleak as a tomb.

Connor could hear Tallulah in her room singing with her record player. He often couldn't make out the words of her music, but this one, a ditty by a band called Steppenwolf, stood out. "Born To Be

Wild." Tallulah called it her theme song and would amusingly repeat the chorus in words if challenged with an argument she couldn't win. Connor flipped on the television so he wouldn't hear the music and sat on the couch, laying the rifle Mom had given him to clean at his feet. His mind exhausted, his thoughts swayed like tree limbs fighting two different winds.

One of Randi Jo's favorite TV shows, *Truth or Consequences,* played. The host, Bob Barker, questioned audience members and, if they couldn't answer, made them face the consequences. Connor felt like he might throw up. He went to the kitchen sink and wet his face, then pulled a rag and some oil from a shelf underneath and returned to the living room. He wiped down the rifle barrel. Anything to keep his hands moving. Any activity to keep from thinking about what had occurred in his bedroom. Mom wanted him to divorce Randi Jo. Tempy would be right there behind her, agreeing. He wasn't sure he wanted a divorce, wasn't sure Rusty Haskew was worth losing his marriage for.

His marriage, a union he'd been tricked into. That's what it really was. But for Tallulah, he might not have married Randi Jo. He thought of Rory . . . what would she have said? Connor clasped his hands around the rifle and stared at the floor between his knees. He knew what she would say . . . He hadn't thought of Rory in years, but he knew she would tell him to think of his daughter . . . that in all, he hadn't had a bad life, and one mistake, well . . . his child would be all that truly mattered.

The front door swung open, and Randi Jo hurried in, shaking the rain off herself. She discarded a coat he'd never seen her wear before without hanging it up. "I'll get dinner started," she said, hurrying toward the kitchen "Tempy has Baylor sweeping out the storeroom from now on, so I am not going back." She paused at the kitchen door. "Told you that would happen."

From his position on the couch he watched her at the counter, untying a Wonder Bread package. Rain pecked at the windowpanes as if to get his attention. Aiming the rifle, he pointed into the center of her chest. He could blow out her heart with one squeeze of the trigger . . . just like she had his own. Tallulah's voice started a new chorus of "Born To Be Wild." Bob Barker forced players to face the consequences. The Black Dahlia licked her lips and disappeared into his mind's darkness as quickly as she had appeared. Connor twirled the rifle around, steadying the butt on the floor, and wiped the barrel with the rag. He held his breath.

Randi Jo leaned into the room. "Want some coffee while supper cooks?" She gasped, eyes glued to the rifle.

Connor's hands squeezed the rifle barrel and he said, "Uh-uh."

"Where'd you get that?" she asked, taking one step toward him

"Store. Mom wanted me to take it." He looked up at her, knowing she recognized the same rifle she'd used to shoot Luther Ballard. He wondered if she'd realized the other man was likely her brother Pug. Now, let her be worried, he thought.

"You got plenty hunting guns–"

Connor stared into her eyes, and his finger squeezed the trigger. Through the flash of discharge, the sharp crack of the bullet hitting the ceiling, the odor of gunpowder, Connor never looked away from Randi Jo. Her expression froze in a confused panic, telling him everything he needed to know. His wife had betrayed him, and she knew that he now knew.

"Connor!" she shouted.

He laughed, not knowing why and not looking away from her until Tallulah ran into the room.

"What happened?" Tallulah asked, looking from one to the other of her parents.

"Hair trigger," Connor said. "No wonder you killed a man so easy." Connor watched Randi Jo take it in, enjoying her petrified stance.

"I'll be in the kitchen," she said, turning slowing as if unwilling to have her back toward him.

"Crack a window," Connor yelled after her. "I keep smelling cigarette smoke in the bedroom."

Tallulah came up next to him, inspecting the hole in the ceiling. "Gonna have to put a bucket under it when it storms."

"I can patch it," he said, looking down at her, a slather of freckles across her nose that he'd never noticed before.

"Daddy, might as well change out the whole panel." She anchored a foot on the couch and lifted herself up to measure a knuckle against the bullet hole. "Once the integrity of a thing has been tampered with, it's never the same."

"Ain't it the truth," he said, and wrapped an arm around her shoulder after she jumped down. "Let's store this ole gun in the cellar."

The damp basement had a hollow feel that made his ears ring. Tallulah cleared a place on a wall shelf while he re-checked for ammunition. His daughter didn't speak while they stood in the dark. He wondered if he'd frightened her. That hadn't been his intention, and now a new set of worries invaded his thoughts.

"Honey," he said as they returned up the steps. "I like your music."

She didn't answer him, but followed him up and ran past him to get out of the rain. She held the door open as he trotted behind her. "Born to be wild, Daddy." She smirked. "Must have gotten it from somebody."

Back inside, Randi Jo had set out ham sandwiches, a bowl of potato chips and bottles of soda. She left a small dish of dill pickles on the side the way Tallulah always liked it. Connor sat, ready to further enjoy the discomfort he'd cause his wife. They'd both bitten into their sandwiches when his daughter lowered hers, staring at the table. She didn't speak or look up at him. Connor didn't see at first, only when Tallulah took a second bite, her jaw chewing in slow deliberate motion, did he notice there were only two plates, two glasses, two napkins.

"Guess Momma isn't hungry," she said, her voice soft and somehow small. A breeze lifted the napkins, and one from the stack flew off the table.

Randi Jo didn't want to be near him, Connor realized. Her shame had driven her to hide from him. He stared at the round dish; the overhead light reflected a crescent moon down the middle. He got up, not looking at his daughter. If he and Randi Jo were both going to stay in this house tonight, they had to talk. He looked for her in the bedroom. Empty. A few doors away, the bathroom was empty as well. He'd built this bathroom for them, for their family when they moved into this house. Prior to that, there was just the outhouse that used to hang over the creek bank. Looking in Tallulah's room, he checked the window. Locked.

He continued on to a rear room they used as storage. No one there. Randi Jo wasn't in the house. The back door was open, a chilly wind blowing through. He flipped on the porch light and saw footprints in the mud, a wide gait. She was running. Cold settled on his skin. Rain sliced through the darkness like blades. This scenery was not unlike that land in his mind where dead women lived. Tonight, he'd almost sent Randi Jo to that place. He stepped outside, the world pressing in on him. Bending over, he threw up. What was happening? What was he becoming? He didn't know, didn't care. He stared into the dark, no answers coming from the hateful night.

Randi Jo had run out into that cold gloom. She had no place to go. No one to turn to. No one to help her. Good, he thought. His wife was gone, and oddly, he didn't care. He stepped back into his house, looked out into the ancient dusk, its blueness full of trickster images that his ancestors thought were magic, and closed the door.

27

July 1969

As the months passed, Connor Herne obsessed among the grim melancholy of his inner demons. He lost himself in the counsel of dead women. Seeking out the phantoms, he asked them no questions, instead spent time sitting beside their purple-rippling creek, watching these professional victims live their faux lives. When he opened his eyes, the real world seemed dull and gray, his day filled with senseless chores, his nights with dreams of exploding worlds and scorched earth that upon waking left him exhausted. He spoke to no living being about his despondency, but instead let the community think he was as well as any man. His mother and sister turned the situation to their advantage, telling tales of woe wherein they were the victimized. If Tallulah was upset, and she must have been, she didn't show it, not to him. He believed that in her way she was trying to protect him, and in later years, he would wish he'd handled the situation with her differently. He started to speak to her about Randi Jo, tried once or twice to explain his position, but each time his voice sounded artificial and faraway, and he only ended up blaming Randi Jo in an effort to keep his daughter on his side. So he lived a murky existence, hoping the passage of time would fade his quiet despair. Summer arrived with warmth and promise, but Connor couldn't shake the notion that he was a man whom the town pitied.

A grainy TV picture flipped several times as Walter Cronkite took off his glasses and rubbed his hands together. Astronaut Neil Armstrong stepped onto the surface of the moon. Tallulah leaned forward on the opposite end of the couch. She tried to appear interested, but Connor could tell by her restless squirming that her focus was elsewhere.

"Daddy," she said, "is Momma ever coming home?"

"No," he answered without reflection.

She continued staring at the TV, crossing her arms, feet tapping the floor in unison. Connor watched the historic event: a man on the moon, moving across the barren landscape where no soul had ever gone before. He'd never expected to see something like this in his lifetime. He tried to work up a measure of excitement, wanting to explain to his daughter what humans could do in this world. But no amount of amazement could uplift his spirits as he returned again and again to the thought that life on earth was still painful, and compassion was for the helpless. He would not show weakness, not to his neighbors, not to his friends, not to his daughter. He'd push himself and his child forward to a new life, even if it killed him inside.

"That's one small step for man, one giant leap for mankind," Armstrong said.

228

Connor leaned on the couch arm, resting his head on the palm of his hand. He was as isolated as the man on the moon. "You'll remember this day all your life, Tallulah," he said. "Someday your children will ask you about it."

"I'll still see Mamaw Gaylor, won't I?" Tallulah asked. "And my uncles and aunts? Collette and I go to school together. What do I say to her?"

"I don't know all the answers, Tallulah. Watch the show."

"It's not a show. It's real."

He rose and went to the kitchen, poured himself some juice and set out canned chili that he'd cook for dinner. Randi Jo had bought it before she left. Tallulah's favorite. Still, the house was not the same without his wife. Randi Jo had moved into her mother's house. She had tried to re-open communications with him and insisted on a relationship with her daughter, but he'd cut her off at every opportunity. Even managed to get full custody of Tallulah with no alimony payment to Randi Jo. His wife's mistake had cost her everything. He'd gotten rid of the bed they'd slept in, the bed where she and Rusty had betrayed him, throwing it over a fence into Rusty's front yard. His former friend had come out and they'd cussed each other, and only Lynn and their three children crowding the door of the three-room shack they lived in stopped the men from coming to blows. The new bed was hard and kept him awake the first week he used it, until he realized it wasn't only the bed but the whole house, even its good memories, that had soured for him. He hated coming home. Blank walls, with dusty, square outlines where once there'd been a photo containing an image of Randi Jo felt like report cards of failure. He couldn't keep up with the cleaning, the laundry, all the things she'd once done, and soon he looked past what had once been immaculate. Why not? All the Notown folks let trash gather in their yards. Why did he try to keep up? Nothing, not even a man walking on the moon, could hold his interest.

Mom had been after him to buy a house in Contrary where she and Tempy could help out. Terrified of being stricken with the same disease as claimed her own mother, Wallis wanted family closer to her, and it was obvious that she didn't trust her daughter. He'd considered the move and rejected it a hundred times. Part of staying in Notown had been to distance himself from Wallis, but he'd never admitted that to himself until now. Now, he needed his mother to lend him her strong backbone. He'd never have thought that he would have been this broken, but this night, thoughts of all he might have done to change his life pricked his motives. Randi Jo had always wanted to live in Contrary. If he'd moved the family years ago, might the affair never have happened? Would she have been happier? Would Tallulah? He no longer saw the honoring of his father in this Notown house. He only saw the room where his wife had betrayed him. Move to Contrary . . . that's just what he would do. Escape this place, these memories. Escape Notown. Notown. He'd tried to do right by her. But Notown was a mean bitch and she'd knocked him on his ass.

28

Contrary was a different kind of woman. Showy but comfortable. A tidy English-style main street, home to a community of haves and have-nots who all knew their place. Avenues named after English towns led to deep-forested hollows on the southern side where people of the land lived; miners coming home each night coated dark with mineral, farmers planting hillsides until the earth no longer sustained root or held water, hunters searching out game that could no longer be found in stores. Their families followed the men's lead, brothers and sons into the same livelihood, and women as their helpmates. All of them looking in from the outside and envying the townsfolk. Life is about fitting in, in small towns where there is no room for mavericks. Connor joined the Rotary Club, the Kiwanis, and had an application in to the Red Men Masons. He managed to avoid becoming a deacon for the First Baptist, preferring to spend his Sundays hunting with Herman when the weather was good.

The big news of the last year was the trial of Willie Carmack's father for first-degree murder. Absorbed in his own problems, Connor had paid little attention to it other than consoling his friend with the empty words that *everything would be okay*. Woken in the middle of the night by carousing partiers on the property behind his, Lucius Carmack had shot all six men as they drank beer and partied around a campfire. At first Lucius denied any knowledge of the murders, even attended the funeral of one of the men who, it turned out, worked for him. When the shotgun that'd ended those young lives was found in his tool shed, there was no denying the truth, and yet the elder Carmack maintained his innocence despite being identified by a neighbor who'd been woken up by the ruckus and watched Lucius march, weapon over his shoulder, back to his house.

But justice favored the guilty that summer, and walking out of the courthouse a free man because of a hung jury, Lucius Carmack bragged to reporters, "You only need one juror to see the truth." He punched a fist in the air, sneezed, then fell dead on the steps of a brain aneurysm. Irony was lost on most Crimson County citizens, and the old curmudgeon's funeral brought in governors from three states, a few East Coast senators, one Saudi prince, and a host of businessmen hoping to buy the Carmack mining interest. Willie considered his options, then decided to take a stab at running the business his father had ruled with an iron fist. He soon discovered that he was no Lucius Carmack and lost half of the company to a secret partner that he refused to name and that he'd never known about when his father was alive.

For the less connected Contrary folk, summer wound down. Connor and Rusty managed to avoid each other most of the time and exchanged mutual glares on those rare occasions when they ended up in the same place. Pop's store continued on as a legacy to him, and Mom and Tempy were overjoyed to have Tallulah living closer. Father and daughter made the adjustment to the big town as best they could, and the last of the summer parties would seal their admittance into that rarified society.

As Connor and Tallulah stood at the entrance of the Carmack mansion, they might have been thinking that they were out of place at such a house after the years of living in Notown. Connor, in a suit he hadn't worn since school had ended the previous May, and Tallulah, in an all-in-one rainbow-colored jumpsuit that made him dizzy. Fireflies lit up the warm August evening, and the fragrance of honeysuckle and roses permeated the air like overly perfumed ladies working behind the counter of the local Woolworth department store. Tallulah glanced up at Connor. She held a loaf of banana bread Tempy had helped her bake.

"You should have worn Sunday school clothes," he said, his finger holding above the doorbell.

"This isn't a suit party, Daddy," she whispered. Quickly, he loosened his tie and shoved it into his pocket while she took off a sash wrapped round her waist as a belt and tied it around the length of her hair, making a ponytail. Switching places so Tallulah would be in front with gift in hand, they shared a glance, nodded approval, and softly tapped the button to melodically announce their arrival.

Their shared discomfort eased with Holly Carmack's uncomplicated smile. "Come in, my new Contrary neighbors!" She hugged Tallulah and patted Connor on the arm. Behind her a dozen people stood in loose groups, drinks in hand, as Aretha Franklin belted "Chain of Fools."

"For you," Tallulah said, holding out the bread.

"Bless your heart, buttercup." She pointed to a room where several teens chatted. "Some girls that'll be in your class are in the den, why don't you go make friends? I'll put this bread in my secret place where nobody can eat it but me." Holly watched after Tallulah as she joined the kids, then turned back to Connor. "And for the adults, liquor's on the patio."

Connor glanced around the room, seeing only people who lived in Contrary: the McDaniels, Blalocks, Gentrys, and Blackburns. "Ah, elections are next year, right?"

"Sly puss," she smirked.

"Rusty and Lynn aren't here?"

"Promised you they wouldn't be." Holly took his arm and led him further into the room. "Something you need to realize, Connor. Now that you live in town, you need to think mainstream, and there are people you need to know."

"Meaning?"

"Those two would never rate an invitation to this party. Look," she said, a hint of justification in her tone, "we have pizza with Rusty and Lynn when Willie needs him to do something. I don't mean anything bad by it, but they're Notown." She nodded to Charlotte Gentry, who'd recently been appointed to the town council after the death of a town patriarch who'd held the position most of his adult life. "Rusty's for the dirty part of town," Holly explained, "and for doing the dirty work that needs done."

Connor remembered Randi Jo had always told him that town people thought this way, inclusive in their egalitarian speechifying in public and elitist behind closed doors. He'd never believed her, thinking she imagined the slights and enjoyed playing the part of victim, or maybe he had believed her and just hadn't wanted to own up to it. "I don't want to run into him."

"No worries," Holly's singsong voice lilted. "Willie's out on the patio. Has something to talk to you about, and before you leave, make sure you see me. I gotta tell you something." She brushed past him when the doorbell rang, but leaned back and whispered, "In private." Holly reminded him of a movie star in her A-framed mini dress that hid the curves of her body and square-heeled shoes that gave her an inch of height. She embraced the town persona as if she'd been born to it, and though he couldn't help but wonder about an unseen cost to the affluent life she'd chosen, if there was one, he couldn't see it.

Connor shifted, uncomfortable in the notion of spending the evening with people who once had thought him from the dirty part of town. He guessed they'd afforded him some grace because of his parents' store, even though they'd lived above it and not in one of the fancy houses out in the avenues. He glanced into the den to see Tallulah and a few other kids playing a game called Twister. She seemed to be having a good time and smiled at him. He stopped by a table filled with plates of deviled eggs, Swedish meatballs with toothpicks on the side, and buffalo wings with mustard dip. He placed some of each on his plate and looked around at the piles of people, joined in twos and threes, absorbed in conversations that he couldn't imagine were all that important.

On an orange rock veranda, Willie puffed a cigar, gesturing to Alvey Stark and his cousin, Brewster Toland. A knot twisted in Connor's stomach at seeing a Stark, though he'd never had dealings with these two. Alvey operated an insurance company out of a trailer 'longside Brewster's drive-in movie theater. Anybody coming to see a movie had an insurance flyer slid under the windshield wipers, and if you weren't careful, a bumper sticker stuck to the rear of your car regardless of whether you'd bought insurance from Alvey. Far as Connor knew, the law had never pinched them, but that they were Starks was reason enough to be cautious. Willie motioned to Connor to join them. He put the food plate down without eating and exited onto the patio, into an intoxicating scent of privet, spoiled by the pungent aroma of the cigars the men puffed on.

"You know Alvey and Brewster." Willie put out his hand and shook Connor's. "We were just talking about Ed Kennedy and that girl he killed. Reckon he'll never get elected dogcatcher."

Connor exchanged handshakes with the Starks as they chuckled at Willie's bashing Edward Kennedy. "Saw in the paper you're now managing the Regal Hotel," he said to Alvey, not wishing to discuss other politics. "Hope you clean it up."

"I like it just like it is," Alvey replied.

"Being so close to the high school, some of those women have been known to actively solicit the high school boys."

Brewster chuckled as if that was the funniest thing he'd ever heard.

"What do you do?" Alvey asked.

When Connor told him, Alvey grunted like he couldn't think of anything to say, then spat tobacco juice over the side of the wall.

"Splatter them roses and Holly'll have a fit on me, Alvey," Willie fussed.

"Got cousin Clyde running the front desk," Alvey said as he turned back toward them. "He'll keep the rascals in line." Alvey took another plug from a tin can and sucked it into his jaw. "Just rented a ground floor office to the FBI, now how's that for cleaning it up?"

Connor bit the side of his tongue, wishing he'd stayed inside and wondering how long it'd be before the Starks managed to have the FBI in their pocket. He turned toward Willie. "Holly said you want to talk."

"Let's go to the library." He gestured with his cigar. "Good to see y'all." He slapped Alvey on the back and motioned Brewster toward the fountain. "Soak your feet if you get too hot."

Since it'd been the result of an FBI sting along with the state police that'd last incarcerated many of the Stark kin, it amused Connor that one Stark rarely knew what another was doing. Renting law enforcement an office in the same building where they operated their whorehouse could work to their advantage if one of the girls was able to compromise an agent. Or the FBI could have a plan. He wondered who would outfox whom in that unpredictable dance of law enforcement and criminal activity. Still, dealing with any Stark, even one who hadn't been in jail, left a bad taste in Connor's mouth.

He followed Willie to a room that had few books, and those that were there looked as if they'd never been opened. An oversized burl desk anchored the middle of the room, and Willie leaned on the side of it, sucking the cigar and offering him one that he took but didn't light. A colored TV played a newscast, but rather than turning it off, Willie spoke over the newscaster as if to demonstrate yet another way in which to impose his will. "School don't start for a few weeks, and I need somebody to spot-check inventory, run some numbers, somebody I can trust."

"You're offering me a job?"

"Full-time if you'll take it."

"Quit teaching?"

"Come on," Willie cajoled. "You make dink teaching math, got a dense school board, smart-aleck young'uns, half of who'll end up working for me anyways. I'm offering you a career. Make you a man people answer to in this community."

"And all this time I thought I was shaping minds and characters," Connor slyly fussed.

"I need smart people. Who better than somebody I know?"

"Got no experience in mining."

"Took me a good long time to clean up all the mess that Daddy left. Got the IRS off my back, made deals with the creditors, now I got to cut it lean and skinny, and you're the man to help me."

"I'd have to think about it," he said. "I'd be giving up tenure." Even as he said the words, the thought of not returning to the classroom beckoned like a pillow for a weary head.

"Few weeks before school starts. Come in on Monday, do a few days, see if you like it." He paused and leaned in. "See if you like the paycheck. Teaching'll always be there."

"Guess I could," he said, his focus drawn over Willie's shoulder toward the television news showing covered bodies on gurneys being pushed out of a house. "Good Lord, what's that?" Willie turned up the volume, and they listened as the newscaster described the horrific deaths of Hollywood actress Sharon Tate and four of her friends. A picture of the blond actress flashed onto the screen. "She looks just like Holly," Connor said without realizing it.

"I look like who?" Holly squealed, prancing into the library, holding two beers, one of which she gave to Willie.

"Bet the husband did it," Willie said. "Husband always does it."

Holly watched along with several people who followed her into the room. "I saw her in *Valley of the Dolls*," she said. "Hey, y'all, get in here," she yelled to the crowd outside.

"Married to that famous director Roman Polanski," someone behind them said as a small group filed into the room to watch the coverage.

"Five people butchered and an unborn baby," a woman covered her mouth and whispered to another couple who hurried in to watch. "I'd always dreamed of Jay Sebring doing my hair."

"I drink Folgers coffee," Willie said, as the newscaster named coffee heiress Abigail Folger as one of the victims.

"Who'd do such a thing?" Holly put her drink on the desk and rubbed her arms, chill bumps spreading on her skin.

"A monster." Connor swallowed, averting his eyes as he listened to the gruesome details of the murders. "Ought to get Tallulah home," he said, breaking from the group. "She leaves for church camp tomorrow."

"Good thing for her," Holly said, unable to look away from the TV photo of Sharon Tate. The resemblance had shaken her, and an involuntary tremble shot through her body, though no one except Connor noticed. "I'll walk you out," she said, her voice the lowest pitch of the evening.

Outside, Tallulah chattered with two girls about her age as Connor motioned to her that they were leaving. Holly strolled beside him, linking her arm through his. "Probably a good thing she's going to church camp."

"You and Willie seem to be getting along better," he said.

"Willie . . . the man who's sure it's the husband that killed five people to get one wife." Her arm muscles tightened against his. "Yeah, we get along fine. Long as I know his secrets, my bony ass is in designer duds."

"Holly, Willie had a lot of options after high school. He chose you."

"Willie's never appreciated what he had, but, now that his father's gone, he's starting to realize the value of loyalty." She glanced toward Tallulah and turned aside so she and the other girls wouldn't hear. "I'm not out here to complain." Hesitating, she stared aside and took a breath. "Randi Jo's getting married." Her arm, still linked with his, squeezed tighter. "I don't think she's told anybody yet. Not even her mother."

A lump lodged in Connor's throat, holding itself there as if to block the realization that his wife had moved on. "And yet you know."

"I know lots of secrets."

"Who?"

"Man named Simon Tuller."

Connor exhaled a breath, somehow relieved that she didn't say Rusty's name. "Never heard of him."

"Lives in Coalfire. Related to the Starks somehow, second or third cousin, I think." Holly rolled her eyes. "Seems to treat her right, but then, all husbands do in the beginning."

"I never cheated on my wife with her best friend."

"Sorry, I wasn't talking about you." Holly paused as Tallulah passed them on the way to the car. "If you need help telling the little girl, let me know. I can be there."

Connor nodded. Holly did mean well, probably for the first time in all the time that Connor had known her, and her concern for Tallulah seemed genuine. He handed her the unlit cigar and focused on holding his voice even. "I just hope Randi Jo's happy."

As he walked to his car, he realized Sharon Tate was behind him, taunting him for telling a lie. He didn't wish for Randi Jo's happiness. The news churned in his belly. He wanted his former wife to experience every misery she'd inflicted on him two times over. She was getting remarried, building another life, and here he was alone, raising a daughter, haunted by murdered women.

As he got into the car, he looked up at the house of wealth and power. Sharon Tate was no longer there, but he could feel her tortured spirit whispering in his mind. As he ground the ignition, it occurred to him that Herman and Sissy weren't at the party either, but then, he thought, why would they be. They still lived in Quinntown, the slightly grubby part of Midnight Valley, good enough for pizza on Friday nights, but lacking the status to attend a town party. So Randi Jo had married a Stark. Bet that makes her feel all superior, he thought.

Randi Jo was getting married, the words dogged his thoughts. Another betrayal, even if he didn't know the man, even if they were divorced. He didn't care that his attitude was unreasonable. He didn't care that he'd been the one to push for divorce when she'd tried to bring them back together. How could she do this to him . . . to Tallulah? How could he tell his daughter that her mother thought more of another man than she did of them? Visions twisted and ballooned, landing on every bitter memory, and in that bitterness, he knew what he would do. He'd take Willie's job. He'd learn everything he could about money and power and rule. If he had to tolerate the likes of uncouth buffoons like Alvey and Brewster, then he'd do that as well. He'd show Randi Jo that two could play this game. He'd become a more important man than Simon Tuller could ever hope to be. And when he lived in a big house like Willie with a blond wife and threw parties for influential people, he'd rub her nose in it. Connor blew out a breath, letting thoughts of revenge wash over him as he drove. All this vitriol settled into his muscles. He could no longer afford to play fair. He had to go along to get along. He glanced over at his daughter, staring into the distance, head nodding and lips moving to the beat of a Zager and Evans tune that he disliked, "In The Year 2525." His daughter was innocence and light, believing the best of the world, and he would do whatever he had to do to place her at this town's best advantage. No longer would he or his be stepped on by anybody. From now on, he had to watch his own back to protect the people he loved.

Then he saw Her walking along the road, long blond hair slightly lifting with the breeze as his car passed. She didn't turn toward him and the image shattered with the rumble of a coal truck going the opposite direction, but She was alive, here in his mind. No longer alone or frightened, but linking hands with other dead girls who showed her a fantastical landscape. Not on earth though, Connor thought. In this dense existence, Sharon Tate was dead, and monsters were on the loose.

29

Connor followed a hand-drawn map along a winding, one-lane road with asphalt crumbling on every turn. More than once, he thought he might have a flat tire. An oversized coal truck forced him to hug the curve of the mountain, so he knew he was going the right direction. Yellow dust blew up around his car as the truck ripped past him without slowing, sending pebbles crackling against the metal underside.

He drove another mile without coming to the coal mine and wondered if he should have turned into one of the several hollows he'd driven past. Near the top of the ridge, he got out of his car and looked around. The crisp air gave no hint of a mine nearby and the solid blue sky looked like one swatch of paint. Being out in the woods was exactly what he needed to wash away the muck of divorce. He knew he had to make peace with the idea of Randi Jo being remarried, and had even stopped at the drugstore and bought her a card wishing her the best, though he'd been unable to bring himself to mail it. Nor had he been able to tell Tallulah.

The unpleasantries of life melted as he stared out at the waves of mountains, ripples of green: olive and jade, emerald and lime. Morning had yet to warm up, and the martins, starlings, and wrens chirped to one another from the overhead trees. He let the harmony of the environment wash over him and ease into his muscles like soothing salve. Now, he thought, to find that coal mine. He closed his eyes and listened. Underneath the cacophony of nature was a low hum, the drone of machinery. The sound came from the north, ahead of him. He hadn't come far enough along.

When he turned into the next hollow, within a quarter mile the terrain blossomed into a tract of ragged rock as if a giant had snatched a patch of ground out of the earth and thrown it over the hill. He parked amid a line of rusted trucks at the end of the road, grabbed his clipboard and pen, then headed uphill toward a white trailer off to the side of an opening into the mountain. Connor stared at the doorway into the earth. It wasn't very high, squared off by wooden panels haphazardly nailed together. The men rode in narrow railcars to get inside and had to lie flat as they entered the opening. He admired the men who did this work, had never known a lazy one among them. He'd taught many of them through the years. They often came from the poorer families who lived in the hollows, and the good pay of this occupation often came with a side benefit of clogged lungs that debilitated the worker until breathing became a full-time job. A dust cloud blew up around Connor, and he coughed, the air heavy with grit. He moved on, and his knock on the trailer door was followed by a gruff "What is it?"

"Connor Herne," he called out, opening the door, "from the main office."

The man inside huffed an exasperated sigh. "I don't have the inventory list yet," he said, as Connor stepped inside. The nameplate on his desk read Marshall Crenshaw. He was not the man Connor had been sent here to find.

"I'm looking for Ralph Harmon." Connor noted the explosion of paper and files that could have been better organized, but he said nothing, determined not to pass judgment on an industry that he was still learning.

"He's at Little Mack Mine checking the gate. Don't expect him back until shift change."

"I can drive over there," he said.

"No," Marshall said, standing and staring out the window. "It's way back in the next hollow, part of the road is washed out. Best you wait, or come back later. Mr. Carmack'll understand."

Connor shifted to the side, in thought. "I wanted to get a jump on this . . . being my first day of work and all."

"Wait here. Have some coffee." Marshal pointed to the percolator plugged into an already overly stressed outlet. "I'll send somebody to get him." Edging past stacked boxes on his way out the door, he pulled out a half-empty package of powdered donuts and slid them across the desk. "Might as well have a bite to eat."

Connor sat for forty-five minutes, doodled on his clipboard, and flipped through a NASCAR calendar more times than he wanted to admit. Looking out the window there was no sign of Marshall, nor did Ralph Harmon return. Finally, he decided to go up to Little Mack himself. How bad could it be, he thought, turning into a narrow hollow whose trees were overgrown with briars and kudzu. Not like he was some city boy who didn't know how to walk around a washed-out road.

A quarter mile in, Connor still hadn't run into a blockage, and he wondered how the lane could be washed out since they'd had a blistering summer with little rain that he remembered. The road ended at a chain-link fence. He parked, got out, and pushed open the gate, surprised to find it had no padlock. Looking around, he didn't see another car, but heavy tire prints in the soft dirt indicated someone had had a big rig up here. Didn't make sense because this mine had been abandoned years ago. Only reason for a body to be up here would be to check that the entrance was boarded up and the gate locked. Neither of which was done.

Turning in a circle, Connor wondered where Ralph Harmon might be. He called out the man's full name. No response. He walked toward a rickety tipple, sliding down a path created by water runoff. He looked down toward abandoned rail tracks where the coal had once been loaded onto train cars. The sun created a blinding arc across the noonday sky. Near the fence edge, a glimmer of sunlight bounced off something, momentarily blinding him. He shielded his eyes to have a better look. Something metallic. Steadying himself on the chain-link fence, he peered carefully, and seeing no human movement, he moved toward the flickering light.

Barrels. Six metal fifty-five-gallon drums, lined up near a forklift. He looked at his clipboard. No forklift should be at this site. This one was spick-n-span new. What in the world? Kneeling beside one container, he made out faded black letters on the side Nu . . . clear . . . waste. He jumped away, dropping the clipboard and pen. *Nuclear Waste.* Six vats of poison, more dangerous than any predator in these woods.

Connor ran to the car, speeding recklessly along the curvy road. He honked and passed cars, nipping through every red light in Quinntown without one police car managing to see him. Willie would be home, and he barreled into the driveway in such a rush that he didn't notice the police cruiser parked alongside the house. Bounding up the steps, he banged his fist above the brass knocker and pressed his face against a side window. Willie swung open the door, an expression of irritation giving way to raised eyebrows, and he glanced aside.

"Important," Connor exclaimed, his hands trembling in front of him. "We gotta call the police and the federal government."

Willie motioned him in with a wave of the hand holding a whiskey glass. He entered the chilly, air-conditioned room, sweat trickling down the sides of his cheeks. "Little Mack mine, I found six drums of . . ." Rusty.

Rusty stood in the center of the living room. He held his police cap in front of him, stone-faced until he looked to the floor. Connor also cast his eyes down to his shoes, dust covering the shine he'd given them that morning. Holly entered from the kitchen and froze in place as she surveyed the scene. Connor nodded to her. He cleared his throat. "Good that you're here, Officer Haskew." His voice struggled to stay even as he stared at the floor. "We need the police." Connor explained about the barrels he'd found, drew out a map, and noted the location. "Some rascal probably trying to save hisself some money and instead of taking this to a proper disposal site, he's just thought he could dump them in one of your non-workin' mines."

Holly brought him a mug of coffee and sat by Willie's side, eyes shifting in the same triangular pattern between the three men. Willie appeared to be holding his breath, and Connor wondered if they were afraid he'd go off on Rusty. He stayed focused, emphasizing the importance of what he'd found. As much as he detested being in the same room with Rusty, the discarded nuclear waste trumped any discomfort he might feel. "Think we need to call the FBI, too. This is a crime, pure and simple."

"I'll do that," Willie said, and motioned for Rusty to write down the names of the federal agencies Connor had said to call. "Do it first thing in the morning."

"This can't wait," Connor said, his voice rising an octave. "If one barrel gets opened, even damaged, anybody who goes near it could be dead by morning if the things are radioactive." Connor talked about radioactivity, nuclear fission, and theories he remembered Dr. Herzog explaining back in college. "Nobody can go to that mine until this is cleared up and we know whether there's been any leakage and exactly what is in those barrels." He hoped they were taking him seriously, but their blank expressions didn't give him confidence.

"You know," Rusty said, rubbing his chin, "Jasper Owens, that old moonshiner who squats on your back acreage, could just stamp his barrels that way, hoping to scare off anybody who wants to steal from him."

Connor patted the air in front of him. "I hope it's that simple, but we can't take the chance. This has got to be investigated by professionals wearing protective gear."

Willie patted him on the back. "Can't thank you enough. I can see I hired the right man." He pressed his lips together in thought. "This could be all a misunderstanding. I mean, how would nuclear waste end up here in the mountains? And on my land?" He spread his hands as if unconcerned. "Don't you think, Holly? Rusty? I bet it's a gag."

Connor looked at the floor, his stomach in knots. "If that's true then I'll be a happy man, but if not, and this stuff leaks into the ground or the water supply, it'll poison all of us."

Willie nodded, gulping down the last of the whiskey in his glass. "Get things started on your end, Rusty, and I'll honk on the phone to this, uh, person, uh, government people you recommended. Don't worry, Connor," he said. "You know I'll take care of this."

Connor realized he was gripping his hands in front of him, unsure what to do, and suddenly he was uncomfortable in the room with Rusty. He wished he could speak with more authority on nuclear material. If he'd been a Duke graduate, he might have known more about nuclear energy. Might have known what to do next or remembered his lessons from Professor Herzog clearer. He nodded to the two men and reminded them that he'd be a phone call away as he turned to leave.

At home, he discarded his clothing and sat in front of the TV. He wondered if what was in the barrels was radioactive. If so, he could be dead by morning. Probably chemicals, he rationalized, wanting to believe. He knew that nuclear waste was stored in fifty-five-gallon drums, an idea he didn't think highly of, but he also knew they were disposed of in areas where human contact would never occur. They'd never be left out in the mountains like that, sitting there for any curious kid out hunting to open and look inside.

A news report showed a picture of Sharon Tate and reviewed the gruesome details of the murders at her home. "Too many monsters in this world," he said, his head pounding. He fell asleep on the couch. Dreams of fire erupting from the earth plagued him. Waking in the early morning hours, he put on his pajamas and returned to the couch. He wondered if he'd called out in his sleep. Randi Jo often told him he did, and he recalled the soothing touch of her hand on his forehead at the times he awoke drenched in sweat from a dream he could not remember. But now, no wife consoled him, and in those bleak hours, he realized how her touch had steadied his belief that dreams could not touch this reality. Now, he was not so sure.

A white frame on the TV had played, and he'd hardly noticed the annoying tone. He flipped it off, looking outside at the houses across the street. They didn't know, he thought to himself. All the people who lived on his street didn't know that someone had committed a terrible crime against them. Bringing in nuclear waste from where? Oak Ridge, Tennessee was the nearest facility that might have such material. But it could have been trucked in from anywhere and left in their mountains. The gate into the mine property had no lock. Left to chance and a no-account took advantage, he thought. The government would do something. They would help. That's what they were there for.

He fell asleep again, awaking to an insistent tap at the door. He sat up, noticing the six a.m. time on the clock. Looking toward the window, he thought he saw Sharon Tate at the door, and for several seconds he froze in place. Holly, he realized, and hurried to let her inside.

She pushed past him, making no eye contact. As self-absorbed as Holly could be, she paused and looked around the living room. "Nice job decorating."

"Not really a job," he said. "It's a teacher's salary." He watched her. A nervous rumble through his stomach warned him something was wrong. "What is it?"

"You have to forget you saw those barrels."

"What?"

"It didn't happen, Connor. For everyone's sake, you didn't see them."

"I did," he said, coming around to face her.

"You're not even sure what you saw."

"Holly, do you understand how serious this is?"

"We went out and looked for the barrels this morning," she said, crossing her arms over her stomach. "Nothing there. Word gets out that something like that was on our property makes us look bad. Squire Mines have been trying to buy us out since Lucius died. This could destroy us. Feds looking into everything we do, treating us like we're guilty. That's what did in Willie's daddy. The aggravation of it all."

249

"Willie's daddy was guilty. That was his aggravation." Connor paused, turning away from her, trying to digest her meaning not her words.

"Willie has his own people going through every mine, we'll make sure it's safe," Holly said. "We'll take care of this ourselves. Everything will be like it was. It's what's best for us." She touched his arm. "It'd be best for you, too. Just, please, don't call the Feds. We don't need the government in our lives. None of us."

"I didn't expect to see Rusty and Willie in the same room," he said, the words slipping from his lips even as he realized they had nothing to do with their conversation.

"Willie says take the rest of the week off," she continued. "Full pay. You've had a bad summer, Connor. No need to create a bad autumn. I mean, Christmas is around the corner." She turned the knob of his front door, hesitating, but not looking toward him. "Let's all move on."

The door clicked shut, and Connor stared after her, watching the foot impressions she made in the grass. The same hollow echo surrounded him as the night Randi Jo disappeared. He was in over his head, a man swallowing water who didn't realize he was drowning. Clues popped into his head: signs once looked past now shone like brilliant stars; suspicions now gelled into fact. How Willie had reacted, how Rusty had hesitated when writing down the name of the government agency. Their hesitation, their mock confusion. He'd thought they might not understand, thought they might be confused by the science. "Good God," he muttered. They knew. They understood completely. They were part of it.

Connor threw on a pair of jeans and a shirt. He went to Tallulah's room and searched her drawers, finding an instamatic camera he'd given her last Christmas. Thankfully she hadn't taken it with her to church camp. He jumped into the car and raced to the

Carmack Mines. The chain-link fence at the Little Mack now had an oversized padlock and barbed wire across the top. Connor followed the fence line to the place where he had seen to barrels. Gone. The barrels of nuclear waste had disappeared. He turned in a circle, looking around him. Even the clipboard and pen he'd dropped the day before had been taken. He wanted to call out, yell to the heavens, and demand this crime be punished. But who would hear him? The trees, the birds, a fallow earth that could do nothing to protect herself.

He leaned against the fence, sliding down until his fingers sank into mounds of dusty grass. The distant greenery enveloped him in a whirlwind of confusion until . . . a breath, the chirp of a cricket, the large brown eye of a rabbit looking at him from a thicket of weeds. A voice from long ago echoed in his ears, "*Once you've been marked by Hertha, she keeps her eye cocked your way for the rest of your life.*"

"What do you want me to do, Rabbit?" his voice croaked out in raspy desperation. "I'm one man."

"*The hare saved your life. Someday, she'll demand the same of you.*"

"You don't understand . . . these people . . . they . . ."

"*You've been marked—by the hare of Hertha.*"

Connor rubbed his eyes. These voices were from long ago, a child's memory, half his grandmother's earthy twang and partly another voice—a cool, calm vocalization that accepted no excuses. He knew exactly what he needed to do.

Hurrying home, he pulled out an Underwood typewriter that he hadn't used since his college days. Pecking out the letters, he wrote out all that had happened, putting in enough detail to scare the bejesus out of any government official who read it. He knew the agency receiving this correspondence would recognize how dangerous a situation he was describing. They'd have to investigate. He hesitated before signing his name, then took the letter to the post office. If there was no response, he'd find someone to contact. He'd make people pay attention. He'd call the newspaper and the television stations. He'd drive to the state capitol and tell his senator and representative about what was happening in these mountains. He'd not let this travesty go unreported or unpunished.

30

Willie's secretary called Connor late Friday afternoon and told him he'd not be needed the following week as well. Phone calls to Willie went unanswered, and Connor wouldn't stoop to phoning Rusty. Herman took him down to the FBI office twice, but both times they found the door locked and lights out. The next Friday, the same call from a different Carmack secretary told him to stay home again.

Days passed. No one arrived on his doorstep asking for more information. He made several phone calls to the Department of Energy, but ended up in a spiral of bureaucracy, transferred from one lower-level government worker to another. One claimed he couldn't understand Connor's accent and hung up on him; another said the practice of relocating industrial waste to mines was normal and he had nothing to worry about; another swore that every barrel of nuclear material was accounted for and none had been deposited in eastern Kentucky. Connor wrote more letters to government agencies and even the governor, his representative, and both state senators. A polite form letter came back from some of the elected officials that his concerns would be looked into, but not long after that, Connor began getting correspondence from the same politicians soliciting donations for the next campaign, making him realize there was little point in driving to the capitol to shake a realization into these politicians. They didn't care.

Out of a frenzied frustration, he went to the *Contrary Gazette* and told his story. The editor listened politely and said he'd look into it. Connor wasn't all that surprised that there was no coverage. The newspaper never printed a story critical of the coal industry, so why would they cross a government agency? The *Crimson County Sun* was very interested, but they were unable to confirm anything of what Connor told them. One of their reporters took a beating from some miners after asking too many questions when rumors began to spread that the mines were shutting down because of an activist troublemaker who was going around saying coal was radioactive. While the editor was willing to continue looking into the story, without solid facts he wouldn't be able to print it.

But the story did get out. Miners talked, wives worried that their husbands would lose their jobs, and stories circulated about a crazy schoolteacher who'd been given the opportunity of a lifetime and bit the hand that fed him. Connor received hang-ups all hours of the night, his tires were slashed twice, and finally a letter from the payroll officer of the Carmack Mines informed him his services were no longer needed. He called Willie's office to give him a piece of his mind for not firing him to his face. Willie wouldn't take the call, and when Connor called his home, he discovered the number had been changed.

Connor Herne was again only a teacher. When the school year began, students stared at him like he was the peculiar oddity in a sideshow circus tent; they snickered behind his back and made faces when he wasn't looking. At least there was camaraderie with the other teachers, few of whom had anything to do with the coal industry. One of the science teachers wrote a character reference that Connor included with his next set of letters to the government, which vouched that he was a man of integrity who would never make up such a story, and that the very least the state officials owed the community was an investigation. No response ever arrived.

By December, he'd mailed out over a hundred letters. He no longer discussed them with his colleagues, some of whom pressed him to let it go, but every Friday night, he went to the library to scour magazines and congressional reports. Upon finding a new selection of names, he'd come home and type into the night so that his correspondence would be ready for Saturday's mail. He never gave another thought to the rabbit, or Hertha, or why he was doing this. He only knew that he had no choice. It was winter again. He was frozen in this way of life he could not change. Sometimes he wanted to give up, and his days of apathy made him angry. He never would have accepted this situation as a child or young man, but this was what life had done to him. He was a man who didn't know what to do and who lacked the cunning to come up with a plan. The people who had perpetrated this crime would get away with it.

Other times he thought about Sharon Tate, who'd taken up a forsaken residency in his mind. Sharon Tate, victim of the Manson monsters whose names would plant seeds of fear for a generation. She twirled in a circle, surveying the lilac sky. Mrs. Worden nodded to her, and Bette and the Dahlia waved her over but she stayed to herself on the edge of the landscape. There was nothing he could do to change how life had turned out. Just as there was little Sharon could have done to change her fate. Monsters. All monsters.

On the night of December 31st, a knock on the door startled Connor. He rose from the table as he pulled out a final letter. The last he would write for many years. His sister stood on the porch, back toward him, holding the fur collar of her coat tightly around her neck. It was almost midnight. What was she doing here?

"Get in. It's freezing out," Connor said to her as he cracked open the door.

"I think I'll not," she responded and sat on the porch swing.

Connor gabbed a coat hanging behind the door and a throw from the couch. "It's late." He sat beside her, noting that her eyes were red-rimmed and her shivery breath was not because she was cold. "Gonna be a new decade in a few minutes."

"I came from spying on Iona and her husband. They're at the Little Tunnel Inn, living it up." She crossed her arms over her chest. "Can't let Mom see me come in this late. Can I stay here tonight?"

Connor inhaled a breath of cold and slowly arranged the blanket around Tempy's knees. "They have a baby now," he said. "I know that hurts, but it's a reality."

She suppressed a short burst of laughter with a hand, then wiped her nose. "I hate my life."

Connor twisted forward, no longer looking at his sister. The two false siblings stared at the frozen road in front of the house. To the left, the sound of parties from houses down the lane competed with an occasional howl of wind. "Me too," he said.

Firecrackers and the whistle of fireworks popped in the distance, announcing the new decade. The 1970s. Connor envisioned the coming days as if they were a movie playing out on the wall. Souls would fall and lack the understanding of what had happened to them, families would focus on the sorrow and not the horror. He would wait for the killer to strike, watching the innocent living out their days not knowing that the sinister was seeping in around them, ready to slit their throats.

PROLOGUE FOUR

March 8, 1975

On this day, the United Nations declared International Women's Day. They had, in fact, named 1975 as International Women's Year. Tempy Herne eye-rolled a sneer when she read it in the news. Like a bunch of diplomats gave a flying fig about the female gender. Now and then she was heartened, like when Margaret Thatcher defeated Edward Heath to become England's first lady Prime Minister, or when Ella Grasso was elected governor of Connecticut without having replaced a dead husband. However, those wins paled when she considered the power of men. She watched Crimson County boys come back from Vietnam, some with maimed bodies and nearly all with crippled minds. Now that that backwards country was about to fall to the Communists anyway, Tempy couldn't help but shake her head and think that their stupidity had bloodied their noses. All of them. Even ole Dick Nixon, with his promises to get the country out of the war, hadn't survived his own foolhardiness as he resigned the presidency amid the Watergate scandal and his henchmen were sent to the poky. They deserved what they got. They were just men . . . and more stupid men would replace them.

From the Lester Street Bridge, Tempy stared at what used to be the Rhine. It was a field now, patches of crabgrass with a marshy path that had been mashed down by teenagers from the east end of town taking a short cut to Crimson County's high school. *Shit pit*, she thought, remembering the muddy streets and clapboard shacks leaning into one another. A fire had taken the whole neighborhood one night, long after her family moved away. A car roared over the bridge, radio blasting Jethro Tull's "Bungle in the Jungle." She turned her face away. Not that anyone would recognize her in Quinntown, but why take the chance? As that music faded, it was replaced by a melancholy violin descant. She looked around but couldn't figure out where the melody was coming from.

Looking at the Rhine from the perspective of a child and from where she'd stood when houses were still there, she realized an orange rock lay over the area where Mom had buried Connor, the real Connor, her brother, and the woman who'd given birth to the child who'd replaced him. Why did she keep this secret? She'd hinted at the deception and poked at the fake Connor over the years, but she'd never outright told him what happened that night, not in a way that she could prove it to him. Part of her had always wondered if Mom had killed that woman, but she'd rejected the thought as beneath Mom's religious dignity. Now, stealing the baby–that, her mother could have justified as Christian compassion. In her more cynical moments Tempy knew why she'd never told Connor the whole story when she'd been on the verge so many times. Telling him would gain her nothing, she rationalized, and why give away information that significant without getting a little something back?

Word was that a Louisville contractor had bought the land that used to be the Rhine and was planning on building a coat factory.

"Imagine that," she said aloud. "Quinntown now has industry." She wondered if they'd find the bones.

"Another mountain mystery." She stared into the muddy canal water, knowing her mother would never admit what she'd done all those years ago. So what would be the point of telling fake-Connor, even if someone found the bones? She enjoyed having a secret on her false brother. She'd been forced by Wallis to tell Connor about Randi Jo's indiscretion years ago. She hadn't meant to tell her mother, but the words had come tumbling out of her mouth like spit-up. She'd enjoyed the look on Mom's face, something between glee and nausea. *If I'd kept that one a secret, could have waited for a bigger blowup,* she mused, but she'd caved under her mother's relentless haranguing. No matter. She still had this one truth that would blow his world apart. Better to make it real when it could inflict the most carnage–maybe after Tallulah left for college. No need drawing her into this. She wouldn't hurt that girl for the whole world.

It was a bold thought–inflicting damage–even as Tempy knew she didn't possess the guts to take any responsibility in Connor's being kept in the dark. Maybe she'd find a way to blame Mom. But not while her mother was still in her right mind. Tempy could never face her mother's enraged glare and cold fury. No matter. She was patient. Tempy had noticed little slips here and there where Wallis was confused about the day of the week or whether or not she'd already been to the bank that day. It was happening . . . that brain-eating disease that would slowly eat holes in her mother's mind until it was like Swiss cheese. Tempy wondered if the same would happen to her. Maybe some day she would forget all her own secrets, struggle to know her given name, then wistfully meander those hazy streets with Grammy's ghost, letting go of the misery of living in a world that deemed her devoid of moral purity–another dirty secret.

The setting sun glared into her eyes, and she turned east and looked at her watch. Where was Iona? A scrape from below caught her attention. She moved to the end of the bridge and peeked over the railing. Someone in a black coat was digging on the creek bank. She watched as the figure dropped to his knees and stuffed a hand down the front of his pants. At first, she wrote off the scene as another gross man doing disgusting things, but as she watched him, she noticed he dipped his head down and sniffed the dirt. As if he could sense her, the man's head whipped around and he looked up. Tempy jumped back, her heart pounding, and for several seconds she fought a primeval impulse to run. She held still, waiting to see if he crawled up the canal bank. She'd have plenty time to run down Marcescent Street if he chased her. The air around her felt hollow, and she realized the violin no longer played. She held her breath, praying that the man didn't see her.

"Over here!" Iona called to her from across the street.

Tempy trotted to her side, leaving behind any thoughts of her former neighborhood and whatever trash was buried there.

"Wish you wouldn't wait on the bridge; you know that's where my cousin was killed."

"I'd forgotten," she lied. "I like getting a drink of mineral water."

"Don't know why. It makes your breath stink."

"So you don't want to kiss me?"

Iona flicked her shoulder, pointing toward the Regal Hotel, managed by her cousin Alvey. "I didn't say that."

"Besides, you knew Bette Moss all of a day and a half."

"I decided not to like her when she kept correcting my verb syntax."

Cousin Alvey kept a room for them every Saturday night when both were supposed to be at different churches. In all these years, they'd never been caught, and if Iona's simpleton husband even suspected, he was at least bright enough not to challenge his Stark wife. Iona knew he had a girlfriend on the side, a waitress at Critter's Pool Hall. They'd eaten there once to look her over. The tramp was a mousy-looking dirty blond who walked like she had corns, and Iona had just laughed.

Upstairs in the room, Tempy looked out on the Lester Street Bridge as she undressed. The black-coated figure had climbed up the bank and was drinking from the artesian fountain. He was a spidery thing. A killer, she realized, re-living his glory days. She turned on the radio and found a station playing The Hollies' "The Air that I Breathe." Humming along, she watched the gangling figure stretch like a gorilla about to beat its chest. Oddly, she wasn't shocked or even fearful in realizing exactly what she was witnessing. It never occurred to her to tell Iona. Not like her lover cared who'd killed a cousin she'd barely known and didn't like, and besides, that conversation would only disrupt their evening. What the man did next did surprise her. He walked to the place Wallis had buried the blond-haired woman and knelt down. Digging his fingers into the earth, he leaned forward and kissed the rock. He must've been there that night, she figured, must've watched Wallis bury the woman. All these years, Tempy had thought the unidentified woman starved to death on the creek bank as so many had in those days. Now, she realized Connor's mother had met up with the same man as Iona's cousin. Must've been young, she thought. Connor's birth parent might have even been his first. By the time he'd decapitated Bette Moss, he was an old hand. "My, my," she said. "That is interesting."

"What?" Iona asked, coming out of the bathroom in a silky white gown as the next song transitioned–Steve Miller Band's "The Joker." That's what she was, a knave that fooled all the men who thought they were so smart.

"Nothing." Tempy swallowed, letting one more secret fill her belly. "Just thinking, we live in a hell of a place."

That Temperance Herne felt no compulsion to share what she suspected and in her heart knew to be true should not surprise the mountain citizenry. She was sure the monster had no interest in her type. She was aware that he would kill again, and she was certain that she could care less. He kept his secrets in the dirty part of town and so did she. In a way, she even understood his compulsion: to smell dirt; to know joy through remembering seconds of old ecstasies; to drain life from what you hate, what sought to destroy you. In the end, the jokers of the world would prevail. Deviants had to stick together. And so what? Yes, she did live in a hell of a place.

HOLLY

31

Six years later, Connor stared out his window at Sharon Tate walking up the sidewalk to his house. Had the starlet come out of his interior world and into the real one? For several seconds he willed himself into that surreal otherness to see if she was still there. Yes, Sharon was there . . . staring into a glittering, lavender sky. A brisk knock jarred him from his imagination. Holly. Holly stood outside his house. Her long blond hair, parted in the middle, and her softly angled cheekbones made her favor the deceased actress even more than she had in younger years. He sipped hot coffee, looking at her through the sheer curtain. His radio played "Waterloo," an ABBA song that he knew would stick in his head for the better part of the morning. Holly pressed a palm on the window and dipped her head as if to say *Please*.

Connor opened the door, holding the coffee cup between them, mesmerized by her allure. An aura of leonine prowess had replaced the peacock showiness of her youth. Her hair, now ash blond, hung in loose curls around her shoulders. She wore no makeup and her azure eyes cried out an injury as she studied him.

"I need a favor," she asked.

"From someone you haven't spoken to in ten years."

"Six," she said, gaze glued to him. "Can I come in?"

He looked out at the road, swallowed a drink of coffee, then reluctantly held open the screen door. "Have to leave soon. Picking Tallulah up from choir practice."

"Can you believe so much time has passed?" Holly moved around his living room, touching photos of Tallulah, surveying the furniture as if they were still friends and a visit from her should have been expected. "She'll graduate soon. Going to college, I'm sure."

Connor didn't answer. Frankly, he didn't care to give her any information about his family. Holly had made her bed, a life of Crimson County society, such as it was, and he wasn't about to help her with anything. He flipped off the radio to edgy silence.

She pointed to a black sedan parked on the side of the road. "See that man in the driver's seat?" Her slender hands came prayer-like to her lips. "He's an FBI agent."

Connor put down his coffee cup and closed the door. "What's this about, Holly?"

"I want you to take him to the place you found those barrels."

"Barrels!" The word burst through his lips. "You'd know more about them than me. Come join me being a prized ass of this town."

"That's unfair. I'm here to help you."

"Yeah, back me up, why don't you. You're ten, oh, I'll give you, six years too late."

"It's not too late."

"No way to prove anything, other than my word, and I grew weary of being the whacko that put the town out of work."

"The FBI has ways, scientific-fangled methods. Let them do the dirty work."

"And why are you turning against Willie now?"

Holly bit her lip and exhaled a shivery breath. She blinked, tears filling her eyes and drying up just as quickly. "We've split. Willie stays in Atlanta almost full time. Set up a leggy model in a place down there. I'm divorcing him."

"So, this has nothing to do with doing the right thing." Connor chuckled, letting her feel his disinterest. "You just want leverage against your husband."

"Don't act so high and mighty, Connor Herne. I knew you when."

"I reckon I will." Connor opened the door, pointing for her to get out. "You were the one to tell me to stay out of it, and now I'm supposed to help you with your little plan for a bigger divorce settlement?"

"Willie's cut me off. I got nothing. Stuck in a studio above Selma's Beauty Shop in Quinntown. Quinntown, for God's sakes. I'm a step away from being back in Notown. Connor, I need your help."

Her voice tore at him, begging for the camaraderie of their youth. He wanted to shake her until she realized her greedy grab for legitimacy still landed her in the dirt, but the image of those barrels, hidden like rodents waiting to spread an unstoppable death tied his hands from dusting themselves of her. "You made a sorry deal with the Devil, Holly."

"I know what I am. I know what I did. But you know what you are, too, and regardless of my reasons, this is your chance to right a wrong."

Connor blew out a breath. In the end, no matter how many betrayals or lies, the two of them were outsiders, and to prove anything, they were all the other had, each of them needing what the other knew. "Tell me what happened."

Holly stared at the floor, biting her bottom lip. "Contractor," she said, clearing her throat. "The contractor was supposed to deliver the waste to a place in Utah where they deal with that kind of stuff, but the train had to stop on the other side of Cumberland Gap, something about the rails being stolen by one of the fraternities at Kingsley University, a prank, I guess. While he waits, Darius Stark meets the guy in a bar, completely by chance, gets him drunk, finds out what he's about and works a deal with him to put the barrels into one of Willie's defunct mines. Contractor saves transportation cost, Starks and Willie get a payoff." She coughed, hand trembling as her nerves betrayed her. "We were having bad times. Needed the money." A cynical chuckle was followed by a weary sigh. "That's how the Starks bought into the Carmack mines. They hide what they own under Willie's name."

"How many barrels, Holly?"

"I don't know."

"I only saw six, an entire train filled with those . . . how many?"

"Do I look like I'm good at math?"

He grabbed her by the shoulders, shook her. "Do you know what you've done?" What was hidden in that mine, melting the muscle of the earth formed image after image of horror in Connor's mind: *A white hare fleeing through fire. A woman, on her knees, begging a killer to spare her.* "Even one of those barrels leaks, the catastrophe could last for generations . . . cancers, deformed babies, agonizing death."

She jerked from his grasp, crossing an arm over her chest and a hand to her mouth. Tears wet her eyes again, but not for sorrow of her inaction. Holly didn't like being blamed. "It's not my fault," she said. "What could I have done? I'm a woman. He was my husband."

268

Connor turned away from her, wishing distance, wishing he hadn't heard her story. "That's a sorry excuse."

"I don't know how many barrels," she said, voice trembling, "but Willie and Darius both bought vacation houses in Daytona Beach afterwards." She paused and cleared her throat. "They . . . they might have had an ongoing relationship with this man, once he knew how easy it was to do."

Connor held his hand to his stomach, a wave of heaviness coming up in his throat. "I'll go," he said, "but not to add fuel to your divorce settlement." Connor picked up a jacket, stashed his .22 in an inside pocket and headed out the door.

In the black sedan, the FBI agent didn't speak as Connor directed him to Hemlock Mountain toward Little Mack mine. The local radio station played country music and he turned it off, giving Connor a look to make sure he didn't object. Connor stared straight ahead. There were no communities along the road, a few deserted shacks collapsed under their own weight. Vines and kudzu encroached, slowly claiming back any territory where a lone human had hoped to make a solitary life. "Think anything'll come of this?" Connor asked.

"Agent Parilla," he finally introduced himself. "I'll do my best."

The man's accent wasn't of the mountains or even the Southeast that Connor could tell. He wondered how Holly had managed to get someone to take her seriously after all his efforts had been ignored. He guessed she'd made some powerful contacts as Willie's wife, but whether this man possessed the know-how to take on the Carmacks and the Starks had yet to be seen. An outsider would be blocked from truly effective change, and Kentucky politics being crooked as a mountain creek, well, no telling who was in a Stark pocket. Only a federal official might stand a chance. Connor thought of a Wendell Berry poem called "Eastern Kentucky, 1967." Tallulah had once memorized it for an assembly program. He remembered she'd been booed afterwards. As the car hung on to the winding curves underneath dangling kudzu vines and massive ridges shadowing the road, he prayed that he'd have a smidgen of his daughter's courage.

They parked at the chained-off entrance between a bullet-riddled route sign and a billboard advertising a tent ministry in Jellico. Connor paused to read about last month's Bryson Pomeroy revival, giving a silent prayer that Little Preacher Boy didn't come any closer to Contrary than that, then he and the agent walked the quarter mile inward on a weedy road. The gate around the abandoned mine had rusted through the years. Connor pointed down the hill where he'd found the barrels, and they walked the gate line until the agent found a weak section an animal had dug under. He pulled a small jar from his pocket and took a soil sample. He studied the dirt, narrowing his eyes, and capped the container.

"Likely put the barrels in the mine, or they could have taken them somewhere else since they knew I was on to them," Connor said, indicating the boarded-up entrance. "If what Holly says is true, there's no telling how many other mines have been filled."

"This is all I need," he said and faced Connor. "Any residue in this dirt, our analyst'll find it." He shook the dirt, then put the jar in his pocket. "That'll give us enough to get a search warrant for the mine."

Connor looked aside, the agent's words not entirely making sense, but he explained it off as the agent probably not having a scientific background. "You know it's not likely they'll find anything in that dirt, only if a barrel was leaking, and I don't have any reason to think they were. Time and rust is the enemy."

The agent smiled a closed-mouth grin and looked off toward the distant hills.

"I've got my gun," Connor said, pulling out his .22. "I can shoot off the lock. Maybe if we go look inside–"

"Gun," the agent repeated and locked his gaze on the firearm.

Connor realized it might not have been a smart idea to pull out the handgun without warning the agent and returned it to his front jacket pocket. The agent again looked around the wooded landscape, heavy with green and overflowing kudzu that had overtaken the abandoned metal.

"Guess you have to have a warrant for us to go in, huh?" Connor asked.

"You've done a brave thing," Parilla said, showing his row of straight, white teeth. "The right thing." He smiled, the frozen, knowing mug of an outsider patronizing someone he thought was naive. "I'll be back once we know what we're dealing with."

"Will they know it was me?" Connor asked.

"Naw." The agent waved a hand and put the jar in his pocket. "I'll never tell."

"I want them to know," Connor said. "They made me look like a fool all those years ago. Their denials nearly destroyed my life." He had little confidence that this agent knew what he was doing, but maybe if Connor's name was thrown around in the right places, it might stir up some fear. Fear, he knew, could force Willie into a mistake. His old friend would not want to walk his own father's path. Willie would make a deal with law enforcement and give up the Starks to keep himself out of trouble. That was Willie's way, even as a teenager. "You're gonna have to put some pressure on Holly's husband. He'll squeal to stay a free man. It'll rattle him to know I'm backing her story." Connor's confidence began to return . . . until what came out of the agent's mouth next.

"A thing like this," Agent Parilla bared his teeth and nodded like he knew better, "best keep the whistleblower's name secret. Too many of 'em end up dead."

32

Herne's Food Market was worn around the edges, an antiquated but still functional building. Tempy usually worked the sole cash register while Mom, in her uncompromising style, ran the place with the flexibility of a drill sergeant. Baylor Grubb had stayed with the store, despite Mom's meticulous nature, and now was part of the family. They'd hire on extra help when needed, and Connor had sent some of his ambitious students to work weekends and during the holidays. Most business had gone to the Kroger and Piggly Wiggly out on the highway, but loyal customers and frugal practices kept the Hernes' store afloat.

Connor parallel parked across the street from the grocery in front of John's Store, a countrified clothing mart that had been here as long as the Herne's. A yellow and black lettered going-out-of-business sign was slashed across the window. Connor thought back to all the tightly-woven blue jeans and work shirts he'd bought here through the years, landing on the amusing memory of a gray cap he bought to cover his bald head after Pop shaved his hair to clear a lice infestation when he was a young boy. He looked through his reflection in the window to the elderly owners sitting behind a counter staring forward at no one. The image sent a wave of sadness through him. The places of his youth were changing; some stores disappeared into strip malls while others sat like empty walnut hulls. The old town looked like a ragged pair of dungarees that could no longer be patched. He trotted across the street, though there was no traffic. Baylor was at the cash register and gave Connor a wave as he headed toward the apartment door.

Upstairs, he found Mom at the kitchen table writing a list. "Here are the items we need to get done before Tallulah's graduation," she said, handing it to him.

He glanced over it. "Most of this is done."

"I'm sure it isn't." She stood and gestured toward the paper.

"Tempy already made the reservation for the graduation dinner. Tempy!" he yelled back toward the rear bedroom.

"Tempy's gone," Mom argued. "The library or something."

"No she isn't," Connor said and pointed. "She's right behind you."

Mom turned around, looking at Tempy as she stood in the doorway with her hair half up in a ponytail, one hand twisting it into a topknot.

"What?" his sister said, irritated by having been called out of her room.

Mom swerved from one to the other of them, her expression confused and alarmed. She sank into a chair and covered her face with both hands. "It's happening to me." She sucked in air and expelled it in a wheeze.

Connor and Tempy were immediately at her side, rubbing her shoulders and trying to give assurances they did not believe. "One spell of forgetfulness doesn't mean that," Connor said.

"I've made lists that I've forgotten the same day," Tempy said, sitting next to her mother and watching her closely.

Mom pressed her thumbs to her temples. "I've always had a mind like a steel trap. I'm losing it little by little."

Connor and Tempy linked a gaze over their mother's head. He wanted to tell Mom that what she feared wasn't happening, wanted to comfort a person who'd always been so self-sufficient, but he knew the truth and didn't dare speak it. "I forgot where I parked the car the other day," Connor lied in jest.

"I don't have a car," Tempy said. "Still have to borrow yours."

"Look at you," Mom snapped at her daughter. "You act like this is happening to you, and in your selfish mind, I guess it is."

"That snapped you right out of it, didn't it?"

Connor chuckled, negotiating the tense landscape between his mother and sister. The three of them were a lopsided triangle fitted into an exacting space. He wiped the complexity of their relationship from his mind, keeping a simplified version that played out in 1960s sitcoms as his vision of family. He knew he lied to himself but didn't have the motivation, the time, or the focus to untangle the tightly woven habits they'd fallen into over the years. He kept the peace with folksy humor, knowing in his gut that it gave him an escape for one more day. "Why don't you bottle that, Tempy? We'll sell it downstairs."

"I'm going to take a nap," Mom said, pushing slowly up from the table. Clasping her hands in front of her, she commenced a long, slow walk to her bedroom, looking at photographs on the wall along the way.

"It could happen to all of us," Connor said wistfully after Mom was out of hearing range.

"Maybe not all of us," Tempy said.

"I have the same genes as the two of you. We both have a fifty percent chance."

Tempy stared at him, bit her lip, and looked aside. "You should know–" She paused, her Adam's apple bobbing in her throat as she swallowed, considering. She shifted in the chair and crossed her legs. "There's an extra seat at the table for Tallulah's graduation dinner."

Connor nodded, somehow feeling that was not what she'd meant to say. "So there's room for Randi Jo to bring her husband."

"Oh joy," Tempy remarked and rolled her eyes. "I was hoping Iona could come. She's been around Tallulah as much as anybody. Tallulah even calls her Aunt Iona."

Connor shoved his hands in his pockets. That his daughter had a relationship with a Stark via his sister still irked him, but Iona was probably the least troublesome of that family. "I have to let Simon have a seat. Randi Jo might not be able to come otherwise."

Tempy huffed, "We'll squeeze in somehow." She stood and looked at her watch. "I have to go babysit Iona's girl. She's taking Wayne to the doctor in Knoxville. He's in menopause or something." She checked her topknot in the mirror, then hesitated at the steps and looked toward Mom's room. "Who's going to take care of me?" A hand covered her mouth as the flooding realization vibrated from her core.

"I'll always take care of the two of you. You know that," he said, resting a hand on her shoulder. "When you don't want to work the store anymore, we'll sell it. That'll be more than enough for you to retire, and Mom can move to my house. With Tallulah gone this year, we can do that any time."

"Connor, you remember what it was like taking care of Grammy. It took all four of us and sometimes that wasn't enough. I think we should consider a nursing home. Someplace we can stash her to be sure she's fed and cleaned."

"I'm not going to warehouse Mom."

"She's not your mother." Tempy's voice broke, and she looked up at him with glassy eyes. "She's mine."

His sister rushed down the steps, slamming the door so hard a photo of his father skewed sideways. Connor huffed an exasperated breath, leaning against the wall. Why did life have to be so hard with these two women? Nothing he did ever seemed to be enough, and they both fought him no matter how much he tried to help. He straightened the picture of his father, staring into his kind eyes and wishing that Pop were still alive. Down the hall, he could hear Mom talking and moved that direction. Connor peeked through the cracked door. Back toward him, Mom sat on the bed, photo album open. She pointed to each picture, naming the person and reciting memories of each of them.

"And this is my husband. I married him in Johnstown, Pennsylvania and we moved here after the flood in '36. This one is my mother, Matilda. She was a difficult woman . . . but then, I guess so am I. This one is my son, Connor. The picture was taken when we first moved to the Rhine, before Asa left for Europe to get my mother out of Germany. I was frightened all the time, but I didn't dare show it. Connor stopped breathing one day. I loved him. This is my daughter, Temperance. I pity her. She's made a hard life for herself."

Connor closed the door and put a hand over his mouth. It took him several seconds to take a breath. Perhaps just like that day as a baby. Mom had never him told him about an incident where he'd stopped breathing. He wondered if she had resuscitated him or if he'd started breathing on his own. He had died and come back to life. No wonder Mom was always so protective of him. Maybe that was why he saw the dead so easily, why they flocked to him, taking up perdurable residency in his mind. Or was this confirmation of Tempy's childish hints that he was not a Herne? Her vitriol had peppered his life since he was a boy, and despite his efforts to ignore her, the hurtful suggestions lay like open sores on his confidence. He didn't know what to believe. He wasn't sure he wanted to know the truth.

He wondered if this was the beginning of his mother's memory fracturing the way Grammy's had and her life becoming a series of mishaps until they would have to confine her for her own safety. He wondered if he would go to that murky land as well and lose all that he was. Connor walked back toward the stockroom, closing off the apartment behind him, and for the first time in his adult life, he cried.

33

After the incident with Mom and Tempy, Connor was heartened to come home to the chirpy babble of six teenage girls spiraling to a feverish pitch as they yakked about the nuances of high school verses college. They were staying for a sleepover. He'd promised to go out for the evening and not return before midnight, and she'd promised there'd be no alcohol or boys. He didn't know why he made that useless rule. She would be in college for the summer session in a few weeks where she'd have to make her own decisions about boys and booze. He tried not to think about it, telling himself that she was a good kid, a smart girl, the best daughter he could have imagined. Still, his stomach churned when he thought of his own college days, knowing she was walking into a world more uncertain than his university years. He closed his eyes and willed himself to think that she was smarter than he'd ever been.

As the half dozen sprinted toward Tallulah's room, she turned back and gave him a hug. "I'm about to be a high school graduate!"

she said to no one. Pushing back from her father, she twirled around and held both hands against the side of her head. "I can't wait to get to college. No insult should be inferred."

She was on a light beam, he realized, excited and forward looking as if no shadow would ever darken her path. "Rehearsal went well?" he asked.

"All except Theresa Cullen goes flat on the high notes of 'Arches of Roses.'"

"It's the little things you'll remember all your life."

Tender seconds of silence passed as she looked aside, her profile a soft pastel of youth that has endured its scars. She was thinking, and he could have predicted her next words. "Did you talk to Momma?" she asked, a hesitant tone slipping into her confidence. "I've told Aunt Tempy that she and grandma have to stay in line and be nice to her and Simon. After all it's my, my, mmmyyyy day, and the other one hundred and thirty-two people in my class, so, family-kins, take note."

"I'm writing it all down," Connor said and motioned her into the living room. "Got you a present." He pulled a package from the side table drawer and handed it to her.

"Think Simon will start up?" she asked. "He will let Momma come, won't he?"

Connor didn't answer, hoping the gift would distract her. "You can open it now."

"I think he hits her, Daddy." Tallulah picked at the tape on one end of the box, waiting for her father.

"Open your present."

"Can't you do something, Daddy?"

His breath caught in his throat. "No, Tallulah. It's not my place." Her needy tone and pleading expression tugged at his gut. He, too, had noticed the bruises that Randi Jo covered with makeup. He wished he could do something, but she was another man's wife . . . She lived in a different territory now, and it wasn't his to cross into.

"If not us, then who?" Tallulah said, more a statement than a question.

"I don't want you to be disappointed if they don't come to the graduation dinner. I'm sure she'll make the ceremony, but the dinner might be more difficult with all of us there. Simon would be uncomfortable, and she knows that."

"Momma would never miss my graduation dinner. You just wait and see." She ripped the wrapping paper off in one stroke and held up the box, looking at him, open-mouthed with peaked eyebrows.

"I used to think you were going to be a scientist, maybe a doctor," he let out an audible sigh, "but I've accepted it."

"A Montblanc fountain pen!" she squealed. "I'm going to write until the end of time."

"They're not going to make these much longer," he said, pointing at the pen, "so I bought up a lot of ink." He handed her a second package from his pocket.

"I will use it frugally and only when writing masterpieces."

"Tallulah!" yelled a girl from the bedroom over the ever-volumized Rolling Stones. "Get your ass . . . I'm mean be-hind in here . . . Sorry, Mr. Herne."

"Go," he pointed toward her room, "and wipe worry off your list."

The strange sensation of the world spinning too fast swept him up as he looked at a stand of photos of Tallulah as a babe, toddler, pre-teen and now, a young woman. When had that happened? In the reflection of the glass he could see the age in his jowls, a spread of wrinkles around his eyes, his hair more white than blond, and he could hear the silence in the house once she would be gone. Connor took a deep breath, not knowing what he would do, but these few days she'd have at home, he wanted to make them the best for her. The most memorable.

He picked up the phone and started to dial, then hung up before finishing. He hushed a tremble in his chest, unsure whether it came from the sorrow of sending his daughter out into the world or the uneasy apprehension of what he knew he needed to do. He dialed three more times before finally letting the connection ring through. He hoped Randi Jo would pick up. No such luck. Simon Tuller, her husband, answered. "Simon," he said. "I was calling Randi Jo to make sure you got the graduation dinner invitation."

A sigh. More of a huff. But no answer.

"Is Randi Jo there?" Connor asked.

"None of your damn business," Simon responded and hung up.

Connor held the receiver against his ear for several seconds, his chest pulsing with nerves that ran into anger. Calling Simon a few choice names, he clipped down the receiver. He'd never had one easy phone call with the man, and over the years had come to avoid any encounters with him. Just another Stark hothead, quick to accuse and always on the defensive. Tuller avoided any outright conflicts with Connor, and he gave Simon no reason to engage him, even though he might liked to have told off Randi Jo's husband a time or two for his surly behavior. As far as he could tell, Simon avoided Tallulah whenever she and her mother visited, and Connor refused to allow her to stay at their house.

More often than he liked thinking of it, Connor wished he'd been kinder to Randi Jo after the divorce. Maybe she wouldn't have married again so quickly. Maybe she would have chosen a better husband. Maybe with the passage of time they might have . . . He squashed the thought even as it flooded his emotions. Maybe, he thought, maybe he'd talk to Randi Jo after the graduation. A few words might wake her up to the life she could have . . . away from fear, pain . . . away from a man who disrespected her. Connor caught his thoughts. He'd never been physically abusive to Randi Jo, but he'd never done right by her either. The way they grew apart was as much his fault as hers, maybe more his, and it was his guilt that kept him from reaching out. He couldn't change the life she had now any more than she could.

The harmonies of the girls singing ABBA's "SOS" wafted through the house. Yes, Randi Jo needed help, had needed it for a long time, but he didn't know what he could do. Still, his daughter's words echoed in his mind . . . *If not us, then who?*

34

Good as his word to leave an adult-free house for the evening, Connor picked up Herman Cahill, who left the gas station in the hands of his cousin Troy, and the two headed to the Pinnacle, a mountain overlook with a panoramic view of three states. Connor and Herman had been here only a few times since Pop had brought them the first time as kids. A teardrop-shaped patio now hung over the most panoramic view of the Kentucky, Tennessee, and Virginia mountains. As part of the Cumberland Gap National Forest, the park attracted scores of visitors yearning to see where the longhunters challenged the wilderness and the native Indians, and where Daniel Boone cut a path for pioneers to head West. The men gazed out on the spread of rolling hills toward Powell Valley, the sharp ridges around Middlesboro, and Fern Lake reflecting in the distance like a mirror turned toward the last of the day's sun.

"Needed this today." Connor nodded toward the mountains. "Wish we had the time to go hunting."

"Me too. Can't stay long," Herman said and sipped his brew. "Jason's had a tummy ache, and never know when Darius is going to want something–like his car washed on a rainy day."

Herman and Sissy's son, Jason, had been a miracle child. Sissy had nearly died giving birth to him, and now, almost seven years old, he ruled their hearts like a pint-sized prince. But with every joy, it seemed a sorrow hung over them. For Herman, it was the long shadow of Darius Stark. Once out of jail, the vengeful Stark had managed to put himself on the board of directors for the bank that owned the loan on the Cahills' gas station. With a few other cousins, he bullied his way into getting whatever he wanted, which eventually led to his owning the gas station. Darius hadn't thrown the Cahills out . . . no, Darius was more inventive, leaving Herman right where he was and keeping him under his thumb for whatever humiliation came to mind. He ordered Connor's friend around like a military general, giving his cronies gas at Herman's expense, using his vending machines as free lunch whenever he or another Stark passed by, and each time letting the Cahills know he could do far worse.

"Ever think we've made nothing of our lives?" Connor asked, not expecting or knowing an answer.

"Never thought I'd be beholding to a Stark. Not like this. Funny that, they stole Daddy's car and we get the blame for their going to jail." He rubbed his face, turning toward the sinking sun. "If it weren't for my boy . . ."

"Maybe we should've moved out of the mountains."

"Everybody digs a hole, whether here or in the city."

It was true, the years had passed faster than either of them had realized, taking with them any dreams they might have had of a better life somewhere else. Their flesh, their bone, their memories, and their grit had knitted itself into the fabric of the land. They hated it as much as they loved it. For better or worse, this was their hole.

"How do you stand working for Darius?"

"Daddy always said he'd blame us once he got out of the pen." Herman squeezed the railing with his calloused hands, rims of his nails embedded with car oil. He was a simple man, a loyal man, and as Connor watched his friend's tightened grip he thought, *A man who doesn't deserve this.* "He even brings up that we buried a dead body once like he's holding that over me. The nerve."

"Your father knew better than we did. I always thought when he went to jail, that'd be the last we heard of him, but bile keeps coming back like a filthy wave."

"Damn tyrant is what he is. Last week, he orders me to drive over to Tennessee and bring him a case of liquor 'cause he's too lazy to go get it hisself. Tells me to advise my customers to vote for his cousin Floyd next mayor's race." Herman paused and grinned. "Had to give out flyers last year. Guess which trash can I threw them in."

Connor chuckled. "I always thought when Tallulah graduated, I might leave." He hesitated, hardly believing he'd said the words. "But with Mom going downhill, Tempy . . . I don't know what'll happen to her."

"Sissy and I can't leave. It's 1975, economy is in the toilet. Go to a big city and get swallowed up. Tell you who ain't hurting. The Starks. Starks always end up on top."

"That's it, isn't it." Connor shook his head, agreeing. "The economy. Still, seems like we're due a little justice."

The bottom of the sun dipped into the mountains. The men shifted toward the east to avoid the blinding rays. If there were thoughts of how they might make their world a little more even against the forces of barbarism neither spoke them. They were as two prisoners of war trying to get along with captors in order to survive one more day. Connor wondered how long it would take the Feds to act on his and Holly's information. He wondered if they would pursue the information at all.

"Waiting on justice," Herman said, pointing toward the mountain range. "Until then, we have this."

A tooting horn drew the attention of a few tourists admiring the view. The parking lot was an eighth of a mile downhill, but trees obscured the area. "Herman Cahill!" a voice yelled from that direction. "Herman Cahill!" The two men trotted toward the parking lot as the call continued. They caught sight of a man standing on the roof of a blue Pinto, hands cupped around his mouth. "Herman Cahill!"

The man saw them and jumped to the ground in a running sprint. "Troy?" Herman called out to his cousin.

"Gotta hurry," Troy said, grabbing Herman by the shoulders. "Jason's been taken to Fort Sanders Hospital in Knoxville. Sissy rode in the ambulance."

"My son," Herman said, as the words froze his muscles. Connor pulled him along. "His stomach?"

"Sissy said yes," Troy babbled, giving Herman the keys to the Pinto. "Take my car. She said something about they might have to operate."

"The gas station," he muttered.

Connor could see Herman's mind flooding with all his responsibilities, all the worries that could become problems. The stress etched in his forehead of what could go wrong next. "We'll take care of it," Connor volunteered. "You go. Drive careful!"

Connor and Troy watched the Pinto zoom down the mountain. Then, the sudden quiet of the land . . . then the birds in the trees overhead chirped like wildfire, all seeming to say, *Hurry, your child needs you.*

286

Back at the gas station, Troy showed Connor how to work the cash register and fill out receipts if anybody asked for one.

"It's mostly a cash business, Mr. Herne," Troy explained, eyeing a backroom whose door was padlocked, "so you won't have any troubles. Anybody want something you can't handle–a fan belt or tire rotation, just have 'em come back when I'm here."

"I think I can handle a fan belt or two," Connor said, making a mental note of the supplies hanging on the wall. The men agreed to split the shifts. Troy took the day when Connor was at school, and Connor would relieve him at six p.m., keeping the station as normal as possible to avoid drawing any Stark attention.

Early evening Herman called. Jason had a burst appendix. The worry in his friend's voice vibrated and caught in his throat. Connor assured him that his son would be fine but wished he felt the confidence he expressed, knowing the precarious medical situation this was for the boy. The worrisome situation drew his heart closer to his own daughter, who he guessed was swinging to the ceiling at her slumber party. Before hanging up, he assured Herman he'd keep a low profile, and likely the Starks would never know he was gone.

"I don't know how to thank you," Herman said.

"Not necessary. That's what friends do, along with drinking all your coffee." He sat at Herman's desk with folded hands after he'd hung up, thinking about the years he and Herman Cahill had behind them; he thought about the blue devil prank from childhood, the trashy blond whose life they'd saved, and how he'd ended up with Darius Stark's silver lighter; he remembered the evenings out at the pond at Copperhead Fields, and then, faster than they'd realized, the mundane responsibilities of adulthood seized them and they bore it like heavy loads of coal. Life had lived itself, and here they were, middle-aged men who railed at their own excuses for not making better choices. Connor dropped to his knees and prayed for his friend's son. When he opened his eyes, his gaze fell to some papers stapled to blue cardboard underneath the desk. He leaned lower and looked at them, seeing that a fake shelf had been fashioned under the main drawer. Connor hesitated, knowing that whatever was there was Herman's business. He figured the Starks had made him compliant in some of their scams and wondered how deeply his friend might have been pulled in. Gently, he took out the papers. Looking through the documentation stunned him, inspired him, and gave him more respect for Herman Cahill than if he'd been a war hero and Superman combined.

Herman was keeping track of every dollar the Starks ran through his business. He had a detailed list of stolen merchandise and dates that matched robberies as far away as Lexington. Connor looked toward the padlocked room at the back of the station. There was a card of an FBI agent named Zachary Gates and one for a federal prosecutor, Nolan Greer. There was also a sales document for the gas station where it appeared Herman had tried to buy his business but Darius had written over the purchase price the words *Not Accepted*. Connor bristled as he looked at the *DS* initials, red-inked letters that reminded him of blood.

Some day, he thought, Herman Cahill is going to hand you your ass just the way I did years ago, and you'll never even know what hit you, Darius Stark. Connor replaced the papers just as he'd found them, then gave a couple of teenagers a free few gallons of gas, he felt so good.

Around seven o'clock, George Perkins brought his Monte Carlo in for its weekly detailing. Connor found coveralls hanging on a nail and donned a gray work cap before beginning to vacuum the rear seat. He stopped for a cup of coffee, and his gaze kept returning to the padlocked door. He went over and fingered the lock, looked around the side of the building but didn't find any window into the room. Far as he could tell, the room was an add-on to the original building.

Back to vacuuming, alarm shot through him when he caught sight of a red-haired man in the car's rearview mirror. Simon Tuller, Randi Jo's husband. Connor switched off the vacuum, his muscles tensing as he wondered what he should do. Tuller glanced his direction but showed no recognition. Connor dipped his head and adjusted the cap low across his brow.

"Going to the backroom, Troy," Simon called out toward him.

Connor nodded, restarted the vacuum cleaner, and watched Simon reach to the top of the doorframe and pull down a key. He entered the room, not bothering to shut the door behind him. Leaving the vacuum running to cover any sound, Connor glided toward the open door and peered inside. Stacks of boxed TV sets lined the wall as well as radios, air conditioners, toaster ovens, and several slot machines. Gambling had been outlawed since the 1950s, but that a law had been passed would never deter a Stark, as the money-eating machines were stashed in most of the businesses they owned.

Simon worked at opening a crate sitting on the floor between a file cabinet and a safe. He pried open the top and pulled out a slim red stick. Dynamite. Connor's breath caught in his throat as he watched Tuller flip it in the air and catch it with his other hand. Inching his way back to the Monte Carlo, Connor continued vacuuming, peeking over as Simon carried out the box and replaced the key on the top ledge.

A tremble shot through his limbs and he held his breath when Simon carelessly anchored the box against his hip and ambled toward a van parked out on the street without a word to *Troy*. Soon as he pulled away, Connor retrieved the key and opened the room.

Relieved that he found no more dynamite, he eyed the stacks of stolen goods, a few boxes marked with the name of a Lexington store. Along the far wall were stacks of papers. Peeling through them, he found insurance claims for burnt buildings, deposit tickets for more money than the gas station would ever have taken in, and a ledger of payoffs to state and local politicians, even a few area police chiefs. Insurance fraud, money laundering, and a little payola on the side. Connor shook his head at the brazenness with which the Starks operated and, unbelievably, got away with. Other than Herman, he was sure no law enforcement had them on the radar. Connor hoped Herman would get his federal friends to move on the Starks soon before they did something as foolhardy as put more dynamite in the back of his business.

After finishing up Mr. Perkins's car, Connor decided to check on Tallulah. Before he could pick up the receiver, the phone rang. He listened to a man swearing at him, and figuring it was a wrong number, hung up and called his daughter. "Sweet Home Alabama" played in the background along with hysterical laughter and over-talk of teenage girls.

"We're fine, Mr. Herne," one of the girls yelled over Tallulah's own assurances that all was well.

"Except your daughter dances the hustle like a she's on seventy-eight speed. You're old enough to remember that, aren't you, Mr. Herne?" another called out, making Connor laugh aloud.

He no sooner hung up when the phone rang again. The same cursing man. "Buddy," Connor said, "slow down, can't make out a decent word you're saying." The man continued to cuss. "Sure you got the right number?" The tirade continued and Connor hung up again. He waited for a few seconds, but the caller didn't call back.

Evening traffic slowed around nine o'clock, and Connor sipped a second cup of coffee. He looked over the sales document to the gas station again, wishing there was something he could do to help

Herman. In the distance, a siren, no, a horn beeping, then a long whine as if someone were pressing it non-stop. Connor wondered if an alarm was going off; maybe the bank on the next street was being robbed. He watched the empty street. No movement other than the changing traffic lights. A car shot through a red light on the distant block and the sound of the horn grew louder. The driver careened through the next light as well, swerving into the filling station, missing the pump by inches, and stopping short of the front door at a perpendicular angle. Connor stepped back, shocked that the car hadn't plowed into the building.

The car door opened and a disheveled man held on to it to keep himself standing.

"Where is that dang sonnavagun, sorry-assed slacker?" Darius Stark weaved toward the building, pausing to steady himself against one of the gas pumps.

Connor stayed put, waiting until the portly man staggered to the open bay. For several seconds Darius seemed confused, then circled around to the office and slung open the door like he didn't care if the glass broke or not.

"Can I help you?" Connor asked, realizing that the swearing man from the phone calls now stood before him.

"Who are you?" Darius swayed, his lips smacking together as if he were eating. "I don't know ye."

"I'm helping out. Herman had an emergency with his–"

"Blast his emergency! I had an emergency!" With one hand, he swiped half the desk clear as if to make a point rather than being aware of what he was doing.

"His son was rushed into surgery, taken to Knoxville by ambulance."

"You ever tried to have a party and no liquor? Herman Cahill, blast him, was supposed to deliver five cases to my house by six o'clock, not a second later!"

Connor paused, wondering what part of *emergency, son, surgery,* and *ambulance,* the swaying man was not hearing. "I'm sure he'd have done it, if not for Jason. I mean, it's his child."

"Blast his son! He works for me, and nothing comes before me!" He plopped down in a chair opposite the desk and belched. "Not a pretty sight, party with no booze. Not a pretty one a'tall. Got a mind to fire Cahill's rear end. If not for me, my sister would be over here haranguing his ass." He stared toward the open door into the carport. "There's devils back there." Swaying and blinking his eyes, he seemed to forget that Connor stood beside him.

There was no smell of alcohol on Darius, who had the glazed look of an impaired man.

"Want some coffee?"

"Shoot. Coffee. I wanna wake up, I pop a handful of yellow jackets." He sniffed, wiped his nose, a hand on his stomach now and then as if he might upchuck. "My brother Jonas said he'd shoot Doc Manley if he wrote me another prescription. I told Doc I'd shoot him if he didn't!" Darius succumbed to hysterical laughter, slapping his knee and repeating *shoot him if he didn't.* He reached for Connor's coffee and struggled with unbuttoning his shirt pocket. Pulling a red pill from his pocket he snickered and looked at Connor. "Need me a little red devil to calm my nerves."

Connor handed him the coffee and watched him wash down the red pill.

The phone rang, interrupting a slur of mumbling. Darius sat straight and stared at the receiver as Connor picked it up. George Perkins said he was on his way to pick up his car. Staring down at Darius as he swallowed another red devil, an impression formed in Connor's mind. An idea . . . he wasn't sure it would work, but if it did . . . if it did . . . If it did, there'd be no more waiting for justice. He would knock Darius Stark back a step or two. With Darius's wasted state, Connor might just be able to pull it off. He was no stranger to devils . . . a red devil indeed. In his mind, he heard a chortle of girlish giggling.

"You know my sister," Darius said to no one. "She's got no use for me."

"Know the feeling," Connor said to him, keeping the phone to his ear.

"Hell of a thing for your sister to hate your guts."

Connor continued holding the phone after George had hung up and let his eyes widen as he stared at Darius. "Seriously?" he said, an alarmed tone soaking up the words. "Mr. Stark's right here. I'll tell him, but I want to make sure I understand . . . a raid tonight, an hour or so . . . ten to twenty in federal prison if . . . Yeah, I understand." He hung up the phone and wiped his brow, turned away from Darius then faced him, biting his lip as if he didn't know which way to turn.

"What?" Darius asked, holding out his palms.

"That was your cousin . . . the one that's spying on the FBI, least that's who he said it was . . . don't think anybody would play a trick, do ya?" He bet that in Darius's impaired state, he'd not have the faculties to reason out what Connor would tell him. Stark's paranoid and suspicious nature would be fertile ground for planting seeds of confusion.

"Stop wasting my blamed time! What'd he say?"

Connor swallowed hard and bit his lip, letting his chest heave up and down in a nervous tremor. "Said the FBI was gonna raid this place tonight, got a tip about some illegal goings-on." Connor raised his hands, patting the air, but kept darting glances toward the padlocked door in the back of the station. "I don't know anything. I just filled in for the emergency. Maybe I ought to go home. This is your property. You're the one who should stay."

"No, wait." Darius stood up, paced from the door to the wall, washing his hands in the air and looking as if he wanted to vomit. "Damn it! I always knew this place was cursed. Got ghosts, you know, weaving all around the tire section." He dug deep in his pocket and mouthed a couple of yellow pills, not bothering with liquid to wash them down. "How in blazes did the FBI find out about this place?"

"I don't know, and I don't care." Connor held out the keys to the building for him to take. "This is your building. You need to be here when they come. You need to explain."

Sweat popped out on his nose and forehead, the thought of returning to prison sinking into his trembling muscles. "Cahill's the tenant. How would I know what he keeps in his building?"

"'Cause he don't have a key," Connor said, hoping he could bluff the addled, drug-festered man. His eyes shot toward the padlocked room then back to Darius. "But, you know, hmmmm. You know what you could do . . ."

"What?" he demanded, his breath quickening. "Got an idea, let's hear it."

"Well," Connor piddled, letting the tension settle into Darius's bones. "What if you didn't own the building?" He reached under the desk and pulled out the deed. "I was organizing these papers and found this. What if you sold it to Herman Cahill right now? His signature's already here. If you sold it to him, then he'd own it, not you."

"Yeah, he'd own it. It'd be on Cahill's back." He rubbed his chin. "Blamed ghosts would haunt him then, not me. Blamed devil take him as well as the FBI."

"Guess they would at that," Connor agreed, and nodded his head feverishly.

"Oughta call my attorney first."

"Your cousin said the law was on its way. Not much time." George Perkins opened the door, and Darius jumped back a foot, expecting the full force of the FBI to throw him in handcuffs. "Mr. Perkins here can witness," Connor said. "I'll be the other witness."

Darius grabbed the paper and scrawled his signature, nervously looking out at the street as if expecting law enforcement lights and sirens to enter blazing. "There," he said, thrusting the paper at Perkins to sign. "I don't own it. Nobody can say I own this building."

Connor walked Darius to his car. "I'll make sure the FBI sees it. I mean, I'm just a fill-in for the night. Nobody can hold me responsible, right?"

"Right, son," he said in an affable tone, letting out a hearty chuckle. He slapped Connor on the back, shooting him a wide smile. "You tell Cahill I'm pissed about that liquor, and I expect to be paid every cent on that deed, and hey, thank you."

"Don't mention it," Connor said and smiled back. "That's what friends are for."

After he'd gone, Connor retrieved the pen that he'd signed with and marked the amount *paid in full*. He initialed Darius's elaborate *DS* and stuffed the deed in his pocket. George Perkins wasn't sure what he'd walked in on, but like most Quinntown residents didn't cause a fuss over anything a Stark wanted to do. Connor would take care of all the legal paperwork and have it all done before Darius sobered up from his drug haze. If he even remembered what had happened that evening, he might be in jail before he realized he no longer owned Herman's garage.

Before he left that evening, Connor took the home number of the federal prosecutor and drove over the state line, then found a pay phone at a gas station in Harrogate, Tennessee. Since he'd started the ball rolling, he might as well finish one last poke at them.

He dialed and cleared his throat when the federal prosecutor answered.

"Man named Simon Tuller's got a box of dynamite in his van," he said to the sleepy man, who was instantly alert after hearing his words and asked for more detail. "Don't drive around with something like that unless you're gonna use it. You might want to investigate. You know Tuller . . . he's a Stark."

35

Perhaps there was no reason for Connor Herne to remember the particulars from his college physics classes so long ago, but the lessons about cause and effect might have served him well about now. For what he'd set in motion that night at Herman's gas station would haunt him more than any specter that lived in his imagination. A few days passed and hubris set in. Darius Stark had yet to discover he no longer owned the gas station. The more time that passed, the less claim Darius could prove. The sole other witness to the deed, George Perkins, was an old man who suffered from bouts of gout and had already had one kidney removed, so if the ruse could outlive him, then Darius would have little recourse. Connor filed all the necessary paperwork with a nod and a wink to a high school buddy who worked at city hall. He'd pulled one over on a Stark without a drop of bloodshed, nary a bruise or any hoopla of argument. He'd gotten away with a prank for the ages.

But today, the friends and family didn't worry about the battles to come. Today was about celebration. Herman and Sissy had returned from Knoxville with a healthy child and a reason to celebrate, for Sissy had found out she was pregnant again, and Tallulah would graduate high school and take her first tenuous steps out into the world all on her own. She had been well trained, prepared, and educated, and yet . . . Connor worried as he watched his daughter standing at the door of the steakhouse waiting for her mother. At the table, Wallis, Tempy, and Iona struggled to make conversation with two of Tallulah's girlfriends along with Herman and Sissy. Connor scooted out of his chair and came up behind her. "I'm sure she'll make the graduation, 'Lulah. Come back to the table now. Derby pie is being served."

"I think she bought me this white dress I really wanted." Tallulah scanned the parking lot, gaze shifting to the highway as far as she could see. "Maybe she's late because she's at the store buying it."

"That's probably it," Connor said, wishing he could take this anxiety away from her. "I'll call their house again."

At the pay phone he noticed Herman excusing himself from the table, but instead of going to the men's room he circled around to where Connor was searching out dimes for the pay phone.

"They may not be coming," he said, and glanced to the floor then back to the table. Herman dipped his head and whispered, "Sorry I couldn't tell you before. It's all happening tonight."

"What did you do, Herman?" Connor asked. "Please tell me you're not trying to take on these people by yourself."

"Last week when Jason got sick, and Darius cussed me like one of his dogs, I decided. I turned in everything I had on the whole bunch of them and told the FBI where to find every slot machine, every bootlegger, every warehouse full of stolen merchandise, and boxes of cash that have never been taxed."

"FBI pushed you into this too soon."

"My son's not going to live under Stark rule. None of my kids are, ever again."

"They'll come after you. We needed more time to prepare, to round up people on our side to protect our backs."

"I'm not hiding anymore."

Connor shook off a nervous tremor as the knowledge of what was about to happen to the Starks settled into him. "We could have taken on Darius, but all of them? We both need to be carrying our guns."

"I thought about what you said–about our wasted lives. I remembered what you did all those years ago . . . calling the state police on Darius. That was brave. I couldn't have done this without knowing you. Without looking at the example of what a man is."

"But they never knew my name," Connor said, putting a hand on his friend's shoulder, more to steady himself as he absorbed the information and implications. "You're the bravest man I know, Herman Cahill." Breath shivered from his throat and he swallowed hard. "I'm proud to call you my friend."

"FBI put some protection on me, but that won't last forever, so I'm making my stand."

Connor grinned, hardly believing what he was hearing and knowing the dangerous line they'd both crossed. "You must know Agent Parilla," he said, looking around to make sure no one was listening. "Holly had me show him where I saw those nuclear waste barrels long time back."

Herman crossed his arms, one hand stroking his chin. "I know everybody in that office, Connor. Nobody named Parilla."

"You're sure?"

"There's a task force over the whole of southeast Kentucky looking into this stuff. I even met the Washington, DC folk."

"They've set her up," Connor realized, shaking his head at the gall and remembering the odd way Parilla had looked at him when they were alone up at the mine. Connor wondered if Parilla had taken him up there to kill him and realized he'd lost his chance when Connor pulled out his own firearm. "I gotta warn Holly." He glanced back at the table. "Randi Jo. What'll happen to her?"

"Starks don't tell their women nothing, and that's not who the FBI is after anyway. Simon gets caught up in this and arrested, probably be the best thing that ever happened to Randi Jo." He paused and looked at the floor. "I'm sorry it had to happen today," he nodded toward Tallulah, "on her day. Wasn't my call."

Connor watched his daughter, her gaze returning again and again toward the parking lot. This was for the best. Randi Jo could be free of the Starks today, even if she did miss Tallulah's graduation. A soothing relief flooded Connor's chest as the two men walked back to the table, taking their seats among the people they loved. He glanced briefly at Iona, who was chatting about velvet cake recipes with Sissy. She held her teacherish superiority even in her off-time. Being a Stark only enhanced it. The clan would be taken by surprise, but Connor was under no illusions that they would hit back hard. He and Herman needed to get organized, surround themselves with their own posse, people who were sick of the Starks. There were plenty of them around. Tallulah looked up at him with an expectant and hopeful expression. He leaned over and whispered in her ear, "I know she'll be at the graduation if she can, and you know that, too. We'll have to be satisfied with that for now."

She nodded, trying to smile.

Connor loaded the three kids in his car to drive to the high school while everyone else made their way in their own vehicles. He hoped Randi Jo had driven over by herself and would be waiting at the auditorium. If there were mass arrests of the Stark family tonight, then better she not be at home, better she be kept in the dark until the Starks were behind bars, hopefully her husband as well. Maybe he could talk some sense into her, convince her to come back to Contrary. He'd help Randi Jo get a place to live, a job, whatever it took. Connor's thoughts drifted to the years he and his former wife spent together. He landed on happy thoughts: the graze of her hand across his back, the care she gave to mending his clothes, the way she studied a recipe, trying to make the most tasty meal for the family. Family . . . she'd been his family, and he should have taken better care of it. *If not him, then who?* Yes, him. He would help get Randi Jo out of the mess that was the Stark family. Now, he had a second chance.

"Are you nervous?" Connor asked Tallulah over the babbling of her friends, excited as they checked each other's golden-colored graduation gowns.

"Taking deep breaths," she said, and adjusted her cap, the tassel swaying and tapping her cheek.

Amused and grateful that the teenage chatter kept his daughter occupied, he began to feel hopeful as the girls' excitement rubbed off on him. It was a good time for them, and he told himself to keep focused on the future.

"Kids," Connor called out. "Brief detour, but we won't be late." He parked in the library parking lot and left the radio on for them. "Gotta run over here for a minute but I'll be right back." He glanced down the street before crossing, his mind registering someone at the corner phone booth as he trotted across then headed toward the rear of Selma's Beauty Shop. Holly lived in an apartment up above. It'd only take a few seconds, but he had to let her know to stay away from the fake FBI agent.

As he approached, Holly came speeding down the back exterior staircase. He called out to her but she kept going, her blond hair flouncing with each step. "Holly!" he yelled her name again.

She turned but did not stop. "My sister's in the hospital. I have to go!" She opened the car door and slid in.

Connor stopped advancing toward her, hoping she'd stop as she drove past him. He looked back toward his own car and the girls moving their hands in animated speech . . . but they weren't alone. The Black Dahlia was lounging against the front of his car. She slid off the hood, and he froze in place. Rushing toward him, through him, white noise filled his ears and his mind spun in distorted images: Bette Moss, Mrs. Worden, and Sharon Tate circled him, a vortex of death that sucked breath from his body like a deflating balloon as they sang a song with words he couldn't make out.

"Holly," he said, just as a force of air knocked him to the ground. There must have been a sound, a crunch of metal. He must have seen the explosion, for he'd not covered his eyes, but even many years later he had trouble remembering the exact event. What memories stayed with him were like flashes of an ill-cut movie: The teenagers running to him. Ushering them back to the safety of the car. Sprinting to the corner pay phone, dialing, dialing . . . it hit him. Someone else had dialed before this. Who? The Black Dahlia? No. A man. A policeman. Cap pulled low. Rusty? He wasn't sure. He wouldn't know until later that Holly's sister was not in the hospital. A ruse to get her into her car that had dynamite rigged to the starter? Dynamite carried by Simon Tuller from Herman's garage? Given to whom . . . the boy who liked to blow things up? He would wonder for many years if Rusty had made that call.

A few men from a nearby grocery store worked to lift wooden beams from the collapsed garage roof off the hood of the car. Connor squeezed underneath after the men braced the roof and reached inside the car to hold Holly's hand. Her face turned toward him, eyes wide, mouth slightly ajar, the shock of what had happened blinding her to reality. Oddly, the radio was playing, an Elton John song, "Candle in the Wind." Connor reached over her and turned it off.

One side of her cheek was raw from the windshield exploding into her face. Her gaze fell onto the side view mirror and Connor quickly angled it away from her.

"Why'd you turn off the radio?" she asked.

"Help is coming," he said, not knowing if it was true.

"I can't hear you. Talk louder. My hair's all messed up." She hiccupped for air, eyes averted to her twisted, broken body. "They've killed me, Connor," she said. "They've killed me."

The smell of charred flesh mixed with a gunpowder odor, and Connor worked feverishly at pulling open the car door so he could get her out, but it would not budge. "Call the fire department," he yelled behind him at the men who'd worked to free the car from the rubble. They all gathered around him, and Connor realized there was no more to do. Expressions of shock gave way to a churning sense of horror. One man covered his mouth with a hand; a younger man turned and threw up.

Holly looked down at her fragmented legs, a bone torn through the skin of her thigh, the other leg hanging more than connected to her body. Connor put a finger under her chin to hold her head in his direction. "You still got breath in you," he said, wanting to will his strength into her broken limbs. "Live, Holly. Avenge yourself on these people." He wanted to believe that somehow she might make it, but his rationality knew that she was right . . . *they* . . . had killed her.

The fire truck pulled up, followed by an ambulance.

"It hurts, Connor. It hurts so bad."

"Can't you give her something?" he asked, nodding toward the band of firemen as they surveyed a scene for which they had no experience.

303

"She can't feel anything," one of them said. "It's not physical pain she's talking about."

Connor leaned as close as he could get to her and whispered, "Holly, there's a place and I'm going to take you there." She stared into his eyes as he described the amber hills shading the cabin, the lavender sky and bountiful daffodils more gold than yellow. Then, in the last minutes of her life, Holly began singing. The sound, a hoarse whisper, soared with the power of heartbreak, as if her essence were floating away with the music of her voice:

"Lord, you know I love everybody,
Deep down in my heart,
Lord, you know I love my brother
Deep down in my heart
Lord, you know I love my sister
Deep down in my heart
Lord, you know I love everybody
Deep down in my heart."

He recognized the words of a gospel song he hadn't heard since he was a child going to Notown Baptist, then Holly Waller, a daughter of Notown, looked beyond him and smiled just before she died.

❧

Tallulah didn't make it to her graduation, but then neither did Randi Jo. His ex-wife disappeared that day. So did Simon. Whether she was alive or dead, he would not know for many years. The FBI and state police swooped in that night, arresting several Starks and a bucketload of their kin and henchmen. Through the coming months, he would hear of the indictments, follow the grand jury rumors, and delight in handcuffed Starks proclaiming their innocence. Herman would be the chief witness against them, and for a while, he and his family were placed into protective custody. Finally, it seemed a little justice had filtered down to the ranks of the ordinary men and women of the town. But despite the arrests and investigations, no one would ever be charged with Holly's murder.

Two weeks after Holly's death, Tallulah left for college. She stood at the bus platform, waiting to be the last to board. Turning to her father, she chose her words with a deliberate focus. "I know the good life you've given me," she said to him. "And I won't waste it. One day the reckoning of these evil men will be laid open for the world to see, but I see it now. I see what you always knew, and I'll never forget it." She hugged him and got on the bus, choosing the seat closest to the front. After she sat, she touched her palm to the window, and he nodded to her. As the bus pulled away, she stared forward and did not look back.

Behind him, thunder rumbled. He stared into the darkening sky. Gray clouds moved toward him like an angry goddess plotting her path. As he turned to look after the bus curving down the road and out of sight, tears rose in Connor's eyes as he repeated her words to himself: *"One day the reckoning of these evil men will be laid open for the world to see . . ."* His daughter just might be the wisest person he'd ever known. She was on a light beam, riding out of the mountains, and he prayed to God that she never came back.

⁓

Back at the Pinnacle, far above the clatter of their world, two men shook hands. Today would be the first day of a holy siege. From this day forward, every act, every deed, every thought, every word would be directed at bringing worry and trouble to the Stark family.

Connor Herne and Herman Cahill declared war. As they drove away in separate directions, armed with a mission, they dedicated themselves to that hallowed judgment day. They lived under the radar by day and took notes by night. Feeding information to law enforcement under the code name Blue Devil, the two men laid waste to the stronghold that had once ruled Crimson County. By the time they were done, more than thirty-five Starks were in prison.

PROLOGUE FIVE

September 1, 1981

The happiest day of Tempy's life was the morning Wayne Bacon died. During the following days of bereavement, she acted the sympathetic and consoling friend, but when she was alone, her joy burst out in a gleeful rendition of Peaches and Herb's "Reunited." After Wayne's cancer-infested carcass was lowered into the ground, she let loose a sigh that caused Iona's uncles to glare at her. Recovering by dabbing her eyes, she nodded deferentially toward them. Hateful, repulsive men, fat and slovenly pigs, unable to show the decorum of controlling their revulsion toward her, much less their raucous appetites. Tempy wished every misery of old age upon them. Far as she was concerned, the sooner they were dead, the better.

Every Sunday for a month, Iona was required to deliver flowers to her husband's grave and stand reverently at the headstone in gracious prayer. On the last day of that long month of mourning, Tempy waited in the car, feet jacked up on the dashboard, singing "Me and Bobby McGee" along with Janis Joplin on the radio. Yes, freedom was just another word. And surely, the two women had nothing to lose. Iona had done her duty by family. Finally, she was done. Emancipation. Iona had her freedom, and now, Tempy wanted hers.

⸎

It was not Wayne Bacon's grave that Tempy found herself duty bound to visit again and again, but rather her own brother's and that woman buried with him. Standing on the Lester Street Bridge, she pondered the orange rock embedded in the ground marking the spot. It was not so much the idea of death that preoccupied her thoughts, but rather the power of knowing this secret. She'd held on to this information for so long that it festered like a nasty cut that wouldn't heal. But now, time had come when she needed to use it.

She watched the man who used her brother's name park his blue Oldsmobile '98 in the alley beside the Regal Hotel. Looking both ways before crossing the street, he shot her that quizzical expression that always annoyed the bejesus out of her. As he approached, her grip tightened on the straw handbag held in front of her like a shield and she fought the urge to crack her knuckles. The tight bun of her hair caused a headache that she ignored. She needed every bit of her wits, and she let the rage of a lifetime fuel it.

"My mother never loved me," she said to this Connor Herne. As expected, he had no response, only the flat-faced anxiety of having been caught off guard. "You were such a charmer as child. Not a Herne trait. Mom and Pop fell in love like you were a lost puppy."

He dipped his head, a familiar frustration easing into his brow. "You brought me out here for this old fight?" Anchoring his arms on the bridge rail, he stared into the brackish canal water and shook off a shiver as his eyes darted toward the dark underneath the bridge. "I'm not having it again."

"What you think is of no importance. No one's left to sing your praises or hang on your every word like you were Moses watering the burning bush. You're just a humdrum school teacher who's failed at what should have been a brilliant life."

"You have got to be the cruelest women I have ever known, and I have no idea why I've put up with you for as long as I have."

A cackle of laughter erupted like a pot boiled over. "I am not cruel, but I'm not good either. I'm only what this hypocritical town made me. I've bided my time. I've waited and I've acted the part just like everybody said I should, and now I am going to take what I want, do what I want, and there is no one to stop me."

He held his breath. No dumb one, the pseudo-brother of hers. He knew how to divine between the lines. Standing straight and forcing his body to turn toward her, he whispered, "What have you done?"

It must be her smirk, she thought, that told him she now owned the day. She held his gaze longer than necessary, enjoying his apprehension. "I put the old bat into the rest home, and I've sold the store." A short giggle escaped her lips. More nervous energy than mirth. Another giggle slipped out as his uneasy expression changed to misery.

He stepped back, looking at her as a person he didn't recognize. "The doctor said Mom should stay in familiar surroundings. Tempy, think on this." He leaned toward her, hands slicing the air like an ax chopping wood. "Keeping her at home was the plan. We discussed it. You agreed."

"Then keep her at your home, I don't care."

"I keep her weekends. You know I have to teach." His eyes narrowed as a white feather drifted through the space between them, then another, as if an exotic bird had shed its outer layer just for them. "And to sell the store, without even telling me. What about Baylor? The other people we hired? What about. . ." He stopped, appearing to realize that he argued with the wind. He caught a third feather and looked up to the sky. No bird. Only white clouds mushrooming into gray.

"I've put half the money in a bank account that will pay my part of the nursing home, the rest I'm taking, and Iona and I are moving to Florida. After our vacation there last year, we decided to go back and stay."

"You can't make decisions about Mom without me."

"Want to fight me, go ahead and try." Now she turned on him, filled with the power of blasphemy. "You're not their son," she said, arm outstretched, pointing to the orange rock without realizing it. "Tangle with me, and I'll drag that old lady through the mud with a story that'll make the Herne name rhyme with evil for a generation." Her legs trembled, and she placed a hand on the bridge railing to steady herself. "This gives you legal control of Mom," she said, pulling an envelope from the straw purse and thrusting it toward him. "Once I'm in Florida, we're never coming back."

"She's your mother." His mouth slightly agape, Connor was stunned. "I don't understand."

"You wouldn't. You've always floated in this little bubble of perfection where nothing gets dirty. You've had a wife, a child. I got nothing but resentment and puritanical judgment. It's me that's got to live what life I have left." She shivered out the last of her breath and inhaled anew. He stared at her, his expression grown more toward confusion than hurt as he struggled with whether or not to believe her. She knew he wanted proof, but this Connor Herne hadn't convinced her that he was worthy of it. "You back off. Let me live free and the way I want. Then, when Mom dies, I'll tell you where to find the bones of your mother."

"I would have let you live however you wanted without blackmail."

"Maybe," she said, fighting a tremor of her lower lip, "but you've never helped either." She weaved around him, determined not to look back, every step a march on the path to freedom.

"What do you want me to tell Tallulah?"

Tempy halted like someone had struck her. A gloved hand covered her mouth, trying to hold in the swell of emotion that burst out in one sobbing howl. Turning, she clenched her hands into fists, shook them in front of her, and willed the return of her self-control. She heaved breath in hoarse gasps. "Don't be so smart as to think this hasn't cost me." She stared at his shoes, unable to look up into his eyes. A cool breeze flowed from the upstream. "You and I, we made of life what we could. And now, I'm calling it quits. I'm taking my fifty percent, and I'm going to live the rest of my days happy." She coughed, hacking up yellow bile that she spit over the side of the bridge. Wiping her lips on the back of her glove, she closed her eyes and steadied herself. "You try and do the same, but know this, Connor . . . I don't owe you anything. You came into my life and you took. Even if you didn't know it. Even if it wasn't your fault. Infant that you were, you still took everything that was mine. Be grateful for once that I left you the money I did." Tempy sniffed again, a quivering wave of emotion shooting through her chest. "Tell Tallulah I love her, and I'll send a postcard."

And with those true words, Temperance Herne walked the length of Marcescent Street and settled into the front seat of Iona Stark's Mercedes-Benz. As they drove the winding road across Cumberland Mountain, neither woman spoke. In the backseat, Iona's daughter read a *Teen Beat* magazine from a pile they'd bought her for the trip.

Tempy cracked her knuckles, then reached over and held Iona's hand as they cleared the mountaintop and faced the rising sun over the mellow hills of Powell Valley, Tennessee. They were off and they were free. And yet, the spell of the past hadn't cleared from their damaged souls. No more than thirty miles from home, Tempy's hand left Iona's and went to her throat. Another choking fit overtook her, and Iona pulled the car to the side of the road. Tempy jerked open the door and fell onto a grassy bank. Heaving racked her body as she sucked in air. Iona and the girl raced to Tempy's side and began patting her back and stroking her arms. As the two women looked into each other's eyes, the pain of their half-lived lives seeped like fake tears from a conman's Madonna. Neither could speak. It was the child that read their thoughts. "We have to go back."

DOROTHY,
DOMINIQUE,
AND DIAN

36

August 1982

Holly's death changed everything for Connor and Herman. The war the two men declared brought down a dynasty of corruption and shifted the tempo of Crimson County. Law enforcement moved in the night of Holly's murder, leaving two dead in a shoot-out on the outskirts of Coalfire and a missing FBI agent whose body was never found. Stark compatriots went on the run, including Randi Jo's husband, Simon, who was captured in Arizona a year later and charged with kidnapping his own child from a woman he'd never married. Connor had no idea what'd happened to Randi Jo. As the years had passed and she never contacted Tallulah, he wondered if Simon had killed his ex-wife and she might lie buried in an unmarked grave far from home. It hurt him inside to think about her, and he wished he'd done more to help her escape that Stark marriage. On those days, he'd say a silent prayer for the little girl with the big green eyes who put cardboard in her shoes and sang songs to the sun. He'd finally come to a place where he'd forgiven Randi Jo for what happened with Rusty, and with the grace of time, he could see his own part in the way their marriage had fallen apart. Connor still kept a distance from Rusty, who'd floundered after his Stark bosses lost control of the county, but he managed to stay in the fringe of those who were left and picked up crumbs whenever a Stark needed to keep their fingertips clean.

The FBI looked into whether the dynamite used to blow up Holly's car could be connected to the Starks, but nothing came of the investigation, and neither Willie nor Rusty were ever connected to her murder. Floyd Stark managed to hold on to the mayor's office by grace of a supporter named Gentry; others fled to Coalfire, where their nefarious deeds were more tolerated. They weren't gone, but they were beaten back a step, and for a while, life unfolded in a predictable, though imperfect, existence.

Connor spent his days nurturing his most gifted students and looking after his mother, but his most enjoyable time was when he and Herman hiked the deep woods. Here the men found the stillness of peace where the only conflict was watching the birds battle for territory in the overhead tree limbs. Thinking that after his mother's death he might leave Contrary and move closer to Tallulah, he adapted and bided his time. His daughter would soon be taking a job with the *Washington Post* after having worked at the *Lexington Herald* since graduating from the University of Kentucky. But plans have a way of shifting with the circumstances that drive individuals: injustices they've seen as youths that they want to make right; a gutful of ire that yearns for a dose of comeuppance; a vengeful goddess determined to balance the scales. As an old man, Connor would look back on this day as the time Tallulah *laid down the law.* It was the week of her Granny Gaylor's funeral. Throughout the service, he could tell she'd been in deep thought, hoping her mother might show up, watching the entrance of the funeral home the way she had the door of the restaurant years ago on graduation night.

But in August of 1982 the events that shaped Connor Herne's old age hadn't yet lived themselves out. The day began with the last class of Crimson County High summer school, a place where the friendless sought refuge for the vacation months and those with no interest in applying themselves during the regular school year sought to catch up with the more ambitious of their classmates.

Connor hadn't looked at a dirty magazine since his college days. The glossy he confiscated from Knox and Kyle Pomeroy was a doozy. Yes, Pomeroy, twin sons of the Little Preacher Boy, who'd opened a tent church out near the highway. It was an old, tattered issue of *Playboy.* Dorothy Stratten was on the cover. Stratten's husband had viciously murdered the young starlet, and Connor figured that was the reason the boys had found the back issue and passed it around. Butchery stirs the testosterone as much as nakedness. He paused short of the principal's office. If it'd been up to him, Connor would have let the matter pass. After all, he and his gang's youthful obsession with the Black Dahlia hadn't been all that different.

Inside the principal's office, a gray-haired Bryson Pomeroy, a smidgen taller than his sons, came to pick them up, razor strop in hand. Bryson's pale blue eyes worked the room as he passed out business cards with his twenty-four-hour prayer line printed on the back. "I wanna personally thank you people for bringing my boys' indiscretion directly to me, but I also want you to know you can beat their butts any time they're out of line, and I've brought my personal razor strop to leave with you."

Connor locked eyes with the principal and guidance counselor as the two teenagers slumped in their chairs. "Maybe we should discuss this with Knox and Kyle waiting outside." Principal Martin O'Brien pointed to two chairs in the hall opposite his office. "And no listening at the door," he called out after them.

Another glance from the principal told Connor that O'Brien wasn't sure where to go after that proclamation. "We love when parents are concerned enough about their children to partner with us," he said. "But we try to measure discipline so as not to humiliate but to instruct."

"That's the Devil's book," Bryson said, pointing at Dorothy Stratten's face lying on the principal's desk. "Not the first time I've tangled with Satan."

"I think what we want to impart," said Clara Shipley, Contrary High's just-out-of-college guidance counselor, "is that things like this book, well, you might say they're a rite of passage, but we still can't have them on school property."

"So, no razor strop is necessary," Connor picked up after her. "We thought we might set up a few sessions with Counselor Shipley and a couple of after-school detentions that I'll direct."

"Exactly my way of thinking." Pomeroy stood up and slapped the razor strop against his hand, the hard snap of it causing Clara to jump. "You do your sessions and detention. I've got to put the fear of Jesus in my boys, and along with you good people, the man who's going to help us do it will be here any minute." He slung the razor strop across the back of a chair. "These ole things never worked on me either."

The stunned quiet that followed caused the school officials to glance different directions, and finally to the floor, as Pomeroy opened the door and directed his sons. "Get in here, and don't give me no guff!" He paused and looked down the hall, then folded his arms over his chest as he paced in front of his children. "Now you're going to see the wages of sin."

Around the corner stepped Rusty Haskew dressed in full Contrary police officer regalia. His nightstick struck the door handle as he swaggered, while the boys eyed the pistol secured to his waist. Garbled voices muttered on the walkie-talkie anchored onto his belt, and he smiled and shrugged as he silenced it and pushed his cap back from his forehead. "These my two charges?" He walked a circle around Knox and Kyle, who appeared more intrigued than afraid.

Connor stood. "Police aren't necessary to this situation."

"I agree," Principal O'Brien said, standing at the same time. "A city policeman has no jurisdiction and shouldn't be here without our expressed invitation."

"Ain't that always the case," Rusty said, shaking his head. "The law is always the town dog until you need them."

"Now, now." Pomeroy patted his hands against the air as if the teachers were toddlers. "Officer Haskew is going to give these kids a taste of what it is like to be in jail. A full-fledged night in the pokey."

"Dad!" both boys said at once, looking back and forth at each other.

"We've got choir practice tonight," Knox pleaded, looking up at his father as doe-eyed as he could.

"And I promised Sister Wynona that I'd lead prayer circle." Kyle clasped his hands together.

Rusty stepped behind the teens and took hold of each of their collars to give them a shake. "This is gonna be an education to you boys." He didn't look at the teens, but instead stared at Connor, his flat grin lifting to a smirk, a dare.

"Wait," Connor said, putting a hand on Bryson Pomeroy's shoulder.

"A father has every right to choose how to discipline his clan," Rusty challenged him, stepping between the men, his equipment causing him to take up more room than he needed. "Don't you have a sayin', it's not what you teach kids, it's putting them in the right circumstances to learn. I'm just providing educational conditions."

"I'm begging you, Mr. Pomeroy, don't do this to your children. You can't guess the scars that an experience like this could cause."

Rusty laughed. "You might coddle little boys at this school, but when they go out into the real world, they need to know the stuff of men."

"Guess we have a different definition on what makes a man," Connor said, a hard edge to his voice. Principle O'Brien stepped between him and Rusty, physically nudging Connor back.

Clara Shipley leaned into the circle and whispered, "Gentlemen, remember we set the standard."

"I am astounded and honored that men from our finest and most difficult professions have such a protective interest for my sons." Bryson Pomeroy clasped his hands and shook them like a winning athlete. "Think on it," he said. "A policeman and a teacher. Could there be two more difficult jobs in this world, and both of you, looking to mold children into the best citizens they can be." He yanked his boys up by their arms. "You are indeed lucky young men."

After they'd gone, the principal, guidance counselor, and teacher sat around the desk, a stagnant silence squeezing the room. "This isn't a loss," Clara said. "A setback."

"A disaster," Principal O'Brien said. "You haven't lived here long enough to know Rusty Haskew. He and I," he pointed at Connor, "went to school with him. You were even his friend back in the day."

"Long time ago." Connor rapped his knuckle onto the chair arm and let out a aggravated breath. The final bell of the day rang, and they sat, ignoring the shuffle of students hurrying to exit the building.

"So who gets this?" O'Brien said, pointing at the *Playboy*.

Clara shifted in her chair and scooped up the magazine. "Really."

❧

As Connor pulled into his driveway, he was surprised to see Tallulah's red Ford Falcon. Near the corner of the house, a blond-haired woman gestured. He didn't feel any surprise as Dorothy Stratten urgently motioned to him. She'd slipped into his mind with such ease that he hardly acknowledged her as a dead woman. Walking toward the house, she faded like a ghost into its white exterior. Turning the corner, he saw his daughter standing in the side yard, her back to him. Her hand moved in angry, animated gestures. Connor started toward her just in time to see her slap Simon Tuller.

The frozen image of the strike and the unlikely prospect of Randi Jo's husband being at his house made him doubt his own sight. Tuller's round, black eyes reminded Connor of a shark's. With age, his sharp red hair had faded to a pasty orange, touched with white at the temples. He'd served three years for the kidnapping of his illegitimate child, then returned to Coalfire to work for Jonas Stark, the family patriarch, who'd barely managed to avoid the penitentiary. Springing forward, Connor ran toward them just as Simon turned to leave. The hunched man held his gaze as he walked past, but did not speak. Connor watched after him as Simon jumped into a van parked on the side of the road and screeched out.

"Tallulah, what in the world?" Connor asked, fear spreading through his limbs like fast-running water. As he observed his daughter, he didn't see fear, he saw contempt. "What are you even doing home?"

The young woman's hands clenched in fists. "Uncle Greg called me, Daddy," she said, pulling him to a patio at the rear of the house. "Granny Gaylor passed. Visitation is tonight."

"That's not why you hit Simon Tuller." He leaned toward her, but she stared at the ground, her lips pressed in a full grimace.

"You're not going to understand what I'm about to do," she said, "but I need you to know that my mind is made up."

"I know what you're going to do," he said in his best authoritative teacher's voice as some inner knowing told him he would not like what she was going to say. "You're going to take that job with the *Washington Post*. You're going to stay five generations away from a Stark."

"I've taken a job with the *Crimson County Sun*."

"No!" Words would not come fast enough from his mouth. She had opportunities outside of the mountains. Why waste her life in this corrupt little town that offered no future?

"Somebody has to speak the truth," she argued. "The *Sun's* been the only paper in Eastern Kentucky brave enough to take on the politicians and offer solutions for the problems."

"Its offices have been firebombed twelve times in the last two decades."

"More like twenty," she said matter-of-factly. "Mr. Ausmus is selling the *Sun* to retire, and I've talked a friend of mine into buying it."

"This friend know the pile of dung he's about to step into?"

"One other thing. I'm going to marry him. The friend, that is, not Mr. Ausmus." She held up a hand to keep her father from speaking. "He doesn't know it yet so don't you say anything, but when the time is right, he's going to propose to me." She paused, lips pressed firmly together. "Anything else you want to say about dung?"

Connor didn't have words that would have mattered. His daughter had lost her mind.

In time, he would meet Justin Fairgate, the classmate who purchased the *Crimson County Sun*. His family owned a string of newspapers throughout the Southeast, and the *Sun* would be an acquisition he would personally manage along with his star reporter and sometime managing editor, Tallulah Herne. In the early days, Connor feared the local and state political machine would bury his daughter, and they tried with lawsuits, threats, and a few more firebombs, but the Fairgates had a passion for freedom of the press and with their backing, every threat was met with more light than the Starks could eventually stand. Simon hovered in the background like a tiger eyeing meat. Other Starks paid off reporters on competing newspapers to blast Tallulah's reporting as vicious lies against upstanding citizens while the Gentrys ignored her as unimportant. Connor had stayed in the shadows when he'd taken them on, but Tallulah stood in the sun, and he was afraid that her speaking truth would eventually burn her. Then again, with that pen of hers, maybe, just maybe, it would be she who would slay them.

Tallulah never told him what Simon said to her that day, but he figured the Stark relation was pestering his daughter for Randi Jo's whereabouts. That pleased Connor. Perhaps it meant his former wife was alive. But she was right to hide, for if Simon ever found her, Randi Jo's life would be short. Rumors around town were that she'd been the reason Simon had been sent to federal prison for a little girl's kidnapping. Randi Jo had gotten the child back to her mother and led the police to Simon. That sounded like Randi Jo. Too often she got herself in thorny situations, but she always did what was best for the innocent–whether it was giving up custody of Tallulah to him or returning the kidnapped child to her mother. And he knew both decisions had cost her. If Simon or a Stark threatened Tallulah, she never showed it, and the *Sun* flourished under the Fairgate management. True to Tallulah's word, Justin proposed on a snowy Christmas Eve. While she said yes, Tallulah put off picking a date. Connor didn't have to wonder what she was waiting on. He knew. She was hoping her mother would return.

37

Halloween decorations were still up at the Songbird Nursing Home four days after the celebration. Six a.m. was quiet. Connor sat in a rocking chair beside his mother's bed. Her eyes were open as they always were when he came in this early. He was never sure she was awake; only when she looked at him or spoke did he try to interact with her. Between himself, Tempy, and Tallulah, they'd made the room as homey as possible, putting up photos, dressing the room with her favorite rocking chair, and using her own bed sheets and comforter. He wondered if all these homespun touches were more to assuage their own guilt. The family had kept Grammy at home all those years ago. Mom had managed, yet between the three of them, they could not. Their failure was a testament to Wallis and Asa Herne.

Visiting hours weren't until ten a.m., but the weekday floor nurse, Patty Mills, a former student, allowed him in, knowing that his day was spent at the high school. Tempy came in the evening hours, and Tallulah on weekends. With that, Wallis had family around her every day. Some days were better than others. Her inter-actions were childlike; and on the bad days, really, the sad days, she simply stared, unaware of who they were.

Today, Wallis wasn't talkative, so Connor read the previous day's newspaper, noting a series of burglaries on the east end of town and an attack on an actress he'd recently seen in a movie, Dominique Dunne. Her estranged boyfriend had strangled her the night before Halloween. Connor flashed back on the night he'd pulled a shotgun trigger and put a hole in the roof of his Notown house. The paralyzing fear on Randi Jo's face had frozen in his memory for years, and he felt ashamed. It was unfair the advantage men had on woman. He had terrorized Randi Jo, and Dominique Dunne's boyfriend had strangled the life out of her in the same rage as he'd experienced when he pulled that trigger. The actress with the promising career was in a coma. Her family must be heart-broken, he thought, and he hoped she'd come out of it and put the fiend in jail. He wished someone had straightened him out when he had been a younger man. He thought of his father, wondered if he had lived what counsel he might have given him. Perhaps life would have unfolded differently. He looked at Mom, staring straight ahead at the wall, then took her hand in his and kissed the palm. "See you in the morning, Mom. Tempy will be here around three o'clock."

His mother clutched onto his hand and pulled him toward her. "Tell her not to say anything," Mom blurted.

"About what?"

"About what?" Mom parroted, looking at him confused and agitated.

326

"It's okay, Mom," he said. "I'll tell her."

"The Rhine is so dirty. I don't want to go back there."

"You won't have to. The Rhine is gone."

She put her fingers to her lips, pressing them prayer-like as her expression grew into a child's who knew she'd done wrong. She whined and rocked to and fro, as if frightened, as if she didn't know where she was, then would giggle as if someone had whispered a joke into her ear.

Connor loosened the belt that stayed across her when she slept, a security measure taken so she wouldn't wander away. He hated it, but of late it had become necessary. "Honey, nobody's going to take you to the Rhine. I won't let them."

"They kill girls there, you know."

Connor petted her forehead, letting his fingers entwine through his mother's snowy white hair. "I know. Don't think about it."

She pulled the covers close around her neck and squeezed her eyes shut. When she opened them again, she turned toward the window and pointed at the rising sun. Connor re-tightened the belt and waited a few minutes to see if she remained calm.

Walking down the empty hall as he had nearly every day for the last year, he paused at the sound of a voice. Looking into a room, he saw Bryson Pomeroy standing at the foot of a bed. His hands were raised, eyes skyward, and his lips moved in fevering prayer. Perhaps sensing he was being watched, Pomeroy turned toward the door, and Connor swiftly walked on.

At the nurse's station, he waved to Patty. "Noticed there's a minister in one of the rooms."

"Pastor Pomeroy," she said. "He often comes to pray with the residents."

Connor glanced aside, a rush of blood heating his cheeks. "I don't want him having access to my mother."

"He means no harm, and many of the guests enjoy talking to him."

"I must insist," he said.

"Got it, Mr. Herne," she said. "I'll see to it."

He nodded thanks. "Tempy'll be in later."

Patty smiled flatly and looked to the floor. "She doesn't come in anymore, Mr. Herne."

Connor paused. "At all?"

"I shouldn't have said anything. We take good care of the residents whether people visit them or not."

Connor's jaw clenched. Sometimes, he wished Tempy had left Contrary that day she'd threatened him. Part of him was amused at her feeble attempt the previous year, and part of him knew the stranglehold that chained people to this town. He didn't quite understand it, but he knew it, knew it like a comfortable sweater or a person he didn't like but couldn't let go of. "I'll be back after school," he said to Patty.

࿇

Pulling into Crimson County High's parking lot, Connor noticed a Contrary police cruiser idling beside a two-door Mercury Cougar. Driving slowly around, he watched Rusty barking at Knox and Kyle Pomeroy, his hand pounding the steering wheel as he spoke. The twins were sophomores, and he wondered if they were even old enough for a driver's permit. Connor parked and watched while his radio played a Neil Young song, "After the Goldrush." The school bell rang, and he waited in front of a teacher's lounge until the boys came toward the school. They hopped up the steps in sync like disciplined soldiers.

"Pomeroy squared," he called out as they passed.

They stopped in unison. "Present and accounted for, Mr. Herne," they answered.

"Saw you with Smokey out there. You two in trouble?"

"Not us," they said together.

"Then why are you talking to law enforcement?"

The boys looked blankly at him, the familiar emptiness of teenagers trying to fabricate an explanation. Knox, the better liar of the two, smiled his father's jovial preacher's grin and said, "Some of the cops work security with Daddy's revivals."

"We were telling them if they wanted to be saved, Daddy would preach a special sermon for them," Kyle continued, picking up on his brother's tale without hesitating.

Connor stroked his chin and stared at them silently as they fidgeted under his best teacher's glare. They were lying, not very good at it at that. He motioned them to class with a nod of his head. He didn't like the idea of Rusty being on school property without an official reason. Something to keep an eye on.

At the end of the day, Connor returned to Songbird Nursing Home. The Pomeroy boys were on his mind. Nothing good could come of a continued association with Rusty, but there was little he could do about it. He rolled his mother down the hall in a wheelchair, fed her dinner, and made arrangements for her to get a haircut and manicure. He pointed out the Thanksgiving decorations that had replaced Halloween, and waited while she stroked a calico cat that roamed the hallways. The night nurse came in to get Wallis undressed and into bed, then Connor sat by her and read the day's edition of the *Crimson County Sun*. Another home burglary. This time in Marleybone. The homeowners had been on vacation, and had even asked the police to keep an eye on their property. Connor let slip an involuntary chuckle and thought that request had been the poor folks' first mistake. He looked for any information about

Dominique Dunne but didn't find any. Tallulah usually took national news directly off the AP wire, so it could be several days before anything new came in. Tempy didn't show up. He pondered whether to say anything to her. Not caring for another fight with his sister, he decided to leave a testy message on her answering machine.

The early dark crept up onto the day, and he felt winter's depression seep into his bones. A memory of Tempy calling him a failure flashed through his mind. Well, wasn't he? A cog that did its daily turn. A man who'd accomplished nothing. He stood by the bed and held his mother's hand until she closed her eyes. Unsure whether or not she slept, he stayed a while longer. Dominique Dunne sat next to him in the rocking chair that creaked with each roll.

38

When a Russian chemist, Dmitri Ivanovich Mendeleyev, developed the periodic table, he changed fragmented slivers of knowledge into an orderly branch of science. Yet Mendeleyev was smart enough to know what he didn't know and left gaps where he predicted elements would someday be discovered. Connor wasn't an expert at chemistry, but when Mrs. Downey came down with an attack of appendicitis, he jumped at the chance to teach her class, not because he wanted to brush up on his skills, but because it offered him an opportunity to fill in the blanks where he smelled something rotten. The Pomeroy twins leaned on opposite arms, bored as they awaited the next instruction.

"When I was boy," Connor said, "me and my friends would go to the Lester Street Bridge and get us a drink of sulfur water. Lunchtime, some of you go over there and take a sniff, see if it smells like this." He waited for the students to look up at him.

"Everybody ready." The students simultaneously dropped the iron sulfide in their beakers of hydrochloric acid. "What do we have?" he called out.

"Rotten eggs," yelled a boy.

"Real name gets five points on the pop quiz at the end of class," Connor challenged.

"Hydrogen Sulfide!" a front row student said.

The odor of rotten eggs filled the room and drifted down the hall and into the whole wing of the school.

"We gonna get expelled for this?" a student asked, holding her nose and breathing through her mouth.

"Naw, we do it every year," said another who was repeating the class for the third time.

"I'll confess a little secret," Connor said, walking among the students. At the back of the class he could observe every movement. "Been a long time since I had a chemistry class so I practiced this at home last night, and now my kitchen smells like decaying rat." The students chuckled and watched as their chemicals bubbled.

"I won't be practicing this at home," the repeater said.

"Luckily I'm leaving on a hunting trip tonight, so I can leave the kitchen window open to let it air out."

The empty piece of information Connor dropped presented itself like a missing element when the Pomeroy brothers sat straight up and shot each other a knowing glance. He watched as the twins turned to look at him but stopped mid-glance, turning back to their chemistry experiment as if nothing had happened.

After school, Connor pulled out five old guns: a Smith and Wesson revolver, two .22 pistols, a Browning semi-automatic 9mm, and a hunting rifle that was lacking a scope and trigger mechanism. He'd cannibalized them for parts over the years, and none were operational. Laying them out on the kitchen table, he positioned them as if he'd been considering what to take on the hunting trip. Then he packed his car, left a porch light on, and drove away.

Just after nightfall, he returned and parked on the street several houses down from his. The Warwick neighborhood where Connor lived had only a handful of teenagers. Around midnight, the red and white Cougar slid past, both boys' heads turning to look into his driveway. Connor hunched down. Soon it returned, passing a second time, then parked at the corner. Two figures slipped out, leaving the car doors ajar only enough to keep the inside light from coming on, and sauntered up the street as if they belonged to the neighborhood. He observed the boys dart into his yard, look both directions, then sneak into his side garden. He gave them three minutes, then, making his way toward his house, he swung open the front door and hit the living room lights in one motion. "Yeah, I'll tell you, Herman," he called out loudly. "It's a darn shame to have to put this off, but I understand if you're feeling rotten."

A scurry of movement in the kitchen. Connor peeked around the corner. The two had fled out the window, taking the five guns with them. He hadn't allowed them enough time to take anything else. Connor rushed to his car and caught up with the Cougar on Laynchark Avenue. Following at a distance, he was not surprised to be led to Darius Stark's rustic cabin out in the county. There was no way to approach without being seen, so he parked and walked in via the hunting path behind the house. Watching as the Pomeroy boys entered as if they lived there, Connor circled around on the hunting path and peered through the rear window. The brothers were drinking beer, laughing, bantering until the phone rang and Knox answered it. Darius Stark was still doing time in prison, so he didn't live here, but Rusty likely had access. Tonight he'd know for sure. After the call, the twins made a leisurely stroll from the house as if their night's work was done.

Connor waited for another twenty minutes, then snuck up to the back door and peered inside. No movement. He checked the barn. No cars or livestock. Returning to the back door, he slipped his pocketknife into the crevice and jimmied the lock. Using his flashlight, he looked around. TV sets, record players, radios, and toaster ovens. The kitchen table was covered with jewelry–watches, rings, necklaces–and containers of medications. Slowly making his way to the living room, he tripped over a mini-refrigerator. Three of his guns lay on the couch. A note beside them read: *Tonight's haul.* Looking around, he didn't see the other two weapons, and chuckled at the thought that the brothers had held out on Rusty.

On a shelf above the couch, a copy of Dostoyevsky's *Crime and Punishment* stood out of alignment with the rest of Darius's books. Oh, the irony, Connor thought, pulling the novel out with a dishrag so he'd not leave any fingerprints. He slid it back into the bookcase, but it jammed. Connor peered into the dark corner and found the same pearl-handled pistol he'd seen years earlier laying beside a sleeping Darius Stark. He carefully moved the gun upright to get the book in the same position that he'd found it, then drove to a Texaco gas station and called the county sheriff, describing how he'd walked in on a break-in and followed the thieves to a cabin outside the city limits. When he described the five stolen guns, he knew they'd act quickly, never wanting a firearm loose that might be used against them.

Sheriff Jacob Rollings and four deputies arrived within the hour, and Connor took them out to the Stark cabin. Lights were on in the kitchen. If Rusty was inside, he'd be caught in the act.

"That's a Contrary police car in the side yard," Sheriff Rollings said.

"Ah, surely a policeman wouldn't be involved in such a thing." Connor shook his head to feign disbelief. "But if he is, well, I know how you feel about the city police, Sheriff, so I'll just let you do your duty."

It wasn't long before the sheriff had Rusty spread-eagle against his own patrol car. They walked him past Connor on the way to the sheriff's car, and the fear in Rusty's eyes matched the humiliated slump of his shoulders. "These your guns?" Sheriff Rollings asked Connor.

"Three of 'em," he said loud enough for Rusty to hear. "Five were taken. Guess whoever stole them held out on their fence."

"I ain't no fence for stolen goods," Rusty hollered. "Not been at this cabin since last year."

"*Pfff,*" a deputy spit. "You drive your dang police car over here every weekend, you really think that's not noticed?"

"Had no way to know criminal activity was going on here," Rusty tried to explain.

"You invited me in," Sheriff Rollings said. "If I happen to see half the merchandise that's on my list of the latest burglarized houses, you gotta know I'm gonna have questions."

"I was just keeping an eye on the place for the owner," Rusty said.

"Who is where?" the sheriff asked.

"Prison," Connor piped up. "Isn't Darius Stark still in prison?"

"Not for much longer," Rusty said in as vicious a tone as Connor had ever heard.

"No doubt he'll be concerned and confused as to why his home is being used as a warehouse of stolen goods." Connor shrugged his shoulders. "You'd think some people ought to know better."

"Some people ought to," Rusty said, his glare never leaving Connor.

The sheriff rolled his eyes and nodded for a deputy to drive Rusty to the county jail. "Have to keep these guns for a while," he said to Connor, putting the firearms in the trunk of another vehicle. He let out a slow stream of breath and rubbed his forehead.

"What's wrong?"

"Don't know if I can stick a charge, but I'll try and serve him up a few months in jail. 'Bout all I can promise."

Connor nodded. He thought about the Pomeroy boys. They were minors, and he didn't really care to get them into trouble, only scare them away from the criminal life Rusty was leading them into. They could testify if he named them. That would convict Rusty. Corrupting minors, sons of a preacher. A good jury wouldn't let him walk but twelve honest people weren't a guarantee. Connor thought about Kyle's and Knox's future. Rusty was out of business, and he'd have a piss-poor time of throwing back any retribution toward Connor with all these county sheriffs as witnesses. That left the boys with no Fagin, and by the time he was out of jail, Pomeroy's traveling ministry would have moved on, so Connor left, never naming them.

39

When Connor found his mother's room empty the next afternoon, his chest muscles seized up with fear of the worst. As he hurried to the nurses' station, blinding sunlight shot from an adjoining lounge. The glare through a skylight drew him toward the room where Tempy and Iona stood on each side of a mirror, looking into the eyes of the other's reflection. Mom, strapped in her wheelchair, was between them. Whatever they spoke about ceased as Connor approached.

"You might have left a note," he said. "I thought–"

"That all our troubles were over?" Tempy smirked. "Got your scrappy message."

"I don't think of Mom as trouble." Connor knelt down in front of the wheelchair. His mother stared vacantly, then one finger lifted and touched his nose. He took her hand and rubbed it warmly between his own.

"We'll come on Saturdays from now on," Iona said. "Of course, if you'd like that day."

"Come whenever and as much as you want," he said, lifting his gaze to her, figuring she was the reason Tempy had shown up at all. If anything, Iona was the icon of family responsibility, and he figured the caustic message he'd left about visiting Mom had caused a fight between the two women, but his sister was here and that was what mattered.

Tempy plopped on a Naugahyde bench. "Grand of you."

"You decided to stay in Contrary, Temperance. You live with what I've decided." She didn't argue with him, whether from disinterest or lack of legal standing he didn't know or care.

Iona stepped away and picked up a *Time Magazine* with Jimmy Carter on the cover. "I'll give you two some visiting space." She ducked into an outer lobby, glancing back as if to tell Tempy to behave.

Connor turned the wheelchair so he could sit on the same bench. He bushed his mother's hair, curling it around her ear. Her eyes followed the trail of his fingers.

"You know, I guess we don't always have to fight." Tempy scooted a half seat closer, reached out, and patted her mother's shoulder.

"You saying that to me or her?"

"You, of course. She has no idea who I am."

Connor watched his sister as she opened a jar of applesauce and fed it to their mother. He wondered at her contradictory nature, at times harsh, then her better nature coming through, as she wiped a bit of sauce off Mom's cheek. He wondered if he could have been better toward her, more accepting. Maybe he'd deserved some of her ire.

"I think I know why you stayed." Connor leaned back against the mirror, resting his head. "You want to tell yourself that you're trapped by a family connection that won't let go of you. I used to think that, too. Was terrified Tallulah would be ensnared by the same trap. But it's not that, Tempy."

"Dropped the Temperance, did you."

"You stayed because behind that sarcastic façade of a personality you spit up on people, you have a heart. You love her. Maybe you even love me."

Tempy scoffed, letting her lips puff out a playful insulted breath as her hand raised and slapped against her thigh. "I suppose there are worse things."

Her answer made Connor smile. Sometimes, he saw that sister who'd prayed for him the night he was poisoned by wild berries. He remembered wondering if she had been praying for him or herself. Some part of that prayer had been for him. He knew there was caring in her heart, deep down. As they both got older, they had to make this fragile relationship work for the sake of their mother. He made a promise to himself to help her out any way that he could.

In a grande-dame gesture, Wallis sat up, straight and dignified as she might have in her younger years, and pushed the jar of applesauce away. She pointed, not at either of her children, but into her infinite reflection caused by a mirror on the opposite wall. "I know you," she said, eyes narrowed as if warning the image.

Connor and Tempy glanced at each other, their postures coming to attention. "Mom?" Connor said. Brother and sister followed the direction of her pointing finger. She smiled at her likeness, tracing the outline of her face.

"So many selves," she said. "So many dead women." She looked back and forth between the two of them. "You should be good children." Her hands clapped in front of their faces like a parent getting a toddler's attention. "Take me to my room. I'm ready to die now."

339

"Her heart seems fine," the nurse said after they'd tucked Wallis into bed. "I'll have her blood pressure in a minute." As she fastened the strap around his mother's arm, Connor couldn't help but pace the length of the room. Tempy sat in the rocker, pulling it as close to the bed as she could.

"That's pretty normal, too," the nurse said. She glanced at both of them while Wallis followed her movements, tracing her finger in the air. "You're sure she was lucid? I mean, sometimes–"

"She was lucid," Tempy barked. "My brother does not lie."

"I wasn't saying that." The nurse glared. "I meant to say that sometimes near the end, patients have a few minutes of clarity."

"So you're saying she's going to die?" Connor asked, his heart beating rapidly.

"No, I'm not saying that. Her vitals are good. I don't know." Their confusion melted into the nurse. Wallis clasped her hands over her stomach, turning her head toward the window, and stared at the view of a railroad track and a swath of houses. "I'll call the doctor." The nurse left the room, the hefty silence marred only by the hum of the Black Forest cuckoo clock that had once hung in Herne's Grocery.

"I'm going to stay here tonight," Tempy said.

Iona entered, bringing two cups of coffee that she handed to each of them. "She said anything else?"

"She said enough," Connor said, taking the cup. "I'll stay with you."

Tempy looked up at him, a grateful expression, then took hold of his hand. "I'll show you where," she said, her voice trembling. "I'll take you to where your mother is buried. Never should've hid it from you. I'm sorry. I'm sorry. Please Jesus, if I do this thing, give my mother her life for a little while longer."

The cuckoo clock announced the hour. Connor didn't like thinking about his own mother, didn't like admitting a truth he couldn't deny since seeing Wallis's AB blood type on the medical forms on file with the nursing home. He was type O. He remembered at the time his great relief that Temperance was not his sister. The realization that Asa and Wallis were not his parents held itself in the distance. He loved them. He loved the memory of his childhood, every birthday, every Christmas, every discipline, every pat on the back. Whatever the truth of what they knew and kept from him, he accepted as their right as his parents. They must have done what they thought best. How easily he might have ended up in an orphan house. All the same, he wished he'd tried to get information from Wallis when he was younger. But for now, in this snug room, surrounded by knickknacks collected over a lifetime, they were related, bonded as mother and son. He'd sit with this woman who listened for the final tick of the clock.

The doctor came, confirming Wallis's strong heartbeat and normal blood pressure. "Likely the ramblings of her disease," he said, and left them to the stillness of the room. Whether from hope or fear, Connor and Tempy stayed by her bedside like sentinels, knowing their mother had emerged from the wanderings of her sick mind for those few seconds. Wallis had said she would die tonight, and neither of them questioned it.

Before nightfall a tap on the door jarred them from the trance of the deathwatch. Bryson Pomeroy peeked into the room. "I've heard this might be the night," he spoke softly. "Can I offer up a prayer for her well-being?"

Tempy waved him away. "No need. Our Mom is an exact person. If she says she's kicking it tonight, well, I've never known her not to do something when she's determined." Tempy's voice wavered, caught in her throat, and a hand covered her mouth. "I'm not ready."

Pomeroy stepped inside. "Perhaps for her salvation, then?"

"Not necessary," Connor said, glancing in Little Preacher Boy's direction but avoiding eye contact. "Thanks all the same." Connor and Tempy's gaze froze into one other's as an old nervousness infused them. His sister's shoulders scrunched up into her neck as his stomach muscles clenched in an automatic response. Neither looked at Bryson, expecting him to launch into a sermon the way he had as a child. Wallis twisted in her bed, moaned, and smacked her lips. Her eyes fixed on the cuckoo clock.

Pomeroy studied Wallis, resting a hand on the bed rail. "She's giving you the chance to say good-bye. You two are digging in like you're playing tug of war with the angels."

"Holding on to what you love is worth knocking down an angel or two," Connor said. "All the same, your kind words have helped us know what we're facing." He hoped with that, Little Preacher Boy would move on.

"I know you," Pomeroy said. "My sons' teacher. That day they sinned."

Tempy's shoulders visibly fell as if relieved that Bryson Pomeroy didn't remember them from their youth. "Now isn't a good time for us to catch up," she said.

"Of course." Pomeroy nodded and moved toward the door. "If you need comfort, I'll be here for most the evening." He hesitated, then swung back. "It was kind of you to take the side of my sons, and I want you to know they are back on the path of righteousness. Why this very night Officer Haskew has them ministering to children who've lost their parents."

"What?" Connor turned full-bodied toward Bryson.

"The same police officer who took them under his wing has guided them to aid the most troubled in our town."

"You must be mistaken," Connor said. "Rusty Haskew is in jail."

"Don't know why you'd say such a thing. He came looking for my boys around lunchtime, and I sent him over to pick them up from choir practice."

Connor bolted from the room. Running down the hallway, he heard Tempy call after him to come back. As he jumped into his car, his mind raced to what he hadn't considered before. The larger crime. The organization supporting the crimes. Sheriff Rollings had said he'd have trouble making a charge stick, and somehow, Rusty's cohorts had gotten him out. The stash in Darius's cabin showed organization beyond what the twins were capable of. More merchandise than two boys could have procured. Rusty needed kids he could train and control. He'd been looking at the wrong set of boys. Instead, he should have considered–

"Meanest bunch of orphans in Notown," he whispered to himself. And those boys weren't ones to tolerate a snitch. That Rusty was looking for the twins meant he believed they were set to testify against him.

Screeching around the corner to Herman's gas station, Connor left the car idling while he ran inside. Troy lowered the hood of a Toyota to see the commotion. When Herman came out of the office, Connor grasped onto his arms, waking to the trembling in his own muscles. "I need help finding the Pomeroy twins," he whispered. "They're about to be butchered."

40

Judge Rounder's two-story house had been painted black with gray shutters. Resembling a tombstone at night, its wooden porch leaned toward the left like it might separate from the house with a heavy push. Patches of dandelions and mud holes made up the yard and a tall hedge bordered the street so passersby couldn't see inside. Connor told Herman about the incident at Darius Stark's cabin and his realization that the local burglaries were probably part of a bigger operation. "Rusty doesn't know that I didn't name the twins. He'll hold them responsible for leading me there."

"He'll be beholding to somebody up the chain," Herman agreed.

"Somebody who won't be happy with him getting pinched." Connor's jaw clenched as he thought about the ramifications. "Somebody who'll want him to clean up the mess."

A nervous lump settled in Connor's throat just as it had the first time he mounted these steps as a kid. That Rounder's orphan house still existed disgusted him. Rubbing out any fear of the tyrannical man who still called himself a judge, Connor rapped on the front door, then pounded, a hard, insistent knock.

The Judge's black hair was now white, still slicked back from his face in a close-cut cap. His arm and leg came around the doorframe, holding to it like a spider. "Gentlemen." He eyed them with just enough anxiousness to assess if he had customers or trouble. "We only allow couples to adopt," he said, his high-pitched voice scrunching his words like vowels were unnecessary. "But if you've got special needs, some of our older boys do hire out . . . as handymen, painters, that kind'a work."

"You've got trouble in your house," Connor said in a slow drawl.

"I don't think so." Rounder pulled back, using his arm as a crossbar over the entrance.

"Some of your boys taught a couple of town kids to pick locks, been burglarizing houses across town."

"You the police?" He eyed them up and down.

"I'm their uncle," Connor lied.

Holding to the house frame and the door, Rounder continued to block the entrance. "None of my concern what boys do in the school lavatories."

"It will be if I get the state to come down here and look at your little den of handymen that only adopts out to couples, oh, and, special needs."

"What do you want?"

"I want to find out where my nephews are tonight, if they're not right here learning some other criminal trade."

"I can't allow that, and I assure you no one is in this house that doesn't belong here."

Connor pushed past him and sprinted up a staircase, glancing from room to room until he found a cluster of bunk beds where a dozen teenage boys gathered in a circle. As a set of dice tumbled across the floor, Connor hit an overhead light. The boys scattered to corners and bunks, each staring at him with innocent wonder. He didn't see the twins. Connor held up a twenty-dollar bill. "One of you taught Knox and Kyle Pomeroy how to pick a lock. The first man to tell me where I'll locate them gets this twenty. If I find them where you've said, I'll bring you another twenty tomorrow."

The boys looked from one to the other, surly and suspicious. "Never heard of them," somebody called out

"Not for a twenty anyways," laughed a younger boy.

Connor had dealt with teenagers his entire working career. He knew they were more bluster than bite, and that to back these tough kids down, you didn't give an inch. "Okay. Let me put it this way." He quickly counted the boys and the beds. "Hmmm, eight beds, seven boys. Someone is out on the town." He turned in a circle, catching as many eyes as he could. "Say I bring Judge Rounder up here with his belt. See if that loosens any tongues. So what's it to be?"

The boys avoided each other, stared at the floor, the wall, picked at a bedspread, each of them sneaking glances at a boy of about fifteen who lay on a top bunk studying the ceiling. Connor grabbed him by the collar and jerked him to the floor. "I think maybe you know."

"You're crazy!" He started to strike Connor, who shoved him face-first into the wall and held him there by anchoring his arm across his back.

"Go on, Tom," said the younger boy. "Pomeroys ain't nothing to us. Been nothing but trouble since they joined the crew."

"Might find 'em at the Rosa Drive-In," Tom volunteered, a suspicious eye never leaving the money as he jerked out of Connor's grasp. "They hide there when they're supposed to be working. Now give me the money and bring back that other twenty tomorrow if you know what's good for you."

Connor handed him the twenty, making him tug it from his grasp. For several seconds, he observed the room: peeling paint, water-stained corners, the rank smell of unwashed flesh, bunk beds that creaked with every movement. Rusty had grown up in this house, probably this room. Everything that had made the man started here, in this claustrophobic den of festering futility. Together those kids could have taken him down and rescued their friend Tom. They didn't because they were ruled by fear; they didn't understand strength lay in their trust of each other; they'd never been taught loyalty. All they knew was survival of the belly and obedience to the gun with the fastest draw.

Downstairs Herman had kept Judge Rounder occupied by sitting on the bottom step and refusing to move. The cantankerous Judge paced like a cat circling hanging meat.

"I hope you got what you came for. Now, never darken my home again!" Rounder slammed the door behind them.

"We gotta close this place down," Herman said.

"Next on our list."

41

Connor caught sight of the Pomeroys sitting atop their Cougar in the back row of the Rosa Drive-In. A Hercules movie silently played, though he caught parts of dialogue as they passed cars whose windows were rolled down to anchor food trays to the sides of the vehicles. Connor T-crossed in front of their vehicle. The twins leaped up and sprinted diagonally through the acreage of parked cars. Connor and Herman chased them, weaving through the automobiles, whose occupants honked their horns as their shadows appeared on the screen. The men couldn't keep up with the younger boys when they jumped over a fence and sped up the hillside into a copse of woods.

"Maybe we should be looking for Rusty instead of chasing teenagers who are faster than us. You know he's bound to be looking for them, too."

Connor bent, resting his hands on his knees to suck in air. "Are we getting old and fat?"

"Yes," Herman said. "I got a better question. Why'd those boys run?"

"I'm a teacher." Connor straightened up, wiped a curtain of sweat from his brow. "I inspire fear and loathing of extra homework. Sad day when you run from your teacher and friend up with the local mafia."

Herman chuckled and slapped him on the back. "Makes me glad my biggest problem is finding parts for Iona Stark's Mercedes-Benz Ponton."

"They'll come back for the car," Conner said, between gulps of air. "Let's hide out front."

"Don't even bother," Herman said, still catching his breath as he pointed to the Cougar skidding out of the drive-in and onto the highway.

The men retrieved their car and drove around several restaurants that the local police were known to frequent, then circled the police station to see if Rusty's cruiser was parked in front. After an hour, Connor had an idea. He called the police station and left a message for Rusty that packages were waiting for him at the bus station. "Confusing enough for ya?"

Herman nodded as they watched Rusty pull up in front of the bus station. "There," Herman pointed. "That message got more that Rusty's attention." They watched as the chief of police got out of a black car and waited by the door. When Rusty exited empty-handed, they observed the chief rake him to the point that Rusty stood head hanging down.

"Good to know what side he's on," Connor said.

"He must hate that he can't fire him," Herman agreed.

"Not any more than knowing a handful of his officers don't really work for the city. Hate to think the Starks are making a comeback."

Having gotten his pound of flesh, the chief left. Rusty looked back into the bus station, still confused by the message they'd left. As Connor and Herman followed him, it became obvious that Rusty was searching for the Pomeroy boys. He cruised around Pinkie's, slowed down, and inquired of groups of teens hanging around the bumpers of parked cars. After talking to a group of boys smoking in the back of a pickup truck, the police cruiser sped up with more direction.

"What was that?" Connor pointed toward the police car. "Behind him, something moved."

"He couldn't have them already, we haven't taken our eyes off him."

"Does he have a dog in the backseat?" Whatever was moving dipped below the window line. "Keep your eye on that," Connor said, then pointed to the glove compartment, "and jack a bullet in my gun."

The traffic pattern thinned out as they followed Rusty onto a curvy road toward Quinntown. Connor slowed down to put some distance between the cars as they approached town. "I know where he's going," Connor realized and turned off the main street. "And we know the short cut."

Parking beside the Lester Street Bridge, the men held onto foliage to shift themselves down the embankment. A cluster of red berries came loose in Connor's hands and he paused to look at the juice between his fingers as Herman slid down to his side. A sad violin melody played from somewhere above them. Jumping across ankle-deep water, they sped upstream toward Copperhead Fields. By the time Rusty drove, catching streetlights and evening traffic, they could beat him there. Connor looked behind, ghosts of the dead, fireballs, and white hares stirring in his memory. He grabbed onto the tree where he'd found Randi Jo retching after having drunk too much and pulled himself up the hill.

The park where he'd once gathered with his own gang of teenagers was overgrown with weeds, and strands of kudzu overhung all but the evergreens. No one met up here like in the old days, and the deserted patch of land had returned to the wild. A snaky fog streamed through rusted swing sets and monkey bars. The men came up behind a picnic table. They listened. Quiet. Connor kicked a falling barbeque pit. "I was wrong!" he shouted.

"You weren't," Herman said, and pointed toward a parking area on the other side of a swing set.

Rusty's cruiser turned into the area, his lights catching the red Cougar parked on the far side behind a trash container nailed to an oak tree.

"Give me the gun," Connor whispered to Herman just as someone popped out of the cruiser's rear door. Connor's mind flew back: the wrong set of boys, dice rolling on a wood floor; eight beds and seven kids; an empty bed, empty. *The eighth orphan!*

"No!" he shouted and jumped the picnic table as a figure moved into the headlights of the police car. Tackled from behind, a hand mashed across his mouth as shattering glass mixed with screams and the pops of gunfire.

He struggled to get loose as the boy unloaded into the Cougar, and his captor voiced a "Shhhh" in his ear. Herman? Herman was holding him down. They shifted upright and Herman's arm reached over his shoulder and pointed. Connor could hear moans and a weak cry of someone calling for their mother, but that was not what Herman pointed toward.

The orphan turned toward the police car, his frame dancing in the hazy light. He bobbed his head and raised both arms, shaking the gun toward the sky. "I did it," he said. "See me do it. I'm in now. Right?"

Behind Rusty's car, two other police cruisers flashed on their headlights. Four men joined Rusty, standing like a wall of initiating elders. Connor hadn't seen them. His focus had been toward the children. He knew in that second, slaughter would be unleashed, and he knew with certainty that Herman had just saved his life.

"I passed the test," the orphan squealed. "I'm on the force now, right?"

Four policemen raised their guns. Rusty stood there watching.

"What'd'ay doing?" the boy asked, facing the men. "I did what you said, I–" He swung up the pistol but before he could shoot, a blast of gunfire cut him down. What bullets didn't hit him, popped the Cougar's wheels and blew up the engine as smoke streamed from the car hood.

☙

As Connor made his way down the nursing home hallway, the fluorescent lighting cast a sickly yellow haze. He passed the nursing station without speaking. The calico cat jumped from the counter and followed him. Connor swallowed; heaviness in his chest threatened to drop him to his knees. How would he find the words? The next time he would feel this torturous anguish was two years into the future when John Sweeney would be sentenced to six years in prison for choking the life from Dominique Dunne. Unfair. Maddening. Hopeless fury heated his blood. On this heartbroken night when the tracks of sorrow were the only ones to follow, Connor steeled himself to tell a man that his sons had been murdered.

Mom's rocking chair had been pulled out into the hallway. Tempy rested in it, her hands folded prayer-like, pressed to her lips. Bryson Pomeroy knelt beside her, one hand on his sister's shoulder. They looked up in sync when they sensed his presence. Pomeroy stood, opened his palms toward Connor and spoke softly, "I'm so sorry to have to tell you this, Mr. Herne, but your mother has made her final journey tonight into the hands of our Redeemer."

42

Rumors that float up and down the streets of small-town America are the fireflies of discord. Disappearing in a flash only to reappear closer or in the distance, they are as impossible to hold as a solid image until the observer is unsure if his sight deceived him. Word of murder spreads fast, reconfiguring the town's social structure like winding creeks hit by flood waters. A murky undertone invades conversation where everyone knows the truth, but dares not speak it. Whose side you are on today might be your enemy tomorrow, or at least the person to avoid in case his bad luck rubs off on you. Connor Herne was aware of the stares, the judgment, and whispers that he knew more than he would say. He stood across the street from Bryson Pomeroy's tent ministry. Knox and Kyle's funeral had started an hour ago, and he couldn't bring himself to go inside. If guilt was his cloak, then anger held it about him like chains.

Another solitary soul looking as if his gut was full of ire was Contrary's police chief. He leaned against a stone fence built into the ground, lit a cigarette, and inhaled deeply. From the tent behind him "Trust and Obey" played and the voices that sang wailed with grief. The story the police pieced together was one of hate and betrayal: the eighth orphan shot the Pomeroy twins because they had cheated him. Police who came upon the scene tried to intervene and the orphan fired on them. They returned fire, killing everybody. The officers were cleared. Higher-ups agreed it was a good shoot. No charges to be filed. Only funerals to attend.

Connor turned to leave and found himself facing Rusty. He stepped back, hand unconsciously going to the firearm in his pocket. Rusty squared off his stand, his eyes squinting, full of challenge. Connor wondered how long he'd been there watching him.

"You killed those boys," Connor accused Rusty. "I knew you to be lowdown, but murdering children?"

"You know jack." He jammed his finger into Connor's shoulder and left it suspended in midair until he realized his hand trembled. "I was cleared. My gun never fired."

"Rusty, think, think what you're doing, what you'll now have to live with. Those kids were no different from you and me." Connor's voice softened, a hand covered his heart. "Could have been us, 'cept for adult influences. I had my father, and you had–"

"Judge Rounder, yeah, that's a role model."

"Me," Connor said. "You had me."

The two men stared at each other, the quiet reflective like a mirror that might break. Rusty let out a shivered breath. "Those times are over. No need remembering."

"I hadn't named those boys," Connor said. "They wouldn't have testified against you."

Rusty made a *pffff* sound to the side. "You don't know what you're talking about."

"I saw the gun at city hall, the pearl-handled pistol you put into the orphan's hand. I know it was in Darius's house."

"Can't prove that, but you go ahead and tell your little story. Tell 'em about being in Darius's house. Bet you didn't say that when you called the sheriff, did you? Breaking and entering, I'd say. Maybe you were even the one dealing in stolen goods." He chuckled, his face a twisted mask of fear and bravado. "Go ahead, crazy man, tell everybody. I look forward to it. You'll get worse than you got last time, crazy fool." Rusty's mouth curved into a frown and trembled at the corner. He sniffed and looked away.

"You could still walk away from this."

"You want to know why those traitors are dead? Not 'cause they might have testified against me." He wiped an eye. "They held back two guns. Held back booty. Nobody holds back from Darius Stark. Nothing I could have done about it even if I wanted to. You wanna blame somebody," his voice slurred in hiccups of air, "blame yourself." He marched across the street without looking for traffic. A truck driver blew the horn at him, and Rusty raised his middle finger as it swerved around him.

The police chief inhaled his cigarette and blew out a long line of smoke without looking toward Rusty as he entered the tent. Connor followed, nodding to the chief, who stared blankly ahead, tossed his cigarette, and lit another.

The congregation was singing "Blessed Assurance." Connor sat in the back row with Tallulah, who was taking notes for a story on the shooting. She touched her father's arm and pointed toward the front row where Rusty had sat. Bryson Pomeroy stared at Rusty from across the aisle. As the song ended, Pomeroy stood in front of the coffins and motioned for the mourners to sit. He was red-eyed, his lips pressed as he wiped his cheeks with a handkerchief. "As we say good-bye to my sons, we who are left can only live the life that the good Lord has given us. I ask each of you to know truth in your hearts. Even when we are powerless, we can still fight by knowing who to embrace and when to shun evil." He cleared his throat and stared at the pictures of his boys set up among floral arrangements. "I ask that I be joined by a man who tried to make a difference in my sons' lives, a man who tried to save Knox and Kyle from the path on which they'd fallen, a man who fights the devil."

Rusty was half up from his seat when Bryson said, "Mr. Connor Herne, would you come up and stand with me as my friends say goodbye to my boys?"

Connor froze upon hearing his name. At once he knew what Bryson Pomeroy had done for him. He'd taken away the stares, destroyed the rumors, and elevated him to the side of right. He glanced at Tallulah, who was equally surprised. She pushed him into the aisle. He went to Bryson's side, stood with his head high.

As the mourners passed, eyes studied him, but this time they were filled not with accusations but curiosity. He met their gazes, his mouth dry and his grip firm as he shook hands with the mourners.

Rusty was the last in line, and as he approached Bryson turned his back and spoke to Connor. "I want you to do two things for me, Mr. Herne."

"Anything," Connor said, his voice a whisper.

"I want you to forgive that man."

Connor felt tears in his eyes, blinking them to his cheeks. "I don't think I can."

"Try," he said softly. "Because if you don't, I'm afraid Officer Haskew will kill you. I don't want that on my conscience."

Rusty froze upon hearing Pomeroy's words. His eyes darted from side to side and he turned briskly to exit the tent.

Connor burst into a sob. "I'm sorry," he said. "It's not right that he gets away with murder." He swallowed and rubbed his eyes,

"But he will." Pomeroy said, his voice deflated to near tears. "I'm not a fool, Mr. Herne. I've learned too late what goes on in this town. But now, my sons are buried here, and here I'll stay until my dying day. I'm building a ministry in their names. For them, yes, but also because true evil lives here, and I am needed." He returned to his sons' caskets, stroked the shiny exterior as if to polish it. "They were not the first to fall to evil. They'll not be the last. I'd be honored, Connor Herne, if you'd let me call you friend."

Connor sniffed back congestion. "You said I could do two things for you."

"The other, I want you to forgive yourself."

As he stood at the graves of the twins, Connor no longer felt guilt. Inside of him a seed of resolve planted itself into the fertile soil of responsibility. He and Herman would shut down the orphan house. He would teach. For among his students were the next Knox and Kyle Pomeroy. As for the men responsible for this tragedy, including Rusty Haskew, Connor had waited for his day before. He would wait again.

43

Holding up Dian Fossey's book *Gorillas in the Mist,* Connor Herne made sure to hold eye contact with his thirteen physics students. He'd received the book as a Christmas gift from Justin Fairgate, a man he considered his son-in-law, even as his daughter procrastinated in setting a wedding date. He liked Justin, a Louisville-raised chap who'd adopted the mountains when he could have easily settled into one of his family's larger newspapers. "A citified hillbilly," he called himself. Justin had gone out of his way to get Connor information about Dian Fossey's murder, including a little known fact that Connor was about to impart to his students.

" 'When you realize the value of all life, you dwell less on what is past and concentrate more on the preservation of the future.'" He paced the length of the room, holding the book for all to see. "These are the last words Dian Fossey wrote in her diary. I want you kids to consider her life, her zeal, and her commitment to a continent that to most of us might as well be the moon." The television behind him played footage of astronauts exiting a building. Christa McAuliffe, a social studies teacher from New Hampshire, held a thumbs-up sign as the shot cut to the Challenger spacecraft on the launching pad at Kennedy Space Center. The astronauts had waved toward the camera and Connor couldn't help but wave back, drawing some giggles from the students. "Dian Fossey embraced what was uniquely of our earth. Here, seven more adventurers go forth to explore what will be uniquely our future." Christa McAuliffe would be the first teacher in space. He'd applied to the program, hoping to demonstrate the physics of sound waves, but he hadn't been accepted. Maybe next time, he thought, enviously remembering McAuliffe's infectious smile.

Turning up the television sound, he answered a few questions as the news went live and focused on the Challenger spacecraft heating up its engines. The voice from Launch Control counted down: "*Four, three, two, one, and liftoff of the twenty-fifth Space Shuttle mission.*" Connor couldn't help watching the second hand on his watch, waiting for those future seconds when Challenger would slip into outer space. Partly visualizing himself inside the spaceship, he barely noticed as Dian Fossey sat at the empty desk next to him, her arms crossed over her chest, shaking her head. A few more seconds . . . .

The white ribbon of smoke spiraled like a noose around the neck of humanity. At first, what had happened wasn't clear. Then, students looked from one to the other, and then at him. The voice from Launch Control confirmed they were assessing the situation. "*Obviously a major malfunction,*" the voice said. Connor rose from the desk and walked toward the television, himself unsure of the truth of what he'd just witnessed. He reached up and turned off the TV.

Unable to turn around, he stared at the black screen, eyes filling with tears he knew he couldn't show the students. He wished for time to reverse itself. Afraid words wouldn't come to him and knowing he must explain to children about the fragility of the world, he cleared his throat. "I'll be here for an hour after school if any of you want to talk."

In the black reflection of the TV screen, he could see a couple of girls covering their faces; others stared intently at the television even though it was not on.

"They're still heroes," one girl said, her voice almost a whisper.

"Are they really dead? Can they get out of that?" another student asked.

Connor shifted to face the class and leaned on the edge of his desk. "I don't think so."

"God doesn't want us to challenge the universe," a boy slouched in his seat called out, letting his hand slam onto the desk.

"God?" another argued. "You sound like the Almighty wanted this."

"That's not what this is about." A girl in front twisted around in her seat.

The furor of argument rose up into the heavens, circular reasoning that led nowhere except back onto itself. Dian scampered in and out of the lines of desks, studying the teenagers as if they were specimens. Connor stepped into the hall and saw two science teachers looking down the corridor. Their stunned expression speaking to their shock, as they too must have wondered what they could possibly say to their students who'd just witnessed a global tragedy.

A hand on his shoulder broke his trance. It was Dian's.

"We're going to spend the rest of the hour talking about purpose," he said to the class. "I felt it the first time in my life when

360

my father explained to me what it was to be a man; later when I voted for John F. Kennedy; watched his brother Robert take on the Mafia; and again, when I heard the speech of Martin Luther King." He moved to the center of the classroom, all eyes upon him, and he felt the first tear drift down his cheek. "Then, my dad was murdered; President Kennedy was assassinated; so was his brother and Martin Luther King; all gone. I didn't think there was a reason to care any longer, thought the world was lost, and I was left with memories of words that would be forgotten for all time. We die. Few of us live without suffering. We rarely understand the whys and may never know if our deeds will have an effect upon this earth or fade with our memory. Those men . . . my father, President Kennedy, his brother Robert, Mr. King . . . they gave my life purpose as they did to many of my generation; their deaths marked not my loss but my awakening that I am just as responsible for what happens in this world as any man that I might have seen as great. You'll remember what you saw today when you are as old and white-headed as me. And I hope that all of you will live each day of what is left of your life choosing what you're willing to die for."

At the end of the day, he waited to see if any students needed to talk. The quiet of the room weighed heavy. He looked at his watch then up to the wall clock. No one came.

The *Crimson County Sun* was in chaos when Connor entered their editorial office. Justin Fairgate barked out orders as the staff scrambled to redesign the front page with stories of the Challenger explosion. He waved at Connor and pointed toward Tallulah's desk. "She's should be here any minute, out all day tracking down . . . something, I can't remember." He held up his hands in a *who-knows* gesture.

"She heard about this?" Connor asked, pointing toward the silenced television that played coverage of the exploding spacecraft over and over.

"Don't think so. Left early this morning. Doc Huber's been waiting for her over an hour," he said, pointing to a gray-haired man sitting erectly across from her desk, holding a briefcase on his lap. "They had a four p.m. appointment." A staffer yelled his name and Justin nodded that he had to leave. He paused, turning back toward

Connor, and said in a lower voice, "I haven't forgotten about Dian Fossey. I talked to a reporter this morning from South Africa. Looks like she might have known her killer."

Connor thanked him for the information that somehow he'd already suspected. A shadow of Dorothy and Dominique clouded his mind. All killed by someone they knew. People you know bringing death. "I'll leave Tallulah a note," he called after Justin, shaking himself from the hold of the murdered women. Sitting at his child's desk, he nodded to the doctor sitting opposite. "My daughter's usually punctual," he said to make conversation. "Sorry you've waited so long. She left me a message about something important to tell me. Guess I'll have to wait on that."

"Sad times," the doctor said, glancing up at the television. "Hell of a way to go." His hands held to each side of a briefcase balanced on his knees, and he shifted to adjust the position.

"If that's heavy, you can put it on her desk. She won't mind."

The doctor pulled the case closer to himself. "I'll keep hold of it, thank you."

Connor was writing out a note for Tallulah to call him when her voice rang through the room like a cat screeching for attention. "I need the back conference room for me and Dr. Huber for the rest of the day,"

"Can't. Had to re-do the whole issue. I need every available table!" Justin called back to her.

She dropped in the chair next to the doctor and let out an exhausted breath. "Some day. I heard on the radio on my drive back."

Connor noticed a slight darkness under her eyes as if she hadn't slept. "I thought you were taking off a few nights."

"You have it?" she said to Dr. Huber.

He patted the briefcase.

Tallulah turned toward her father. "It's here," she said, reaching over the desk and touching his arm. "Everything you said would happen, Daddy."

Locking off the men's bathroom and telling the few males who tried to enter to cross their legs and hold it like a girl, Tallulah spread out maps Dr. Huber pulled from the briefcase. He'd marked various hollows and written the names of people and their diseases. In one hollow, every person had some sort of cancer. In another, birth defects were thirty percent higher than they had been the generation before. He pulled out heartbreaking photos of infants with cleft lips, withered limbs, and showed Tallulah a hollow where every newborn that year had died for failure to thrive.

"Wait," Connor said, the scientist in him arguing with the man who'd been called a fool for making these predictions. "Any community in a coal-mining region is going to have a higher than normal disease rate."

"Not like this," Dr. Huber answered. "I've written letters to every government agency I could find that might have some sort of jurisdiction. Also wrote to some state politicians, but I don't expect much there."

"I wrote those same letters years ago."

"But now there's proof," the doctor said.

"Now," Tallulah said, her voice part quiver, "now, we have bodies."

Connor turned his back on his daughter and the doctor. His reasoning didn't want them to see the panic bursting in his chest, but there it was, terror owning his reflection in the bathroom mirror. The horror of what might be inside all of them. Dr. Huber moved to his side and put a hand on his shoulder. The shade of Dian Fossy doing the same just a few hours earlier fluttered in his memory.

"All this time," Connor said, his voice a scratchy whisper. "It shouldn't have happened. I might have stopped it. If I'd fought harder. Yelled louder."

"They would have killed you," Tallulah said. "You know that's true."

"And now, they'll come after you." He turned, grabbed his daughter by the arms and pulled her close. "Tallulah, promise me you won't chase this. Only report what the officials tell you after they've done an investigation."

"Really, Daddy. Really." His daughter pulled away, fists anchored on her hips. "It's too late. I've been in all these hollows for the last six months, interviewed people, listened to stories about the agonizing deaths of their loved ones, learned about how what medical attention they could get came too late. You didn't back down years ago, and I'm not going to now. I am making this happen." She rested both hands on the sink, exhaling a breath that seemed to exhaust her strength.

"Are you okay?" Dr. Huber said, putting two fingers onto her wrist. "Your face is flushed and your pulse is racing like a rabbit's."

"Just excited," she said. "Just angry." She looked into the mirror at her father's reflection. "I'll be careful. I've lived with the same enemies, Dad."

"Right now, we have our secrecy," Dr. Huber said. "But when this goes public, your father is correct. We'll all need to lock our back doors."

"Remember my cousin, Collette Gaylor, the one who works for the Senator in DC? She found all your old letters, Daddy," Tallulah said, putting a hand on his shoulder. "She'll take them and all this research to an undersecretary at the Department of Energy. She's dating him, long story. We'll get the investigation we deserve this time."

Connor rubbed his eyes. "When Justin said you had something to tell me, I thought maybe you'd learned to cook the chicken recipe I gave you."

She chuckled. "This isn't what I was going to tell you."

"Didn't really think so," he said. "Not sure my spleen can take much more today."

"The invite of the decade." She pulled a cream-colored envelope from her back pocket, putting it into his hand. "I set a date. Justin and I are getting married on Valentine's Day."

❧

In the weeks that followed, Connor shadowed his daughter's comings and goings. Followed her home from the newspaper. Followed her as she drove to work. He'd sit outside in his car watching as she took her turn as managing editor, while the same Neil Young song signed off the radio night after night. Justin had put on extra security, but Connor trusted only himself with her safety. He wished he could stay with her throughout the day. She promised that she'd always have someone with her, but Connor knew her tenacity when she found a lead and needed to jump on it.

When the first article hit, the town rolled over, pulling the covers tighter around its neck. People walked down the street without looking each other in the eyes. Those from the hollows filled the health department hallways, demanding to know what was wrong with them, only to be sent home with no answers. The next few articles brought a wave of denials from local officials–*the same ole stuff the reporter's father tried to hoax this town with years ago.* A dead cat was left on the doorstep of the *Crimson County Sun.* A rock bounced against the window. Rival newspapers ran stories that the *Sun* was trying to blame the coal industry for diseases that everyone got, and some owners were threatening to shut down, putting hundreds of miners out of work and destroying the local economy in the process.

It was an unequal tug of war. But they were not alone this time. Bryson Pomeroy opened his tent for community meetings where Dr. Huber led workshops and showed his maps. He taught those who lived in the hollows how to sanitize their drinking water as much as possible, and several churches opened their spigots to anyone who showed up with empty bottles. Was anybody safe? No one knew the answer to that question. And that was the point. The seeds of fear sprouted. More people wrote letters.

Demanding editorials in Kentucky's major newspapers called upon the federal government to step in if local and state officials did nothing. A game of common sense was afoot, and whatever broad strokes were painted to cover it up, a steady wash of acidic letters to the editors punched right back. Connor acknowledged the different feel of the fight this time around, like a rough and tumble ambience of snarling dogs circling each other. After learning Collette Gaylor had pushed through several levels of government to get Senate and House hearings, his battered heart relaxed, letting others lead the charge.

On the afternoon of Valentine's Day, Connor felt hopeful as he waited outside a choir room in the First Baptist Church that had been transformed into a dressing sanctuary. Several of Tallulah's high school and college girlfriends flitted in and out, the last one shaking her head and whispering to him, "Her Aunt Tempy is what my momma calls a prickly wicket."

Finally, Tempy came to the door with as wide a smile on her face as Connor had ever seen. "She's ready for you to escort her to her doom."

Inside, a cascade of white flowed out of a corner shadow. His daughter's blond hair curled over her shoulder and peeked out of a lace veil framing her face. Tallulah's eyes always had a cat-like quality, penetrating yet wistful, not like his or Randi Jo's, and he wondered from whom she'd inherited such beauty. "You're beyond words," he said. She stepped into the light, and Connor couldn't help but notice the thinness of her arms, the drawn hollows of her cheeks that the girlfriends had tried to make less noticeable with peach blush. Tired, he rationalized. She'd been working much too hard. "Promise me. After the honeymoon, you'll take it easy. You're managing editor. You don't need to chase stories."

She nodded and looked aside as if a thought was hiding in the tea roses of her bouquet. She exhaled a small breath, her eyes narrowing but looking at no one. "I just realized." She paused. A hand to her throat as if she were having trouble swallowing.

"Don't be nervous," Connor said. "I'll be right beside you."

"Daddy–"

At first, he thought she'd bitten her lip. Blood droplets fell from her nose, cascaded down the front of her white dress. Bridesmaids stood silent. Tempy froze as did he. Her hand brushed a strand of hair from her forehead as she collapsed in a swirl of white fabric. Her body convulsed. Tempy screamed. The bridesmaids hurried to Tallulah's side, steadying her against the floor. Connor fought the image of his daughter in the heap of white cloth, scarlet blood staining the purity of the color. A dying white rabbit. A sacrifice. A goddess demanding her due.

Tallulah reached out for her father as she desperately tried to speak. The words crumbled like caked earth as she pushed them through her lips. "Blue man."

Connor found himself pacing the same waiting room as when Tallulah was born. Arms folded across his chest, he counted the tile floor squares backward and forward, forward, backward. Any distraction to keep his mind from going into that comforting place of dead women. He thought about the rabbit's foot he'd pulled out of the trashcan that night so long ago. What had happened to it? Had he tossed it out? Had it finally disintegrated and returned to the wormy earth where all dead things go? Justin stood at the window in the same gesture, arms folded around himself. Both men were holding in their fear. Tallulah's bridesmaids heaped in a corner, tearful, worried. He finally told them to go home. He'd call when they had information.

Tempy rocked back and forth in her chair with Iona rubbing her shoulders. "She was too stressed," Tempy said, her eyes glaring toward Justin as she stood and stepped toward him.

"It's not Justin's fault," Connor whispered.

"You should never have pushed her into that wedding, Justin."

"Tempy!" Connor spat. "For once in your life have some compassion!"

"Yes, she was working too hard." Justin turned toward them. "On one particular story." He looked at Iona, who stared at the floor. "A story whose roots are in this room."

Tempy swung her purse, hitting Justin on the arm. "Don't you blame her! Don't you dare blame her."

Connor pulled her back just as Tempy broke into a sob. He wrapped his arms around her, holding her as she cried.

Iona pushed up from the chair in a slow meander, eyes still lowered. "Perhaps it's best if I'm not here."

Tempy slipped from Connor's hold, her hands trembling in front of her. "Me too," she said. "Maybe it's better if I wait at home. I don't think I could stand it if–" She wiped her nose, glancing toward Justin. "I'm sorry. It's my way to blame what I can't control. I've always been like that. Connor will tell you. Sometimes I can't help myself." Her breath shivered through her lips. "Call me soon as you hear."

The women left them circling the room into another lapse of quiet, their eyes darting to the hall with each set of footsteps. The unbearable burden of time. A flurry of snowflakes drifted past the window. Justin watched them. Connor paced.

As the hours passed, he called Dr. Huber, who promised he'd be straight out. Justin's parents and brothers stopped in, then left to await word at their hotel. Connor revisited every detail of the afternoon, the past months . . . Had she been sick all along? Had her family and loved ones missed important details? Would she die because they hadn't been paying attention? Something was missing. Something he'd seen as his daughter crumpled to the floor. Her lips moving. Words floating like bubbles. *Blue man?*

A doctor stood at the threshold of the hallway. Connor's mind blurred with fear when he saw Dr. Huber come up beside the other physician, his expression a dour seriousness that spoke his concern.

"She's fighting a massive infection," the doctor said.

"Her blood test from last year was fine," Dr. Huber said. "Now her white blood cells are skyrocketing."

"Blue man," Connor said under his breath, hardly accessing the meaning of the words. That was what Tallulah has said to him.

"Mr. Herne, is there any family history of leukemia?"

Connor hesitated, his mouth so dry he was afraid he couldn't say the words. "I don't know my family history," he said. "I'm not a blood member of the Herne family. Just me and my daughter." He stepped back, watching both doctors study the clipboards. For the first time, he'd spoken aloud the certainty that rooted him to this earth. He and Tallulah were alone in this world, and if she died, who was he but a withering limb fallen from a nameless tree? Without her, his life meant nothing. That knowledge was harsh, even ruthless, but it was truth.

Justin came up beside him. "Maybe you should sit down. You don't look well."

"She's been poisoned," Connor said, his voice scraping through his throat "And I know where."

As much as Connor didn't want to leave the hospital, he was the only one who knew the way to Blufred Hollow. At daybreak, a caravan set out, driving the winding road of Beans Fork and turning toward a series of hollows into the deepest parts of the mountains. Three ambulances followed him as well as Dr. Huber and three of the most experienced emergency room doctors. A collection of others had been called to the hospital to prepare for . . . well, they didn't exactly know.

As they passed enclaves of clapboard houses with tin roofs, Connor shook off the dread of knowing the disaster that was headed their way. He turned on the radio to help wipe the gloomy thoughts crowding his mind. Neil Young sang a song about Mother Nature being on the run. The same song the radio station always played when they went off the air each night. Turning onto a dirt road, he led the ragtag band across February's frozen ground to a pocket of shacks spaced around a covered well. His only thought was that there was no smoke coming from the chimneys.

He parked and motioned for the others to pull in beside him. One of the ambulance drivers opened his door. His radio drowned out the howl of the wind, and the DJ announced a Neil Young tune, "After the Goldrush." Haunting music lifted into the air, the same tune that had played on his radio moments before. The two men stared at the cabins, waiting for the other cars to come to a stop. A blue man sat on one of the porches, wrapped in a blanket; another on the ground, his arm draped across the wall of a well. The gathered living huddled in the clouds of their icy breath, unsure of what to do first, when a murder of crows lifted from the trees and scattered.

"It's the radio," someone said. "Scared them."

"It's a spaceship!" An ambulance driver pointed toward the sky.

Coming down toward them, one, two, three crafts hovered. The wind of the blades blew the men to a stoop, holding on to their hats and scarfs. Soldiers slid from ropes and landed on the ground in front of them. A fourth helicopter steadied itself and landed in a dried-up garden patch behind the cars.

Several soldiers hurried toward them, their faces covered with masks. They pushed Connor and the others back behind the cars.

"There are people sick in there!" he yelled to them as all but one of the helicopters flew away.

A dozen soldiers advanced toward the houses, holding out instruments that he recognized as Geiger counters. They swept through the area like worker bees, covering the houses, sheds, and a barn. One of the men turned back and waved toward a group of people who'd come from the helicopter that had landed in the garden. "Dr. Ressler," he called out. "Doesn't appear to be radioactive, but I want to test as far to the top of that hill to be sure."

"Can we get the people out?" Dr. Huber asked. "For god sakes, they need help."

The soldier looked past him as if to get permission from the group who were coming toward them. Six men and one woman. The dark-haired woman stepped forward. "My name is Dr. Rory Ressler," she said, "from the CDC. I'm taking charge of the care of these victims. If there are doctors among you, please raise your hands, and let's begin the triage." She spoke confidently as she divided the work between the locals and the doctors she'd brought with her. She moved between the ailing and the helpers, showing skill and self-assurance, her voice commanding and professional, but her eyes never left Connor.

Back at the hospital, Connor held Tallulah's hand as he told her the wild tale of spaceships to the rescue. "Turns out to be headed by a woman I went to college with that year I was at Duke."

"What did she have to say about being several years too late?"

He paused, the last words throwing him back to a time when the sight of Rory Parker had electrified every mental muscle he had. Ressler, she'd called herself. Married, he thought. "Didn't have time to talk to her. They had lots to do."

"Collette told me something big was about to happen. I'm going to want to interview this college pal."

"You are going to rest. You are going to get better and get married. Remember."

"I forgot," she said with a tired smile.

Connor wiped a damp curl of blond hair from her forehead. Her skin, pasty to the touch, glistened with beads of moisture. He pulled a tissue from a side counter and dabbed her hairline, but it was her green eyes he focused on, a starburst of amber shooting out into a ring of green–her mother's eyes. Connor wished he knew Randi Jo's whereabouts. She should be here with her daughter. Part of him inwardly cringed at the self-accusations that he'd been complacent in keeping them apart, but mistakes were like scars, fading blemishes to be faced day after day. One lives with the wounds, or bleeds to death from them. "You figured it out, Tallulah," he said. "Something I tried to do all my life."

"I'd been thinking about it all day. Some of the hollows where people were getting sick had no relation to each other. How could one hollow have birth defects and high cancer rates and not the next one? Then, I realize it had to be the ground water. Remember when I won an award for that science experiment where I demonstrated that water can flow uphill?"

"Water doesn't follow a straight line." Connor nodded, remembering

"The hollows whose land are affected are sucking it up from an underground source, either a lake or a river. Somehow, that same water source is not affecting the other hollows. That should help, right?"

"I'll go tell my friend Rory, and we'll re-set Dr. Huber's maps. See if we can figure out where those barrels are hidden." Connor shook a finger in the space between them. "Still doesn't tell me how you got sick."

"Almost every house where I stopped to talk, people offered me cider or coffee or tea. I even had a few sips of moonshine."

"All of that needs water."

"And of course, I realize that as I'm fainting on my wedding day."

A tap on the door drew their attention. Rory wore a white doctor's coat and a stethoscope around her neck. Her features had not so much aged as matured, and Connor thought if he'd run into her on a street in a distant city, he would have known that smile after a hundred years. He noticed her quick glance toward his left hand. He'd already checked to see that she wasn't wearing a wedding band.

"The government should read its mail more often," Connor said, pulling up a chair for her beside Tallulah's bed. She remained standing, fingering the stethoscope and averting her eyes each time their gaze linked. "We've been waiting a long time for some help."

"We are mounting a massive cleanup," Rory responded, picking up Tallulah's wrist and feeling her pulse. "Evacuating some of the other hollows."

Tallulah glanced from one to the other. "Dad can give you lots of unsubstantiated facts that nearly everyone will deny. He can even give you names and places, but he'll need witness protection afterwards. I'm not ready to lose my father."

Rory nodded. "The kudos goes to your cousin, Collette Gaylor. She managed to pull together federal, state, and county officials who normally hate each other. I've got the National Guard, scientists from the CDC, the Army Corp of Engineers, the local coroner's office, and a federal prosecutor with me. Let's see if that doesn't give a few people indigestion."

"Rory, don't underestimate the venom of these snakes," Connor warned her. "I've seen these people get away with murder. What's killing a few hollow people if it protects their pocketbook? I'm more concerned with finding those barrels and cleaning that up."

She gazed downward, a hard swallow as she bit her lower lip. "It's likely the people in those hollows won't be able to return." She paused, unable to look at him. "It could be decades before the ecosystem restores itself."

"Where will they go?"

"They can file lawsuits against whoever is behind this once we find the barrels and have indictments."

"You don't understand. These people don't have money to do that."

"There's no choice, Connor. They'll have to leave."

"If the government had responded all those years ago–"

"This isn't my fault," she said.

"Well, really, it is."

"I came as soon as I saw your name!"

Tallulah waved her arms between the two of them as if to chop off the words. Connor and Rory stared at each other, breaths held, arms crossed. The years disappeared as one struggled to prevent the curl of her lip, the other covered his mouth with a hand.

"So," Tallulah said. "You two used to date?"

46

The hard February ground softened with the April rains as two hundred fifty people in all had to be moved out of the hollows of Crimson County. Twenty-five people died in the first days and others were so ill they would be bedridden for months. Rory's team scoured the mountains, mapping creeks and glades, worming through caves and abandoned coal mines, while a federal prosecutor subpoenaed the bejesus out of Willie Carmack and Darius Stark. Just as the heavy fog hid entire mountains, the barrels remained elusive. The story of the search found brief segments in regional news, and the glare of that spotlight sent Willie and Darius fleeing for the shadows. Darius installed a wrought iron gate around his cabin, avoiding the news crews from Lexington and Knoxville who waited out on the county road for him to make a statement. Willie fled to Palm Springs, where he was photographed with buxom younger ladies at his side, then, like Darius, barricaded himself in his Contrary home, hoping that in time the story would fade away.

Connor hadn't the time to keep up with their movements. He spoke his piece with the press, encouraging them to keep the pressure on the guilty, whom even when called before a federal prosecutor, managed to lie their way to more security. They were tiptoeing on burning coals while Connor spent his time at his daughter's side.

While the majority of the stricken hollow people were on their way to recovery, Tallulah was not one of them. He held his daughter's hand as it thinned to bone over the weeks. Every rally had its setback. Every time she left the hospital, she returned within days, weaker than before. Now as she lay in a hospital bed surrounded by plastic sheets that distorted the view of the outside world, Connor often would slit the side nearest the window so she could look out onto the mountains. The world passed him by, and he hardly noticed when the bodies of the Challenger astronauts were found, or when Russia launched the Mir space station. Finally, he took a leave of absence from teaching so he could be with his only child.

Sitting at her bedside swaddled in medical garb–mask, gloves, plastic encasing his every limb–he watched her without blinking, prayed in a fever, and devoured every medical article he could find. He hated the thought of her eyes opening and seeing no one at her side. When he wasn't at the hospital, Justin was, and Connor respected the heck out of the way this young man's love focused on his daughter and took on her fight as his own. Rory had taken charge of Tallulah's care, treating her for an impaired immune system. He knew Rory believed she had full-fledged leukemia but didn't want to tell him. Tallulah's bed was draped with plastic, a drip bag hanging over her head delivering poison to fight poison. She'd lost most of her hair, strands of blond falling out each time she moved her head. Connor matched his breath to hers, wishing he could take her place.

A tap on the door drew his attention. Standing there was a familiar-looking man. Connor couldn't place him as he exited the tent around Tallulah's bed and stepped into the hall. "Toomey!" he said, grabbing onto the man's hand and shaking vigorously. "You're white!"

"As a widow's pearly teeth," Toomey said, smiling widely, his other hand stroking his cheek. "Thank your doctor gal for that."

Connor stepped back, taking in his ivory visage and pink palms.

"Turns out there's a name for people like me." He sounded out the word in syllables, "I got me a dose of meth-e-mo-glob-i-nemia. Yep, methemoglobinemia."

"That's a mouthful."

"Doc Ressler got me set up with some pills that'll keep me in a snowsuit, if'n I want."

"Never thought you looked so bad as a blue man."

"Thinkin' maybe I'll just take the cure on months I need to come to town. Aside from that, I'm a-cheered to be blue."

Both chuckled with the weary titter of people who had been through too much.

"How's your kin?" Connor asked.

"Last of us is headed home today. Government moved us into trailers toward the backend of Bean's Fork. It'll do, but we'll miss the ole home place."

"I'm so sorry this happened."

"Connor, if it hadn't been for you and Doc Ressler . . ." He paused as his voice cracked.

"Is that my name being bandied about?" Rory called out as she strolled down the hall. She rubbed Toomey's shoulder and nodded approval of his appearance. "You're looking ghostly and sprite."

Connor noticed she'd had her hair styled, the gray once at her temples now raven-toned as he remembered from college. "Toomey and I got in a bit of trouble when we were kids, and he was blue."

"*Pfff,*" Toomey shot aside. "This'ne didn't even show up." Toomey pulled out a bag of Red Man chewing tobacco and offered her some. "Missed all the fun."

Rory politely declined the tobacco but comically nodded to Connor to feel free and partake.

"Reckon we'll ever be able to move back home?" Toomy asked.

Rory glanced to the floor, lips pressed together. "If we can find the barrels, the ecosystem could eventually repair itself by the motion of the water moving downstream."

"If?" Connor said. "When Knoxville, Chattanooga, Atlanta, all the way to the Mississippi and Gulf gets the poison that originated right here, then maybe we'll get somebody's attention."

"Makes you want to go beat the petunias out of Willie Carmack." Toomey punched a fist into his palm, his gray eyes narrowing as if seeing his knuckles connecting with Willie's face.

"Don't think it's not been considered," Connor agreed. "He could save us some time by fessing up about where the barrels are, but he's lawyered up like the coward he is."

"May be he needs a visit from a blue devil," Toomey smirked and poked Connor on the arm. "Give you a discount on my services for that job. Just one bag of candy this time." Toomey glanced past Connor into Tallulah's room. His expression softened, a flush of purple coloring his cheeks. "Gotta pick up my Aunt Zella," he said, pausing at the door and bowing his head. "We'll say a prayer circle for your daughter."

Connor thanked him and watched as he ambled down the hall toward the elevator. The image of a blue devil played with his memory, bringing back recollections of boyhood mischief. Toomey was one of a kind, and Connor thought his blueness a positive feature. As Rory stepped closer to him, he inhaled a whiff of her rose-scented shampoo. In so many ways, all of them were still the young people they were all those years ago. Idealistic. Optimistic. Naive. But now, the world was theirs to sort out, and the C+ students were running it. "And why can't a division of soldiers, a legion of engineers, and who-the-heck-knows-who-else you've got out there, find the barrels?"

She didn't answer. Looking at a clipboard, then up at the wall, she was still avoiding direct eye contact with him. "I thought we would have found them by now, too."

"It is kinda ridiculous."

She pulled him into the waiting area across from Tallulah's room. "We're doing the best we can."

"I fought this battle for so long, by myself. Just thought the federal government could do a little better."

"Perhaps your expectations are a smidgeon too tough."

"Words worthy of Fitch."

She slapped him. Twisted away, then swiftly turned back, and kissed him.

The contact of her lips on his released every frustration and every desire as he pulled her to him in a faultless fit. A nurse ran past the room, then returned. They broke apart, and Rory raised her clipboard to suggest they'd been merely talking.

"I can't believe it," she said to Connor. "Mr. Fairgate is in the emergency room."

"Go," Rory said. "I'll stay with Tallulah."

At first, Connor assumed Justin's father, who'd stayed to help with the newspaper and support his son, had had a medical emergency. His concern turned to blinding anger when he found Justin getting stitches on his forehead, welts swelling around his eye.

381

"Is he okay?" he asked the doctor.

"I'm fine," Justin croaked out.

"You likely have a concussion, Mr. Fairgate, so hold still," the doctor ordered.

"Do what he says," Connor said, steadying Justin's shoulder. "Who did this?"

"Who didn't?" he said, gritting his teeth as the doctor gave him another numbing shot. "Four goons. Looked like Coalfire types. Tattooed. Muscled like gorillas. All on motorcycles."

Coalfire and its ne'er-do-well neighborhood, Spit, was Stark territory, a haven that hid hoodlums and protected well-manicured trash. Justin's father rushed into the room and halted at the end of the gurney. Viewing his son, he steadied himself against the wall, temples pulsing and jaw clenched. Connor shared his fury but didn't know what to say.

"This is war," the elder Fairgate said it for him.

"War," Connor agreed.

ᴄ⁓

Connor pushed his way past Willie Carmack's distressed secretary and kicked open the office door. She trotted behind him, squealing threats to call the police.

"Don't bother," Connor grunted. "They're already here." He pointed out a window at two state trooper cars parked on the opposite side of the road. Then he waited as the three men assembled around the desk swiveled their heads toward him. Rusty Haskew. Willie Carmack. Simon Tuller. A fourth man lay on a couch, head draped off the side over a trashcan. The smell of vomit wafted off Darius Stark.

Connor eyed each one of them. Rusty stood in the center, stance wide as if expecting a fight. Willie's glazed expression belied his fear when his lower lip trembled, and he clutched the arms of his chair to hold himself steady. Simon wouldn't acknowledge him, eyes averted, resting his chin on a fist. Darius threw up, afterwards peering upward and pointing at Connor. "I know you," he slurred, words enveloped in a drugged laughter. "Pumped gas for me, over at the Texaco." He laid his head back down, kicking out at the end of the couch where Simon crossed one leg over his knee. "Place is haunted. Worst devils I ever saw." He hacked and spit into the trashcan.

"You're going to find that those troopers are eating their lunch there every day," Connor said, "maybe even their dinner. A few others will find their way to Coalfire lunch counters, and don't be surprised that the Attorney General is having a talk with the Contrary police chief and county sheriff right now. I believe they're going to have to make a few arrests before they find new places to eat."

Rusty looked aside, his stance relaxing when he realized Connor had come in alone. He wasn't dressed in his police uniform, and, for the first time in months, he had no weapon holstered around his waist.

Simon glared, eyes squinting, head bobbing in a quiver of rage. "Harassment," he belched, "pure and simple. I know people who'll talk to the governor. We'll see who ends up in a cage."

"Now that doesn't really matter to me," Connor said. "You see, I didn't get them here. Oliver Fairgate did. Believe the old man had a little talk with the governor himself, who, as it seems, is up for re-election, and you know how many newspapers he owns." Connor leaned back on his heels, letting his gaze sweep the room in a dare. "But that's not why I'm here."

"I'll get this scum outta here." Simon started up from his seat, but Rusty pushed him back down with one hand.

"Shut up, Simon," Rusty said.

"I ain't afraid of him!"

"That man'll take you out before you know what hit you."

"Who the hell's side are you on?" Simon spit but did not try to rise up again.

Rusty leaned against Willie's desk and opened his hands palms up. "I don't know what you think we've done, but I've been with these men all morning. Nothing illegal going on here. No need for the state police dogging us. We're here helping a friend." He pointed to Darius, who motioned with both hands as if he were conducting an orchestra.

"I came to tell all of you where the state police aren't going to be," Connor said, letting his words melt in the icy air. "My house." Connor let the information sink in. Simon stared at the floor, slumping deeper into the couch. Willie fidgeted like the broken, used-up man that he had become, while Darius hissed at some creature beyond this reality.

Rusty glanced at the others as they sat in silence amid Darius's manic giggles. "We've done nothing," he said. "Got no reason to start trouble with anybody. We're just trying to get through this like everybody else."

"All the same. Anybody wants to pay me a visit, you know where to find me." Connor backed from the room, pausing at the door. "I'll be waiting."

47

War. He had declared war. Shown them his face. Offered himself up. Ready for combat. Yet no one approached Connor Herne's house. Not that night. Not any night. He found himself disappointed. Spoiling for a fight, he could only battle inside his head.

Oliver and Justin Fairgate waged their own crusade. Competition between newspapers may be fierce, but when freedom of the press was at stake, the big guns were going to have their say. Editorials in major newspapers held officials to task. Clean up the corruption. Sunshine the government meetings. Protect the health of every citizen of the state, not just the ones in urban areas. Television news, both regional and national, had cameras on every corner, and a few documentary filmmakers asked to follow Justin and his father around. Connor was relieved, believing the spotlight would at least keep them safe.

The days also renewed the bond between Connor and Rory. He heard the story of how her husband and son were killed in an auto accident and only the charitable acts of medical colleagues and a Siamese kitten had kept her from ending her life. She joined Centers for Disease Control and Prevention after she realized she was tired of the dead living inside her head. Connor had nodded, saying he understood. She told him of returning to Contrary for Aunt Edna's funeral and watching him as he walked out of the high school and got into a car with Randi Jo and Tallulah. She said she'd wept, finally grieving for a lost teenage love that she'd never gotten over. They laughed about their college memories, and Fitch, who'd ended up a headmaster at a private boys' school. Then, they kissed, and years evaporated, making this turn of life seem as if it had always been destined. Life had played out for her as it did everyone, with its pain and its glory, and its demand to be lived.

Connor shifted in his bed. Sleep eluded him between dreams of his dead women running from their attackers while he was unable to help. He drifted away, following the Black Dahlia to an ebony lake with a stone shore bereft of wildlife, where the only sound was the echo of a scream. He twirled around, looking for her, lucidly realizing his imagination had created this landscape. Slowly, snaking out of the water, a woman's forehead appeared. The Black Dahlia rose, suspended in air, covered in the black murk of the lake's depths. She pointed at him.

He jerked awake, his room claustrophobic and spinning. A scrape outside his window brought him upright. He looked over at Rory, curled sideways and clutching her pillow. He stoked her hair and twisted around to face the window. Hyper-vigilant whenever she stayed, he peered into his yard. Early morning was tinged blue just before the sun would slide above the mountain. Fog kept the days cloudy, moist, and sleepy. He didn't like putting Rory's safety at risk by staying with him, but he didn't like being without her either. She had overridden his insistence that she stay somewhere else for her safety by proclaiming "*The government put me in charge, and you have to do what I say.*" Her curt smile had invited sparring, but on this one issue he had been unable to argue.

A slow movement caught Connor's attention and he reached for his bedside pistol. Sprinting down the staircase, he clung to the wall as he peeked out the edge of the curtain at a cow. A cow. He opened the front door, stepping out onto the porch. A brown cow was munching on his lawn. He sat on the swing and watched her.

A few minutes later, Rory came out and sat beside him, bringing two mugs of coffee with her. "There's a . . . why state the obvious?"

"There is at that."

They sat quietly as the cow ate contently, moving over closer to them and watching the couple with her auburn eye. Rory shifted toward Connor and touched his arm. She fidgeted, avoiding his gaze as if holding back something that needed saying. She set her coffee cup under the swing, then leaned forward.

Connor rubbed her back as she gulped deep breaths. As he pulled her body into his arms, she clutched the collar of his robe and trembled. "She's not getting better," Rory whispered. "And I don't know why."

"Don't tell me to prepare myself because I can't." His jaw clenched as all vitality left his muscles.

She pushed back from him and wiped a tear from her cheek. "Something else has happened. I got called about it late last night, and there's not much information. Come inside, you need to see what's on TV."

The sound was turned low. "The Soviets," she said, her finger on the dial. "They're not admitting much, but this reeks of a major nuclear accident. Probably near Kiev in the Ukraine. There's a power plant there called Chernobyl."

"The Soviets," he repeated as he watched the news anchor report about radiation being monitored through Finland and Scandinavia. "It's horrible," he said, "but I have a hard time watching the world rush to their aid when we have our own Chernobyl right here and nobody cares."

"It's more than that," Rory said, her fingers intertwining with his. "They'll call all of us back. That radiation cloud has to be monitored. Every government agency will be on high alert for–"

"A catastrophe. A worldwide health scare. Once again, we don't matter?"

"I can't change this," Rory pleaded, and stroked his arm to calm him.

"The world screws up and my daughter has to pay!"

Rory looked at the floor. She had no answer.

"You haven't even found those barrels yet. Poison seeps into this land like baby's milk, and we drink it and say thank you!" He waited, hoping she would say something, find a reason to stay. She avoided his gaze, and he turned to go outside. "I'm going to sit with my daughter. If you're leaving, don't bother saying good-bye."

At the hospital parking lot, Connor remained in his car. He regretted how he'd spoken to Rory and fought the urge to go back home. He hadn't been able to find those barrels over all these years, why should he have expected outsiders to crack the oligarchy that was the Starks? He saw Rory park by the entrance and head into the hospital. She gazed downward as she walked, in thought perhaps, and hurt by Connor's words. At least she hadn't left yet. He could still make it right, but Rory couldn't fix the world for him. It must have been agony for her to tell him that Tallulah wasn't going to make it. Connor held his breath, those words chewing on his insides. What would he do without her? How could he live without his daughter in this world? Oddly, the person in whom his thoughts found comfort was Randi Jo. When he found himself with unanswerable questions, Randi Jo had always had a comforting answer that made the pain bearable. What he would give to have her here at her daughter's side at this time when their child might take her last breath.

His steps into the hospital were weighted and precise. The elevator opened on a nurse who eyed him suspiciously and seemed nervous. Rory was ahead of him in the hallway and he called out her name. She didn't turn, but instead ran down the hall. Connor saw another nurse and medical personnel follow her, one pushing a cart. The next few seconds were a jumble of thoughts he denied, and realities he wished he could punch. Tallulah had died, and he knew it, felt her essence pass through him. At the room's doorway, a nurse pushed a dark-haired woman out of the room and she retreated to the visitor area across the hall.

"Randi Jo?" He squinted to make out the woman's features. Connor's feet were moving as if he were stuck in mud. The continuous sound of machine beeping and Rory shouting orders invaded the hollow frenzy of despair that swallowed him. *Run*, he told himself. *Get to your daughter.*

He turned into the room just as Rory placed paddles on each side of Tallulah's chest. "Clear," she said, her features tightened and focused. His daughter body lifted up off the bed in a spasm. The machinery hummed, blaring like a trumpet in Connor's head. "Again," Rory said, and pressed the paddles.

Connor blinked his eyes, half of him fading off into the country of dead women, who regarded him as an invader to this land he'd created. *She's dying*, someone said. *Dying*. "Save her," Connor whispered. *No one saved us,* they answered. "Save her." Hands pressed to his head, he opened his eyes wide, returning to the hospital room where everyone seemed frozen, staring at a monitor. A beep, waiting, another beep. The tone returned to evenly spaced heartbeats. Rory returned the paddles to the cart, telling the intern to leave it in the room, then she turned to Connor, stood in front of him, and looked up into his eyes.

When speech was inadequate, the worth of tears spoke all he needed to know. Gathering around Rory's blue eyes, one after another trickled down her cheeks. She put her arms around Connor's neck, breath shivering out of her. He squeezed her to him, letting his fingers entwine into her black hair. "I won't leave," she said. "I'll never leave you or her. Never."

The silent pact they made to each other was to see through this struggle of sickness to its uncertain end. Over her shoulder, he watched his weak daughter battle the chemicals that stripped her body of everything you could call life. Her eyes opened, focused as if in thought of a new and original paradigm. She lifted her hand and pointed to the side of her bed. "Momma was here," Tallulah said.

Connor and Rory rushed to the bedside even though they hadn't draped themselves in sterilized clothing. "You're dreaming, honey," he said, pressing her hand to his lips. As they talked, he noticed her eyes were now a deep green. She studied the two of them as she spoke, something she hadn't done in days. Her speech was focused, where before she'd dreamily mumbled nonsensical mutterings. "Rest now," Connor told her after a while, even as he looked up toward the hallway, half thinking he would see Randi Jo. But that wasn't possible, was it? Had he seen Randi Jo? Had Tallulah? As his daughter slept, he walked over to the visitors' lounge to the place where he thought he might have seen his former wife. His imagination. Had to be. The stress of the episode had conjured Randi Jo's image, for both of them. He sat by Tallulah the rest of the day and into the evening. A hand squeezed his shoulder and he looked up at Rory, her face lined with exhaustion and worry.

"I'll stay here the rest of the night," she said. "I won't leave her side. She won't die. I promise you. Go get some rest."

"Justin is on his way," Connor said as he stood, shaking out his stiff muscles. "I do have somewhere to go."

"Connor?"

He touched his daughter's cheek. "I have to talk to the darkness."

48

As Connor stood on the Lester Street Bridge, he fought the feeling that this confrontation had been set in motion long before his birth. A gibbous moon hung in the night sky like a chipped coin. Fog snaked up the bank, leaving a misty wet coat in his nostrils. He leaned over the bridge and stared into the shadowy underside. A chill took hold of his limbs.

At the bridge's edge, the artesian water pipe had been placed in a rock fountain. He bent over it and sucked in the sharp-tasting water. A car passed, causing a shuddering roar from underneath the bridge. Can't put this off, he thought. Tonight, he would battle the monsters in his mind. Tonight, the dead women he'd let live in his imagination would face their killers and finish their macabre dance. He had fought their battles, and tonight the Hunter of Hertha would demand his reward. A single thought grasped his being: In this world, if there was bad, then there had to be good, too. Tonight, good needed to help him. Letting his grip loosen on the cattails and rushes, he slid down onto the canal bank and stepped into the dark.

Connor's shoes skidded in the loose pebbles and he crouched, letting himself settle onto the ground. A sharp odor drifted from across the canal, and he turned an ear toward that direction as if he could hear it. The black water occasionally caught a gleam of moon or headlights from a passing car, but in the dead center there was nothing but dark. He stared across the canal at the place where Bette Moss had died. There was no form in the darkness, only a ghostly movement that appeared wavy each time he blinked.

"I'll trade you," Connor said. His voice rang hollow against the ground, water, and steel above him. "I'll give you myself for her." He waited. Of course, there was no answer. He hadn't expected one. Though maybe he could will himself into that other world and bargain with whatever overlord held life and death in its hands. He stared into that inkiness until his eyes watered. An ambulance siren pierced the veil, and the vehicle made a clunky stop somewhere on Lester Street. After a rumble of activity, another silence.

He thought about the dead women who'd stood no chance against their monsters; perhaps his mother had been one of them. If Tempy's story was correct, she might have lost her life in this very spot. Above him, someone played a musical instrument. A thorny, haunting sound as if to toast the dead of night. Connor inhaled the ambience, for only then did it occur to him that he had misunderstood the dark. It waited. It didn't cause death or toy with the frivolities of the living. It simply existed, accepting offerings when they were ready. In microseconds, the dawn layered the air before him with a shade of light. Across the canal, from the beams of the bridge, hung a dozen violins.

The realization that the whine above him had been the squeal of a violin being tuned brought back to him a background sound that might have been in his head his entire life. The sensation was new as he negotiated it, brought to reality from an old memory he could only grasp as slices. The sound ceased, and across the canal, rocks moved. On the spot where Bette Moss had lost her life, stood a cloaked form. Connor blinked, unsure if what he was seeing was real or if he'd entered that other land. He stepped closer to the water. The form's stillness formed a patchy gray against black. Stacked on rocks surrounding the violins were cans. The pungent smell. Paint?

"I see you," he said.

No sound or movement. The canal was too wide for him to jump, and not knowing exactly what he'd walked into prevented him from moving closer. "This is a cursed place," he called out. "Or maybe you already know that." A car crossed the bridge, causing a thundering echo. "Let me see your face."

The figure stepped backwards, clutching a violin and bow in front of him. Connor could see the paint can better as morning slid under the bridge. It was a varnish called Dragon Blood. A memory circled back to his childhood . . . seeing the Dragon Blood wrapper half buried in the sandy bank. This man had been making and painting violins for a long time. Likely then hanging them under here to dry.

"I'm not leaving," Connor said, "until I know what you are to this place." Looking down into the water, he assessed it to be a few feet deep. He could jump into it and be on that side of the canal before the man had time to get up the bank.

The figure brought the violin up to his chin and crossed the bow upon the strings in quick jerks. The tune slid, rising like an eagle headed toward the sun and drifting like a leaf whose only destination could be the earth. Connor raised a hand at the sound as if he could stop it. The music filled his mouth, his throat, every cell of his body drowning in its essence where the music was a story. A flash of blond hair. A smile. A cat-eyed woman tickling his tummy. His nose dug into a hair braid and the smell of lye soap as if it'd just been washed. Connor found himself choking, unable to pull in breath. He turned to his side and coughed, crawling on his knees toward the light.

Once he made it from under the bridge, he turned to look. The form was gone. Connor struggled upright. What was this memory that had taken him to his knees? Who was that man who disarmed him with a tune? Connor held to the ground, muscles twitching. This was not his imagination. This was real. That violinist was real. He held on to the rocks of the earth, determined to regain his composure. Go back under, he told himself. Get one of those violins. As much as he tried, he couldn't. The darkness had won.

49

Two days later, Connor sat on his front porch swing, hands shaking after he'd repeated the story of the Violinist. Beside him, Herman held a coffee mug and a flask of liquor. "Take a swig," Herman said, pouring some whiskey into the cup.

Connor waved him away and rubbed his palms over his eyes, hoping to still the tremble. Daylight hadn't calmed the horror he'd felt under the bridge. "I have never experienced that kind of terror." He leaned back, fighting a nauseous wave through his innards. "The music suffocated me. Like I'd heard it before. It was real and not real, a place where memory is more a dream. I know I'm not making sense."

"Sense has been kicking your ass lately. No wonder."

"I know I looked into the face of a killer," Connor insisted. "Not like the people we know. Something, somebody more dangerous, something that kills without reason, something that likes it."

Rory's car pulled into the driveway. When she opened the door, she stayed seated, looking over at them with a guarded expression. Her steps to the porch were measured and hesitant. "Eleven," she said, and cleared her throat. "State forensic teams have pulled eleven skeletons from under the bridge during the last two days of digging. They let me into the site and from what I saw . . ."

"They were female," Connor finished the sentence for her.

"No violins," she said, "so he'd taken them, but there were enough varnish droppings to determine that human blood was mixed with the paint."

"Sick," Herman said, shaking his head.

"Did they find a skull with no body?" Connor asked, thinking of Bette Moss.

"So far not. But since you mentioned it, there was a woman there asking the same thing."

"Renita Stark," he said.

"She was a handful. State police had to call one of her relatives to pull her away and take her home."

"Her daughter was murdered under that bridge. Head never found." Connor and Herman shared a glance, seeming to understand that they'd keep their youthful obsession to themselves.

Herman leaned back in the swing, taking the flask with him and sipping. "This killer's been living among us. No telling how long. Using our land to hide his trophies. Connor, you were probably lucky not to be killed yourself."

Connor shook his head. "No, I'm not what he was looking for. This piece of work crafts a song for each victim, weaves those women into his spell." Connor stood, taking the coffee mug from Herman and drinking deeply. "There's another skeleton there," he said. "One the police haven't found."

"How do you figure?" Herman asked.

"There were twelve violins. One for each body, so one is missing." Connor finished off the whiskey even as his stomach twisted in knots. "And he was playing a thirteenth," he said and held to the porch post. "Every prey has her own death song. He's already picked out his next victim."

"There was one feature they had in common." Rory said. "They were all blonds." From the side yard, the cow lumbered out, a handful of grass clinging to her mouth. She mooed as if surprised by their presence, her soulful eye glancing upon them, then she continued to munch. Rory stopped a giggle by pressing her fingers over her lips. "Perhaps it's time to show you some good news." She pulled a Polaroid from her jacket pocket and handed it to Connor.

Justin and Tallulah. She sat up in bed, his arm around her supporting her back. Looking into the camera like she was trying to read the lens, her smile was less tired and she lifted one hand as if to wave. Connor was filled with joy despite her fragile appearance. This was the first time she'd sat up in weeks.

"I need to head down there," he said, hopping off the porch and into the path of the cow. "Just as soon as I find out where Bessie here belongs before she eats me out of grass and home."

◌◠

Figuring the cow hadn't strayed far, Connor looped a rope around her neck and led her down the street toward a series of fenced-off lots where Warwick merged with the Suffolk neighborhood. As they walked, she nuzzled up beside him, and he scratched her behind the ear. It wasn't long before the cow took the lead and turned into a field where the gate lock had rusted off. He followed the cow to a pond and lifted the rope from around her neck. She slurped water, joined by her sisters, who mooed at Connor

398

as if to tell him to get along. Connor chuckled, and used the rope to tie off the broken lock mechanism. As he stared at the landscape, peaceful except for the vivid colors, he couldn't help but think how it resembled the land where his dead women lived. He corrected himself: it wasn't a real place. He knew well that he had created it; his imagination had resurrected those victims as icons he depended on to aid him in seeing beneath the surface of human reality. It no longer bothered him that his mind had turned toward the macabre. If Einstein rode on moonbeams, his fantastical landscape had served him in curious ways. The cow turned and mooed, then a bell rang and the entire herd trotted toward a barn in the distance.

Connor walked back to his house in thought. The cow and the walk had dispelled the shakiness of the last few days. As horrible as the thought of a killer burying his victims in their town, it was the business of the police. He hated that he'd been unable to give them more of a description of the man under the bridge. One of the state patrol officers had pointed out that there was no direct connection to the man Connor saw and the bodies. It could have been a coincidence, someone who liked to play under the bridge for the unique sound it created. Connor didn't like how the officer had eyed him for knowing there would be victims, but the first several had IDs dating them to the 1940s, when he was a child. That alone had probably prevented the police from taking him in for questioning.

A green car passed him, slowed, and reversed. He fingered the gun in his pocket, stepping quickly to the side of the road where he might hide behind trees if he needed to shoot. The window rolled down and a blond-haired woman leaned out. Serena Lawson, now Gaylor. She'd been a student of his and had married Greg, one of Randi Jo's brothers. In the backseat, strapped into a baby harness and squeezing a stuffed buffalo, was Butch, another of Randi Jo's brothers, who now lived with Greg and Serena. Butch reached out his good hand toward him and made a high-pitched squealing sound that Connor had learned was his *happy to see you* vocalization. Despite his many disabilities– near-blindness, deafness, withered legs, and bent arm–Butch never seemed to forget anyone who showed him kindness, and had a way of sucker punching people he disliked.

"Mr. Herne," she called out in the way of former students, who never became comfortable with his first name. "You need to come with me, quick as a hare. Dr. Huber sent me to get you."

"Tallulah?" he said, a stabbing fear shooting through him.

"No, your daughter is fine. We visited her a few hours ago. That's when we ran into Dr. Huber and figured it out." Serena leaned over and unlocked the opposite door. "It's Randi Jo," she whispered as he got in. "She's come back."

50

Connor stood in the doorway of the hospital room, unsure of what direction to turn his eyes: toward Randi Jo lying in bed, eyes swollen shut, cheek crushed, jaw broken, arm tied up in a sling, or the circle of dead women ringed around his ex-wife, singing out to him: *save her, save her, save her. Find a way to save her.* Dian broke the circle and challenged him, *Save her and we'll save you.* This was what they wanted him to do.

Dr. Huber slipped from behind him, explaining that she was found near the outskirts of Coalfire, beaten, raped, and near death in a hovel of trouble called Spit. "Had her in surgery twice," Dr. Huber said. "I don't know if she'll make it."

"If she'll make it," Connor repeated, not wanting to acknowledge the words. "Simon finds out she's here, he'll end her."

"She'd gone back to using her maiden name on her ID," Dr. Huber said, moving to the bed and checking her pulse. "I contacted the only Gaylors I knew, the ones who owned the corner flower shop. Had no idea, Connor. Had no idea of the connection to you."

The dead women looked at him, imploring his help. He cleared his throat, approaching the bed, and touched her finger on the one spot that wasn't purple with bruises. Yes, there was something about her: her sweetness, her kindness, her bravery, her tolerance. He'd never appreciated the life this woman had lived, never realized until this moment that her every action had been to protect her daughter or him. He was ashamed of himself. He'd played a part in how she'd come to this hospital room. How dare they, he thought. How dare they do this to this woman he had loved. And he loved her still. A welling of pity overwhelmed him as he took in her broken body. He hadn't the courage to imagine what this had done to her spirit. Shades of the dead clasped hands and formed a protective circle around her. They knew, he realized. They knew the horror Randi Jo had been through. "Get her through this, Dr. Huber. Get her through this and I'll keep her safe. I'll find a way."

Dr. Huber crossed the room to Connor, drawing him out into the hallway with Greg and Serena. Butch clutched his stuffed buffalo, and Serena shifted him for a better hold. The boy turned his head away from the room, as if he realized the damage no human being should ever suffer, and other than a whine made no sound.

"Got a colleague with a clinic up North," Dr. Huber said. "He can hide her under a fake name. Some of the cost'll be donated, but she's going to need time and money to get out from under this and start a new life."

Greg and Serena looked at each other. Connor, too, was at a loss. All of them thinking the same thing—none of them had that kind of money.

"We could get a loan on our business," Greg said. "Corral in all the other brothers and sisters, ask them to pitch in."

402

"No," Connor said. "The fewer people know of this, the safer she is."

"I know a man who can make her a new identity," Dr. Huber said, "but none of it's cheap."

Connor scratched the back of his head. "I have some house equity."

Butch reared back his head and conked Greg in the nose, making a whining sound. "Sorry," Serena said as Butch wound his arm around and smacked Connor on the cheek.

"Butch!" Greg said, "Stop that." Butch backhanded Greg, causing his lip to bleed.

"I don't know what's got into him," Serena said, stepping back to keep him from striking anyone else. "Unless . . . I know what he's trying to say."

"Honey," Greg said. "Butch can't say anything."

"You know as well as I do that he has his way, and I think he's telling you that he'll give you the money."

"Butch has money?" Connor asked, rubbing his jaw.

"Sitting on a bundle," Serena explained. "His mother set up a trust at the bank. Remember the black-lung settlement from your father's passing?" She nodded toward Greg. "She set some of it aside, and the banker invested it. With compounding, he's a little tycoon."

Connor and Greg looked at one another, then at Butch, who was winding up his arm again. Both men stepped back.

"Think you better take him up on your offer," Dr. Huber said, "or I'll be treating the two of you for cracked noggins."

Serena jostled Butch to her other hip and touched his nose with hers. "We'll take care of Butch the rest of his life whether he has a dime to his name or not." She reached out and touched her husband's arm. "He wants to do this for his sister."

The four of them looked into Randi Jo's room. A blade of moonlight struck the edge of the bed and blended into a worn floor tile, giving it a reflective quality. Her legs jerked and she moaned as she reached out with her one uninjured hand. Serena sniffed and held Butch close. Greg's expression hardened as he watched his sister struggle against an invisible culprit. Connor could only look away, blaming himself and hoping he could live up to the expectations of his shades. In that cacophony of painful thought, he realized they were not alone. Connor shifted to his left to see Rusty Haskew hiding in the stairwell with the door cracked open. He'd heard everything they said.

Connor rushed the door, knocking Rusty backwards. Grabbing him by the collar, he flung Rusty into the hallway and pinned him against the wall. "You did this to her, you sonnavabitch!" Shaking him by the collar, he realized Rusty was not fighting back. Stepping away, Connor let him fall to his knees.

"I didn't," Rusty said, his voice a weaving slur. "I'd never have done something like that to her."

"You might as well have." Greg leaned over him. "You destroyed her life."

"I didn't know. I didn't realize this could happen." His swollen eyes were red-rimmed and his lips trembled. "When I heard whisperings, I went out to look for her. Was gonna try and get her out of town. I've learned things."

"You tell anybody about Randi Jo being here, and I'll kill you with my bare hands." Connor jerked him upright and shoved him toward the stairwell.

"You don't understand what it is to be me," Rusty said, hand to his forehead as he struggled to keep down a sob. "You don't even know the things I've prevented!"

"You're pathetic," Connor spat. "Like I need your help."

"You do," he croaked. "You might not realize it, but you do."

"I swear, Rusty. I swear, anybody finds out she's here . . ."

"There's a truth you need to know."

"Rusty, every word out of your mouth is the seed of a lie. There's nothing you can tell me that I don't already know."

Rusty hesitated and stared at the floor. "Here's truth for you. Simon's looking for her," he said. "Count on that. I've been trying to find her so I could head his crew off." Rusty sniffed and wiped an eye. "Trust me," he said, holding a hand up at if pledging. "They'll not hear about her from me. But whatever you're going to do, do it quick. After that, when she's safe away, we need to talk." He looked into Randi Jo's room, lips frowning as he limped toward the exit. As the door swung closed, Butch threw his buffalo and it bounced off Rusty's back.

Connor fought the urge to spit in Rusty's direction, but why waste energy on a rascal like him. "How fast can you get things in motion, Dr. Huber?" Connor asked, knowing that time might now be against them. "You can't count on Rusty not running straight to Simon."

"I'll make the calls. We'll move her soon as she's stable."

"I'll get somebody here to stand guard. In the meantime, Dr. Huber, you know how to use a gun?" Connor pulled his own firearm from his pocket.

Dr. Huber pressed his lips together, observing the gun. "I come from the Scarlett O'Hara school of pistolry. I can shoot straight, long as I don't have to shoot too far."

"Good enough." Connor turned to Greg and Serena. "Get the money together, whatever you can, and bring it to Dr. Huber."

"Can't believe he showed his face here." Greg glared toward the stairwell where Rusty had left. "We'll do our part."

Connor held out a hand to Butch. "Thank you, young man. I'm buying you a spanking new buffalo." Butch high-fived him.

After they'd gone, Connor stood in the doorway, watching Randi Jo. The curious little girl she had been played in his memory, and recollections of her as a young woman danced like fireflies in his thoughts. The lightness of her touch; freshness of her kiss; the aroma of honeysuckle after she'd washed her hair. She was a woman without a friend in the world. If she lived through the night, the four who knew would carry the secret of her survival to their graves. He'd have to confront Rusty. Offer him something to keep quiet. The Black Dahlia stroked Randi Jo's forehead, and then she was gone. So were the others. In his mind, Connor thanked them for holding him to task. He realized that the dead women were in every woman that he knew, because any of them could be the victim of monsters; but with everything in his power, he would make sure Randi Jo was not going to join them. Outside the window, the mountain range seemed to breathe, rising like a goddess–the only woman with the power to take her vengeance on mankind.

Connor clenched his fists, nails biting into his palms. Randi Jo had given him one last gift: anger . . . the final ingredient for the cauldron of wrath percolating in his mind. He knew exactly what to do to find those barrels, take down Willie, Darius, and anybody else who got in his way.

51

Tearing through drawers he hadn't opened in years, Connor finally found an old cigar box. Flipping it open, he smiled at the contents–a 1938 penny given to him by his grandmother on his eighth birthday, an old worn-out key to the grocery store, and a blond lock of Tallulah's baby hair–but it was two other items he had been searching for: a rabbit's foot and a silver lighter engraved with Darius Stark's initials, *DS*. He clipped the rabbit's foot to his keys, *for luck*, he supposed, and held the silver lighter in front of him. Now, all he had to do was gather his gang, his group of motley warriors. He'd known most of them since childhood. He trusted all of them with his life.

Looking at their faces, he smiled, knowing they could implement his plan like no other people in the world. His pupils sat upright in the table-armed desks that likely brought back anxious memories of high school days. Connor was at home in his classroom. On a blackboard behind him, he diagramed out his plan like an algebraic equation. Arrows and boxes filled the board with contingencies and false starts; what to do if one element fell through or another went in an unexpected direction. "We can't give him any time to think," Connor said. "Darius Stark is ruled by superstition and his drug-addled mind. We gotta let those be his motivator." Connor tapped the endgame, then nodding to his compatriots, he erased it all. "We're going to cut off the head of the snake," he said. "And we start with my mother's bones."

Despite all the misery that had taken place at the Lester Street Bridge, in the afternoon sunlight it looked friendly. Local community groups had built a walking path on the high bank and a garden club had planted an assortment of perennials. Tiger lilies were flowering now, with a few out-of-season tulips and daffodils scattered along the edge. Connor stared at the still water as he waited. A paddling of ducks caused a vector of ripples. Beneath, all shades of russet and umber. From the east, Tempy approached, Iona Stark half dragging her.

"Thank you for coming, Iona," he said. "My sister will need all the support she can get in this troublesome time."

"You said this was about murder. Is Tempy in trouble?" Iona wrapped an arm around his sister's shoulders. "I warn you, a Stark attorney will defend her like she's one of our own."

Connor exhaled, nodded and let the tension build. "It's about my mother."

Tempy expelled a shivery breath and looked out onto the canal. "Maybe it's best to leave the past buried," she said. "Ever thought of it that way?"

"I'm only surprised that you do."

Tempy shifted beside him, their shoulders touching. "I'm not angry anymore, not the way I was when I was young." She touched his hand. "I call you my brother," she pleaded, biting her lip and cracking a knuckle for the first time that he'd seen in years.

"But I'm not your brother," Connor replied, keeping his voice stony. "Your brother is out there, buried in unconsecrated ground with a woman he never knew."

"How did you guess it would be here?" she asked, her lower lip trembling.

Connor leaned against the bridge railing. "It always came back to this bridge. Here was where you threatened to leave the past behind. You held on to the place where something happened to you. Something awful that you can't let go of. Was the Rhine house next to this canal? What happened all those years ago that has scarred you so deeply that its played in your mind like a looping horror movie your entire life?"

Tempy pressed her fingers to her lips and squeezed her eyes closed. "You think that man who killed those woman also killed your mother."

"It would seem plausible, don't you think?"

She looked up at him, shaking her head. "Mom was lucky he didn't kill her, too."

"No," Connor said. "He wasn't playing Mom's song that night."

Closing her eyes, Tempy's hand drifted in front of her face, waving gently like the drift of algae in deep water. "There was music that night. A violin played the saddest tune I'd ever heard. It broke on the high notes and drifted down as if it was the lowest pitch a sound could make. I thought the musician must be playing to the moon as it dissolved, a slice at a time." Both hands adjusted her glasses, then she shaped the houses in the air. "We lived there," she pointed. "I hid under the porch. I walked out into the dark, worried Mother would never come back. I'm afraid to be alone. All I wanted was Mother, her touch, her voice, then I'd feel safe." Her hands clasped at her heart as tears drifted down her cheeks. "I don't think I've ever felt safe since that night." She held her breath. "There," she said, pointing at the orange rock down the shore. "You'll have to dig deep. That's why she wasn't found when they dug up those other women. Mom wanted my dead brother never to have existed. She wanted him to be you. You'll have to dig deep." She sniffed, lips pressed to seal in emotions she didn't want to show. She glanced at Connor, her expression one of hope that she'd done what he wanted.

"Why don't you and Iona wait in the hotel lobby," he said, pointing at the Regal Hotel. "I'll let you know if we need anything else."

He nodded to Rory, waiting down by the edge of the bridge with a crew from the county coroner's office. Pointing to the orange rock, Connor walked to the corner telephone and called Herman to tell him the next part of the plan was ready.

Less than an hour later, the first bone emerged from the malleable earth. Connor looked down into the hole as the coroner dusted off a skull. Her blond hair trailed around her shoulders. Some of the clothing was still intact, a navy serge suit, from what he could tell. As the remains took shape, two arms wrapped around a small skeleton made him want to cry. He sucked in the congestion and looked at Rory, who came over and held his hand.

"You can do this," she said. "I'll go get the others ready."

He leaned down and scooped up a handful of dirt, then walked toward the hotel. He'd never been inside the Regal Hotel. Its red velvet couches and deep purple drapes gave it a movie theater ambiance. With its stories of fallen women and marauding

410

gangsters, he suspected that many of the skeletons that lay buried underneath the bridge had once lived here. He hadn't seen any women going in and out of the hotel as long as he'd been here and figured they'd all been told to check out until the police presence had died down. Connor sat next to Tempy and rubbed her shoulder. Her eyes were red rimmed and her shoulders trembled. "It's not them," he said, looking at her directly as he lied.

Tempy shook her head. "How could it not be them?"

"They might be buried deeper, but the skeleton they've come across has a silver lamé purse holding a driver's license that identifies her as Brenda Crider." He sucked in air, noticing the slight twitch of Iona's eyes.

"Deeper then, I told you to dig deep."

"They'll keep going," he nodded. "Seems this Brenda went missing years ago. I recall it being talked about in some bars I used to hang around at back when I was home from college." Connor pulled a plastic bag from his pocket and pointed to a silver cigarette lighter. "County sheriff deputized me, asked me to take it down to the state police lab so they can analyze it." He held the lighter up for both women to see. "This is one that can be solved. See that DS engraved in the side? Not her initials, so probably belongs to the last person who saw her, probably the person who killed her. Might even be fingerprints."

Iona leaned forward, eyes snapped onto the lighter. She coughed aside and touched her forehead. "Good Lord, I've forgotten I was supposed to teach seniors' Bible study tonight," she pantomimed. "I need to make a call and get myself replaced. Best I stay with Tempy with all this upset going on."

"Kind of you, Iona." Connor leaned his head to one side to acknowledge her. He watched as she frantically dialed from the hotel desk and covered her mouth with a hand as she talked.

Connor stroked Tempy's shoulder. "It's going to be okay," he said. "I am your brother. I'll always be your brother." She leaned into him and wept, holding to his neck as if she didn't want to let go. Now, all Connor had to do was wait.

ᐧᐧ

"I come to preach for the dead," Bryson Pomeroy said to the heavens as Darius Stark emerged from a black sedan parked in front of the Regal Hotel. He glanced sideways at the minister, then slammed the car door. Lingering on the opposite side of the bridge, he leaned over the railing and peered into the water, then glanced both directions down Marcescent Street.

"For the dead have no need of their secrets and the living carry them like a curse. I am here to say to you that God above sees all, knows all, but what you mere mortals forget is the devil himself knows every detail of what we try to hide from the world. He's out there waiting to claim you as his own." Bryson stood on a fruit carton just as he had as a child, letting the twilight settle around him. A smattering of people stood around him, calling out an occasional *Amen*. "Old blue devil tempted me once. Almost dragged me down to the brimstone palace!"

Connor stood on the lower bank at the end of the hole, looking into the darkness. Darius slid down the side hill in what was now a well-worn path. He tentatively looked around as if this were something he did every night.

"Evening," Connor said, tipping the front of a cap that he hoped Darius would assume was law enforcement. "Can't be down here. Place is still under police control."

"Crazy preacher." Darius nodded toward Bryson up on the bridge.

"Just words of comfort."

"Of foolishness," Darius chortled and spit aside. "Hear they found more than one person's remains. Thought I'd pay my respects. See if there was anything my family could do."

"Your family?"

"I'm a Stark. You know who we are?"

"Ah." Connor nodded, then pointed. "Eleven under the bridge." He stepped onto lower ground, keeping himself at an angle and his cap tilted down. "One here." He nodded toward the hole. "Still looking for evidence over there." He pointed to some marshy reeds near the edge of the bridge.

"The ghosts of the dead will have their vengeance. Our better angels will see to it," Bryson preached.

Darius studied the reeds, then stared into the darkness under the bridge. "You see that?" Darius said, pointing at the shadows.

"The Blue Devil taught me that there was no escaping the sins of the past," Pomeroy continued, his voice sliding up and down a musical scale.

"Wish that fool would shut up."

"I don't see anything," Connor said, coming up behind him.

Darius jumped. "Hellfire, man! Don't sneak up on a body!" The heels of his boots slid on the rocky shore, and Connor reached out to steady him. "How long they think this body was down there?"

"Maybe a few decades. Be a guess, but I think I saw that same sequin gown in a movie from the late 1950s."

"Gown," he repeated. "Sequin? Poor girl. Evidence, I'd say."

"Guess if the preacher there is right," Connor let his voice lower, "devil take whoever did this." He held out Herman's whiskey flask, and Darius grabbed it, drinking deep.

Nervously, Darius looked underneath of the bridge. "Whoa!" he squealed, and jumped behind Connor. "What is that thing?" A woman, tattered dress lifting with the breeze, stood at the overhang of the bridge. Her blackened eyes and sunken cheeks gave her a skeletal appearance. Slowly she raised a hand and pointed to Darius. "You see that?"

Connor turned to face Darius and block his access to the bridge. "I don't see anything but the bridge."

"No, that woman!"

"What woman?"

Darius pushed Connor aside and ran to the edge of the bridge, but didn't go underneath. "She was here."

"Nobody's there. You can't go under there," Connor said, coming up beside him. "Area's taped off by the state police."

Darius rubbed his eyes. "Awfulest thing I ever saw." He drank again from the flask. "Giving this stuff up starting tomorrow."

"Blue Devil scrambled around my feet and tripped me at my lowest point," Bryson bleated from his perch above. A car rumbled across the bridge, causing it to quiver with the timbre of his voice.

"Heard they found some things among the bones might identify the person buried."

"Evidence that'll bury the killer," Connor said. "Bet the Blue Devil like to get his hands on that sinner."

"Never judge what I don't know about."

"The Blue Devil is watching you now, ready to pounce on you sinners!" Bryson let his voice raise amid the *Amens* of his listeners.

"Shut up, you old fool!" Darius yelled and turned. He froze mid-breath as he faced Blue Toomey squatting on the canal bank, making like a demon ready to eat his prey. He pointed at Darius, letting his grin spread into a spooky leer.

"Don't you tell me you don't see that?" Darius hollered.

Connor turned around, face-to-face with Blue Toomey, grateful to him for allowing his inky blueness to return. "I don't see a thing," Connor said, and winked. "Only the canal bank and the preacher."

"At least he's real."

"Good words he's saying, don't ya think?"

"I gotta get off the pills and juice." Darius rubbed his head. "Get away from me, demon. I already know what you've got to say."

Blue Toomey moved to the side and jumped toward Darius, who fell backward into the ankle-deep canal. He popped up, scrambling for the opposite bank, whining a high-pitched squeal as he ran.

"Repent to the honest Lord or die!" Pomerory preached.

Toomey mimicked Darius's run all the way up to the road as he ran to the hotel.

Connor hurried under the bridge and met Justin, Rory, and Tallulah. "Get her back to the hospital now!"

"I'm fine, Daddy," Tallulah said, rubbing her cheek. "See, this is mostly makeup. Who else had the body frame to pull off a ghostly girlfriend?" She held up her scarecrow arms and laughed.

"I don't want to take any chances," Connor said.

She put her arms around him and hugged. "What you're doing is brilliant. You're riding on moonbeams."

Connor shook hands with Toomey Manfred and Bryson Pomeroy, assuring them he didn't need them for the rest of the evening. He followed Darius's path to the Regal Hotel and waited in the side alley until Herman pulled up.

"Got the phone call right on schedule," he said to him. They entered the hotel and the desk manager nodded that Darius was expecting him. When Connor started to follow, a baseball bat came between him and the wall.

"He didn't say you," the desk manager interjected.

"I'm security," Connor showed his pistol strapped to his waist.

"And I'm Yogi Bear." He held out a box. "Drop it in, or you don't get on that elevator."

415

Reluctantly, Connor set his gun into the container, glaring at the manager, who shoved it under his desk.

The manager glared back with a surge of *humph* to his expression. "Jonas Stark sets the rules here, not little brother Darius. Remember that when you next visit."

They got on the elevator when it hit them that the desk manager thought they were going to party with Darius and visit the girls that worked the hotel. "Rules to visit hoochy girls," Herman said, "who knew?"

The elevator door opened at the fifth floor to an empty hallway. Herman knocked on door 509 and entered at the command of a gruff "Yeah!" As he turned, he left the door ajar, and Connor saw a single room that looked out toward the bridge; liquor bottles covered a side dresser and overfilled trash cans evidenced Darius's love of fast food.

"I was having dinner with my family," Herman complained. "Don't like getting ordered over here."

A faucet ran and water splashed as Darius either wet his face or washed his hands.

"You know something," Darius said, "I don't ever remember selling you that gas station."

"Well, you did," Herman said. "So I don't work for you anymore. I put enough Starks in jail to break a mafia, so maybe we ought to take a vacation from each other for the rest of our lives."

"I don't hold a grudge," Darius snickered, glass clinking. Herman must have set some cups between them. "Yeah, but me and you, boy, we got a little secret, don't we?" Herman was quiet, and the sound of a bottle opening indicated Darius was into the liquor. "Take a seat now."

"That was a long time ago, Darius."

"Don't be a crybaby."

"I was a kid. If'n it'd been today, I'd do it all different."

"Want you to tell me where we buried her."

A scrape of a chair against the floor indicated that Herman had sat down. "I have no idea where we were," he said. "You did the driving."

"Go over it with me again. My memory ain't so good."

"You were pilled up out of your head, wonder you can remember anything."

"And you let me drive? Thanks a lot, friend. Now, tell it to me again."

As Herman relayed the made-up details of that long ago evening where Darius had knocked a young woman through a window, he embellished the story, leading Darius to believe that he had buried the girl in a place where she'd never be found, a place Herman had never seen before; a place where Darius said she'd always be hidden.

"So that can't be her out under the bridge?" Darius mused. "Unless one of my idiot relatives found her and moved the body there." Silence. The scrap of a chair, pacing, sound of a bottle opening. Liquor being poured. "And you don't know where we buried her?" Darius asked.

"You buried her. I waited in the car."

"Hmmmm. Must've been on the yellow sunshine that night, 'cause all I recall is waking up the next morning in Critter's with a hangover."

"You did the driving, made me pull my cap down over my eyes so I wouldn't see where we were going," Herman said, his voice a polished sincerity. "Elsewise, I could tell you more, but you said only Starks could know this place. That's why I had to wait in the car."

"She smoking that night? She use my lighter?"

Herman shrugged. "I guess so. Why would you care about that, of all things?"

Connor smiled at how well Herman played Darius. Starks weren't ruled by common sense but by their own hubris. Each time Herman laid out a generalization, Darius filled in all the blanks.

A scrape from behind him caused Connor to turn quickly. The hallway was empty and the door to the attic tapped in its frame. He took a step and listened. His imagination? He peered into a dark passage up a narrow staircase leading up to the attic. A light switch didn't work, so he listened, hearing nothing. A whiff of a sharp odor wafted by him, mixed with the musty smell of a sealed room. He quietly closed the door and looked out a window at the street below. Opposite the hotel, Rory waited in a car, ready for him to leap in and follow Darius . . . if their plan worked. And it had to work. Right now, Connor was betting on Darius Stark's paranoia running his show. He returned to the room and leaned back into the cracked door.

"Don't you remember you told me we'd bury her where no one would ever find her?" Herman said.

"Yeah, yeah, that'd be the smart thing to do," Darius said. The bounce of a glass against the table indicated he was drinking heavily. "Where nothing would ever be found."

"Where would that be, Darius? Where would you put something that nobody would ever find?"

A chair scraped along with the thud of a bottle hitting the table. "Come on, Cahill, you're driving me. I'm going to dig up that bitch."

Connor hurried to the end of the hall and hid on the attic staircase. He peeked around, catching Herman's eye as the two men waited for the elevator. Now it was a matter of letting Darius go to the place *where nothing would ever be found.* Connor would bet all he owned that the barrels would be in that same location. As the elevator door closed, he stepped out to follow them. A flash whipped past his eyes and caught him around the throat. His fingers touched a grainy wire before he realized his air was cut off. Connor gasped, trying to turn, but whoever held the garrote around his neck controlled him, dragging him up the attic staircase. He found himself whaling backwards, and the more he tried to fight, the less breath he inhaled. He was being strangled . . . to death.

52

Connor clawed at the tightening noose around his throat. A hand clamped onto the side of his head and twisted. His neck strained against the motion as he struggled for air. Grabbing on to a sinewy arm, he lifted his feet and pushed off against the wall. Disorienting his attacker enough, Connor fell, landing on his knees and hands. He pulled a stringy band of wire from his neck and struggled to rise as he sucked in air. Above him, a shadow with a shock of white hair was regaining his balance. The man ripped a violin bow off the wall and sliced it through the air. From the end shot a bronze-colored spike.

Moving sideways, Connor steadied himself against the wall and assessed the direction of the staircase. Too far to get to without engaging the man. He backed up toward a fireplace mantle where a burning half candle illuminated the attic. Violins hung on every wall and rafter. Connor cast his gaze around at a worktable where wood shavings piled in heaps and horsehair hung in bundles. Cans of Dragon Blood varnish lined a shelf, an open can scenting the air with its astringent bloom. On a separate desk, piles of sheet music formed organized stacks. Pages littered the floor from their struggle.

"Sit down, stupid man," the Shadow said, swishing the blade toward a chair. He stepped into the candlelight. A hazy, golden glow revealed a face older than Connor had expected, given the enormous strength it must have taken to drag him up the steps. An oversized forehead sporting deep wrinkles seemed to sit on his head like a hat. The rest of his face squished together like an out-of-proportion line drawing: a hawkish nose overhung a mouth that looked like crumpled-up scratch paper, wobbly jowls surrounded a thin white mustache and goatee, but there was no mistaking the black shark-eyes of a Stark.

Connor moved in the direction of the chair but didn't sit. Upright, the man's wiry frame looked oversized, as if he were a skeleton walking. He held the bow like a fencing sword, and Connor saw it was no wooden bow, but rather metal, strong enough to pierce him. Scooting the chair between them, Connor wiped sweat off his upper lip. His fingers touched his throat and he realized it was wet with blood.

"Gut strings," the man said, glancing at the violin strings he had used to choke Connor. "Sometimes you use whatever you can find." He kicked them aside. "Too rich a sound for the likes of you. I once decapitated a flutist with a gut-string garrote. A fella like you, steel cord would make you dance." He tapped the tip of the bow on the back of the chair, keeping the spike toward Connor. "I said, *Sit*." His hard-clipped accent sounded like stones dropped in water.

"You killed my mother," Connor said, trying to discern the man's choppy accent, "Was she the first?" He motioned with his hand toward all the violins mounted in lines across the roof rafters.

"You were the ghost under the bridge." The Violinist narrowed his eyes, studying him. "Why do you haunt there?"

"I was in her arms. Was she trying to run away from you? Did you know her, or was she a stranger who took a wrong turn?"

The Violinist's eyes fluttered for a moment as he was remembering.

"Someone interrupted you," Connor said, reviewing the distance to the attic door as he spoke. "She took the baby and buried the woman." Connor coughed out the words, reliving or imagining the past, he wasn't sure.

"I followed her from the old world. She was a challenge. Delicious." His voice stretched out like a note held too long.

"You followed her," Connor repeated. "What was her name? Why her? What did you want from her?"

"Questions. Always questions. People would do better to hold their tongues. Not that it changes the final sonata." He reached up and took hold of a child's violin from the wall. "That one was for you, hmmm?" He scratched the bow across the strings, making a full-bodied sound. "Had it not been for you, she would have been mine for life, in life. It was her choice, and my song. Let me play for you. The song I wrote holds her essence. We can end this sweetly, and I will allow you to know her again. Know her as I knew her."

Connor breathed in the notes, mesmerizing tones that linked one to the other in a deep resonance of sadness. He put out a hand out as if to say *Stop*. His voice froze inside of him, the music binding him as it had under the bridge. Was this the song the murderer had played all those years ago? Had his mother been bound by the hypnotic notes as well? Had she gone to her death trying to protect him? On a crowded shelf above the desk, a copy of *Letters to Solovine* stood out. The Einstein book shook him back to reality as the Violinist leaned in toward him, weaving his body like a snake as he performed the mesmerizing tune whose notes hung in the air like teardrops. "Come now," he said, nodding toward the chair. "It has always been destined."

"Only thing," Connor said, "I'm not a slave to the song." He kicked the chair forward, catching the Violinist in the chest, the bow swishing toward his neck. As the blade came back, it cut Connor's underarm and he called out, grabbing the wound. He lunged forward, catching the old man's wrist on the downswing. The violin crashed on the back of his head, stunning him. Connor grabbed for the man's knees and pulled up, taking him down. The Violinist's head bounced on the floor, and Connor kicked the bow-blade away. Flipping him onto his stomach, he kneed him between the shoulder blades and grabbed a handful of violin stings to tie the Violinist's hands and feet, anchoring him to a steam pipe.

"Those are E stings," the Violinist complained. "You know how hard it is to get a decent E string?"

"Sometimes you use whatever you can find."

"I'll kill you for this."

"Who are you?" Connor asked as he reinforced the bonds with his own belt. "I don't ever remember seeing you, but you've been here a long time."

The Violinist chuckled. "Invisibility is my gift, stupid man," he said, straining against the binding. "You think you have won. You have not. You think I don't see your childish games from my window, a blue man, a ghostly woman. I see them come up the other side of the bridge." He chuckled again. "I told Darius everything. You have killed your friend." His low maniacal laughter sent chills through Connor, and he bolted for the door, the man's final words echoing in his head. "Better that you would have died under that bridge!"

When he hit the lobby, Connor screamed at the desk clerk, "Where'd they go? What direction?"

The clerk stood and sneered at him. "None of your business where Mr. Stark goes."

Connor swiped his hand through the desk, spilling all the contents onto the floor. "Give me my gun!"

"You get!" he hollered, bringing up Connor's gun and pointing it. "I need no cops to take care of the likes of you." The clerk fired into the wall.

Connor ran outside. Rory's car was gone. She would have followed Herman and Darius when he didn't come out. Why? he thought. How could this have gone so wrong? Darius knew they'd tried to trick him. He'd kill Herman, and if he saw Rory, he'd kill her too. He'd put his friends in danger. He looked up at the attic of the Regal Hotel. Maybe the Violinist was right: *It would indeed have been better if he had died that night so long ago.*

Out in the street, he turned in a circle. What could he do? Who could help? The desk clerk had followed him out, baseball bat over his shoulder, pointing the pistol into the air and shouting obscenities at him. Connor ran. Sliding down the canal bank, he raced toward Copperhead Fields, every demon of his life chasing him.

As he entered the woods, pulling himself along the tree line, his chest burned from exertion. He paused, sucking in air, and held to a tree. The elbow cut had soaked his shirt in blood. He ripped off the opposite sleeve and tied it around the wound. Trudging forward, he thought if he could get to Contrary, he could get help. Call the state police. The FBI. How would he even explain this? His friends had trusted him. Guilt plagued him that he'd lost track of Darius. Where could he have gone? Connor had no idea what direction to go.

Closing his eyes, he focused past the pain in his body, the terror in his mind, and spoke to the dark: "If any part of you has ever been real, help me. Help me now."

He saw them in his imagination. Beautiful, talented, and with a wealth of gifts to offer the world. Taken down by monsters at a time when their lives should have been the most full. Connor no longer fought the heady sensation of the dead, the whispering voices, lingering stares, sad and yet poignant as if waiting on the next experience of his life. Beautiful Dorothy Stratten, barefoot and walking amid daisies, didn't appear to have a memory of the horror of her death at the hands of her ex-husband; the talented Dominque Dunne, as well, had taken her last breath at the hands of a boyfriend who should have loved her, should have protected her, and instead choked the life from her. Now she swung in a tire swing from an apple tree in the side yard. Dian Fossey, macheted to death in her sleep, most likely by those threatened by her work, by a mission that defined her. Now, she studied salamanders sunning themselves by the creek. Mrs. Worden rocked on the porch and knitted, while Sharon Tate rested in the grass, letting the lilac sun warm her face. Bette Moss twirled in a circle, letting her arms dance in the soft breeze. The Black Dahlia chased a butterfly until it landed on a Rose of Sharon, then blew a gentle breath, watching it take flight again. Over the years, the women had brought color to this world, and they flourished, continuing their lives as if they had never died. He turned around, looking at the fantastical creation of his own mind. They saw him but ignored him, and yet every moment seemed to have meaning. "You said you'd save me," he said to them. "Save my friends now and do what you will with me." Coming together, they joined hands around him and began singing a lullaby, sweet and whimsical, a tune sung to a baby.

"Hush-a-bye, don't you cry, go to sleepy, little baby.
When you wake you shall have all the pretty little horses.
Way down yonder in the meadow lies a poor little lambie,
bees and butterflies, picking out its eyes, poor little
thing's crying."

Something knocked Connor sideways. He sat up, blurry-eyed from his vision, half wishing he could go back and never live in this real world again. Beside him, a gray rabbit hopped over him and up the hill, jarring him from that other reality. Connor forced himself up and climbed upwards, ignoring the foolishness he'd grabbed onto in his stress. He had no time for the dead. Every ounce of strength pushed him forward. At the top of the hill, he crawled onto the grounds of Copperhead Fields. In the parking lot sat a Contrary police car. Rusty leaned against the hood, smoking a cigarette.

Rusty angled his head for a better view of him, and Connor realized his bloody shirt, mud-caked shoes, and torn clothing probably caused Rusty not to recognize him. Connor limped forward, and Rusty threw the cigarette away.

"What happened to you?"

Grabbing him by the collar, Connor pushed him back onto the hood of the car. "Listen to me! Darius has Herman, and probably Rory too. He's going to kill them at the place he hid the barrels. You have to take me there, Rusty. For once in your sorry life, do the right thing, do this one thing! Take me there!"

Rusty laid his hand on top of Connor's. He didn't struggle against him. He held his gaze, taking in Connor's words, then peered up into the mountains. "I don't know where the barrels are. That's the God's truth. I don't know. I've never known."

Connor turned aside, hands on his hips, tears crowding his eyes. How could his plan have come to this? How did it all go awry? He should have thought this out more. He should have realized all that could go wrong, known that lives could be lost. He had no ideas on what he should do next.

"Willie," said Rusty, breaking the night's silence. "Willie knows." He ran around the side of the police car. "Get in."

53

Swerving the car into Willie's driveway, Rusty turned to him. "Let me do the talking," he said. "He's afraid of me more than he is you."

Connor nodded, his pulse racing so fast that he was unsure words would form. He followed Rusty up to the door and clasped his shaking hands as the pristine tone of the doorbell dinged. Rusty banged on the door after the third ring. Willie peered through a side window, bleary-eyed and in a robe.

Rusty mouthed the words *Open it.*

"What the hell, Rusty!" Willie shouted as he swung open the door.

Connor pulled Rusty's service revolver in one swipe and pressed it against Willie's forehead, backing him up to the opposite wall.

Willie squealed, eyes wide, holding his hands in the air. "Rusty, get this maniac away from me." Rusty stood to the side making no movement.

"You're going to tell me where to find those barrels, or I'm going to put more than one bullet into your pea-sized brain." Connor pressed the gun harder to Willie's forehead.

"Way to let me do the talking," Rusty said.

"Rusty!" Willie screeched.

Connor looked stern faced toward Rusty to gauge if he'd make a move.

Rusty stepped back. "Uniform's just been cleaned. Don't want to get it spattered with Willie's brains."

Connor pulled back the hammer of the gun and pushed it into Willie's crotch. "It might as well hurt before I kill you."

"Wait!" Willie screamed.

"You got five seconds, Carmack!"

"Wait! You know it!" Willie babbled. "You know it, you've been there. That day you worked for me. Little Mack Mine. Back of the hollow."

"That's not it," Connor spat. "All those guardsmen and engineers went through that mine."

"It is, I'm telling you it's there. I've never been inside a mine. I don't know where they put it, but I'm telling you it's there and it's not been moved in all these years! That was always Stark land. It was never a coal mine, only made it look like an abandoned mine on the outside. They only sold it to me so their name wouldn't be associated with it. But I never go there. I leave the Starks alone." His lips trembled. "Come on, now, Connor. I wouldn't lie with a gun pointed at me."

Connor glanced over to Rusty.

"I think I know what he's talking about," Rusty said. "You get me there, I can get us inside the secret room."

"If we're wrong, they're dead." Connor dropped Willie, who crumbled in a heap at his feet.

Rusty stared at his revolver in Connor's hand. "We're probably all dead anyway," he muttered.

In the seconds that followed, a cacophony of voices filled Connor's mind. Dead women. Goddesses. His father. Mother. Bryson Pomeroy yelling at him as a child. Judge Rounder cursing him. Professor Herzog advising him. The din gelled into a single tone. A song. His song. Right now, he needed to trust himself with a man who had betrayed him. He looked into Rusty's eyes. This man could have shot him in the back many times, but never had. Why? In that instant he realized their hate for each other was a construct that was expected of them. "I forgive you," Connor said.

Rusty stared at him, confused. "You know the way?" he asked. "To the mine?"

Connor grasped the gun by the barrel and held it out toward Rusty. His reach for it was tentative, and when the firearm was between them, they locked eyes. Connor held his breath, then let go. Rusty re-holstered the pistol. "Let's go," Connor said.

Sirens blasted and police lights flashed until they reached the base of the mountain. The curvy road slowed them, adding to Connor's anxiety. He'd wasted too much time with the Violinist. Connor prayed that Rory stayed out of sight until he could catch up with her. Herman was more than capable of taking care of himself, but didn't know that Darius had been clued in to what they were doing. It only took one bullet to take a man down.

Connor pointed to the cut-off, a tattered billboard with Preacher Boy's face half off its frame marking the entrance. "Park here, and let's walk in."

"Better he not hear us coming," Rusty agreed and handed Connor a flashlight along with a green rag he pulled from the glove compartment. "Tie it around the beam. If he sees us, it'll look like foxfire in the mist."

A heavy fog covered their feet as they walked up the tree-canopied road. "There," Connor said, pointing at his Buick. "Rory followed them in." His heart raced as he crouched and made his way toward the vehicle.

"Don't suppose you'll let me do the talking this time," Rusty whispered.

They checked the car. A rush of relief hit Connor when the trunk was empty. Taking another flashlight from the glove compartment, he then searched underneath the seats for his spare pistol. It wasn't there, so he could only surmise that Rory had taken it with her. At least that's what he hoped. "You know Darius better than I do. If anybody'll influence him, it'll be you," Connor said. "But Rusty, Herman and Rory's lives are in your hands. Can you do what might be necessary?"

Rusty didn't answer him. "You hear that?"

Connor cocked an ear. The hollow sound of night mixed with the call of a night bird, a thrashing in the underbrush, a trickle of a faraway stream, then a moan. "Over there," he said, and pointed the flashlight without its green covering. Moving uphill, Connor tripped over a shovel. Blood covered the edge. Nearby, they found Herman tied to a tree, a gaping wound on the back of his head. Connor pulled the rope loose and took a handkerchief from Rusty to press against the wound. Herman coughed and reached out, clasping his hand on Connor's arm.

"Can you stand up, buddy?"

"Think so," Herman mumbled, and fell on his first attempt. "Gotta get Rory," he said. "He's got her. Coming back for me."

"I hate to say this, Connor," Rusty said, "but she may be–"

430

"Not dead," Herman said. "Same reason he didn't kill me. Said he wanted, and I know it sounds strange, but said he wanted the Violinist to interrogate us."

"That'll give us some time," Connor said. "The Violinist will miss his curtain." He anchored a shoulder under Herman's arm and helped him toward the road. "Rusty, in my car. There's a towel in the backseat."

Herman's gaze followed Rusty down the slope, and he held Connor back out of hearing range. "You kidding?"

"I know," Connor whispered. "Not a lot of choice."

"You got a gun, at least?'

Connor shook his head that he did not.

"You can't trust him." Herman dug deep into his coat and pulled out a Boy Scout pocketknife. "Not much, but don't let him get the high ground on you."

"Keep it," Connor said, pushing the knife back at him. "If I don't make it back here, you get out of this hollow, even if you have to crawl on your knees."

"Connor?" Herman squeezed his friend's shoulder.

Connor helped Herman onto the road as Rusty approached carrying supplies. "Stay to the edge of the road," Connor whispered. "Hide if you hear any noise." He tied the towel around Herman's head, fastening it with duct tape Rusty had brought back with him. Every heartbeat throbbed in his ears, each pulse awakening senses he didn't know he had. Stars shimmered though swaying tree limbs; a hawk's cry told him the night fowls disliked their presence; his boots on the overgrown road crunched unnaturally. Connor inhaled the night, willed all his might to become part of it, merge with the darkness to fight the darkness. Still, he didn't know who could and couldn't be trusted as he and Rusty hiked toward the mine.

54

The rusted gate padlock had been dropped to the ground and the gate stood ajar. Scuff marks in the gravel indicated Darius had forced Rory into the mine. A boarded door across the opening tapped against the frame. Rusty put an arm across the opening.

"You're not going to like what you see," he said, his expression guarded and fearful. "I've heard of this place. Stories Darius told me. I thought he was making it up, one of his drug-induced hallucinations. This Violinist. I met him once. He's Darius's kin. Scared the crap out of me." He swallowed and looked aside. "Things I learned, things about the past, they changed me."

"Will you help me get Rory out alive?" Conner asked. "I don't care about anything else."

Rusty bit his lower lip, staring into the dark tunnel as a cool breeze whipped past them. "Yes."

They scooted on their hands and knees with only the flashlights in the pitch darkness until they reached an area where they could stand. "Think it's far?" Connor whispered.

"Not far, just hidden." Rusty pointed at a miners' cart shoved into a carved-out hovel. He approached it and studied its position. "I don't know if this will work or not." He pulled the cart back several inches, then turned it clockwise. It tilted, acting like a lever to twist a wall-size door open into a cavernous room illuminated with a string of bulbs hanging across the ceiling. They stepped inside, and Connor fought the reflex to gag.

Human-sized cages lined the walls of the room. Rory was locked in the one nearest him. The smell of blood and human excrement mixed with a palpable curtain of fear. A single chair in the center of the room was outfitted with leather straps to hold arms and legs in place. A side tray was filled with instruments of torture. His back toward them, Darius Stark stared at the two of them from the reflection in a mirrored wall. "Well, sonnavagun. Wasn't expecting you." He turned and smiled at Rusty.

Connor's heart pounded in his chest, and he moved sideways to keep both men in sight. Rory pressed her face against the bars, her lips trembling as she reached out for him.

"The Violinist call you?" Darius asked. "You bring him here?" Watching Connor with the cool eye of calculation, Darius cocked his head to one side. "Somehow, I got the feeling that you've been the spit in my beer for a long time, mister." Then he raised two guns, one pointing at Rusty and the other at Connor. "Well, now, what have we here, a conspiracy of stupidity?"

Rusty raised his gun in the mid-space between Connor and Darius. "I don't take to being aimed at, old friend."

"Apologies," Darius said, without lowering either weapon. "You brought me this one as a birthday gift?"

Rusty bit his bottom lip. "Maybe some truth needs to be told here."

"I got all the truth I need in my trigger finger." Darius held his aim firm.

"The other one is out on the road," Rusty said. "He could get help. I should go back and bring him here."

Connor's heart hurt hearing those words. Was Rusty turning on him? A sideways glance showed Rusty's gun wasn't pointed either way. Connor reached out and took Rory's hand, at the same time looking around for a weapon. There was only one way to win this fight . . . in darkness. Cupping his hand to her cheek, he whispered, "Behind you, can you reach it?"

Rory glanced toward the wall and a single extension cord connected to the overhanging light bulbs. The intensity of her gaze told him she was measuring off whether her arm could reach the electrical socket where the cord was plugged. She pressed her face into the bars and kissed him.

"Ah, true love," Darius mocked. "Let's leave 'em alive. I want to see how much romance they can muster after a few weeks of smelling each other's piss." He nodded toward the next cage. "Rusty, wrangle that rooster."

Connor spun around and laughed. "You're a fool, Darius Stark." He stepped off-center to keep the focus away from Rory. "With your fear of ghosts and devils, it's a wonder you didn't become a TV evangelist." Connor jacked his foot up on a chair, thinking to kick it right into Darius's face. But what would Rusty do? He hadn't made eye contact with him, but he could tell his pistol was still raised. No telling where it was pointed. "You're right," Connor said. "I'm the one you've been looking for all these years. I'm the specter that has been haunting your every step. I called the police to alert them your barn was full of stolen cars. I got Brenda Crider out of town and back to her family. I got you to sign that paper giving Herman Cahill the gas station, and I was the one who's had the FBI on your tail from the beginning. The Violinist is tied up in the attic of the Regal Hotel waiting for the police to pick him up. He won't be playing a tune tonight."

"Yeah, well." Darius bit his lip, hatred flaming up into his expression. "Nobody's ever gonna hear that story."

"Now!" Rory screamed.

Lights went out, and Connor dove behind a desk. Flashes of gunfire matrixed from all directions. Then, quiet. The dark that could not be blinked away. Connor held his breath, trying to perceive any sound, any movement.

"What?" Darius said. "It's got me!"

Connor moved toward the voice, staying low, aware that Darius still held two guns. He knew Rusty would be moving the same direction, but for who?

"Let me go! Who are you? I'll kill you!" Darius's voice crumbled in terror. Shots zinged out again.

Connor scrambled toward the flickers and pounced, knocking Darius onto his stomach, hearing a gun shatter on impact. A flash. A shot passed his head. Sound exploded in his ear as he struggled with flailing arms. More arms than his. Rusty? Connor's hand came to rest on a solid object that he raised above his head and brought to the ground with all his force, again, and again, and again until Darius lay motionless beneath him.

Connor felt for Darius's hand and dislodged the pistol, putting it in his coat pocket. He felt around for the other one but couldn't find it. "Rory? Rusty?"

"I'm okay," Rory called out.

"Hurry up," Rusty said. "Hurry up."

"Stay where you are, Rusty. I'll be right there."

"Ain't going nowhere," he said, followed by a short chuckle. "Bringing buttered biscuits, ain't'cha?"

Connor felt his way to the cage, pulling Rory to him. She led him over to the side where a key hung on the wall. He released her, and they held to each other as tightly as they ever had. Darkness swallowed them and all they had was touch. "Rusty," she said, pushing back from him. "I think he's hurt."

"Rusty, call out to me," Connor said.

"I said over here, cousin," Rusty said impatiently. "You need to give me a lift up into the catfish 'fore ole Judge Nobody irons us out."

Connor and Rory felt their way to him. Leaning against a cage, Connor felt the wetness that was Rusty's blood pooling around him. Rory searched for the flashlight, hissing when she cut her finger on glass from the broken light bulbs. "Found it," she said and pointed the beam.

Rusty had been shot in the forehead and chest. His eyes were open and he mugged at Connor, one side of his mouth staging a grin. "We're cousins," he said.

Rory pulled off her sweater and held it to the chest wound. She glanced at Connor, then away, shaking her head.

"Take this," Connor said, handing her the gun he'd taken from Darius. "Herman is making his way to the road. Get to Rusty's police car and call for help."

"You'll be in the dark," she said. "When I pulled that cord, all the bulbs fell to the ground and broke." She waved the flashlight about. "I don't see any other source of electricity." The beam shone on Darius's body. A chunk of coal was embedded in his skull.

"It's okay," Connor said. "Go now."

In the ebony dark, Connor Herne pulled his old friend to his lap, holding him as they talked about old times; they remembered the fun and the pranks, Rusty chiding him about missing the blue devil episode. His speech soon devolved to single phases. "Didn't mean to . . . . Get better . . . . Hurt . . . . Cousin."

"Friend," was his last word. After a while, he moaned, trying for words, his breath slowed, and Connor held him close and wept.

Connor didn't know which way Rusty's gun had fired. He'd probably never know, but he did know what he wanted to believe. He stared into the dark, thinking that Rusty could not have been the person holding Darius down. Seemed as if he was too far away. Or maybe that too was his imagination. The dark revealed no answers, though once he thought he heard a woman's laughter. He wondered if it was the dead women. Had they joined with the darkness one last time to save him like they'd promised? Or was Darius a victim of his own irrational fears and superstitions? When light reached them again, he looked down upon Rusty Haskew's face. Connor didn't see the policeman or the man who'd betrayed him, he saw the boy Rusty had been. Eager, defiant, with all of life against him, and this was what he'd made of it.

$\rightsquigarrow$

The Violinist escaped, probably helped by the hotel clerk, who also disappeared, along with Connor's gun. The state police brought Connor back to the attic room in the early morning hours. The violins were gone, his workshop clean. All that remained was the half-finished violin he'd been working on. The paint was still wet, selected strings set off to the side. Connor wondered whom it had been for. Had he been able to prevent a tragedy? Or would the Violinist begin anew somewhere else? He knew he would watch his back until the day that man died.

The next morning, Connor and Rory watched as law enforcement and engineers entered the mine. Connor paced impatiently, wishing he could go inside with them.

"We scoured this mine before," an engineer complained before entering the mine. When he came back out, his pale features were more humble. "There's no barrels in there. A lot of torture equipment in the private room. We can't detail it until law enforcement okays it, but I don't think the barrels are there." He coughed, looking as if he was holding down vomit. "Looks like this Violinist did Stark's dirty work."

"Is there any other kind of work the Starks do?" Connor stepped forward, staring into the dark puddle of the opening. "They're there," he said. "We've just been searching the wrong way. Looking with the wrong eyes." He bit his lower lip, scuffed his feet in the gravel. "We don't need searchers," he said, turning toward Rory. "We need coal miners."

It took a few days to gather the right people–those who weren't on the Stark payroll–but soon more than a dozen men led by Gene, Melvin, and Casper Gaylor went into the deserted mine. Their eyes were wizened, backs stooped, wiry arms carried picks and shovels, leaving behind any mechanized armaments; full of gnome and earthworm, they promised to crawl through the bowels of this earth until they found every hidden space. Within the week, the barrels of hazardous waste were unearthed behind slag mounds hiding a false wall. Discarded around an underground lake that fed the hollow streams, the leaking barrels yielded enough evidence to prosecute Willie Carmack and all those who had a hand in this disaster.

Connor knelt onto the ground the day the word came to him, pushing his fingers into the dirt. His heart felt he'd not done enough, not acted soon enough, and floundered when he should have stood strong. He only hoped that the good earth would, in time, forgive him.

The cleanup began.

55

True to her word, Rory gave notice to her employers and began the paperwork to become a practicing physician in Kentucky. Contrary Hospital allowed her to keep treating the people who'd been poisoned by the spill and look after Tallulah Herne, who grew stronger each day. No one had more skill and knowledge than she, and with each day, the love that grew between her and Connor rooted like the oaks of the deep forest.

Tallulah rescheduled her wedding on the most beautiful June evening. In the afternoon, a banquet for the hospital workers who'd saved her and the many others who'd survived was celebrated with dignitaries from across the nation. With promises that this disaster could never happen again and assurances of better oversight, they shook hands and ate, and ate, and ate.

Just as the sun set, leaving the sky a brilliant mixture of blush and vermillion, Connor and Rory followed a group of bridesmaids and his daughter to the First Baptist Church.

"Watch for cars," he called out to the girls as they struggled with an unruly veil in the traffic island outside the church. The joy and the sadness of the journey to this day was not lost on Connor or his daughter. The bridesmaids assembled in the inner foyer, and Rory went to take her seat. Connor stood outside the church, looking down each direction of Laynchark Avenue. Music hummed from inside the church, mixing with the giggles of the bridesmaids.

Tallulah poked her head out the door and studied him. "She's not coming, Daddy."

Connor smiled and looked at his shoes. "I know," he said. "I hoped . . ."

"She'll be fine," Tallulah said. "Momma knows we love her. She knows she can never come back."

Connor nodded, biting his lip, tears rising up in his eyes. One last glance as a white van pulled from a parking space across from the church. As it drove away, Connor watched after it. The avenue was quiet. A bluish twilight seemed warm and peaceful. In many ways, this was the happiest day of his life.

PROLOGUE SIX

In the years since Temperance Herne had attended her mother's funeral, she often thought back to that day when she'd almost made her escape. The road out had stretched before her like a grosgrain ribbon, Iona at her side, nothing holding her to this tiresome town except the choke-collar hold that had looped itself around her neck and dragged her back like a whipped dog. She didn't understand why she'd returned, but she rarely bothered to analyze herself or her decisions. Age had brought a certain grace to her life. Watching her contemporaries drop dead from overeating, smoking, drug use, mine work, drunk driving, and any other number of bad decisions, she felt proud that in her seventh decade, she had few bad habits. She hadn't even cracked a knuckle in the past ten years.

She and Iona had made a home for themselves, and raised Iona's daughter, who now lived in Cincinnati and made her living as an accountant. A good career, she'd thought at the time, and just hoped her raising had taken the Stark larceny out of her blood. The community accepted them as the widow women who lived together to conserve money, even though Tempy had never been married. She didn't correct the perception, and it was an easy lie to live.

Only hard time she and Iona ever had was when Connor used her to set up Darius Stark. Iona hadn't spoken to Connor since that day, but then, their paths didn't cross all that much anymore. The two women had gotten through it, of course, just like any strong relationship would. Connor had those bones tested for DNA in the 1990s. The baby had matched her, and the woman him, just like she'd said it would, and she had had a day where being proved right brought her some self-righteous bragging that nobody could take from her.

In time, this thing called the Internet had set up databases of people's DNA, and Connor found family living in Pennsylvania who produced a photo of a cat-eyed blond woman named Hertha Hunter. She was the spitting image of Tallulah. What a tale they spun of the determined young librarian who along with her husband and sister brought a trunk full of books to the mountains, planning on setting up a library. The family's disappearance was a mystery told to each generation of relatives. Now they knew what had happened to one of them. Now the tale had a partial ending, though they would never know how her path crossed that ugly Violinist's. Oh, that one had found his comeuppance as well, not all that long after his identity was known. At times, Tempy found herself laughing at the irony that the little disabled Gaylor boy had had a hand in taking him down in a most undignified manner. Because Iona's family had harbored the Violinist, she didn't like talking about it, and that was all right with Tempy. It was past, and she really didn't give a flying fudge.

In the meantime, Connor laid his mother's bones and those of the baby boy to rest beside Mom and Pop, and had bought extra plots for himself and, well, she guessed for her. In these end times, Tempy didn't argue the way she might have when she was younger. What did it matter what happened to you after you were dead?

What mattered was the life you lived while you were still kicking and had your senses about you. At this advanced age, she woke every day with a smile. She knew her name. She knew where she lived and whom she loved, and she knew as clear as a mountain stream that her mind would never leave her.

What years might be before her would pass easy knowing that at this advanced age she had not shown signs of her mother's and grandmother's disease. She and Iona were the matrons of the block, the old biddies that youngsters called Aunt; grade schoolers could depend on them to buy their Girl Scout cookies; teens could call upon them for church donations; they were the elders whose memory could be relied upon when newcomers wanted to ask how something or other might be done. They taught Sunday school, volunteered for the Red Cross, rang bells for the Salvation Army at Christmas, put their time in at the pet shelter, and no one cared that they lived in the same house. It looked normal. It seemed to the world that no harm was being done.

Today, she longed for a change. Any kind of change. Her hair was tight in the bun atop her head that stretched her scalp, and she strained from the throbbing behind her eye. It seemed she'd had this same headache her entire life. And she was tired of it.

Tempy flipped through the pages of *People* magazine, pausing at a picture of actress Bernadette Peters. She chuckled at Bernadette's spirally tresses that matched hers, except Tempy's were gray, and she doubted Bernadette had a bald spot on the crown of her head the size of a Kennedy half dollar. She glanced out the window at daffodils sprouting like sunny little faces, thinking, *Everybody needs a spring romp.* Impulsively, she tore out the photo and jumped in the car, sped all the way to Middlesboro, Kentucky, parked in front of Collins School of Cosmetology, then barged into Juanita's Beauty Salon next door to the school, where the most experienced beauticians worked. Willie, Brenda, Regina, and Faye all looked at her hair and her bald spot and each showed her a style that would cover it up without her having to tie it up in a topknot. They even threw in some crystal hairclips when she told them to dye it red.

Her mother would have thrown a fit to know she was dyeing her hair red. Iona would laugh, saying she was silly to spend money on such a thing at her age. Tempy didn't care. She was doing it because she felt like it. She rested back in the hairdresser's chair, watching Faye mix the scarlet dye. She no longer had to answer to anyone. She was a woman who had her senses, her right mind, and her God-given right to choice. Happy. Satisfied.

NICOLE

56

Connor Herne figured he would take his leave of this world having done all that was required of him. In the last decade, he had watched a dynasty fall and another rise. The Gentry family wormed their way into city politics, aiming at the state level, only to be knocked down by bigger money. At least they seemed less violent than the Starks, but Connor distrusted their shifty words and above-it-all attitudes. They were slick and superior, but they also had thorns in their sides; a curmudgeonly lawyer by the name of Joddy Paradise peppered them with lawsuits until his passing. Then his young associate, Jefferson Bingham, picked up the gauntlet. Toward the turn of the century, Connor watched the first woman win the office of Commonwealth Attorney. Alma Bashears had won against a Gentry. Connor had voted for her. Change rose and fell in Crimson County, and no doubt would again with the next political cycle, but Connor acknowledged his time of fighting was over.

Sitting in his yard, looking through a photo album of his grandchildren, he took measure of the life he had lived through their eyes. Graduations, awards, marriages, and careers. They called him Pop, and he liked that. When Rory retired, they took a second honeymoon to Europe. Herman and Sissy had joined them there, and the highlight of the trip was a visit to the Einstein House in Bern, Switzerland. Connor stayed alone after the others had left, soaking in the ambience of the place where Albert Einstein had developed the theory of relativity while working as a clerk in a patent office. Connor sensed wonder in the small flat, imagined how Einstein had lived, what he thought, how he came to such miraculous conclusions. He wondered about imagination and why it gave one man a theory that changed the world and another the ability to conjure the dead. Walking back to the hotel, Connor concluded that imagination, wherever it leads, is a gift not a curse.

After serving his stint in federal prison, Willie Carmack had died alone and broke in his mansion. The dilapidated structure fell to pieces with a roof cave-in that he didn't have the money to fix. He lived in three rooms on the main floor, the house becoming a place for kids who wanted to throw a rock and break a window. The morning his body was found, a pack of raccoons had tunneled through the wall and made a mess of a stash of cash likely hidden by Willie's father. Two hundred thousand in all, enough to have given Willie a new start, but all too late.

Rusty had been buried in the Rose Hill Cemetery, his headstone reading: *Orphan of Midnight Valley*. Before his casket was closed, Conner had put the rabbit's foot key chain in Rusty's hand. "*For luck,*" he'd whispered, then kissed Rusty's cheek. Connor occasionally visited the gravesite, but found he never had words for his childhood friend. He stared at the tombstone, reading his name over and over, then left, sadly depressed for the rest of the day.

Rusty's wife, Lynn, moved to Florida with her children and grandchildren soon after the burial. She left a letter for him saying she never wanted anyone of her blood to live in this awful town again. Connor couldn't blame her. Maybe in time she would forgive her husband and the children might remember the good that was deep within their father.

Simon Tuller disappeared, and no one ever learned of his whereabouts. Connor prayed the evil man never found Randi Jo. The sweet girl who always seemed to know what he was thinking was also never heard from again. Connor knew that she had recovered in the northern clinic that Dr. Huber had arranged for her. The doctor had gotten her fake IDs and set up an account with Butch's money for her to make a new life. Connor hoped she had. He wanted a happy life for her. He wished her safety and peace.

As for the Black Dahlia, Bette Moss, Mrs. Worden, Sharon Tate, Dorothy Stratten, Dominique Dunne, and Dian Fossey, Connor never saw them again after that night in the mine; and he saw only one other dead woman in his lifetime. A golden goddess of a woman, blond hair lifted in the breeze. At first, he thought perhaps she was Death coming for him, but she walked past his house, nodding to him as she disappeared into waves of heat drifting up from the asphalt road. Connor rose from his lawn chair, holding on to the photo album as he leaned across a fence and looked the direction she'd walked. Nothing there. He wondered if she'd drifted into that invented world of fantasy and color that he'd created long ago and could no longer see. He wondered what seeing Nicole Brown Simpson meant. He wondered if those beings would awake again or if they lived in someone else's reality. He swallowed, his mouth dry, and hoped she found the place she was going to.

Looking the opposite direction, heat shimmered in a hazy screen and a figure walked sure-footed toward him. Connor held his breath, awaiting another specter, but as the boy got closer, his blue skin was unmistakable.

"How-do," Connor said as the young man, possibly around ten, came into his yard.

"You the one and only Connor Herne?"

"That I be," he said. "Got kin by the name of Toomey?"

"Be my great-uncle. We're good and close 'cause looks like I'm the last of the Blue Freds."

"You must be Sam," Connor said. "Last time I saw your uncle he said you were fixing to come to the town school."

"Yep, hope I don't scare the little kids. I can take the pill if'n I want," the boy explained, "but I'm partial to being blue. Think it makes me unique."

"I think it makes you unique, too," Connor agreed, and the boy smiled widely.

"Uncle Toomey sent me looking for you 'cause you're the only one he trusts to help."

"Do my best," Connor said. "But I'm an old man, not much I can do these days." Connor motioned for Sam to follow him to the swing on the porch.

The boy wiped his brow and nodded that he'd take the glass of lemonade that Connor offered. After a long sip, he said, "Somebody has stole the mountain on the other side of ours, and they're working their way to us."

"Stole the mountain?"

"Taken it, plain and simple. It's gone"

"How can that happen?"

"Come on, I'll show ya."

450

The winding roads brought familiar memories as he turned onto Notown Road. He slowed when they came to the house where he used to live. Looking over at it, he saw a group of kids take turns on a tire swing just as he had as a boy. The house looked good, lived in, and Connor felt a pang of nostalgia as it disappeared in his rearview mirror. At Bean's Fork, he noticed the houses and trailers were well tended, though a few had discarded washing machines and rusted-out cars sitting in the side yards. Over the years, Blufred Hollow had regained its health, and former residents got the itch to move back to the ole home place. He saw Toomey now and then, but like himself, the older he got, the more he stayed close to home.

"Pull over there," Sam said, pointing to the shoulder of the road.

Connor parked and followed Sam up an embankment. The harsh grind of machinery blotted out Sam's voice as he called to him, and dusty pockets of grit blew up into the air, causing Connor to cough. At the peak of the hill, Sam turned and held out his hand, pulling him the last few yards up the hill. What Connor Herne looked down upon took his breath away. Someone had indeed stolen the mountain. What once had been an ancient stand of oaks, walnuts, beeches, chestnuts, and tulip poplars that rose hundreds of feet toward the sky, was now heaps of dirt. The rich valley was flattened as machinery dug into the next hillside, carving it to the nub. The mountains were gone. What was left was a hole in the ground. The devastation caused a physical pain in his chest.

He didn't know if words would come to him as he pulled out his cellular telephone, a contraption he'd been playing with since receiving it from Tallulah and Justin on his birthday. He dialed his daughter at the newspaper, got her answering machine, but chose his words with exactness. " 'Lula, get Justin and my wife and as many people as you can. Set up a meeting down at the library. We got trouble, baby, big trouble. Somebody has gone and stole a mountain. I know how it sounds, but I'm telling you like it is. It's a travesty, a violation. Nobody in their right mind would do a thing like this, but someone has, and we've got to put a stop to it. Wake up, honey. Wake up everybody you know! We've got to get organized!"

Connor knelt down beside the boy, who sat cross-legged on a mound of lime green moss. He put a hand on his shoulder and squeezed, letting the child know he was not alone any longer. Connor Herne didn't know who had done this or what he could do about it. He didn't know if he'd be listened to or laughed at, but he did know that his life was about to get interesting.

The End

Author's Note and Acknowledgements

I have come face-to-face with strangers that I believe had the intention of killing me four times in my life.

The first time I couldn't have been more than seven or eight years old and had wandered away from my grandmother's yard with the plan of going to see my other grandmother, who lived about a mile away. To get there you had to cross a creek that to my young eyes looked about a mile wide. Undeterred, I cut down a dirt path to the creek and was surprised by an elderly man with a walking stick sitting against the bank. He began talking to me, and I must have spoken back to him, though I remember little of what we said. But as I took off my shoes and socks to wade the creek, I do remember his last words, telling me about his daughter who'd had her leg amputated. He put his hand right at the level of his knee, showing me the first cut, then continued up to his thigh, where the next amputation had taken place. "That one killed her," he said.

It would be years before I realized that people kill people. I didn't know that it was inappropriate to tell a kid about amputated limbs and dead daughters. I took the conversation in stride, waded the creek, and continued on my way. My parents and grandparents, in those days, didn't know the words pedophile or child killer. I guess they must have been unhappy with my wandering off, but I don't remember anybody fussing at me about it. I expect I had a lucky day.

At seventeen, I left for college, moving into an off-campus apartment near the University of Kentucky in Lexington, Kentucky (much to my father's displeasure). My boyfriend, Jack, brought me home from a date, kissed me goodnight at the door, and left. I had been inside long enough to change into my nightgown when a knock came at the door. Thinking Jack had returned, I opened the door, and only the security chain kept it from opening wider. A disheveled man stood there. Black curly hair hung to his shoulders, a beard, mustache. He wore an oversized green army jacket and his wide almond-shaped eyes focused on mine. He didn't look down at my body even though I was wearing a nightgown. Instead, he focused his gaze into mine.

He began to talk, saying he was looking for a friend of his. His hands continually rolled around each other, and I realized he kept leaning toward the door opening, eyes still oddly focused on mine. I slammed the door shut in his face. He yelled out, "Hey, I'm only looking for my friend." I ran to the window, thinking perhaps I could yell at the FIJI fraternity house across the street, and someone could get Jack. I don't know why I thought that, the fraternity was kitty-corner to my building and no one would have heard me. In the street directly below my window was a campus police car with the officer standing outside the car. I yelled down to him about the strange man at my door and asked him if he could come up. No hesitation. He ran into my building even though this off-campus building was not his jurisdiction. (Thank you, campus police.) Of course the man was gone, and the officer told me that there'd been a lot of rapes in this neighborhood, and to be careful. I'd had another lucky day.

Three years later, after college graduation, I moved to San Francisco, California, and began working for a local theater. On daytime shift, I was usually in the theater alone, and had to go to a nearby building to get the mail. As I returned one day, a curly-haired, redheaded man called out my name. He smiled and said, "Hi, I'm Lloyd." Then he pointed to the CATS poster on the theatre's wall, at the name Andrew Lloyd Webber. Now, I was twenty years old and had just begun working in theater. I didn't know who the players were or what Andrew Lloyd Webber looked like, but this well-dressed man knew my name and talked as if he'd been told by someone to find me. He kept looking toward the theater door as if I should invite him inside. And I did think about that. If this was the important person who wrote the musical, I should be nice to him. I don't know why, but I rattled off the show manager's telephone number to him, and told him he should contact him to get access to backstage. Another lucky day.

That same year, I finally saved enough money for a television. Taking the Geary Street bus out to the Sears store, then balancing the oversized box, I got off the bus at Van Ness Avenue and began walking the eight blocks to my apartment on Hyde Street, shifting the TV box from one hip to the other. As I walked, one of San Francisco's unpredictable thunderstorms began. There wasn't much choice but to keep walking. I kept noticing a green van passing me. It circled the block, slowing as it passed me again and again. Finally, it pulled over and a man yelled out, asking if he could give me a lift. I was soaked, carrying a box much too heavy for me, so I walked over toward the van. He popped open the door. I said to him, "Thank you. I've noticed you circling, but I don't need a ride."

He was a nice-looking man, clean-cut, white shirt, black hair neatly combed, olive skin, and a beautiful smile with straight, white teeth, a movie-star kind of smile. "Come on," he said, a hand indicating the rain.

"It's very kind of you, but no, thank you."

He continued to smile, talking and making eye contact, the smile never waning. He indicated the seat with a nod of his head. "Come on," he said again, more insistent but still polite.

I was focused on the frozen smile that never changed even as he talked. Now, I'm from a small town in eastern Kentucky, and if I'd been walking down the road in my hometown and a downpour of rain hit, I would probably have taken the ride. In Lexington, I don't know, I might have taken the ride. I had no experience of saying no to this kind of offer. But here in San Francisco, what kept me from getting into that van was his frozen smile. "No," I said more firmly. "I don't want a ride."

I continued home, not thinking all that much about it after that day. Years later, I'd learn that serial killers had just switched from Volkswagens to vans. Lucky day.

In those years, we didn't know the term "serial killer," but now I have a strong feeling that I was looking into the eyes of one that day. And I also believe that the brave campus policeman who ran into my building probably saved me that night, if not from death, at least from terrible harm. Whatever intuition made me walk away from the fake Andrew Lloyd Webber and the man with the walking stick probably saved my life.

Women live by the good graces of men who decide not to kill us. Once that decision is made to kill, there's very little we can do. We're not stronger than them. We might get in a lucky eye jab or groin punch, but then we'd better be ready to run like hell.

Like most people, I watched the news or read about the horrific murders of both famous and nameless women. Oddly, I rarely thought back to the times when, but for a turn of fate, I might have been a victim, too, but when I read about those women's murders I was terrified. I was more terrified of what had happened to them than of what had happened to me or could have happened to me. I could have been any one of those women. I could be killed by a stranger, or unthinkably, by someone I loved. Those women became mythic icons in my psyche; they lived inside my head, telling me to go down this street, not that one; date this man, not that; wear these clothes, not those. I don't talk to the specters or see them the way Connor Herne does, but I know I've created a reality for them in my life much the same as he did, and those women have kept me alive among men who might kill me.

I have many people to thank for helping me write this book: my sister, my editors, production folk, and PR mavens, but I include in that thanks Elizabeth Short, Bernice Worden, Sharon Tate, Dominique Dunne, Dorothy Stratten, Dian Fossey, and Nicole Brown Simpson.

Coming Soon
From BearCat Press
Book Three: The Midnight Valley Quartet

The Mayor of Midnight Valley
By Tess Collins

Renita Stark didn't know that in her veins ran the blood of a Viking warrior, a Muslim pirate, and a French whore. She only knew that she'd lost being cheerleader by one vote and she was pissed. Time to go talk to that creepy cousin that played the violin.

About the Author

A coal miner's granddaughter, Tess Collins was born and raised in a crater. Yes, really, a crater formed by the impact of an asteroid millions of years ago where her hometown, Middlesboro, Kentucky was eventually built. Tess spent her younger years in a one room Carnegie Library reading around the room. She started at *SALLY AND THE BEAR* and ended with *WAR AND PEACE* at which time she thought, "I want to do this."

She is the author of *THE LAW OF REVENGE, THE LAW OF THE DEAD, THE LAW OF BETRAYAL, HELEN OF TROY* and *NOTOWN.* Her non-fiction book *HOW THEATER MANAGERS MANAGE* is published by Rowman and Littlefield's Scarecrow Press. Ms. Collins received a B.A. from the University of Kentucky and a Ph.D. from The Union Institute and University.

Visit her website at TessCollins.com

CPSIA information can be obtained at www.ICGtesting.com
Printed in the USA
LVOW10s0820070515

437511LV00003B/135/P